LOVE
AFTER
MIDNIGHT

Also by Sister Souljah

Fiction

The Coldest Winter Ever

Midnight: A Gangster Love Story

Midnight and the Meaning of Love

A Deeper Love Inside: The Porsche Santiaga Story

A Moment of Silence: Midnight III

Life After Death

Nonfiction

No Disrespect

LOVE
AFTER
MIDNIGHT

A Novel

SISTER SOULJAH

EMILY BESTLER BOOKS

—

ATRIA

New York   London   Toronto   Sydney   New Delhi

EMILY
BESTLER
BOOKS

ATRIA

An Imprint of Simon & Schuster, LLC
1230 Avenue of the Americas
New York, NY 10020

First Emily Bestler Books/Atria Books hardcover edition October 2024

EMILY BESTLER BOOKS/ATRIA BOOKS and colophon
are trademarks of Simon & Schuster, LLC

Simon & Schuster: Celebrating 100 Years of Publishing in 2024

For information about special discounts for bulk purchases, please contact Simon & Schuster Special Sales at 1-866-506-1949 or business@simonandschuster.com.

Interior design by Yvonne Taylor

The Simon & Schuster Speakers Bureau can bring authors to your live event. For more information or to book an event, contact the Simon & Schuster Speakers Bureau at 1-866-248-3049 or visit our website at www.simonspeakers.com.

Manufactured in the United States of America

1 3 5 7 9 10 8 6 4 2

Library of Congress Cataloging-in-Publication Data has been applied for.

ISBN 978-1-9821-8063-8
ISBN 978-1-9821-8065-2 (ebook)

LOVE
AFTER
MIDNIGHT

What to **REMEMBER**,
What to **FORGET**.
What to **CHERISH**,
What to **REGRET**.
What to **HOLD** on to,
What to **LET GO**.
Who to **TRUST**,
Who **NOT** to let close.
When to push **FORWARD**,
When to **RETREAT**.
What to **CONSUME**,
What to **NEVER EAT**.
Which is the **ENTRANCE**,
Where is the **EXIT**.
What to **GUARD** and
Always **PROTECT** it.
Monkey **SEE**
Monkey **DO**
Monkey **ACTS**
Like we do.

1
MOOD

Tonight, I need something stronger than weed. It hit me all at once. After being the coolest, nah, the coldest bitch on the planet, it was like, I was getting hit, by an intense heat wave. Then anger overtook me. Fifteen fucking years on lock and finally free. But right now in this moment, I'm more hateful than grateful. Fuck the bullshit. Hate has its place. Suddenly famous, I'm out of my element. I've been all Brooklyn, da peeps and da streets or the cells. Upon my prison release in January this year, I caught a reality show starring me. The bag was big. Course I was amped about it. But somehow today . . . Fame gotta bitch feeling like comfortable is the most uncomfortable feeling. Blank mind. Blank soul. It's false, empty, and vacant.

I realize I'm addicted to struggle and hustle, moving and maneuvering, fight and fury, action and reaction, pressure and tension. That's how I got here in this dark club they calling a lounge. See, even the scene and the lingo switched up on me. No matter what *they* call it though, it's where I need to be right now. It's hot. The walls are sweating. Every body is body to body. No air, the scent of perfumes and colognes and funk and strong liquor and scented smoke intermingling. Inhale weed, exhale frustration. Music, louder than thunder. This is how I need to party, with hood bitches who can't pay their rent, but got $150 mani-pedis, $500 weaves, and $700 shoes. Fuck cameras and papparazzi and the rich crowd of fame, and children of fame. Whether they young or grown, they all be insecure, suicidal, fake, and psychotic. They perform and talk too much about nothing. Think they know everything but never did nothing real. Don't know the real deal about shit and whine like newborns bout this and that. My party needs to be packed with niggas and bitches who ain't got a damn thing to actually celebrate, but who keep on pushing, rock the spot, make it pulsate, rhyme, sing, scream, or just mouth the lyrics, eat the beats, and make moves that look like seizures, or others who just lean back or glide and ride the rhythm real smooth.

I party with the ones who got no real reason to be confident, but still be the boldest, baddest, and the coldest. I love that. I crave that. But, in the twenty-first century I find myself chasing a feeling I used to feel. So much so, I am wondering if the feeling I felt before is no more in existence. Somehow, wafted away in the wind. *But I'm still here.* Ain't found one man who can make my pussy pump, soul jump, or hips hump. I want to feel something. Make my eyes widen. Make me cry. Make me laugh so hard my stomach aches. Make my nipples plump, my thighs shake, my toes curl. Bite me. Fight me. I'll bite you back. Excite me. Make me cum six or seven times in one night. That's the only way for me to feel right and alive. Cause I am alive and love that fact. But neer nigga got that look, style, clout, or that energy. I know what it looks like. When I see it, I'll snatch it, trap it, and make it mine. But I ain't seen it day or night, night or day in the short amount of weeks that I have been free, awake, and active.

My bodyguard is with me. My investors insisted. They guard

me like gold. My new accountant told me to look at each of my body parts as units of wealth. My time and each and every second as representing a certain dollar amount that I choose as my price quote. *Make all pay to play.* That's the only way to prevent people, agents, businesses, and companies from wasting or interrupting my time, which equals my potential earnings. When I think of my name, Winter Santiaga, as a brand, and my body parts each separately as a unit of wealth, that gives me the power to sift out the diamonds and throw away the ordinary rocks, he says. I'm on my private time now, although I'm mixed in with the public at this club. I mean *lounge.*

Dancing and drenched. My mood and my mind are swirling inside of the music. Don't even see what nigga pushed up on me. I make my bodyguard stand at least six feet or six bodies away from wherever I am. I tell him, "play dead." I don't want him to be a cooler to my hot or my heat or my hunt. He's in my employ. He *has to do* what I say. I'm his boss. That kills my desire to mix it up with him, even though he's all muscle. I don't want my new love or my husband to be under my command. Then when he's coming for me, I won't be able to tell if it's because of money, lust, admiration, or love. I need it to at least be for lust for sure. A man's lust makes my lust multiply. It's okay if he admires me, long as he ain't acting like a fucking freaky fan groupie or stalker. I mean I love my fans, but I need *the man I choose*, to not be a fan or a stalker. I need my man to have his own mind, schedule, and schemes, his own money and things, his own style and swag, Word up! I need my man to have 21st-century legit business, sprinkled with a half kilo of 20th-century murder energy. I laugh to myself. But, I'm serious.

Just then, in a flash, or should I say a glance, I spotted an unusually pretty bitch seated at the bar. I'm not about that girl-on-girl action, but I'm definitely about that beauty. I'm it. But I see myself every day. So, therefore, I'm drawn to other unique, beautiful people and things. So I walked over.

"What you drinking?" I asked. She cut her eyes at me. So I said, "Bitch you by yourself! I'm by myself. So what if we the baddest bitches in da club." She broke out in laughter. I could only tell because of the way the red club light lit up her smile. The music devoured the sound of her laughter. The rough, raspy voice of Jada Kiss rhyming and the Brooklyn flawless flow of fashionable Fabolus sent bitches into a frenzy. The beats through the mega speakers caused the floor beneath my feet to feel unsteady. With one pretty finger, she tapped the bottle seated on the bar top next to her glass. The angle of her hand positioned for me to see her *I'm better than the best bitch* Rainbow Sapphire bezeled, factory set diamond flooded, yellow gold, beautiful black-faced Daytona Rolex Chronograph Automatic, woah. Costs almost a mil. A piece that only a chick associated with top hustler or the president or the king or queen of some country or a nigga that rules the military would wear.

"D'Ussé," I saw her lips mouth. Then her eyes searched me like she was asking if I know the liquor. I'm thinking *yeah bitch*. It just debuted, a big money collaboration between Jigga and Bacardi. Then she used her pointing finger to call me in closer and yelled in my ear, "I can buy my drinks. Just pay for yours." I gave her a look like *of course bitch*. Then I flicked my fingers at the bartender. I pointed to her bottle. Then I pointed to myself to let him know, *I'll have what she's having*. I pulled out two racks, from my thousand-dollar stacks, and placed them on the bar top. Had my drink in my hand in a jiffy.

With her booty on the bar seat and back to the party crowd, she was tapping her foot on the lower level of her bar stool and gulping her Cognac. I was sipping mine but then I figured, *take it to the head* so I could hurry up and fill it up again. After my second drink, I

was feeling more than nice. I know when I'm nice. When I'm thinking less and feeling more. She shifted sideways on her bar seat and
was facing me now. Her green eyes lit up like lightning bugs from
back in my childhood days on the Brooklyn block when we tried
to catchem and sneak peaks at them lighting up in the palm of our
hands. The slant and shape of her eyes, plus the green, gave her an
advantage. *If I spot the man I been hunting for and I'm side by side
with her, he would still choose me,* I told myself. My beautiful brown
doe eyes and naturally long black lashes should never be taken for
granted. And even though females with green, gray, hazel, or blue
eyes get a headstart, the sum total of each of my body parts, including even the dimple in my chin, knocks every next bitch out the box
and I know it. She pointed her finger at me then at herself. "Let's
go!" I saw her lips say. I didn't say nothing back. Just widened my
pretty, big eyes like, *Where?*

   "I got a next spot," she said. "I've gone as high as I'mma go here."
She spoke into my ear. When she pulled her face back she had a nice
smile and pretty white even teeth. I stood up instead of answering
her back. So she got up also. I like a bitch who could drop 2 g's on a
bottle, and leave it behind for the vultures to devour. Now that we
are both facing the crowd, we can both see that the niggas in the club
could now see us beneath the red light where we are standing. We
can feel the niggas bout to move forward towards us. I already know
I am not drawn to any one man in here. However, my eyes landed on
my bodyguard, who had me square in his iris. Meanwhile she must
of saw my eyes lingering on him. She grabbed my hand and pulled
me in to her. "Bitches over niggas," she said. I pulled out of her palm
and hand signaled my bodyguard. Of course he caught my meaning.
We had practiced and used it enough for the past couple of weeks.
He turned and pushed his way through the crowd, moving in the

opposite direction of where me and her were standing, and headed
to the back door. She turned and gave me an *are you coming or not?*
look. I gave her a look back. We both stepped at the same time in
our stilettoes towards the front exit, our hips swinging and pretty
legs and thighs moving, our hair swaying and our titties bouncing.

A blast of summer wind rushed our faces once outside. Compared to the lounge atmosphere, hot summer wind is like air-
conditioning. Feels good. She reached into her Chanel clutch and
pulled out her iPhone. "Beejoo pull up," she said, to whoever was on
the other end before I could put my words together to say, *I got a
whip and a driver.* Tonight I am in the Lamborghini, one of the cars
in Santiaga's Exotic Fleet Dream Car collection. That's right. My
father, who is also my new and first ever business manager, told me,
before I drop a bag on a whip to own, I should drive or be driven
in the most exotic vehicles I ever dreamed of. "Choose to purchase
the ride that complements you. Makes you feel high just looking at
it, and even higher once you get inside." I listen to Poppa. Our love
is legendary. I love the way he always has a connect to whatever I
need. From then on I been changing whips like I change my nail
design. I love not letting niggas know who exactly is in the whip.
Keep them watching, guessing, and most importantly keep them off
of me, unless I want them on me.

A Mini Cooper pulled up, looking like a Coney Island El Do-
rado bumper car. I smiled. That shit ain't it. Ain't exotic, but . . .
I could definitely camouflage in it for my next nightclub adventure. She opened the front door then turned to wave me into the
front seat, saying to me, "You ride shotgun." I thought she would
sit up front herself. I didn't need her opening doors for me. I don't
know the petite little bitch whose driving her whip. I got in anyway. She hopped in the back, threw her legs up to rest over both

back seats, and sat with her back pressed against the driver side rear window.

"Let's hit up The Box," she said to her she-driver.

"I got you," the girl, who must be the one she called Beejoo, said, passionately like she really meant it.

I was both eyes on the front passenger side rearview mirror. My driver had just pulled up behind us. Now I'm watching my big-bodied bodyguard get into the white Lambo. When Beejoo pulled off, they followed. That's exactly what they suppose to do. My bodyguard makes it possible for a celebrity bitch like me to do whatever the fuck I want to do with whomever the fuck I want to do it with, cause I know I always got invisible backup.

"I'm Beejoo," she driver said. She has a weird feeling to her. I take a half glance and quick study. She's very light-skinned, light-weight. Boy hair cut, Caesar style, no titties and small sneaky eyes like a rodent.

"Beejoo?" I repeated even though I had already heard Green Eyes in the back call out her name on the celli.

"I didn't ask you," I said, but then added, "but that's a name I never knew nobody with."

"That's Bijoux, B,I,J,O,U,X." She spelt out each letter of her name with some type of accent spin on it. "It's French," she added.

"Your name might be French but you speaking English just like me and you look the same as the next bitch from my hood," I said, and she took it lightly and laughed.

"True dat! My father is Black American. My mom is white Brazilian," she announced like it was some type of an upgrade from being a regular hood bitch like the rest of us.

"You're mixed. Got it," I said as I took out my phone and Googled Mini Cooper to check the value of this little car.

"Mixed! Oh don't say that," she said like I had insulted her.

"*You said it first.* Like you want to be sure that I know."

"No I was just introducing myself and most of the time everyone pronounces my name wrong and not one person can ever spell my name right and nobody understands even why it matters. My name means 'kiss.' " She puckered up her unappealing thin lips. "It also means 'jewel.' " She raised her hand and jingled the fake crystals she has hanging from a thick thread on her rearview. "But honest kisses are like jewels aren't they?" she asked, and I'm thinking *Is she tryna push up on me?*

"And what is your name?" She slid the question in after saying all that.

"Bitch you know who I am," I said. "You think this is a fucking job interview?"

Green Eyes started laughing, then leaned forward. "Bijoux is mine," she said. "She works for me. Her job is to not do whatever I am doing, so that I can do what I do. She gets me to where I'm going safely and doesn't leave till she tucks me in." She said it like it was normal for a bitch to have a she-butler who's also a she-driver and maybe she even does karate or got an arsenal with switches in the trunk that makes Green Eyes believe Bijoux can get her home safely. Then she opened up the palm of her hand and pushed it right beside my face, then beneath my eyes.

"You, my Royal Highness . . . need to take the edge off. Obviously the Cognac didn't do for you what it did for me." I looked at the pill, then looked at her. I liked being called Royal Highness, by her.

"It's way stronger than weed, and it makes you feel like . . ." She made a sucking sound like she was inhaling the wind through her teeth.

"I'm not no fucking junkie. I don't want nothing that fucks up my look," I said calmly.

"How do I look?" she asked swiftly. She pulled her head back some so that I could take a good look at her. She was smiling like she was posing for a flick. Her eyes sparkled and her teeth were pure white. I had already studied the rest of her, her form and her flesh and her fashions and her angle and attitude. She is top tier. She pulled her hand back and closed her pill palm. Her manicure was doped-off the way I like it. Not nails that are long like animal claws, that make it impossible for a bitch to thoroughly clean her own body or wipe her own ass. Not nails sharp and pointed like knives that make a bitch look like a dangerous beast. And, not raggedy or jagged nails clipped too short, without design or precision, like how some sloppy or boring bum bitch might do hers. I tapped her palm. She lifted it up and opened it again. I picked up the pill and popped it into my mouth. Why not? That was my first thought of the night. *I need something stronger than weed.*

2
AFTER AND BEFORE

A dark sky and I am awake. I'm in the front passenger side seat of my Lamborghini for some reason, facing some bushes. *What the fuck.* I touch my face searching for feeling first and then memory. Confirmed. I have feeling, that's good. But I am missing some memory. That's not good. I pause, searching at least for the last memory that I can remember. Oh yeah. I was in the club last night. That's it. Nah, that's not the last thing. Oh yeah . . . the pill . . . the pill . . . and . . . that *is* the last thing I remember.

Earlier this same year, I got shot. It was the second I walked out of the prison after having served fifteen years for something I didn't do. I was declared dead, revived, and then fell into a coma. That was seven months ago. Ever since I survived the coma, I had to reset my body, brain, and motor skills like a newborn baby in order to fully recover. Now I find the whole matter of sleeping, dreaming, nightmares, waking up, and actual death to be *a really big deal.*

Don't get me wrong. I'm picture perfect and camera ready. *All* sweat my look. However, there are certain things that no one else can see or detect about me, unless I tell em, or unless my doctor tells them, that make me slightly different than my original self. Of course I prefer to be awake, aware, and swift. That's just me. So now, I'm going to test myself to see if I can recall everything that happened yesterday before I took the pill. If I can, I'm good, but not perfect, because clearly I have lost the hours between midnight last night and right now.

YESTERDAY

Friday, July 24. I woke up at 4 a.m. as usual for my celebrity workday.

I ran on my treadmill for one full hour except when I hopped off once because I caught an amazing design idea and had to run to my desk and write it and draw it out before it escaped my mind's eye. Next I took a three-minute shower, followed up by a twenty-minute rose-scented-water bubble bath and then a thirty-second shower rinse. In my bubble bath I felt like a young queen, which is the opposite of a convict.

At 6 a.m. I stepped outside of my front door in a cream-colored, sleeveless, wraparound summer dress made of thin and soft taffeta with a satin cream bow that sat on my left hip. On days where I have appearances as well as multiple wardrobe changes, or even medical checkups, where I have to continually undress, I wear something seductive and exquisite like this. One tug at that bow and the entire dress drops open. I like that.

At 7 a.m. yesterday I had a business breakfast in Manhattan, at the sky-high priced elite and immaculate Midtown Mandarin hotel. I'm not a breakfast person and didn't actually eat. At 9 a.m., I was seated at the dentist, a quick visit and clean sparkling white teeth. At 10:30 a.m. I was fully focused, as my accountant gave me the rundown on money, rules, regulations, and goddamn tax laws.

I definitely recall being blown away by the idea that half of everything I earn is owed to the U.S. government, unless I use my money to create more business, or invest and profit from existing businesses. In that case, what I spend on business is a business deduction, who I employ is a business deduction, my business office, office furniture is a business deduction. Business travel and even the food on the table at my business meetings are all business deductions. Somehow, simply saving and stockpiling my money works against me!!! I never knew that. At 11:30 a.m. I met with my jeweler, gave him a design I drew for a customized very unique charm bracelet, and ordered the kind of diamonds I want him to present to me to choose from. By noon my driver rushed and drove me from the diamond district down to Wall Street to meet with my business and entertainment lawyers. *Whatever*, I was thinking. *As long as I make it to Pizza Hut in Times Square before 3 p.m.* Nah, not to eat. I was headed there for a much more important reason. I heard that one of the girls I was locked up with, who got out one year before me, would start her shift there at 3 p.m. I had promised her I would look her up, hire her, and have her on my fashion team. She's a dope-ass artist who spent most of her time bombing buildings with her art designs. Problem was, she didn't own the buildings, houses, trains, or buses that she bombed. Graffiti is illegal. The city or state would rather lock up an amazing artist instead of paying her for her incredible work. A serial bomber, she lit up the bland city. I'm about to pay her her value. I tapped her as the number two person for the first legit business team I ever formed, that I am super serious about. I plan to show the world how to make millions off the people they eagerly threw away.

Of course I made a wardrobe change. I went from looking rich, sexy, silky ultra girly and creamy, to still looking rich cause I can't help it, but wearing a loose-fitting black satin jumper, black Birkin bag, and black uptowns topped off by black cat-eye sunglasses by Saint Laurent. Didn't end up mattering how blacked out I was. Seemed like my fans can smell me. When I stepped out of the Lambo the thick crowd of everyday walkers took immediate notice. Guess it was the whip. When I entered Pizza Hut, the line was already long. I stood at the end of it but it seemed like a small crowd had rushed in right behind me. New Yorkers try to play it cool. I know. Still I could hear them guessing, whispering, and others outright confirming that it was me, Winter Santiaga. I remained quiet, waiting while ignoring that the entire backside of the Pizza Hut had become filled with onlookers, all the way up to the door. The manager, I guess that's who he was, since he suddenly appeared behind the counter wearing a dress shirt instead of that embarrassingly ugly Pizza Hut uniform, looking surprised at the suddenly super-packed house and the escalating volume of the chatter. My bodyguard was off to my right side as I stepped up, seemingly to place my order. I lifted my sunglasses to reveal my face. The cashier, who had just stepped up for her shift after a quick drawer change, just started screaming to the top of her lungs.

"Ah bitch!!! That's what I'm talking about! You kept your word!!! Word to life!!!" She was so excited her eyes started tearing up. Her manager headed in her direction. She didn't give a fuck. She ripped open her Pizza Hut blouse and tossed it to the floor. Jumped on the counter and did a crazy dance, her titties in a two-sizes-too-small bra, bucking up and down against her tatted up flesh. She leaped off the counter and onto me, her tight grip the only thing that kept me from falling backwards. She eased me up, swung me around, and by that time the crowd and the manager and my bodyguard were all closing in on me to the point where I felt like I couldn't breathe. They couldn't pull her off of me. She was hugging me like I was her long-lost mother or child. "Thank you Thank you Thank you!" she screamed out. All cell phones were up and recording us. I hated that. The police showed up, and the Pizza Hut security were shoving people to the left and the right to get to where I was in her grasp. When they reached, she screamed, "Fuck the police. Fuck the manager. Fuck Pizza Hut. Fuck this ugly ass uniform! I got a new job, health care, and freedom! Winter Santiaga, I fucking love you to death."

Just recalling that crazy scene, and how my girl threw her middle finger up at everybody who wasn't me, as we left the Pizza Hut together, had me, currently laid back in the Lambo, laughing. Now I am sure that I am awake and alive and all is good.

Besides, by now, I fully recognize the groomed bushes. I'm parked at the Elisha Immanuel Brooklyn Estate. That always means I'm safe. Elisha Immanuel is my sister Porsche's husband. He's a young multimillionaire movie director and so much more. He is the one who set up my reality television deal called *Bow Down Starring Winter Santiaga.* He's the one who got me my first big bag. Funny thing though, sometimes the same things that you love can be the same things that you hate. I love that he's a man of the caliber of my father, but not a gangster or convict. I love that because Porsche requested it, he provided a wing of his house just for me, rent-free! He owns four brownstones, two in the front and two in the back, and all of the land in between. That's dope. However, even though I have a separate apartment, my own everything, even front door, mailbox, and parking space in their driveway, the fact is that because it is *his* estate, and because I got shot earlier this year, microscopic

cameras have been installed at all windows and doors and even at
his new security gate that is manned by around-the-clock security
guards. *It became the price of my fame.* It means that there are human
and digital eyes everywhere. Security knows when I come in, whatever time that is. Security knows when I leave out, whatever time
that is. Most importantly, security screens my visitors and knows
who came in, how long they stayed, and who went out. How can a
bitch ever get her freak on like that? I'm monitored and my guest
is registered like a fucking arranged conjugal prison visit! What if
I meet a nigga at the club and want to swing an episode with him,
nothing serious? I want him to come over, come in, and fuck me
right. Then I want him to get the fuck out. Well I can't do it that
way on the Immanuel Estate. Cause first of all, any nigga I invite
here would go gugugaga once he realized that he was at the home of
Brooklyn's favorite son Elisha Immanuel. He would get fixated on
that. Distracted by that. Obsessed with that. Once I see him fan out
like that, I don't even want him to fuck me no more! Besides, even
if that wasn't the problem, this is a family place. It's home to Elisha,
Porsche, and their three children, and now she got one more on
the way. Twenty-five years young and she's on kid number four. I'm
her big sister, Ricky Santiaga's first daughter. Porsche's luxurious life
highlights how many years I fucking wasted in the pen. When I was
locked I didn't focus on that. You can't focus on time while doing
time without losing your motherfucking mind. Now I'm free, living
the so-called high life, and the anger from doing time just down-
loaded into me last night and drove me straight into the club. I tell
myself don't sweat my previous incarceration. It's over. It's done. It's
the past. Get over it. Forget it. Adjust! It's not worth remembering.
But, the fact that I am breaking thirty years old, while looking and
feeling nineteen years young, and not married or even hooked up

with any nigga I fucking love to death, got me heated. Locked up as a teenager and did fifteen years, I'm being outdistanced by my own blood sisters and other bitches and celebrities who were free and doing it and living it while I was held captive.

Matter of fact that reminds me, what had set me off yesterday morning was when I received the hefty red box sent from overseas by a mail service I never even heard of, named Aramax. On top of the package was a red envelope. I picked it up and flipped it around. It was from my youngest sister, Mercedes. She's one of a set of twins. So even though I was pressed for time and had a tight schedule, I was curious. Must be important cause usually packages are not placed inside of my apartment. So Porsche must have put it there. She's the only one with a duplicate key. I opened the envelope. Turned out it was an invitation to Mercedes's regal overseas wedding. Nineteen years young and she's getting hitched. Not in just any ceremony. Her wedding is on a yacht and her invite is shaped like a yacht and engraved with dark gold lettering. "November 11th at 11 p.m. in 2011, In sha Allah ...," and inside of the official invitation was a piece of white papyrus with a handwritten note in dark black ink: "Farasha, I would be so excited for you to be the maid of honor in my wedding."

Now, I have zero idea what Farasha, means or who Farasha is? However, the entire package was mailed to Miss Winter Santiaga and that's definitely me. Her dope note continued, "All first class flights, seven-star arrangements, and accommodations have been set for you to arrive on November 1st, 2011. The early date is so that you can be properly welcomed, loved, fitted, and decorated and jeweled. Our weddings take place over a series of days and I need you at each activity. Please be on time my butterfly. You are the missing peace of my heart."

My mind was spinning. *My butterfly!* The last time I saw

Mercedes face to face, she was three years young. Hell, if she was standing right next to me right now, without someone introducing us or pointing her out, I wouldn't even recognize her. That realization forced me into thinking about how way back then, after our Long Island mansion got raided and my father arrested, I ran from place to place, lawyers and courts. Just a teenager trying to fight back, beat the system that beats damn near all of us. On one of them New York tornado-type days, I came home to our mansion only to be shocked that my three younger sisters had all been stolen, no, handed over to the authorities by our housekeeper Magdalena, who I had left in charge of them till I got back home.

I put the invitation down. I didn't want to get too heated and mess up my energy for all of my early morning appointments. Instead, I decided to open the red box. Inside of it was a varnished, heavy wooden sealed case with five drawers, a gold handle, gold hinges, and a gold combination lock. The tiny tag hanging from the handle said, "The combination is your birthdate." I dialed in the date and heard the box click open. With anticipation I pulled open the first compartment. Even though I knew it wasn't possible under the circumstance, I was hoping the first drawer contained some powerful weed that knocked out the bullshit weed I had been encountering for the past few weeks. Instead, inside, mounted on white satin was a mother-of-pearl Van Cleef lady watch, beautiful. On a tiny rolled scroll, which I unrolled, it read "You are precious. Time is precious. The precious Van Cleef is so precious it must only be worn for a few hours at a time. Keep it safe from water, humidity, and even your own sweat." I paused. In the second drawer, spread out on the white satin were seven pearl bangles. I lifted them to feel their weight. I never thought it would be possible to shape and hold pearl in the form of a bangle. Somehow, it was done with a thin pure dark gold bezel perimeter. I loved the feeling of having something I had not thought of creating myself. Something that I never saw the top designers design. Something that I never saw in a magazine, on a regal or royal or runway model or badass bitch's wrist. I was blown away by the set. Slid them over my pretty fingers and was afraid to let one bangle touch the other or check if they jingled or what type of sound they made when they did. I know all about gold. Pure gold is soft and easy to dent. In drawer number three, I lifted a sexy, curvaceous crystal bottle containing a dark liquid. The bottle top was a crystal crown and it was sealed with a thick gold strip. Amazed at the bottle, and the detailing of each gift, and the overall packaging, which was so creative, I was fucking impressed. I opened the tiny card in drawer three. In her same handwriting it read, "My Umma made you an elixir that I pray will be the scent that attracts the right husband to your heart and soul." I didn't read the rest, just crushed the card in my left palm and tossed it.

Devastated. Is she flossing now? Does she think I need help finding a husband? Of course she's flossing! She could have just FaceTimed me, texted me, or sent me an email or a digital invitation. This special delivery *is to flex*. Of course she's flexing. Probably is the reason that she has never called me or nothing since my prison release and recovery. I heard she refused to do it that way. The next time she sees me, she had said, according to Porsche, would be in person or not at all. Her reason was because she had already waited for way too long for me to come back from that day, long ago, when I left her with our housekeeper at our Long Island mansion.

Now, the fact that she's the younger twin, my youngest sister and a bride to be, and she's sending out expensive gifts that no ordinary bitch could imagine or afford, and complimentary first-class airline tickets and all-expenses-paid exclusive seven-star hotel bookings, which I never knew seven-star hotel resorts existed anywhere in the world, is a strong indication, that she at age nineteen *already has everything*, even the things that money can't buy. *I'm so fucking tight.*

I twisted the crystal crown until the seal opened. The most attractive scent entered the air that surrounded me. It affected my mean mood and moved my feelings in another direction somehow. I had never smelled such an alluring aroma anywhere. I used the crystal stick beneath the crown to spread some of the thick syrup fluid on the front and back of my neck, in between my titties and on the inside of each of my wrists. I even had an erotic thought, squatted, and placed some in between my thighs. I twisted the bottle around searching for the name of the product. How clever. It had no name. Strangely, I began worrying that I had no way to buy more. Needed to use it sparingly. Loved it and hated it at the same time. An elixir whose contents I would never know, that I could not refill unless I did what my baby sister wanted me to do, show up, watch her show off, and somehow ask her for more. In the fourth drawer was a gold envelope shaped like the envelopes a customer receives from a bank. I'm thinking no one would mail currency, not even in a gift box sealed with a combination. Besides, I have money! Mercedes must already know that. *She better know it.* When I pulled out the colorful stack of papers, the note lying on top read:

> "It's a huge and deep and wide world, *explore*. You might find something better, some place better, someone better than what you've experienced so far."

Tucked beneath the note were an array of currencies from a variety of countries, I guess to emphasize that she has already traveled the world and I have not. Whatever, *I'm used to that mean green.* All

American paper money is the same color, same design, same size, even though each green bill represents a different value. I stuffed the funny Monopoly money back in the gold bank envelope and left it in the drawer. I hesitated to look in the last drawer. I pulled it open slowly and saw it was a book. I shut it swiftly. Got zero time for that. Not interested.

Once I got in the Lambo early yesterday morning and my driver pulled off, I hit Porsche on her cellular. I played everything down, wasn't sure she knew what the package contained and just asked her casually instead, "Why is Mercedes waiting a whole year to get married?"

"Because she and her husband-to-be will both graduate first," Porsche explained. "And, you should know, Winter, Mercedes will marry one of Midnight's sons." After she said that, I cut the call and turned my phone off.

The fact that she is set to marry Midnight's son *burns me*. Not just because I know if he is the son of Midnight he is all man, all paid, all that and then some, but she's my little sister, who was adopted by Midnight, the man I loved ever since I was thirteen years young and boiling hot. The man who I still love, but can't seem to ever have, or even see, or ever touch. Now he has become some weird version of my stepfather, while our real father, Ricky Santiaga, is alive, now free and pardoned from his life prison sentence, and living well. That's some fucked up shit that should never happen in real life. I'm back to tight. And I'm swift. Nothing gets by me. I seen how she's getting married in the eleventh month, that's one, one, on the eleventh day, that's one, one, in the year 2011. That's one, one again. It's the same as Mercedes is declaring herself number one. And hell, I'm used to being number one in every category, undisputed, top bitch over all bitches and all of that.

"Winter." I heard Elisha's voice and his knuckles tapping on the driver side window of the Lamborghini. I sat up from where I was leaning back reflecting bout yesterday. My head and my limbs felt heavy. I pressed a button and the suicide doors swept open like the wings of an evil bird. He smiled and ducked and asked, "Why sleep in the whip when you got keys to your villa?" I started finger combing my hair and straightening out my minidress.

"Porsche asked me to come check on you," he said.

"She's up?" was all I asked. He smiled again.

"Look up." He pointed. I looked up and Porsche is in the second-story window all bright like it's mid-afternoon even though it isn't.

"I grilled fish. Come to the breakfast table!" she invited me joyfully.

"It's too early for breakfast," I said in my soft, sleepy voice.

"Well then, I'm coming to you!" she said and then shut her window. I rolled my eyes naturally. Then I noticed that Elisha had his golf clubs bagged and ready to go. I'm thinking damn, I'm used to niggas getting up a game on the basketball court, but never at 6 a.m. Time zoomed by me, and now this fine-ass twenty-seven-years-young multimillionaire is headed out to play fucking golf! He saw me looking at his clubs and said, "I'm driving over to Marine Park for the Police Athletic League Golf Tournament. Santiaga's meeting me over there."

Now I'm thinking, There's three men in this whole world who I love. First is my father Ricky Santiaga. Midnight is my first real man-woman love. Elisha is my hugest gratitude love. Now my sponsor Elisha and my father Santiaga are headed out to playing games with the motherfucking police! I could never have imagined no shit like that.

"Santiaga told me you weren't picking up your calls last night but to let you know that you are scheduled for an eleven a.m. meeting today with the president and CEO of the Network at the Network complex. That's a big one. Don't skip it," he said calmly, but clearly saying for me not to mess up the business he set up.

"I got it, Elisha. I'll be on time."

"Two things. Roll with your bodyguard since Santiaga will be with me. Second, in the CEO's office there is a staircase. Even if he invites you up, which he definitely shouldn't do, decline his offer."

"Got it," I said, although my mind was still not sharp or even all the way awake.

Soon as he bounced, I searched the floor of the Lambo and grabbed my purse. My cell phone is in there. I pulled it out and turned it on. Bells started dinging like I had more messages than I had time to listen to. My cash stacks of crispy new hundreds that I carry just cause I prefer was still intact. Relieved, I grabbed my wrist, and my diamond bracelets are still on me. I put one hand on each of my ears, and my sparkling diamond cubicles are still dangling. My signature platinum hourglass necklace is in between my bare breasts. So what the fuck? How come I don't remember anything about last night after I took that damned pill? Whatever the case, the green-eyed bitch didn't rob me or set me up to get robbed. My driver and bodyguard obviously did their job and got me back here safe. Still I don't like not knowing what the fuck I did or even where I went last night after the lounge. That shit is sloppy. I stepped out of the car. Standing there under the moonlight that was being threatened by the rising sun, I said to myself, *Fuck popping pills. That shit is dead. I don't want nothing that fucks up my look or turns me into a stupid, blitted blacked out forgetful bitch who don't know what's going on around her.*

3
PORSCHE LUXURIOUS SANTIAGA

I grabbed my stillettos from the Lambo front floor, and soon as I stood back up Porsche was standing there in her wifebeater tee, swolled titties, and no bra, wearing Daisy Dukes and Hermès slides, holding a brown paper bag.

"You been throwing up again?" I asked her. "Morning sickness?" She smiled like someone who was definitely not sick in any mild or big way. She held up the bag and said, "Seeds and breadcrumbs, you wanna walk with me to feed the birds?" She asked like she doesn't remember who I am and the difference between her and me, and as though it was a legitimate question.

I was like . . . Then I stopped myself and gave her a look and walked toward my front door. "I'm moving out," I said, surprising myself even though I had thought that thought in my head for several days.

"Why? Don't! What did I do wrong? Did I make you mad? I'll feed the birds and come right back. Let's talk about whatever is on your mind and why. Don't make any quick decisions. At least wait for the sun to come up." She stretched out her arms toward the sky.

"When you see the sunshine and the flowers and the garden you'll change your mind."

I walked in. She walked off. Porsche is like that. She dramatizes, sings, and reveals her emotions whenever she speaks. Plus she don't think nothing like me. I'm doing her a favor moving out. How can a grown woman live in the same property with her sister and her sister's husband? How can especially me, live here with a legit paid-ass, fine Brooklyn nigga who takes care of me like a regular good dude would only do for his own women? A man who checks on me, and talks to me face to face, no matter how large or busy he is, on any matter I bring up, personal or business. What if I feel so grateful to Elisha for everything he has done for me and even for my father, that after a couple of drinks I accidentally fall on his dick and start riding? Real talk. I'm not in love with him or anything like that. He never tried to kick it to me or make any moves on me, and I never ever caught him even giving me a lusty look, even when I was dazzling. Common sense though is that if a man takes real good care of any woman, a woman repays him with her mood and her body. Don't she? I'm not a cutthroat bitch or a fucked up sister. So I would *never do it*. But a bitch never knows what she might do or say if and when she's drunk. If that happened, I couldn't just blame it on the alcohol. It would crack Porsche's mind wide open. She's fragile. It would ruin her. If I let anything like that happen it would be the same as completely cutting ties with my blood. Everybody would side with her. She's the one who works hard to stay in contact and connected and interacting with all of them. If they turned against me, I wouldn't know it, but I do know they would be right. I'm not about that life. My cell phone interrupted my thoughts.

"Hey Bitch," a pretty voice said sleepy-softly. I didn't answer back cause the voice didn't sound familiar. Definitely not familiar enough to be like, *Hey bitch.*

"The guys invited us out for a take two," she said calmly.

"What guys?" I asked automatically.

"Girl, you funny." She laughed. Then said, "The dudes we was partying with last night." Now I was dead silent. I really didn't know what niggas I had partied with last night and I had no intention of admitting it. So I reversed on her. "*No, you funny.* At the club you was all 'bitches over niggas,'" I reminded her. She laughed and said, "Copy dat."

I guess that's the replacement for "true dat."

"Bitches over niggas for me and my girls means when it comes to loyalty—and getting money—we choose and hold down each other first and foremost. Now getting dick is different ain't it?" She laughed.

"Getting dick is definitely different, copy dat!" I said and I laughed.

"We need dick, but we don't fight over it, betray one another over it, and especially never allow the good dick to drive us crazy!" she said and I like her.

"I'm not free till round eight tonight. If that's cool with you," I said to her.

"Me neither," she shot back. "Where should we meet?" she asked. "On Second Avenue and Sixth Street," I told her because I knew my last appointment today is down in the Village.

"And leave that big nigga who was following us around in the Lambo in the dog house," she joked but I knew she was serious. "Who's he, your husband? Don't tell me you're married?" she asked in a peculiar way like that would be the worst thing. I didn't reply. Maybe she had a conflict with my bodyguard cause he peeped that she had me partying with some random niggas. I don't know. I don't remember anything after getting in her car and pulling out.

"Then you leave that butler bitch behind," I barked.

"Deal," she said calmly. "Just because I like Bijoux doesn't mean you have to like her. And bitch you're more my type and my equal, *not my employee*," she threw in.

"Eight p.m. then," I said and cut the call. I was being polite but I know the pretty bitch caught my meaning. Real bitches can look each other over in three seconds and know the caliber. Bijoux ain't it. Why would two gleaming Glocks tote around some bullshit 22.

Porsche pushed the bathroom door open without knocking. I'm in the shower now and immediately felt the cold air-shot that rushed through. She washed her hands and face in the sink and came and sat on the closed toilet seat like it was a comfortable chair and this was her living room. She cocked her legs up and held on to them as she spoke to me. "You gave me a look just like Momma used to do."

I didn't say nothing back. She's always talking about only family and family memories or dreams of family or family plans for the future. That's her. Suddenly she unlocks her legs and jumps up. "Hey let me wash your back," she said as she opened the glass door to the shower stall and stepped in. I was like, "C'mon Porsche. This is too much. I can definitely shower by myself like I do every day. Get out!" She wouldn't listen to me though. She was enjoying the downpour of the water on her hair as it also soaked through her wifebeater tee and denim shorts. Then she grabbed the washcloth, sudsed it up, and turned me round by my shoulders. She began washing my back like it was the best day of her life. "See Winter, even you have to admit that there are some things in life that you will need help with. Everybody does! No one can wash their own back."

"I'm letting you get away with this one time and one time only because you pregnant. If you weren't, we'd be two wet bitches brawling and sliding around the floor," I warned her. She started giggling like I was joking with her, which ticked me off. Meanwhile I was thinking how at eighteen years young I had figured out how to wash my own back in jail on Rikers Island.

"Oh Winter, guess what?" she said, delighted. "We ain't locked up prisoners no more. So we can breathe and relax and love and enjoy. There's no more reason to be angry or mean." She shook her hips and leaned in too close to my face and said joyfully, "We all the way up!"

"Get out. You're soaked for no reason. Now you gon be dripping all the way back to your side of the house."

"Nope, I'm bout to get some of your clothes and put them on. She stepped out of the shower, pulled off her wet denim and eased out of her tee, then reached for my bath towel. She wrapped herself in it, picked up her clothes, and tossed them in my linen-lined bamboo hamper. She turned and said, "I'll be laying on your bed so we can talk!"

Finally alone, in my spacious private customized bathroom, I closed my eyes. My body felt hotter than the shower water. I turned the knob to make the water go cold. A cold shower is the only way to cool myself. I didn't get my right sleep last night. Plus these unscheduled, unagreed, non-mutual early morning talks with me that Porsche shows up for almost every morning are an interruption to me, a bitch who has very detailed big plans, put together over a fifteen-year span, a stacked, packed schedule, a hit list, and way too many things on my mind.

"I don't like your bodyguard," Porsche said. Wearing my summer dress surrounded by sunlight, she was seated in the middle of my king-sized mattress, on top of my comforter, her legs folded Indian style. "The sun is up!" she announced.

"I can see that since you opened all of my curtains and shades even though you know I just got out the shower. And you stole my bath towel," I said, shivering.

"Don't worry. The sun will dry up all of the water drops on your pretty skin. Come let's talk." She patted the comforter wanting me to sit right beside her. "I'll massage some avocado butter all over your skin," she offered. I sat down instead away from her on my eggnog-leather, slim designer recliner. I reached for the mango butter that remained on my vanity table and moisturized myself, inhaling the nice scent.

"I get the feeling he's not really *your body guard*," she said, separating the word "body" from "guard" and saying both words with emphasis. "He seems like he just makes sure you're alive."

"That's what he's supposed to do," I said, defending him although I really don't care either way. He isn't one of my niggas. He was handpicked by the Network and the investors to guard the treasure, who is me.

"No! If I was your bodyguard, I would be doing more than keeping you alive. I would be watching everybody you meet, even the fans in the crowd, even the businesspeople in your meetings. I would be searching for foul looks, fake smiles, or mean mugs and hidden enemies. I would be having my eyes peeled for anybody and everybody who's green," she said strangely. It made me think of the sexy girl with the green eyes from last night.

"Green?" I asked.

"Yeah, I give all of the emotions and certain behaviors a color. I started doing that from when I was eight years young in the cage."

"Cage?"

"That's what I call the prison. Cause that's what it is isn't it? Each of us in a cage, or two or more of us in a cage, or a bunch of us in a space that's in a cage," she said with a rare trace of venom. Quickly, I thought about it. She's right. I found out that she was locked up at the young age that I was princess of the world. But I know one thing. She didn't do fifteen years like I did. She must have read my expression.

"I didn't do fifteen like you did, Winter. But I did ages seven through eleven caged up and behind bars. It was the scariest years of my life. I was a very little girl getting passed around from situation to situation. But, I handled it. I know you think of me as your weird younger sister who overdoes it and adores you too much. Who has a tree house and loves the birds, horses, and all animals really. And, *that* is who I am. But, don't sleep. I formed my own gang at age eight. Then got ganged up again at age ten. I got an entire girl army to this day, and I think you need a sharp and tight security team who knows what they are doing and gives a fuck. Your bodyguard does the minimal, like as long as I bring Winter Santiaga back dead or alive that's good enough. That's how the warden and the co's used to think of us. To them we were just bodies, and they were only responsible for the body count, no matter what condition or circumstance the prisoner's life or body was in." That's facts she was saying right there bout the lockup and the co's and their bullshit. This time I could tell her memories are real. She is not playing or imagining. Still I poked her.

"I have not seen no girl army round here." I looked around like I

was searching. "Just Porsche Luxurious Santiaga, her incredible husband, their three children, her mother-in-law and father-in-law, *and
even her husband's grandparents*," I emphasized and said, exasperated. I
needed to bring her back to the reality of her current happy-go-lucky
life in Park Slope, Brooklyn. After all, the Immanuel property is her
bubble, her world. She rarely even leaves here. Every time I am at the
Immanuel breakfast, lunch, or dinner table, which is where she wants
me to be as often as possible and whenever she checks my schedule
and sees I have some free time. I show up and sit there *in her world
among all of them*. But the truth is, *I just be suffocating*.

"Ain't the dopest army the ones that have the soldiers that no
one has seen? Or even if someone saw them, they had no idea that
they were the baddest and best girl fighters, capable of, but not
known for, violence, but for squeezing their enemies until they surrender. Or as you would say, bow down."

"Squeezing them!" I repeated cause that doesn't sound like reli-
able protection to me.

"Yeah like a boa constrictor, you know, the long wide pretty
killer snake." She jumped off my bed and started doing some dance
moves. Her dancing is unrivaled. I'm not gonna front. She could
move each of her body parts, down to her eyeballs, baby finger, and
big toe, in a way that the person looking might find themselves
hypnotized.

"So when I got shot up at the top of this year," I said, as I eased
into my silk pajamas, "you are saying if your girl army had been
there, they would have *squeezed the shooter to death* before the
shooter squeezed the trigger and shot me?" Then I started laughing
at her ridiculousness. More like cackling at her.

"That's not funny, Winter. I told you I'd prefer if you didn't make
jokes about that horrible incident. And, no, my girl army would

not have squoze the shooter. But if you had them doing your security from the jump, the shooter would have never even gotten close enough to the location to fire at you. Matter of fact, no guns would have gotten pass my girls. They thorough."

"So are you saying it's Elisha's fault because his company did not hire your girls as the security team for my prison release, reality show debut?" I asked calmly, but I knew I had trumped her. Just the mention of Elisha still seemed to give her goose bumps and her mood would be taken over by her intense love for him.

"Definitely not! The Network was responsible for security that day. They hired that security team. I wish they would have investigated every person, every worker, every guest, even everybody on your VIP list before giving them passes to enter the film shoot area. But Network security was more focused on securing all that expensive camera equipment, and their crew, when they should have been securing you! While you were in a coma, I hate to even say those words . . . and during the investigation, the Network passed the blame to the city police officers in Upstate New York. The Network said that since you were locked up and coming out through the release door of the New York State Prison System and onto city property, the city police were responsible. Of course the city cops didn't want to take the blame. They blamed the governor because you were considered 'state property.' But the governor said once you walked through the door, and the fact that you hit time served, meant that you were no longer state property! And, all the different security teams and police agencies and bonders and insurers were busy arguing and passing the buck," she said and then plopped back down on my bed. "You're lucky for Elisha. He didn't run away and hide. He jumped right in the middle and made it possible for all of the agencies to save face and escape the blame. He called an emergency press conference, made a statement to the press about the meaning of force majeure."

"What?"

"Elisha explained to everyone that because of the huge snow-storm that occurred that same day during the filming, no one agency was fully responsible for what happened. Elisha said the storm was an act of God. Therefore all of the agencies should cooperate with one another and fully investigate the *only* crime that happened that day, which was the shooting," she said, and I knew she would defend her husband passionately. *Whatever, I definitely ain't mad at Elisha for a damn thing. That nigga cool as a fuck.* He's dominant in business, like a poker player holding all four aces, or better yet a Royal Flush.

"So Elisha came out the big winner," I said to show her exactly how clever and ingenious her husband is. But then I added, "If those agencies had *cooperated* like Elisha told them to do, they cooperated in never finding the motive or the shooter who almost killed me!"

"It's not Elisha's fault that they never found the shooter. If he were a detective, he would have caught him. But he's not in that line of work. Besides, he made all of the insurance companies pay up, and that's why you got excellent care until you were back to being your same lovely self, all body parts working, and looking like a billion bucks." She clapped. "I still think you need better security. Once you experience my girl army you'll know why hiring them was the best choice."

"Your girls huh . . . I didn't know you had any friends." I laughed. "Just a husband and family." I teased her.

"Look who's talking. You been living it up, being a superstar bigger than the hoodstar you already was back in our Brooklyn hood. But I have not seen you with even one of your girls. Not Natalie, Asia, Simone, Zakia, Toshi, Reese . . ." She was pulling down one pretty finger as she named and counted off each of my Brooklyn project girls who were my friends from before she was even born, when I was five years young, and all through thick and thin. She's right. I have not met up with none of them bitches on purpose.

"After I saw the bodyguard, *not your driver for some reason*, drive you in at 5:40 a.m. this morning, with you knocked out in the front seat and your car seat all the way back like how you're reclining right now, I was convinced. He just parked the Lamborghini, closed up all the windows, and got out. He left you just like that as though his job was done, just enough to get his paycheck. Soon as he left, I ran down and out to you. Luckily he left the digital key on the hood. Otherwise I would not have even been able to get the car doors open. *When I did,* poof! The whole whip smelled like liquor. I pushed on the ignition and turned on the air-conditioning enough for you to breathe. I ran back in the house and got a bowl of cool water and a washcloth and wiped down your face and straightened your hair, and removed your heels. I even saw a smear of blood." She paused. "Like someone had washed away the rest of it, but mistakenly missed that little part. Maybe because it was dark. Through all of that you never blinked or woke or nothing. That horrified me. Reminded me of your hospitalization. I looked at your facial expression and I was like, *What the fuck! What happened to my big sister last night? Where did you go? What did you do? Who were you with?*" She was pissed at the bodyguard and gesturing each of her words with her hands and her eyes, softly, sweetly, which is her odd dramatic signature style.

"So what did *you* do about it? I woke up in that car seat. *So you left me out there as well.*"

"Is that the same thing, Winter? Is what I did for you the same as what he did to you? He forgot that you needed air to stay alive.

It's summertime! And yeah! I did something about it. I investigated. I went in your purse, got your cell phone out. It was off." She gave me a nasty stare. She hates when I turn my cell phone off for even a half-hour. "I turned it on, and right when I did, a call was coming in from an unidentified number. The time was 5:56 a.m. Right when I picked it up, whoever it was hung up. That made me suspicious. So I looked at your call log. The call I had just missed and the last calls that you made and received. I even checked your browser history. You looked up Mini Cooper. I found that strange. I don't see *you* buying *that* car. You got two calls from Poppa and he even left one voice mail." She rolled her eyes. She never speaks on it, but I think Porsche be counting how many times I see or hear from Poppa, and then comparing it to her rare interaction with him. She should understand though. Santiaga and me been mega-busy, making every minute count. Both of us lost way too many years behind bars that we can't ever get back.

"Your last incoming call was from 'Zuzing Zee . . .' "

"Who!" I sat up. "You mean a Scam Likely call?" I swiftly said.

"Funny you should say that, cause if it involves her, it is highly likely that it is a scam."

"What are you talking about?" I urged her to spill the beans, get to the motherfucking point.

"You had her business card in your purse. When I went in your purse to check your phone, and answered the unidentified call, her business card fell out. I found it right on top of your stillettos. It's a deep black mesh fabric card with one tall letter X on the left-hand side, interlocked with one medium-sized letter x, no personal name, no company name, just her full cell phone number. When I looked at the number, it was the same number as the call you had just received. I double-checked. I held onto the card. In fact I left it on my vanity table in my bedroom. I took it up there to ask Elisha because he has this *same business card in his wallet.*" She put her hands on her hips and held them there. I was thinking, *So she goes in her husband's wallet checking on him? Does she suspect him? Nah! I doubt it.*

"So back up a minute," Porsche said. "If you do not know her, or recognize her name, or who she is, yet you have her business card, to me, that means she had her hands on your purse while you were knocked out. She must have put her card in there. She also was the last person to call you, at 5:56 this morning. Who calls somebody at that time if they ain't family? So that probably meant *you were with Zuzing* right before the time you came home. Right?!"

"Damn, Porsche! *You thinking and doing way too much.* And, what were you doing up in the middle of the still dark morning that made it possible for you to see my bodyguard pull up?" I asked her.

"I never went to sleep. You didn't call. You didn't come home. I didn't know where you were or what was up. Or, if you were safe. I checked your itinerary for the Friday workday. You had like nine different appointments but the last one ended at eight p.m. Then you just didn't come back." She struck a pose with her hands up in the air as though me going out to the club, I mean lounge, needed to be reported to my younger sister in order for her grown married ass to sleep.

"Porsche, you doing too much. You know how many people hand me a business card and all kinds of shit every single day? How did you decide someone went in my purse, which I keep in my hand or on my body?" I challenged her.

"See, that's what I'm talking about. I don't like your bodyguard. Nobody who you are not meeting with and who you don't know should be able to get close enough to hand you anything. And what was up with that Pizza Hut riot?"

"It wasn't a riot," I said, completely out of patience. "How did you hear about it?" I asked.

"Are you joking me? Making fun like I'm this stupid young girl who stays in the house and don't know nothing or do nothing, or see anything or hear anything?" she asked still in her soft voice but with a thicker, more intense look and tone in her eyes and voice. "Mad people posted the Pizza Hut thing on the internet. Crazy thing is, since it was different footage posted from different phones and different angles, I watched everything and in not one of the posts that I viewed did I see your bodyguard, but in every post I saw you!" She was pissed.

"Didn't you just say that the best security is the kind that no one can see, or that no one knows is security?" I trapped her in her own words. Now, all she needed to do was get off my bed and get the fuck out so I could sleep peacefully for two hours before my meeting with the Network CEO.

"That's not the same thing," Porsche said even more softly than her usual soft. "And just last week you were filmed at the strip club arguing over some stripper, throwing money, and leaving out with her," she accused, and she's right. I did that, but she don't know why I did. Famous fraudster "Boobytrap" was the first chick I went and got for my new business team. Had to compete with some trick-bitch who was in the club pulling out ones and feeding them to Booby so she could have a monopoly over her big-ass titties and long-ass black nipples. At first I was stuck on trying to figure how a third of the customers in the strip club were bitches competing with the male tricks for the attention of the female strippers. All I recalled from my teen Brooklyn days is people's mothers trying to keep their men out the strip club and being jealous of the strippers. Now people's mothers is at the strip club out-bidding the niggas over the hoes. And the stripper hoes today, a lot of them look beat up, busted, and broke down. So I catch on quick even after being a bit shocked. I started pulling out bigger paper and tossed it in the air over Boobytrap's head and grabbed her hand and pulled her out of there. Once she realized it was me up in the dark-ass club, she got so excited she left out with me, wearing nearly nothing but a string up her ass. Of course cell phones came out, which is the only way Park Slope Porsche would ever find out about some hole-in-the-wall strip joint I went to. Even the club owner came out chasing. I let him bump heads with my bodyguard and went about my business.

"I know I'm your little sister, but none of this is necessary. We don't have to do none of that. We already have everything."

She was right. *She already has everything.* Her and Mercedes are chilling. Now I'm working triple-time putting my own investment-business team and fashion line together, gathering my crew. Somewhere in the process of doing that my way, I'm hunting a man, who's good enough for me to lust, love, admire, marry, and then flaunt and flex.

"Or maybe there is a reason that you are doing all of this, Winter? I wish you would tell me. I can help. You know, I am always on your side."

I didn't tell her anything. I need to build my own Handmade Universe, which is the name of one of my new business companies. The logo that dropped into my mind is an hourglass. That is the reason the piece that dangles from my gold chain is an hourglass. The top that supports it is outlined in sparkling princess-cut diamonds and so is the bottom stand. The sand that pours through it is real gold sand. It's an eye catcher to all whose eyes are allowed to see it, and a reminder to me that life is not guaranteed, and cannot be extended without MERCY, so not to allow myself or anyone else to play with, fuck up, or waste my time.

4
THE ELEVATOR

"Look who's back from the dead." It was Simone speaking as the elevator doors opened up in the main lobby of the Network Entertainment Complex. I'm thinking. There are six elevators operating. How come I ended up with the doors opening up to my whole crew?

"I'm holding the button," Zakia said. "Going up?" she asked me.

"Bitch get in we miss you! How come you didn't come check us first?" Natalie asked me, holding her arms open like she thought we would hug. I stepped in.

"Why you wearing sunglasses?" Reese asked. "Takem off. We wanna see the real you," she insisted.

"Yep, not the Hollywood version!" Natalie said, her hands now on her hips. Then Simone stepped into the left corner of the moving elevator and called out, "Corners!" Then each of my girls dashed into a corner, leaving me standing in the middle, which from back in our days on the Brooklyn block meant the "man in the middle" gets Brooklyn mobbed. Instead of jumping me they rushed in and all hugged me as Simone, the strongest of them, lifted me up into the air. Now they was jumping up and down, all except Zakia, who was yelling, "Don't jump! Don't jump!" But it was too late. The elevator started shaking. Simone let go of me without warning. I could have fell, but luckily I wasn't wearing my stilettos and was able to break my fall with a shorter heel. Then it dropped, same as an airplane suddenly drops during turbulence. I'm thinking *Oh no! I need to stay alive. I'm supposed to be going up, not down. Not down anymore!* Simone is laughing and the rest of my girls were playing until they realized we were actually plunging. Then they each started screaming. Zakia pushed the emergency button. An alarm sounded. Then the elevator rumbled and jerked to a stop, but the doors did not open.

"Do not touch the elevator doors. Remain calm. This is security. We have alerted engineering and you will be able to exit safely momentarily," a calm yet authoritative male voice said through an elevator speaker.

"Remember this shit used to happen to us all the time in the projects?" Natalie, nervous at first, said and then laughed.

"Yeah but in the projects nobody is manning the elevators and no voice comes on to guarantee our safety," Reese said.

"That's facts. At least nobody peed in here and we ain't stuck," Asia said, trying to calm all.

"We are stuck! That's why the doors ain't opening. It wasn't funny when this happened back then. It ain't funny now," Zakia said.

"And this is 'moneymaking Manhattan,' so this ain't suppose to happen at all," Reese commented.

"Y'all pussies don't worry. We got thee Winter Santiaga on this motherfucker with us. If it was just us on board, we might've all been toast, but they won't let shit happen to their top moneymaker," Simone said in her rough voice and manner of speaking. "And I got

a whooly. We can smoke it till they get us out." She pulled her joint
out of her left pocket and her lighter out of her right.

"Don't light up in here crazy!" Asia yelled.

"You gon get us exploded! We already running out of air," Zakia
warned as she snatched the lighter from Simone's hand and began
inhaling and exhaling hard for some reason.

"Don't nobody want that whooly ammonia smell in our clothes,"
Natalie scolded.

"Winter, I am glad you got stuck on this elevator with us," Asia
laughed. "And by the way, *you smell so good*! What are you wearing?"
They all started inhaling dramatically.

Just as I went to say, Natalie jumped in and was like, "Wait, let
me emcee. Y'all know I know my stuff. The stunning Ms. Winter
Santiaga is doing Dolce & Gabbana on this Saturday morning. She
has on black D&G Amore sunglasses and four-inch heeled Palla-
dium mules with the Dolce & Gabbana crossover D&G logo, hot to
death. Her silver lace mini says *This is a stickup, motherfuckers! Give
me all of your money!*" They each laughed.

"And they will give it to her," Simone added.

"Not her outfit, I was talking bout that aroma. It makes me
wanna . . ." Asia was still sniffing my perfume.

"Kiss her ass like you doing right now," Simone spit.

"Shut the fuck up, Simone," Natalie said. "You always got something fucked up to say."

"All y'all need to shut the fuck up," Reese said. "Y'all been saying
everything. Winter ain't said shit since she got in here." And they all
got dead quiet and looked at me.

"Who shot me?" That's all I said and the silence doubled. "I
don't give a fuck if the police never caught the shooter. My bitches
should've caught the shooter. And if any one of y'all loved me after

all the bullshit we been through together, you would've clapped back."

"Stand back. First the elevator will shift and downshift. Then the doors will open."

We all moved back. We all stared at the lighted numbers. I was headed to the twenty-first floor; they must've been all going to the eighteenth floor because that was the only other number that was lit when I got on. The elevator shifted. Zakia pressed both of her palms on the wall as though she didn't believe we would be released and that maybe we would drop down a few more floors without notice. The elevator dropped down to twelve, bounced, and then steadied. Seconds later the doors opened. As they did, we each walked out directly into the movie cameras that were lit and rolling. I was tight about it. This is not supposed to be a filming day. Season 2 of my show doesn't begin until September, right after Labor Day. The PAs (production assistants) were waving us forward as though to say walk in towards the camera, but I was like this is not the floor any of us were headed to before getting stuck. I'm feeling set up.

"This is fucked up," Simone said on camera. "No one said that we were being filmed today. And y'all got us in these velour sweat suits for the softball game, and evidently Winter didn't know shit about the game, cause she the only one camera ready like a mother-fucking movie star. Or maybe she did know, but she felt it was okay for us to look like clowns as long as she was shining."

"These velour Fila sweat suits is dope. Simone, I don't know what you complaining about," Asia defended. "Psst and we rocking Fila 88s. Brooklyn knows that's certified."

"Cause this shit ain't even," Simone replied.

"It ain't suppose to be even stupid. The name of the show is *Bow Down Starring Winter Santiaga!*" Reese blurted back.

"Who you calling stupid?" Simone said at the same time she hooked off on Reese. Now these bitches were thumping. I'm watching two, no three cameras shifting to capture the fight.

"Break it up! Y'all making us look dumb!" Asia said.

"Cut," the DP called out, and everybody knew what that meant and paused like trained monkeys.

"I'm Dana Stern from the marketing department of the Network. I'm here to escort the girls to the eighteenth floor for your brief pre-game photo op."

"And I am Paisley Tosh. Winter, I am here to escort you to the president's office."

The woman Dana whisked my girls away. Rowdy, they were each saying something at the same time, which made it impossible to understand. But I understood. They wanted to know why they were here for some little promotional thing, while I was headed up to the president's office. I wasn't about to explain or interrupt whatever they were involved in. They kept looking back at me as they were directed toward a different elevator.

"Invite us over to the Immanuel mansion," Natalie yelled out. "Then we can talk. I know where it is," she added.

"Everybody know where it is," Asia chimed in. Reese, Zakia, and Simone was just mean mugging me, like they knew for sure no invites to the Immanuel mansion were going to be handed to none of them. And they were 100 percent right and exact.

5
DICK KUNTZ

The office of Richard Kuntz, CEO and president of the Network, took up the entire twenty-first floor and could only be reached by transferring to his private elevator. "He has arranged to meet you in his most elegant setting. That's how special and important you are," Paisley, his polite appointment secretary, made sure to tell me. I didn't say shit. She continued buttering me up. "Even the biggest hip-hop stars and lesser reality show stars only make it to his Chill Suite, which is rather fabulous but totally several steps down from his Icon Pavilion reserved for you this morning."

Ceiling-to-floor panoramic glass walls gave him an *I'm rich bitch* view of New York City. A forty-something-year-old guy, he still had all of his hair and a young man hairline.

"Thank you for removing your sunglasses" was his opening line as soon as he saw my eyes. I gave him my *we making money together* business smile, which is not nearly as inviting or bright as my sincerity.

"I'm Dick," he said extending his hand for a handshake. "Your scent is amazing. I better be careful. I think it has already put a spell on me." He smiled. It is not a smile of desperation. It's the look of confidence and conceit. Like, *Yo check me out. I'm dressed like the Don for you.* He's wearing a white Purple Label Ralph Lauren suit, with suede, white Tod's driving shoes. There's no neck tie choking him. He chose a white silk ascot, which makes him look richer, younger, freer than other wealthy men his same age. *Watch out for him,* I told myself. The way he has outfitted himself makes it doubtful to impossible for anyone to think of him as a man who might do deceitful or dirty shit. His look conceals it all.

"I brought you in on a Saturday. Normally, I never ever conduct business on a Saturday morning. However, I know how in demand you are and exactly what your itinerary looks like. When your business manager said you had an opening on Saturday, I grabbed it."

"No problem. I'm here" was all I replied.

"Great! So let's chat." He walked me over to a Dom Edizioni–designed brilliant white leather sofa. The leather looked thick and soft as butter. So clean, it would make a person question whether or not they should even sit on it. The deep black tightly tailored piping on the work of art boosted the value of the already expensive and exclusive sofa substantially. I lowered my lace mini onto what was as comfortable as a marshmallow and too lovely to be described simply as a couch. He sat across from me on his white Barcelona chair. He looks like a carefree king on an armless throne. So rich is he that he doesn't need a crown to signal that he is the top man in charge. He doesn't need anything. Even Paisley, poof just disappeared after her excited introduction and offerings of water, tea, or almond milk or soy milk, decaf, coffee or cappuccino, which I declined.

"We have a sixty-five-million-dollar deal with Elisha Immanuel. We are extremely excited to be in business with him. *Bow Down* was the first show he pitched to the Network, and much like his independent film endeavors, it is wildly successful. Elisha is a great guy but also a very tough businessman. I respect him. It is not customary for the Network to allow the kind of creative freedom that he demands. We normally produce all of our content in-house. But since I, as you and the crew might say, 'run this motherfucker,' " he leaned forward then continued, "I jumped at the opportunity to collaborate with the Immanuel Group," and he leaped out of his chair and gestured as though he was a desperate runner, exhaled, untied his ascot, then laughed. I smiled politely.

"Your business manager is *also* a stand-up all-round great guy. I know he's also your father. He handles all of your business and negotiated your 2.5-million-dollar contract for season 2 of *Bow Down*. Word has it that you follow his lead. I was told it was not even necessary for me to sit down and chat with you since I had already met with him and agreed upon the broad strokes of every one of his, or should I say *your demands.*"

"I would say our business requirements are for *our* mutual benefit," I said sweetly. He chuckled.

"Exactly. I requested your father to allow me to be the one to inform you that we have put in place a much larger budget for *Bow Down* than for any of our reality and even some of our scripted shows. Mr. Santiaga requested a fat advertising campaign and was quite keen that you get the sixty-by-fifty-foot billboard space at Times Square to announce the debut of season 2.

"There were three reasons why I called you here today. The first was because as president of the Network, I am the person who best demonstrates our commitment to your success not just with words, but by granting you all access and fulfilling your demands. Hence, you will be the only reality show star to be featured at the most expensive billboard location in all of America. The last entertainment icon featured at that location was Angelina Jolie."

"Sounds good. I hear that the Network actually owns that bill-board space," I said to let him know I know that it may be the most expensive advertising billboard location in the country, but that the Network owns it. If they had to pay a different owner, then that would show a real commitment because that cost would definitely burn. I need this guy to understand that I'm grateful, but don't say none of this shit like I owe you a blow job in exchange for special treatment. Some co's be like that. I didn't blow none of them and I won't blow him either.

"You're right. That *is* one of our prime properties."

"You're right, too. It's a great location. Thank you," I said, throw-ing him a bone, like Santiaga taught me to do. Then I crossed my thighs and watched his eyes move.

"Number two, I do see how smart the entire Immanuel team is. So, I'm guessing that you have already figured out that I had mar-keting call in your cast members to appear here at the same time on the same day as our meeting *on purpose*. I hear that you have not met with your friends since your prison release? I'm a pretty seasoned player. I know that friends and relationships can come under pres-sure, or even break and end. I want you to know that who is featured in the cast of *Bow Down* is *your call*. If you say drop them, I'll drop them like a hot potato. They are not contracted as actual cast in any event. They spent the entire season 1 on daily per-appearance pay-outs, very minimal, extremely affordable, unmentionably low sums." He smiled. "I wanted to hear it from you directly. Keep them on for season 2, in which case they would need to be contracted. Or drop them, in which case we would not owe them anything at all?" he said, looking intensely into my eyes. "Miss Winter Santiaga, your friends are my friends and your enemies are my enemies, and either group can switch at a moment's notice. *Everyone except you is disposable.*"

His words were all funnel cake and cotton candy. They were way beyond butter. Still, I seized the opportunity to dump them dirty backstabbing chicks. I was thinking and I had been thinking about what to do with them, my *so-called* friends. Keeping them on would be too nice for some bitches who obviously cut a deal between themselves to remain silent about who shot me. Me dropping them would be too obvious and too easy. I had to fog it up to make them believe it wasn't my choice. Still I knew that no matter who officially fired them, they would all come gunning for me. Besides that, *I need to make them squirm.* They deserve to be uncomfortable. How uncomfortable was I getting shot dead on camera on my own show right after I stepped out of the prison release door? How uncomfortable was I being declared dead, and then waking up from the dead, and then sliding into a coma, and then waking up from a coma? Then having the whole world *watch me* hurt and work to recover my senses, my speech, and my natural-born abilities, and most of all, my stellar stunner look? Then a light bulb went off in my head. "Competition will make for good television I think," I said matter-of-factly to CEO Kuntz.

"Intriguing. What exactly do you have in mind?" he asked in a low-pitch devious cartoon character voice.

"Right before the season 2 opener, episode one, let someone from the Network announce that due to budget constraints Winter is only able to give one of her six friends a role as a contracted full cast member. Meanwhile, the six of them will remain on per-appearance, minimal, unmentionably low, per-episode pay for the first eight episodes. On episode eight, I will say which one is my pick for my best friend who will get the full cast-member contract, exposure, and pay upgrades. Then, we drop the five others completely and continue the remaining eight shows with me and 'my bestie.' How does that sound?" I put it in his lingo. I never called no bitch my "bestie" before.

"I love it!" He balled his fist and shot his arm in the air. His facial expression switched from basically turned on, mildly excited, to very-very amped. He had no way of knowing my plan though. I will make all my girls squirm on an international platform. They will turn against one another for sure, knowing that only one can stay on. When they turn on one another, one of them will say, either on or off camera, who shot me and how the whole hit went down and the reason why. Let's face it. I hated the idea of them being more loyal to one another than they ever were to me. They had locked me out of the clique *that I run*. They had caked up way more than a bitch in the supermarket bagging groceries and repeating "Paper or plastic?" on *my show*. They must have thought I was dead and done. When I was in the coma, they must had been betting that I would never wake up. In what they believed was the unlikely event that I did, they all could and would pretend that we tight and all was the same as we was before. It's not.

"Please allow me to throw some hot sauce on your idea," the prez Dick said. Pacing and gesturing, "Let's not wait until we are filming season 2 this September. I'll have our producers call the girls in, make the announcement concerning the competition as you call it, and we'll start filming the competition immediately."

"Immediately," I repeated, but really to myself. It's July 25 and I am in the mind frame of being off television camera for six more weeks, while continuing to set up my new team, separate from the Immanuel Group team that will be the beginning of my fashion makeover takeover empire. Plus everything that I need to set up to get every aspect of my businesses and even my personal life in motion. My schedule is rammed packed and there was no room for anything else, I thought to myself. "I appreciate your excitement, CEO Kuntz, however . . . ," I said and he stopped pacing and ran towards me. He sat on the table instead of his chair, knee-to-knee with me and leaning in my face.

"You must not have heard?" he said as he leaned back a little and began unbuttoning his sleeves and went on to cuffing them. "My nickname . . . ," he added and then began loosening the buttons of his shirt collar. I don't know what he's doing or preparing for, but I know what he better not be doing and that he is well aware who my father is and wouldn't fucking dare. I remained seated and steel and cold as ice. I could see now his black and silver silky chest hairs that matched the hair on his head.

"I am Dickie 'Let's Make a Deal' Kuntz," he said, then stood up and yanked off his white silk ascot. He kicked off his shoes and walked away towards his desk. I just watched. He came back in a pair of old and worn Asic Tiger kicks and a NY Yankees fitted. "I started off in these kicks with this cap. These kicks and this cap are my lucky moneymakers. They brought me into this million-dollar moment where I own and run more than I could have ever imagined. So let's talk." He pushed his hand into his pocket and withdrew his Tumi wallet and tossed it onto the white marble table. "Seven shows, fifty thousand dollars a show, three hundred and fifty thousand for a seven-day back-to-back summer shoot," he proposed.

"I thought we were friends," I stated to him, and peered into his eyes intensely.

"We are . . . definitely we are . . . ," he said and I cut him off.

"Then why the very minimal, extremely affordable, unmentionably low sums offered up to your top reality show personality and good friend?" I asked softly with very little emotion and no gesturing.

He laughed. "I love it," he said. "You Immanuels are . . . fucking incredible."

"I am not an Immanuel. The name is Santiaga, remember?"

"You're right! You are way different. Porsche, that sister of yours, is like a deep oil well that Elisha Immanuel is sitting on top of, just smiling and whistling while the whole world watches and waits for her to emerge. *So talented.* She refuses to take any meetings, entertain any offers, and only listens to Elisha. You're here." He paused and looked me over from top to bottom. "I can see you. You're more independent, more flexible. I like that," he said like a wolf, then held his arms open.

"Okay, a hundred thousand dollars per episode, for seven episodes that's seven hundred thousand. For only one week of daily shoots that can begin on . . . Wednesday, no Thursday, fuck it. Excuse my French. We are a complex made up of platform and television studio productions. We can begin as early as Monday of this week for seven consecutive days." He paused and stared into my eyes. "Now that's attractive, isn't it?" he asked me and skidded into the couch and was on one knee.

"Make it a mil," I said, purposely avoiding his eyes now, as I looked at my pretty nails and mean-ass manicure instead. I wanted to seem like I am not desperate for the money. I wanted my posture to be all nonchalant and to give him the energy that I could easily take it or leave it but that to be in a business conversation with me about anything, he has to be a "seven-figure nigga."

"Ouch!" he screamed and jumped up. "That's not too friendly!" He smiled then withdrew his smile. "Deal! One hundred thousand per episode for seven episodes," he repeated his offer. "And . . . I'll give the green light to business affairs and keep your girlfriends on non-union, non-contracted, per-appearance, very minimal, extremely affordable, unmentionably low sums. AND, *I'll throw in* the three hundred thousand bonus which I call a 'cooperation fee,' " he emphasized. "That's makes a mil."

"Cooperation fee?" I repeated.

"Yes I should have said happy fee. So if I or my publicity team asks you to do a few promo-type things, meetups, what have you, you're so happy that you won't say no," he said and plastered a forced happy face and big smile.

Swiftly, I remixed his offer. "For three hundred thousand bonus dollars, you get only three promotional or in-person appearances or meetings, but no advertisement requests. That's about as happy as I can get." I stood up. Needed him to feel that I would cancel the whole deal if he tried to talk too much, negotiate too hard, or debate my demands.

He rushed over to his desk and grabbed a red Sharpie. Then from the far corner of his immaculate Icon Pavilion, he pulled a wheeled whiteboard over to where I was standing. He removed the marker cap and wrote out today's date. Then he wrote, "Ms. Winter Santiaga said yes to a 7 day, 7 shows, pre-season 2 Bow Down Starring Winter Santiaga, special summer film shoot in exchange for one million dollars." "Sign here," he said, extending the Sharpie to me. I took the Sharpie and wrote right after the words "one million dollars" that he had just written, "Will be due and paid out by direct deposit on the final seventh day of filming and no later than August 1st." I wanted him to know I'm not playing around. *This is business, not a favor.* I looked at him. He gave me a stern stare. Then he broke into a smile. "Here you initial what I wrote first. Then I will sign," I instructed him. "After I sign, you will write your full signature," I said. He grabbed back his permanent marker and scribbled his illegible signature onto the whiteboard. He pulled out a pocketknife and cut a slight slit on his thumb and put his print in blood on the board. I was shocked by it really.

I took the marker back from him and put my full signature and said, "I'm not going to cut myself."

"Never. You are the perfect product," he said, bowing his head to me and then raising it back up. "Since we have a definite deal, a signed contract, let's finish the other business at hand," he requested.

"Is there more?" I asked him and glanced at my pearl Van Cleef watch.

"Just a little. It won't hurt. I promise," he said oddly. "Yesterday afternoon at your scheduled meeting with the Network and the Immanuel Group combined show writers, I heard a complaint that you had left abruptly after refusing to answer their questions and talk openly about your life, your world, and your feelings. *This is reality television.* They need to have your cooperation in order to write sixteen shows for season 2. Time is of the essence," he said with a seriousness.

"Why do we need show writers when this is supposed to be reality television? I'm at my best when I'm natural. I'm not an actress. I prefer not to be imprisoned by a script," I said.

"That's what your business manager expressed to me, and even when I spoke briefly to Elisha Immanuel about this particular concern, he reiterated your pushing back against show writers. I wanted to say to you face to face that there is a risk in eliminating the orchestrated structure of a show, and the predetermined turn of events. Since *you are the star,* you might want to think about it, and consider that if you use our traditional method and show writers, you have much greater control on what the viewers get to see. If you leave it open-ended, on a live, unscripted reality show *anything* could happen," he said, his eyebrows knitted together with what seemed like worry. I'm thinking, *Does a rich man have anything to worry about?*

"I already took the greatest risk by agreeing to be filmed coming out of the prison release doors after serving a fifteen-year bid. And you saw what happened?" I said calmly.

"Almost a tragedy," he replied gravely.

"Scared money don't make money. That's what my poppa says. I took a bullet yeah, and it made you an even richer man who 'runs this motherfucker.' " I put my sunglasses back on.

"Point well taken. I guess my time with you is up?"

"You said you had three points. You made three points." He laughed. "Did you really mean four?" I asked cutely.

"Three points only, but I do have a few important questions. While you were in the coma and before your father came on board as your business manager, business affairs still had to take care of processing your paperwork. All of your documents and payments were sent in care of the Immanuel Group. Have you retained your own legal representation? Have you formed your own company as of yet?"

"Yes."

"Excellent, let me jot down the name?"

"Lavender Sky," I said, pointing up with my index finger.

"Hmm ... that's sexy." He grunted his approval.

"And your legal representation?" he asked.

"Kai Stone," I replied. "She's with Deutsch, Minter, and Ginzberg."

"We know her and that firm of course. I will have a legal document sent over to your legal team and business manager, with the agreement we made today," he said.

I pointed to the board. "I thought this was it."

"It is, it is," he said, assuring me. "On the whiteboard is what we call the 'short form.' I'll send the paperwork with the details. You don't need to concern yourself with those details. That's why we both have a team of boring-ass lawyers! They love that shit!"

"As long as the details don't interfere with the standard requirements necessary to be in business with Ms. Santiaga," I said and he was silent. "Wardrobe freedom!" I emphasized. "Unlimited wardrobe," I restated.

He smiled and said, "Why, of course." As we walked towards the exit together without talking, he awkwardly stated, "It might be good for me to have your direct number?" He asked it softly as though he expected to be rejected. Because of the awkward way he asked, I thought maybe I should not give it to him.

"For what?" I asked calmly, purposely forcing him to clarify his intentions.

"I like to stay close to my money," he said. "When I call, it's a money call." I pulled out my iPhone and handed it to him. He typed in his contact and pressed call. When his cellular rang, he handed mine back to me. "I won't share your private number with anyone. I'd love it if you did the same for me," he said, whispering for some reason.

"Why, of course" was all I said back.

"What ringtone should I give you? What's your favorite song?" he asked me.

"'Who Shot Ya,' Notorious B.I.G.," I replied without hesitation or thought.

He paused. "You're a very cunning girl," he said. *Whatever that really means*, I thought. He stood still, as though he was waiting for something. Again I walked off. "Hey, you didn't ask me?"

"Ask you what?" I stopped but was still facing forward, away from him.

"What ringtone you should use *only for me.*" I turned and looked at him but didn't ask.

"'Stairway to Heaven,'" he blurted. I paused, remembering what Elisha had warned and glancing towards the marble staircase he had, which was lighted even in the daylight hours. "It's old, but it's gold," he remarked about his musical choice. I had never heard it, so I guess it is old. "Besides none of your friends or associates would have that ring tone, true?" he asked but really not like a question.

"You're right. They wouldn't," I assured him.

"Can we take a photo?" he asked me. "My sixteen-year-old daughter worships you. If you say yes, I'll be Cool Daddy for the rest of the summer," he said, striking a stance.

I smiled. "Sure why not?"

"If you don't mind, please remove your sunglasses once more for our photo." So I did.

"Send me a copy of our pic," I told him. "I'm a fan of Ricky Santiaga, your father. He has the loveliest daughter, who chooses to work with her own father, and listens to whatever he advises. My daughter hates when I'm doing anything aside from transferring money into her account." He laughed. "I'm known as Big Daddy ATM, and she takes pride in taking my cash and then doing the opposite of everything I suggest, request, or tell her to do."

6
NASTY LITTLE NATALIE

"Damn you smell good," some guy said as he entered the elevator on the sixth floor, the only rider interrupting my express trip down from 21, then 18. He pressed B2, left his finger on the button too long, and glanced at me. "Yeah I know who you are," he said calmly to me, but like he was trying his hardest to be sexy. Then he said, "I know you know who I am," and he struck a pose like he was a super-star. The fact is, I have no idea who he is. I only know that this is the Network building. He could be *anybody* in entertainment front stage or back stage.

"Must be meant to be," he said. I didn't say nothing back. I'm glad I'm bout to get off. I'm thinking how I can see the difference between what happens when I am with my bodyguard or my father or any respected man on my team and when I am alone. Since I'm rarely alone, I had not considered it.

"Let me take you to the district," he said and then stepped in front of me as the elevator arrived on my stop, lobby level. I stepped forward bout to bump him if I have to, in order to get off. He then stuck his finger in my navel through one of the tiny openings the lace mini provided. "Let me put a diamond right there," he said. "You're perfect. It's the only thing you're missing. Once I put a big rock in here," he pressed in further, "I own you." I karate chopped his hand even though I don't know no karate. Raised my knee into his balls for standing too close, but of course the elevator door had closed again, and it was heading down to what I figured was the basement level. He laughed, but in a split second before his laughter I saw a painful expression that he swiftly erased and replaced with a smile. "A nigga got on bulletproof draws." He cracked up at his own joke. The elevator doors drew open and he pointed to a polka-dot Ferrari. "Last chance. After you Google me, you gone be sorry you didn't hop on this dick," he said. I pressed the button for up, lobby level. He stepped off slowly like he was anticipating me changing my mind and chasing him. I pressed doors open and held it like he did.

"Save your money. You and your pants are both *too short*. Your colors are *too loud*. Your whip is *whack*. E'erything's too tight." I held my hand up and waved it the brief length of his little body. "Instead of a diamond belly button for me, rush over to your dentist. Ask for a booster seat and get your teeth fixed." Then I lifted my finger and the elevator doors drew closed.

As soon as the elevator doors drew open into the main lobby, I posted the photo of me and CEO/President Richard Kuntz. I didn't type nothing underneath the photo. Everybody relevant knows exactly who he is. I am signaling through all social media and to those rich individuals, independent businesses, and major corporations who have money to spend that I'm in the game heavy. I'm expensive and to place your bets on me, and my brand.

My eyes searched for my bodyguard. He wasn't there though. I checked my calls, nothing from him. I'm like, *what the fuck?* Then I was like, *oh well, good thing he didn't show up*. He might have fucked up the chemistry between me and Kuntz, and maybe the big deal that I stumbled upon and negotiated *all by myself* would never have happened. As I drifted through the revolving door, I saw the boom microphone and cameras set up at curb front. I jammed the door rapidly, but apparently, another person had stepped in a section right behind me and now she or he and I were both frozen in place instead of exiting. The person started panic-banging the glass that separated us from each other. I unfroze and pushed it forward until I was spit out into the street. "What were you thinking!" the pissed off lady who got spit out right behind me said. I turned around swiftly. As soon as she recognized my face, it was all . . . "Oh sorry, sorry you're Miss Winter Santiaga, I didn't mean to . . ."

"You did. But, it's okay," I told the young white girl whose face I'd seen on the twelfth floor when I first arrived. Then I used the opportunity to put my sunglasses on while my back was to the cameras. The boom microphone and the camera setup could have been for anybody. However, just in case it's for me, I finger-combed my hair, licked my lips, and strutted out into the camera like I was on the Paris runway.

"Winter, over here!" It was Natalie's voice. I looked to my right and she was standing there alone calling me over into the corner of the building as though we were gonna have some private convo. How can anything be private on mic and camera? Hell, she's probably mic'd up herself and got the power pack concealed on her backside. I don't like that she knows the cameras are rolling, but acted like she didn't. I sauntered over like I was playing into her hand. When anyone mistakes me for gullible, sometimes I make them believe I'm the sucker they obviously think I am.

"Winter, more than anybody else, me and you is best-best friends. Out of all our girls, I'm *the only one* who back in the day, ever been on the inside of your Brooklyn apartment. *The only friend* who ever slept over. *The only friend* on speaking terms with Momma Lana and Poppa Ricky. I've worn your clothes, your kicks, and your heels. You did my hair. I even took a bath in your tub. Hell, we got our cherries popped together. Remember that? I turned you on to weed, taught you how to roll a joint right, how to lick the Bambú paper back before Black and Milds when that was the shit. I taught you how to tongue kiss and give head. You was almost as good as me at it, too." She laughed. I'm looking at this bitch like she crazy. Who would say that shit on camera? I see how she is trying to take credit for raising me. As though she is the one who made me cool. I hate the way she is talking like me and her are on some same-same or like we ever were on some same-same. We are not. She knew it and she knows it. Slick, she also knows whatever really happened way back when, and whatever happened in lockdown or anywhere for that matter *in real life, doesn't matter.* Because of the power of television, and the millions of eyes that would be watching, if she or anybody else could say some shit on camera, the fact that people saw or heard it on television *makes it true* and real even though it's fake and false. Two can play that "remember when game." So I took my on-camera shot at biting her back. I didn't do the obvious, like talk about how cheap her weave looked, and how other bitches had upgraded to lace fronts or how her obviously new blue eye contacts didn't match with her brown skin and made her look like a clown. I didn't mention how she fucked up her lips with that Botox shit and now she looks like she just got punched in her mouth, or just finished a dick-sucking marathon that left her swolled.

"Natalie . . . ," I began saying.

"Don't be mad, Winter. I feel you and me can say anything to one another, no matter what. Tell the truth, you are *most* comfortable around me. I'm familiar. I'm family. I'm just saying, 'put me on.' I'll be your personal assistant, your trainer, your chef, your stylist, your makeup artist, whatever. *Just take me with you.* Fuck this other shit, sweat-suit endorsements, promotional crap, and community softball games. *You know* I gotta be where the real action is at," she pleaded. I liked that now she toned it down and was begging me on camera. But I'm still hot. It's too late.

"Natalie," I said, " . . . Back on our Brooklyn block you knew if a bitch had a doo-doo stain even if you didn't know her name. You knew who was fucking who, who was fighting who, who was financing who. You knew who was on the low or the lamb, who was on the down low or a she-man. You knew whose rent was paid, whose lights were off, whose phone was disconnected. You knew whose momma was hooking, whose father was pimping or dealing; you knew which nigger pulled the trigger even while the steel was still hot and smoking. You knew all the gambling spots, crack dens, and kingpins. You knew the predators and the victims, the stick up and the stuck up, even the cops and the robbers and the detecks. Natalie, how a bitch like you, who fucking knows it all, every mug, every thug, every roach and every bug in the streets or on the tiers, and even knows what happened to her peers in the courts before the verdict and the sentencing, not know who shot Winter Santiaga? You was there on the scene while the gun was hot, when my body dropped and when the blue blood turnt red and bled into the white snow. Who shot me? That's all I want to know. Until you decide you want to tell me." I leaned into her face close enough to smell her Bazooka bubble-gum breath and see her body mic tucked. "Remember this, 'I ain't got nothing for you bitch!'"

"Cut," the DP yelled out. "Woah! Girls, that was great! Fantastic! Thank you! That was so fucking great!" He was beyond thrilled. So was the little crowd that had gathered there, which caused more people to pile up behind them like bumper cars. My eyes were zooming faces checking for my driver and for my bodyguard. Both of them was a no-show since this morning when I woke up from my bullshit power nap to make it to Kuntz by 11 a.m.

"Come on, don't be like dat," Natalie said, jumping up and down hoping I could still see and hear her after the sidewalk mob had closed in on me. Both of us started breaking through the crowd, our arms moving like we were swimmers bout to drown. As she tried to grab hold of my hand, my other hand got yanked and I was pulled into the arms of some nigga, who then lifted me up and plowed through the crowd like a bulldozer. His grip was strong and his locks were hiding his eyes. The crowd was jeering but not helping. I was in shock but most concerned about not letting my handbag drop. It has my stacks, my cell phone, and a bunch of other little valuables that it took me time to accumulate. I'm like, what the fuck. "Nigga, put me down!" I said the moment I got unshocked. Instead of putting me down he stepped forward even faster, causing one of my shoes to fall off. Now I was having flashbacks of when my sneaker fell off in the subway station while I was being chased by a crew of hoodied-up girls, one who had flashed the burner.

A second dred nigga opened an Escalade door. The one carrying me tossed me inside. The second dred slammed it shut. Then he leaned on it so that I couldn't get back out even though I was pulling on the handle. Then the first one, who had picked me up and carried and tossed me, jogged over towards the driver's side door. I tried to beat him to it from the inside by climbing over the seats, which only caused my mini to ride all the way past my thighs and get stuck on the curve of my butt. When my body was halfway in the front and halfway in the back with my hand on the driver's seat holding me up till I could steady myself, the first dred jumped in, sat on my fingers, and I dragged them from beneath him. I fell backwards back into the back passenger side seat. At the same time as I tried to exit from the rear door, I heard the power locks clicking, preventing the door from opening. The one who had leaned on the back door stepped off casually. All I could see was his back. The driver pulled off. The crowd starting applauding. Dumbasses must have thought we're filming a scene. We are not.

"Your scent is . . ." the guy driving the vehicle said.

"Who the fuck are you?" I yelled.

"Pretty face. Filthy mouth," he said, his light brown eyes revealed to me through his rearview mirror.

I was talking to myself in my mind. Trying not to panic. Already got shot in my head this year. Seems like somebody is trying to break down my natural boldness and fearlessness. I'm telling myself, no one gets kidnapped in Midtown Manhattan from in front of a multimillion-dollar complex and a gathering crowd and television cameras and even cell phone psychos recording and filming everything. No kidnapper is that dumb. *Everything is okay. Everything is okay. Everything is okay,* I repeated silently in my mind. Then I blurted out laughing suddenly.

Joke? the driver's eyes asked me as he kept checking on me through the rearview.

"Yeah, your ass is stuck in traffic. You didn't have to be a fucking genius to figure out that you couldn't get away with all of this from this location." A police siren went off. I turned to look out the back window. The driver couldn't maneuver. He was surrounded by cars immediately in front of him and across the street that were double-parked, and he was jammed between the cop car behind him and the traffic ahead of his vehicle. Two cops got out of the car with the siren off now but the police lights still spinning. I feel crazy. *It's the police*, so I don't feel like they are here to save me. Nope, I feel nervous and worried like I'm about to get rearrested. It didn't matter that I didn't do nothing. I had already served fifteen years for doing nothing. Now there's one at the driver's window and one opposite the driver's window. Both knocking. The driver lowered his window. I didn't yell help or say shit. I didn't know what would happen next.

"License, insurance, and registration," the cop said, and his face looked like *license and registration or I'll kill you.* The cop on the front passenger side had his face pressed against the glass, his eyes searching the car. His eyes landed on me. I just sat still.

"Are there any weapons in the car?" the driver's side officer asked.

"No," the driver said.

"Step out of the vehicle," the cop said.

"For what?" the driver asked boldly. I'm thinking he must not be no New York nigga and don't know how these New York cops get down.

"We received a report of a kidnapping," the cop said as he looked at me.

"Ma'am, are you all right?" he asked me.

"I'm good," I said instinctively.

"See she's good, no kidnapping," the driver said.

"Step out of the car," the officer ordered him again, in an even more threatening tone.

"You got a warrant?" the driver asked.

"I don't need one. Kidnapping is a capital crime, smart-ass," the cop said. The driver got out.

"You got any weapons on you?" the cop asked him as he had already begun to pat him down thoroughly.

"My bad, I don't," the driver said. The cop escorted him to the back of the Escalade. My head turned to watch. I got a first good look at the driver. Diamond fronts glistened in the coming of the noon sun. I knew the cops would hate that, seeing a nigga shining. Jet-black locks that looked like they used to be silky jet-black curls. His edges were cleaned up nice, designed and tapered. That's what gave it away. A handsome young dude. I guess if I'm gonna be kidnapped it should be by a handsome thugged out dude who looks just like him. I saw the cop order the driver to sit on the curb. The second cop had eased around driver side and released the locks that prevented my door from opening. He was still searching the car carefully.

"Remove the sunglasses," he ordered me. I removed them. He studied my face.

"Now that we moved him away from you, you can tell us what's really happening. You're in 'safe hands,'" the cop said with a seriousness as though he thought I thought he could be trusted.

I can't really explain myself. I feel more terrified with the cop leaning into the car than with the dred driver who was the one who grabbed me and carried me in his arms as if I was his willing bride, before dumping me in the car. I'm not answering the cop asking the questions, because somehow I feel like saying anything is the same as snitching even though I don't know these cats who are pulling this caper against me. And I see the crowd gathering to watch. And I assume some of them had seen it all. At least ten of them are still filming with their cell phones. That is bullshit to me because they are not paying me for my appearance and *I cost big money to be filmed.*

"Ma'am, are you hurt anywhere?" the officer asked me. I shook my head no. "Do you know the driver of this vehicle?" he asked me. In my mind I was like, *Oh there go the trick question.* Cops always ask trick questions. If I say no I don't know him, they will try and arrest him for kidnapping. If I say yes I do know him even though I do not, they will try and arrest me for conspiracy to do something illegal with him.

"I would like to call my father," I said suddenly. "I'm going to open my handbag and take out my cell phone." He nodded permission. I took it to mean he wouldn't shoot me for moving my hands.

"Santiaga."

"Baby girl . . ."

"I'm . . . ," I began saying to my father as the cop's eyes seemed glued on my lips like a lip reader when he was definitely close enough to me to hear every word.

"Did he pick you up on time?" Santiaga asked me.

"Driving what?" I asked him discreetly so at least I would know if I was with the right driver in the right vehicle. He definitely is not my usual driver and this ain't the Lamborghini I had this morning.

"In the black Cadillac," Santiaga said. "What's going on? You good or not? Is something stopping you from speaking? Only say yes or no?" Santiaga asked, remaining cool-calm but growing aware that something must have went wrong.

"I'm in the Escalade, there's an officer here who thinks I have been kidnapped," I said softly.

"Put him on," my father said. Once Poppa talks to him, I know somehow that everything will turn out right. Poppa Santiaga is that to me. He's the only human who has my 100 percent confidence.

The officer's demeanor changed with a swiftness. It was as though he was speaking to someone who had authority over him. He straightened his spine and his stance.

"Yes, Chief," I heard him say. "The Network Complex, yes. There was a crowd, Chief. Somebody called it in. We happened to be circulating. No it wasn't like before, sir. No weapons discharged. No one was trampled. Just questioning the perp and protecting the lady citizen." The cop looked like he was losing all his power as the call continued. "Drop it," he said as his face screwed. "Got it." His face muscles unscrewed. *"Apologize."* His two eyebrows joined together and made one evil unibrow. "With all due respect, Chief . . ." Then after that he didn't say shit. I could hear the male voice of whomever he was speaking to blaring through the cellular at high volume but could not distinguish the words. I knew for sure though, it is not Poppa's voice.

The cop didn't apologize. Told me to remain seated. As he walked off to the rear of the vehicle I saw his body having a temper tantrum and heard him saying aloud, "What are the fucking chances!" He informed his partner as I watched through the back window. The driver stood up from the curb. His young chiseled face had a smirk at both cops as though he was saying without words, *I told you motherfuckers!*

"A seventeen-year-old with a fucking Escalade. Yeah right. Great call, Chief. I'm sure this nigger has a great job and that he earned this vehicle the good old-fashioned way." The cop spit.

"I'm eighteen. Check again," the dred corrected the cop. The cop glanced down at the license before handing it back to him. "You're a lucky son of a bitch. Today's your birthday." Young dred driver walked back with his license, registration, and insurance card to the Escalade slowly. Probably he feels about them the same way I do and doesn't want to catch a barrage of bullets in his back for no reason, from the gun of the ones who don't need a real reason to fire.

"Change your clothes," the dred said and raised up a dark glass divider between where I was seated and himself. I called Santiaga back immediately and asked him where this driver was instructed to take me. I reminded him that I have a few appointments scheduled and even a date to go on later tonight round 8 p.m.

"There's a box in the back for you. Dress up. It's 12:15 now. He'll drive you directly to me."

7
MUSTANG

"Baby Girl, I know you're tight that I asked you to take photos with the police," Santiaga said.

"Exactly," I replied.

"In this life, you have to make use of all of the pieces on the board, strategic moves," he said. "Sometimes we have to sacrifice something to gain something," he added and I know he feels bad that I feel bad about it. But I'm still pissed.

"So Poppa ... you sacrificed my street credibility to gain what?" I answered back, probably in a tone I never intentionally use with my father. He laughed a man laugh. I felt even tighter that he laughed.

"Those three photos, one of those guys was the chief of police. He's a fan of yours. The fact that you stood next to him for a photo opportunity *is an investment*. The thing about an investment is you sink your money, property, your work, and your ego into it and let go. One day it matures and you make more than you put up," he said like he was certain.

"Or you could lose it all," I said back to him. I wanted him to know that I had learned some things since before we were both incarcerated.

"True, an investment can become a loss. Are you doubting your father's senses?" he asked me, looking into my eyes. Then there was a pause between us. I understand what he's asking of course. He did seventeen years and still landed on his feet. Aside from his new entertainment management business, my father had miraculously managed to disguise and hold on to some of his non–drug related businesses that are still profitable from back in the day. I want to hear and learn from him exactly how he pulled that off. For me, for obvious reasons, I find it hard to accept that he had friends so loyal and connects so strong that they continued to run certain of his side businesses and somehow had agreed to after him serving seventeen years, give it back to him. Or maybe they gave him back a percentage of it but business was and is so good that it's still a big pay-out.

"No, not doubting you, never that. I'm just saying, there's the before the cell phone days and the after the cell phone days. Before maybe this cop would just have put the photo on his desk or wall at work or at home to impress his kids that he knows somebody cool. Poppa, after the cell phone days . . . one photo travels throughout social media and all around the world. I don't want these streets spreading rumors that the Santiagas sold out or that we some type of rats, plants, or informants or no shit like that."

"Smart way to put it, 'before the cell phone and after the smart phones,'" Santiaga summarized. "But remember this, Baby Girl, there is no one from these streets who has the leverage or the power to doubt the credibility of the Santiagas. Together we served a total of thirty-two years in lockdown without flipping on these streets, or our team, even when some of the players flipped on the Santiagas. Hell, we didn't even snitch on our opposition," he said and I didn't answer back because that's true facts. "But still . . . ," I murmured.

"And, Baby Girl, I have always made use of the police strategically, from young hustler to top hustler. I never allowed anyone's uniform, occupation, or costume to prevent me from using them. I understand men, our ambitions, our appetites, our talents, and our desires, and how to use those desires to move the pieces around the board and win the game," he said.

I thought of how I knew that already. I knew Poppa had cops on his payroll back then and he knew how to spread the cheese around the table so everybody eats, as a means of lessening the amount of ops moving against him and his crew in the hood. I remember being five years young, dressed up in my little girl lace dress with the patent leather shoes and ribbons, and holding Poppa's hand as we walked through Brooklyn Botanical Gardens. I didn't know it at the time, but that was the meetup spot for Santiaga and the police captain and the drop-off of the tucked stacks that up until I was sixteen kept the cops from attacking Santiaga's team.

Sitting in prison I had put so many of the puzzle pieces together day by day. Also, in the letters between me and Poppa, I read between the lines and figured it out and factored in the rest using my common sense and experiences.

"Yes, Poppa, you used them and they used you, true. But I bet you never once took a photo, smiling and standing next to those guys." Then he smiled but didn't deny.

"Winter, there has been a game change. It's not the same game; new players, new board, new rules, new risks, new benefits, new strategies. We're on the main stage now. We are earning legit paper *easily* in amounts that would have been earned in the streets with risks to the extreme and the loss of our time and the loss of my soldiers, and the loss of our things, but mostly the loss of our love, family, and people that should never be gambled or lost," he said solemnly.

"Poppa, where are we headed?" I changed the subject purposely. When we got into the modest Mustang that he was driving today, there was a huge bouquet of yellow roses on the back seat. In my head I was like that's about all that could have fit in that tiny back-seat space. I didn't say it aloud because I was vexed about the photos I had to take. There was also a gift box that looked like it came from Poppa's private jeweler. I didn't get excited when I saw it like I used to. I get so many gifts nowadays, even from people who I don't even know or care about, that it takes much, much more to get my blood pumping and heart thumping. "Poppa, where's Sergio?" I asked him about his missing regular driver. "And why are *you* driving this little car today? There must be a reason." I pouted my lips like letting him know that this li'l joint is not my style and I do not think it is or ever was his style either.

Instead of answering my question he asked me, "Where did your car go early this morning?" I had to stop and think. My head was so blown this morning because of the night before. Oh yeah, that's right, I reminded myself. I was parked in the white Lambo when Elisha showed up at my car window.

"Um, Elisha said you two were going to a golf tournament with the *police* . . ." I said "police" like it was dirty word. He didn't react. Just stared at me for as long as anyone driving a car, who should have his eyes on the road, should or could stare at anyone or anything else.

"Winter, where was I when the driver dropped you off to meet me today after your police incident?" he asked me oddly.

"At a place called 'The Irish Pub,' *with the police*. How come you're asking me? That just happened."

"Put two and two together," he said. I didn't respond because everybody knows two and two is four.

"The chief of police was the guy who got you out of the fake kidnapping incident that happened outside of the Network Complex this afternoon. I handed him my cell phone when you called. He talked to his men and he deaded it. If I didn't happen to be at their post—golf tournament gathering, which I had no interest in, but went to because I made a sacrifice and an investment for the sake of the new business that you and I are in, that whole kidnapping incident could've gotten real messy."

"Yeah but whose fault was that? I didn't kidnap myself. What's wrong with that driver you sent? He could've just walked up and told me you sent him, *let's go!* Why he touched me? Why he had to pick me up in his arms, just to dump me into your Escalade?" I asked nicely but I'm sure Poppa could still feel my disappointment with the whole thing.

"What was the reason that any man could walk up to Winter Santiaga and put his hands on her? Lift her off of her feet, carry her away, and then toss her into a car with a driver who she does not recognize?" he asked me sternly.

I felt like he was flipping the fault back on to me. "Poppa, probably all of that happened and they could do it like that because the Lamborghini wasn't parked outside of my door after I woke up this morning to do the 11 a.m. Richard Kuntz Network appointment. The whip was missing. My driver didn't show up either. My bodyguard didn't either. At the last minute I had to schedule an Uber."

"Why do you think both your bodyguard and your driver failed to show up when they show up like clockwork every day? And, why was the Lamborghini gone? Who do you think took it? And for what reason?" Poppa asked me each question slowly, glancing to his right at me while driving his Mustang.

I didn't say nothing for a few seconds. Then I laughed. "Of course you took it, Poppa! It's your car, from your Exotic Elite Fleet Dream Car Company. And, no one else could've accessed the Elisha estate and removed your vehicle *except for you* or on *your word.*"

"Okay, cool. Why would I take the car that my first daughter needed to be driven in to a major appointment at the Network where we make the majority of our paper right now?" he asked me.

I felt like a little girl, trying to be swift and smart enough not to fall into my father's word traps. I always want and wanted to impress Santiaga. On top of that, in that moment I was thrown off by the fact that we had just pulled up to a place that was a terrible memory. It is the graveyard in Queens where Momma was buried. So I concentrated real hard on not reacting to being at the damned graveyard where now my father is parking this tiny bullshit car with me riding shotgun.

"Winter, your eyes don't see it all. There is so much more going on in a room than what you can imagine, catch, or even see happening," he said like it was a warning. But really, I don't know what he's talking about. *My eyes work.*

"Poppa, of course I can see at least what's going on in a room I am standing in."

"So what have you noticed in the past twelve hours?" he asked me strangely. I raced into my mind. *What exactly is he talking about? Is he bringing up again and blaming me for allowing myself to get fake kidnapped?* I didn't come up with an answer right away. He leaned over. So now we are face to face, eye to eye in the parked Mustang parallel to the last place I want to be on Earth, the damned graveyard. He snapped my seat belt off. I shifted in my seat to face him better as he pulled himself back into his seat.

"Do you need my help? Should I tell you what you didn't see?" he asked, now facing forward away from my direction.

"No, I saw it all, everything that happened to me at least. I'll figure out what you are referring to, just give me only one minute to think about it," I said proudly.

"Time's up," he said and it didn't even feel like a whole minute to me.

"How did the Lamborghini get a flat tire?" he added on to his puzzling questions.

"Flat tire! That wasn't me. It couldn't have been because of me or on my time because I wasn't even in the Lambo ... ," I started to say and realized I just told on myself.

"If you were not in the Lambo, where were you? Who was riding in my two-hundred-thousand-dollar masterpiece aside from my lovely daughter and the driver I hired?"

"No, wait a minute. I wasn't riding in it, but I was in the car in front of the Lambo and your driver was following the car I was in." I cleared that up. No need to get the driver he hired in any trouble or my Network bodyguard either.

"Whose car were you in?"

"It was a girl who I met. Her car."

"What girl? Name? Occupation?"

I felt stupid. I don't know the pretty bitch's name. I damn sure don't know her occupation. But, I can't tell Poppa that. I was rushing to make up a lie. My tongue locked, felt heavy like cement. Because Santiaga is my father, I am not carefree or swift enough. Besides, I knew he would know I was lying. Therefore I didn't say nothing.

"So at what point did you no longer see the whip that your father loaned you?" he asked. All of his questions, he spoke them gently and watched the movement of my eyes too closely for me to feel comfortable.

"Well, I know I had nothing to do with that flat tire because the bodyguard drove me back to Elisha's in the Lambo and parked me safely in front of my villa."

"So why was there a doughnut on the Lamborghini when you arrived at Elisha's?"

"A doughnut?"

"A spare tire, a replacement wheel," he said and then added, "At what point did you get out of the girl's car and back into the Lambo?"

I started stroking my hair and sweating a li'l bit. I don't usually sweat unless I'm purposely working my body. I felt panicked at the idea that I am a disappointment to Santiaga. I can't just tell him that I have no idea and that I had taken a pill and that I didn't know the chick's name who I was with or even remember her driver's name even though I could remember both of their faces. Then I felt mad at myself cause I'm not a fucking pill-popping junky.

"What about the bullet hole?" he asked and I felt startled with the mention of the word "Bullet." That's the name of the nigga who got me locked for fifteen.

"Bullet hole?" I repeated cause that's all I could say.

"There was a bullet hole in the Lamborghini right passenger side door," he said and paused. "The exact seat where you would have been sitting if you were where you were supposed to be."

I felt trapped. "Poppa, there's no air-conditioning now that we are parked. Could you lower the windows?" I asked like I was gagging for air. I was. *Did somebody actually try to kill me again?* I thought to myself. The thought shook my insides and something in my belly was churning. I ignored it. *Porsche had said my bodyguard drove me home. Then the Lambo was gone when I woke up for the Kuntz meeting.* Poppa was still waiting. As I refocused, he began winding down his driver side window. When I saw him do that, I reached for the handle and wound down my side. I get what he is saying and doing without saying it. I did not even see that I could wind down my own window. But that's not fair. This jalopy is an antique. I'm too young to even be thinking about winding down any goddamn windows or any *throw all the way back* shit like that. Hell, a nigga who wanted to take me out couldn't even get me in the car seat of a vehicle that required me to do anything besides touch a screen, press a button, or swipe left or right.

"The bullet hole," he reminded me, but he knew I remembered his question and that I was simply stalling. I couldn't say there wasn't a bullet hole in the Lambo. Yet I couldn't say there was. "Maybe it was there when . . . ," I started saying, but I knew I was talking shit. Poppa would never send me a vehicle with a bullet hole already in it.

"These are *all* things that happened *to you* while you were present but unaware. Tell me . . . why did your bodyguard drive you home instead of your driver driving?"

"I tried to call the bodyguard when I was on the way to meet you at the police party," I said, trying to throw a distraction into the conversation so I would not be the only guilty party. "He didn't pick up. I had called him already three times beginning from early this morning. On the fourth time it said his number was no longer in existence," I explained.

Santiaga smiled. I looked into that smile and I gasped. "Don't tell me . . . Is he dead, Poppa? Did he die in my place? Was that bullet meant for me? Or was it just an accident? No, well, I told the bodyguard not to play me too close. He was just following my orders," I admitted. "I left the club with the girl. That wasn't his call. He did not have a choice. All he could do was have the driver follow behind the car I got in." I was talking too much, which I usually never do with Poppa, who always said, "Less is more."

"You got it?" he asked me. I started looking away from him.

"No one knows it all, sees it all, hears it all. Even when the action is happening right in the same room, the same house, same apartment, on the same block, in the same vehicle, or in the same area. Most of us are at a loss to really know what is really happening. Maybe we figure it out while we're serving time, reading and rereading our paperwork, and comparing it to other prisoner's paperwork who we know."

"Poppa, why did you tell me to leave my cell phone in the Escalade?" I asked, changing the subject. It was just another thing I was ticked off about. I really don't like anybody separating me from my phone. "And if we were going to leave our cell phones in the Escalade, why didn't we just ride in the Escalade instead of this . . . um . . . bullshit old car."

He laughed, which aggravated me again.

"How much do you think this 1968 Mustang is worth? If I sell it, I could earn presidential paper for it."

"Well then sell it! Take the bag and get rid of this thing."

"There's a market for vintage vehicles. Certain cars I don't want to let go of for certain reasons, but I'll rent them out. This one would earn big as a rental, but I never rented it out and never planned or plan to do so."

"Okay, you must've drove Momma around in this one or something like that," I guessed. It was an easy guess since we were already at her graveyard. Still, I would've sold it long ago if I was Poppa.

What difference did it make if Momma had ever been driven around in it? The momma I know wouldn't like this little non-luxurious thing either. Me and her would agree on that.

"That's one level. But the deeper level is that all cars now have black boxes. Meaning your own car is a tracking device, a data collector and recorder of all of your vehicle activity," he said and I just blank stared him. I was thinking that means that the location and activity that happened last night was all recorded in some black box in the Lambo and also in the pretty bitch's car.

"Put two and two together," he said. "Why did I use this car today?" he asked.

"Because it so old that it cannot record your vehicle activity," I answered.

"Why did I leave both of our cell phones in the Escalade?"

"Because you must think that cell phone is a recording and tracking device. But Poppa you could have just asked me to turn my phone off. That would've been better," I answered back swiftly.

"Do you think you know what would have been better?" he asked and I know not to reply to that. "Your cell phone is still recording even when it's off," he said. "Are you sharper than your father?" he asked me.

"I'm not saying that. I would never put it that way," I said softly.

"I match the cars I push with my circumstances, my mood, my schedule, my image, my legal and financial strategy and goals. I chose this old joint because I knew I was going to a golf game. I knew it was sponsored by the police. I knew that no cop, not the little man walking the beat, or higher-ups, are wishing well for an ex-convict who beat a life sentence through a pardon, and somehow in less than six months after his release was living rich. I could've been guided by my ego. Pull up on em in a Bentley or a Ferrari. All the cars are legit, but the envy that they pull out of the hearts of men is severe. So I choose my battles. Sometimes I go low. Sometimes I flash out. It all depends on what I want to make happen, or want to avoid from happening," he explained. I understood.

"And if while I'm laying low, at a golf game, I receive a call saying that one of my most valuable vehicles has a spare tire and a bullet hole, and that my daughter was driven home by her bodyguard and not her driver, I know that I have to bring my daughter in close to me. That I need to be the only one she talks to. I need to shut her down from communicating with anybody because *everybody is a suspect*. I know that my daughter and I need to discuss something that should not be recorded. That's the level the technology is at now. So we are here to discuss privately some matters I had hoped we both left way behind us: a potential shoot-out, a potential double homicide, and how I plan to cover you, secure you from whatever happened last night. I hope I don't ever have to explain myself to you, and that you take it for granted that although I don't see it all, I see more than you. It's my job to protect you from what you don't know."

Santiaga opened his car door and in an instant was opening mine for me. He extended his hand and I gave over my hand. He then removed the bouquet of yellow flowers, tossed the gift box under the seat, and locked each door manually, and we were off to the last place I wanted to be, the graveyard.

Poppa walked ahead of me leading the way, our fingers lightly interlocked. His other hand holding the flowers, the rhythm of his walk was not the movement of someone who did not know exactly where he was headed. It caused me to believe that this must not be his first visit since his prison release to see dead Momma. It is mine. Then that thought changed swiftly as we were both reacting to seeing Momma's tombstone beneath an apple tree and placed in a garden of purple to violet to lavender pansies. But we were paused at the right place. The tombstone was charcoal-colored marble and the name Lana Dominique Santiaga, and the birthdate, February 7, 1963, and death date, July 26, 2000, were all in gold inlay. As my eyes moved down the wording, the next sentence caused me to feel filled up with tears but refusing to spill or explode. It said: "MORE THAN ANYTHING LANA LOVED RICKY," in large capital bold lettering.

Unique and expensive, whereas the other tombstones just listed who the dead person was survived by, Momma had photos beneath a thick plate of glass that were embedded in the stone. First there was a picture of Momma when she was at her peak of perfect. Next to it was a photo of Momma being hugged up with Poppa. The only thing that glistened more than Santiaga's diamonds was Momma's big in-love smile. Next it was weird to see my own photo on a tombstone. It was there though, and all of my photos always look good. Then side-by-side are Porsche, then baby pics of Mercedes and Lexus. Below the glassed photo display written in big bold gold lettering it said "WE WILL ALL MEET AGAIN."

I'm thinking to myself her plot seemed way too big. Aren't graveyards all about space? Nobody cares about the dead. Sometimes they even stack em to get triple the rent, three coffins dropped into one deep rectangular hole in the earth. I read about that moneymaking scandal once in a magazine. I don't remember this apple tree, or any of these flowers. When Santiaga and I both attended Momma's funeral we were both in cuffs and chains, escorted in at gunpoint as though we were somehow a threat to civilization. There was only a heap of black soil and a deep rectangle hole down in the earth with a casket hovering over it, mounted on steel bars. We never got to see the tombstone. We were rushed away as soon as they closed the casket and tossed a shovel full of dirt on her. We were treated as though we were even a threat to our own family. Maybe that's why I had forgotten that I did see Mercedes and Lexus at Momma's burial site. However, they were the least of my focus given my fucked up circumstance and how devastated Poppa was. My emotion shifted from fighting tears to anger. Poppa was placing each rose at the foot of the tombstone. He had not looked at me since we arrived here and dropped each other's hand. I am only thinking *let's get the fuck out of here.*

"Lana," my father said while facing the tombstone.

"Poppa! Do you think that Momma is in there?" I blurted out. But as soon as I asked it, I wished I could have deleted my words. But, I could not. I know and I knew for a fact that Momma is not there in the ground. I learned from my death experience that Momma is surely in Heaven. I have no idea what she had to go through before reaching Heaven, or even why she made it in. I also learned from my death experience that Heaven is not automatic. It's earned.

"Your man is here," Poppa said aloud. Then it seemed that he would make one statement and then there would be a long pause. I wondered if he was imagining her response to each statement he made.

"I admit that I am not on time and I have not been on time for you, Lana, since they first cuffed me. I thought I was Superman. You thought I was Superman. You know how I love you. *I know how you love me.* I admit that I lost you. It was my desire and my job to love and provide and protect you to your last breath. I failed.

Forgive me, Lana. There has not been one day since I was cuffed and removed from your life that I did not think about you. Not you home alone, in the mansion I bought for you. Not you back in our Brooklyn hood being tortured by your ungrateful blood relatives. I thought of you, Lana, as I first saw you, as you first saw me, as we loved and made a family together. I have not had one day even up to this moment that you have not been singing in my ear, dancing in my eyes, laying in my heart, and stirring up my mind." He lowered his head. I did not like that. I'm used to Santiaga with his head held high no matter the situation.

"I'm older now, Lana . . ." Poppa smiled when he said that. "Remember we lived like we would be young forever, rich forever, together forever? Now I'm wearing prescription eyeglasses. Eye doctor says I can see everything that's far away, but not what's right in front of me."

"Momma! You should see Santiaga. His physique is more solid than it was even when he hustled. His walk is so mean in his bright white linen safari suit. He been on the golf course all morning. Can you believe that? And, after the golf course and here to the graveyard your man ain't got one speck of soil on him. Even his white leather Gucci driving shoes look like he just popped open the shoebox and eased them out of the soft sack. They're flawless, Momma. And those glasses he's complaining about happen to be Cartier and they make his already long lashes and sparkling eyes look even more attractive than they already were. You know he was never about bragging but he has all of his jet-black silky, curly hair with mature man streaks of silver that make him look like he's even smarter, sharper than before."

"That's enough," Santiaga said to me calmly.

"Santiaga is still Superman to me!" I kept going. "He's Superman to a whole lot of people. They're even going to make a Hollywood film about him. Picture dat! Momma, there gon be *some bitch on the screen pretending to be you.* I know you hate that."

I had to do it. I didn't like the way my father's mood down-shifted like he was somehow a failure or a lesser man. I couldn't just stand silently listening to that. Now as far as I am concerned, everything at this graveyard is finished.

"Poppa, let's go, I'm hungry," I lied. I left him standing there and walked away hoping that it would cause him to catch up with me as I left this awful location.

"Our first daughter, spicy like Lana, gorgeous like Lana, popu-lar like Lana, made from our young love. I promise, I will not lose her or fail her like Ricky failed Lana. I put that on my life."

8

WHAT YOU DON'T KNOW WILL HURT

Poppa inserted a metal key into the elevator in the luxurious Manhattan building we just entered. The top button lit up with the capital letters PH. My stomach grumbled. So far I haven't eaten a thing. I'm angry though. So I ignore it. Sometimes anger makes me feel full even though I'm empty. "Now, what about our cell phones?" I asked him.

"They're still in the Cadillac. Don't focus on that," he said as the elevator doors drew open directly into a living space, impressive.

I hate that he confiscated my shit. I hate it even more now that I see that he has a second cell phone of his own laying on top of a marble stand that held a vase of fresh lillies. He picked it up as we walked inside. I expect him to keep two or three phones, no problem. *But give me mine.* It has my contacts, my designs, my data, and my everything on it. If there is ever a next time, which there should not be, I'll slip out my sim card before placing the hardware in anyone's hands, even Poppa's.

"Tell me," he said in his calm, masculine boss voice. "What time was that?" he asked. "Leave it there. I'll come through when I come through," he said and that was the end of his conversation on his second phone. I am accustomed from way back to overhearing these short convos that reveal nothing to the person or people standing in the room when Poppa makes or receives a live call, which was not often.

"Take a seat, Baby Girl," he said, and it is the first time I don't like being called by that name anymore. Especially not if it means I live the life of a child while being a grown woman. When I was a child, I knew no one would ever fill in the blanks, bring me up to speed with the details of day-to-day business or family life. Now I am an adult and information is still not being told to me in detail.

Dead or alive, Poppa never told me the status of my bodyguard and driver. On this same day that Poppa had talked more words to me than it seemed in my lifetime, there was so much left out. Too much I didn't know, but I could tell that's how he wanted it to be. On the drive over to this penthouse, he had given me some commands. "I will assign you a new driver." To which I replied that I have an appointment at Motor Vehicle to take the driver's test and get my driver's license in two weeks. I reminded him that I plan to buy my own car and *drive it myself.* "We discussed this already, Poppa," I said to him gently even though I wasn't feeling gentle.

Santiaga had replied, "Get your license, yeah. But it is not time for you to drive yourself around yet. You're a celebrity. It's a different climate. You don't know yet that there can be more than a million more people who now think they know and love you. But if even only one percent of them are haters, you got ten thousand people with negative thoughts, negative intentions, and negative energy, and possibly even negative actions, plotting on your demise. Fame is a double-edged sword. We're richer than before. We are released from prison and freer than before, but more money, more potential problems, and more limited freedoms," he said. I felt trapped. Then I thought about the fact that I have felt trapped since I was thirteen years young.

"I'll put in place two new bodyguards from a security company I choose and trust. No more Network priorities over independent contractors who affect the key aspects of life-and-death matters," he said and I knew he meant it. He had been pointing with his right index finger, while driving the car, holding the steering wheel with his left.

"You don't say nothing. Less is more. On Monday, I will contact Kuntz and let him know that my management company will take over your security details and movements, moving forward, nonnegotiable."

"What about when I get a man?" I asked Santiaga abruptly. "Am I suppose to bring a bodyguard on our dates, no, two bodyguards so they can both sit and stand and watch over us? Should the bodyguard even be in my apartment, in my bedroom?" I asked, a little disgusted to be having the same conversations with my father that I'd had since I was thirteen years young, when he was my self-appointed bodyguard who I didn't ask for and no one hired or paid. It was just his way of cockblocking me from using my body and my time however I wanted to, from thirteen years young . . . and now what? Back then I thought a teenaged girl is the same as a grown woman who can make her own choices. Matter of fact, I still think so and now I'm more than double thirteen.

"You won't get a random man. You'll get a qualified husband. We will size him up, background check him, and watch his choices and actions. If he's a stand-up guy, man enough to handle his business and love and protect my daughter, I'll hand you over to him. But, I have to be sure."

Poppa could not have known that the more rules he threw at me, I was like a shrinking person. I stand five foot, seven inches tall. Listening to him, I dropped down to being only five feet, and then only three feet tall, a little-tiny girl seated in a big chair at her father's Midtown Manhattan penthouse apartment, that *I never knew* he had. That he says he has had since he was a very young hustler who earned and caked up enough paper to buy the condo in his mother's name. His mother! I never met her, saw her even from a distance, and Poppa never mentioned her to me in my lifetime. I never asked. Figured if we don't have no grandparents, we don't need none. Furthermore, I wasn't asking no questions about Poppa that he didn't speak on first. That's a hustler's family way of life. He taught me that.

"Use the bathroom on the left." He pointed. "And you'll sleep in the bedroom on the right." He pointed. "Stay here with me until I hire the best security team and while I do some investigating on everything that already happened involving you regarding last night, the Lamborghini, the driver, the bodyguard, the police, the Network, the fake kidnapping, everything." He was telling me all of this, ordering me to stay here, and stating all of these limits and instructions calmly and politely. I was holding back, but building up like a backed up toilet bout to burst. "You'll like it here. It's not too bad is it?" Poppa asked as he stood and held open and widened his arms to show off his perfect penthouse and all of its spacing, furnishings, and even a glass door revealing his dope-ass balcony. "You shower there. I'll shower in my room and cook us a late lunch." He smiled his charming smile as he walked through and closed the doors of what I assume is his master bedroom. Now Santiaga cooking for me, I love that. On any other day I would've been super excited about it. But today I'm concealing how heated I actually am.

In the spare bathroom, I closed the door and stood looking at myself in the mirror. Not really looking at my fashions or my beauty, more like looking into my own eyes. I began inhaling through my nose like with a dramatic effort and exhaling like pushing the air out by force. I turned on the sink water, but for no real reason. When I broke out of whatever that feeling was all about, I noticed a pink toothbrush in a marble cup. That woke me right up. I'm spinning slowly, taking it all in. Confirming that yeah some other bitch been fully using this bathroom inside of my father's penthouse. Who could it be? It better not belong to fucking Dulce Tristement, that bitch who made my mother break down and the same bitch who gave birth to that bastard, my father's only son, *who I'll never fuck with*. Oh let me *catch her* walking up in here. Does my father think I'm gonna live in here with him and his bitch? I don't give a fuck if he thinks this is some emergency and that I should just adjust to the situation. And is he living with this bitch and taking me by the graveyard talking all that shit to dead Momma!? I pulled the bathroom door back open and ready to charge. In the laid out living room, all I could hear was Poppa's shower water. I peeped that there were a total of three bedrooms. Only thing holding me back from full-on reckless was considering that maybe the toothbrush belonged to his mysterious mother. Maybe this is her bathroom? I stepped into the spare bedroom closest to the bathroom. On top of the not king or queen sized bed was a large suitcase, unlocked and left wide open. It was packed with too many items. I flipped through it. Definitely belonged to some bitch around my same size with clothing I would never have chosen or worn. Most of the shit in the suitcase was regular and unimpressive. So, I opened the closets. When I did, hanging on hangers was all designer outfits with the tags still on them. Fine fabrics, silks and chenille, linens and taffeta, all designed and customized for a young fine-ass female. Not made for a mature man's old mother. Handbags were lined up on the top shelf, completely crispy and totally elite. On the closet floor was a lineup of designer heels *of my taste*. Flipped a few pairs and no wear and tear on the bottoms, *brand fucking new*. It was like Poppa had taken some broke, unfashionable bitch on a shopping spree. Or better yet, he had all of these items purchased and hung them up for her. The drawers were all empty. There was no cell phone or other tech that would give her away. Guess Poppa didn't take her phone. She has it on her cause it's not here and she's not either. "Let Dulce come walking back in here. I'll give her fifteen years' worth of anger, ass whopping that she'll never forget," I said out loud. Then I heard the fly-ass private elevator doors draw open. I stepped out of the bedroom. Soon as I saw her dark eyes and long-to-her-ass black hair I rushed her, pushing her back against the elevator wall and then down to the floor. Now she's looking up to me shocked and horrified, saying some shit in Spanish but that's not the point. I grabbed her long black hair and wrapped it around her neck. I held it tight with my left and slapped her continuously with my right, till I saw her face redden with the print of my hand. She's struggling to get up but choking. I remembered that I'm not a murderer so I loosened my grip on her hair. Then I let her hair go. She tried to unwrap and gather her hair from around her throat. It was so long and her fingers were trembling. Soon as she straightened it all out, I grabbed her hair again, this time from the top of her head so she would feel the pain of being scalped without me having to completely strangle and choke her. I dragged her into the living room. She's kicking and screaming and struggling to stand up. Soon as she's on her feet I cocked my hand all the way back and slapped her like both of us were men. I let go of her scalp and pushed her. As she screamed, and tried to break her fall, I dipped down, got my heels, and cracked her over the head one good time. As she yelled for Santiaga, I screamed, "He's in the shower, bitch. He can't hear you," and laughed an angry laugh. I snatched my handbag off the chair and dashed into the elevator. Feverishly I'm pressing the button to go down. It's not moving. She ran into the kitchen and pulled open a drawer. I could hear the knives clinking. I looked down and saw she had dropped the elevator key on the elevator floor. I picked it up, inserted it the way Poppa had done it when we first arrived. The last glimpse I saw was her rushing forward with a butcher knife. But she did not have the look in her eyes that convinced me she was capable of murder. "Too late, bitch," I said through gritted teeth as the doors closed. *Bitch knew exactly where the drawer with the knives was. Bitch had the key to my father's private penthouse elevator!* She's lucky I'm not no killa. Cause she would've easily been dead.

I still don't have my cell phone, which I hate. But I have my handbag, my Louis wallet, my identification, my 50 bands (50k) credit cards, and everything else I daily carry for two reasons, comfort plus to be prepared for the the expected and unexpected.

When I walked out of the elevator and through his lobby, where the marbled out floors are shining, and beneath the huge throwback chandelier, the concierge or bellman or whatever approached me.

"It was nice meeting you, Miss Santiaga. Your father is the *best* man. His mother was a great lady, may she rest in peace, *and you are a beautiful young star.*" He pushed his hands up as to demonstrate stars sparkling in the sky. "Have a good evening. I hope you'll visit us again soon." I didn't say shit back. Just shot straight out the door of the building. I knew the motherfucker just wanted a tip for doing absolutely nothing but blowing smoke up my ass. Plus, I was recalling how when Bullet and I had our apartment on the east side of

Midtown Manhattan, he used the doorman to surveil me, set me
up, and snitch out each of my movements. That doorman caused
me a lot of trouble. I hated him and I hated that.

My fire-engine-red Dior mini was attracting too much attention. With my Bottega Veneta sunglasses on, and my handbag and
sparkling stiletto heels of the same brand, I couldn't play down my
fame or beauty. Santiaga had sent me this entire outfit as an eye
catcher and game changer for those goddamn cop flicks. It's just
dawning on me that Poppa might have had in mind for me to take
those photos at some point today even before the police incident.
Why else would he already have all of these beautiful items boxed
and bagged, dress steamed and ready to wear in my exact size? The
thought of the cop-pics just kept my body temperature up too high.

I swapped out all of my top designer wear and copped me a denim
mailbag and basic Guess denim overalls on purpose. On my feet
now are a basic pair of blue Pumas. I gathered my hair and tucked
my ponytail beneath a mean-ass Gucci hat, cause I couldn't help
myself. Covering my eyes now are nothing but regular Ray-Bans.
I stepped into a FedEx with a stapled closed Gucci shopping bag
containing all of today's haute couture, and asked for a big box. I
dropped it inside the box and the worker sealed it for me after asking me some dumb questions about whether there were any liquids
or explosives or shit like that in my box. "Would you like to insure
it?" she asked. "Definitely," I replied and paid a ridiculous sum for
a box I was mailing from Manhattan to Brooklyn, the Immanuel
mansion. I didn't fuss about the mail cost though, cause my jewelry
was tucked in there as well.

I'm headed uptown to the Bronx, aka the BX. Fuck everything

else and everybody else. I gotta finish putting together my team and building my business brick by brick. I'm going for securing real wealth in a short period of time. I love that I had flipped a basic meet and greet with the Network CEO into a million dollars, in less than thirty minutes. I'm bout to be boss enough to get what most of us celebs don't seem to have, self-control, deep love, and true happiness.

9

DUTCHESS

No apps, maps, or navigation, fuck that. I asked all my questions at Grand Central Station specifically to not look or act like a dumb vic. This is not my territory. But it's summer and the sun won't go down till late. I'm more determined than afraid of the unfamiliar. Even though I am dressed down, of course I know somebody might still easily recognize me. I'm on TV, laptops, desktops, and phones everywhere. However, dressed down like an around-the-way girl, why would Winter Santiaga, the reality TV show star from Brooklyn, be in the BX, off camera, on foot, looking the same as any hood chick? Nah.

Truthfully, I'm a little nervous. It's a consequence of having been shot dead already, and understanding the randomness of shit happening. But I refuse to be a shook bitch. I fight even my own fears. So I am here to get my *number one girl*, even though she is my third team member pickup. She hit time served three months before me. In my elaborate upon-release plan that I laid out while caged, I had tapped Dutchess as the team leader of my new fashion enterprise. It ain't because she's fashionable. She's not.

I arrived at Randall Avenue in the Soundview section of the BX. That's where she told me her projects are at, apartment 4C.

Her name is Dutchess; she's the opposite of Natalie. We didn't grow up together. She only knows me the convict. I only know her the convict. She keeps her mouth shut at the right time, minds her business, and on lockdown was swift with reading the room and making decisions that didn't backfire. She don't compete with me. She smart enough to know that's a fucking waste of time. Besides she got her own thunder, I love that. Before prison and during prison she earned her own reputation. Nobody can take that from her.

The 1774 building project hallway lights were dim, how I remember this exact lighting from my Brooklyn projects. Projects are projects, no matter which borough they in. I walked up the dark stairwell. I'm not a fan of project elevators. Anything could happen once you step in or out. When I reached the fourth floor, I could hear dogs barking furiously, like they ain't been fed in days. I thought to myself, *I hope they ain't Dutchess's dogs.* Ever since Bullet locked me in the apartment guarded by his trained fighter-killer dogs, I have zero tolerance for them.

I banged the metal knocker on apartment 4C. I heard someone dragging bedroom slippers headed to the door. I heard the metal shutter to the peephole open and swing shut. Then I heard bout three or four locks opening up and finally a chain being dragged and a dead bolt being turned. Yup that's how it be.

"Oh sweat," Dutchess said, then placed her whole hand over her own face.

"I told you I would come for you," I said.

She pulled her hand away from her face. "Ah bitch! Did you think I believed you?" She cracked up.

"Well you gon let me in or what?"

"Well you didn't call so I'm in my nightgown," she said.

"I already seen it all!" I said. Locked up chicks seen every millimeter of nakedness of one another, even each other's anuses. I pushed in the door, past her, and walked in. She let it slam shut and even turned the dead bolt before showing me to her living room.

"I couldn't call ahead of time. You gave me your address but neither one of us had cell phone numbers upstate. Or did you forget?"

"Oh I'll never forget," she said. "How could I?" she asked.

"You got your driver's license yet? A phone? Your Social Security card?" I asked her.

"I got a license and no car, a Social Security card and no job. I got a bogus 7-11 cell phone no internet and no minutes." She laughed. "Hell, I even got a new bank account but nothing in it."

Brickhouse Dutchess is in a greasy short nightgown and her house smells like bacon. The summer sun was shining outside. The dim artificial lights that were on in her inside corridor barely allowed us to see. Facts, inside of her apartment it was cloudy. A dreary fog filled the lack of air.

"Get dressed!" I said. She bolted to the back. I was still standing. She never said, *Have a seat, here's a cup of Kool-Aid* or anything like that.

"Don't you want to know where we going?" I called out.

"Anywhere but here," she screamed back. I heard the shower water come on.

I walked around. Really I was thinking about my Brooklyn project apartment where I lived for sixteen years, before the Long Island move, a so-called upgrade. The layout was the same here. However, nothing else was even vaguely similar. The old and cheap cloth couch that sunk in so deep it had to mean that some big nigga used it as a bed every single night for at least four or five years. No pictures on the wall. A tiny flat-screen that instead of being lodged into or bolted into the wall or perched on a dope-ass TV stand was on the floor, unplugged and leaning. The kitchen was fucked up, holes in the plastic cushioned chairs. Mold in the Tupperware, and the refrigerator let out an odor that smelled like a meat burp when I opened it. *No food, perfect!* I thought to myself. Dutchess is hungry, starving, not spoiled rotten, obviously surviving meal to meal. That means she would appreciate some relief from her circumstance. My Brooklyn girls had gotten spoiled from the spotlight and the small paper that they thought was big paper, from season 1 of my reality show.

I stood looking down into the trash. If my bodyguard was in here with me, I'd have him search through it. I need to know if there are any needles in there, vials, empty baking powder boxes, or any indication that she was on that shit. Three months of being home from prison hell, no money, no job can get a bitch deep depressed. That's when any girl could sink into a cheap high habit that fucks them up for life. I ain't no cop or authority. However, Santiaga taught me that there should be no addicts in my inner circle. He said even if they were not addicts when I first recruited them, I needed to watch closely their behavior and choices so that they don't turn addict after teaming up. "All addicts are great customers, to anybody selling dope, but that's it."

"Can I bring my dogs?" Dutchess asked as she appeared fully dressed and ready to rock. However, I didn't see or hear no dogs inside her apartment. Otherwise I wouldn't even be standing here.

"Where they at?" I asked her. She laughed and turned and went back down the corridor. I folded my arms across my breasts and waited, but I was feeling all like, *Time's up. She better hurry before my patience wears off and the deal I didn't offer her yet evaporates.*

"He's my older brother Duke. He's my younger brother Duel." She introduced them as they approached me coming down the corridor.

"Oh shit, you one pretty bitch," Duel said. Then he turned towards his sister and said, "How you became friends with her? All your homegirls is mad ugly." Dutchess punched him. Then the older one asked, "Where you fit'n to take my sister? She gotta make us some lunch."

"I'm fit'n to move her out," I said using his lingo.

"What we gon eat then?"

"What y'all want. I got a twenty spot. I'll bring y'all back Kentucky Fried Chicken," she offered them.

"Didn't you hear the pretty lady? She's moving you out. You ain't coming back," Duke said. Then they were all looking at me, not smiling.

"How much you want for her?" I asked.

"You crazy. You think we selling the people in our family?" Duke asked.

"Wait, let's hear her proposal. How much you offering?" Duel said curiously.

I went in my handbag and pulled out ten stacks and tossed them to the oldest one who was playing hard to get.

"It's like that huh?" he said. I know that he gets it now.

"Dutch, don't forget to visit," Duel said joking her, but he was not joking.

"Whose your friend?" a nigga asked Dutchess as we walked out the building down a decline that couldn't exactly be called a hill, and off the block.

"Ah nigga stay in your lane. She family" is how she responded. I loved that. Quick thinking is all her.

Today is my first day not chauffeured, and riding on the train and the subway, since my release and since I survived my coma. Although I'm not in my Brooklyn neighborhood, I'm in my element now. I feel more comfortable.

"You're different," Dutchess said.

"Different how?"

"I can't really put it into words."

"We both convicts," I reminded her.

"Ex-cons," she said.

"There's no such thing as ex-cons. Once a convict, always a convict. Everybody always gonna see us that way," I assured her.

"Not if you got money," she swiftly replied.

"No, if a convict has money it just makes people not say how they see it. But, they still see it the same way. Convicts for life," I said calmly but serious.

She smiled the half smile of a young woman who had been through a bunch of bullshit. "You right," she said. "That's facts," she verified it.

At a Manhattan T-Mobile location we walked in. "May I help you?" a young dude, maybe twenty-one years young, employee asked.

"Tell him what you want," I said to Dutchess. She just looked at me hard. "I rock the iPhone, does that work for you, or are you bout that Samsung?" I asked her.

"I'm bout what you about," she said.

"Get her the new iPhone and connect it" was all I said.

"Excuse me, aren't you . . . ?" he began saying to me.

"You already know. Now focus," I said pointing him to pay

attention to Dutchess. "Oh . . ." was all he replied but he was still staring my way.

"No contracts, she's buying the phone." I handed Dutchess two stacks to pay for the phone. "Hook it up and show her how to use it," I told him, then walked away for her to manage the rest of the transaction herself since she had the cash in hand.

Prison taught me a lot of things I didn't know before getting locked. Like, it's impossible to avoid fighting from time to time. Sometimes you gotta punch a bitch in her face first, even though she didn't hit you first. Hit her because you think she's thinking bout hitting you or getting hit. But to keep out of solitary confinement, the box, the hole, protect yourself by protecting the next bitch's space and pride. Don't ask certain questions: *Innocent or guilty? What you did to get yourself in here? You fucking men, or girls? You got any kids?* Wait till she shows through action and tells it on her own. Don't blow a bitch up even when you know she's lying cause there's mad holes in the story she telling and the story her paperwork is telling. Don't stare at a bitch in the toilet or shower or anywhere really. So, I know how to handle Dutchess, a lean brown-skinned bombshell.

"This shit cost more than triple my rent," she said as she exited T-Mobile. She was holding it in her hand waving it back and forth. I knew she was moved, excited, thrilled even. Her face didn't show it. It didn't have to for me to know that my team plan was working so far.

"You good with the BX? Or you rather live in a different borough?" I asked her.

"I can survive wherever," she said. "If you asking if I got beef in Soundview that I'm tryna get away from, nah. King holds it down," she said matter-of-factly.

"King?" I repeated.

"That's my big brother. Duke's my middle brother and Duel is

the baby brother," she said nonchalantly as she stared at the new
cell phone, and played with the functions. "The first two stacks in
the ten stacks you threw at them is gon be to bail King out," she
explained. I didn't say no reply. Once paper leaves my hand, I know
I don't have no further control over it.

"If you asking me if I have a reason to stay in Soundview, I don't.
According to the authorities, I'm in the same house with four convicted
felons, who even though we sister and brothers, ain't suppose to be living together in the projects no how. My mother passed last month.
She was on that shit. The apartment is in her name. Be about five
minutes before the housing authority comes up in there regulating."

See? I didn't have to ask. She voluntarily told me the whole
story, which revealed the reasons why she was going to come with
me and do what I want her to do in exchange for some "money-
power-respect."

In the Hell's Kitchen section of Manhattan, not upscale, but
not a slum, I'm ringing the buzzer after again reminding myself
that I don't have my phone. I had told Dutchess to type on her
browser, "Apartment For Rent, NY, NY," and then the particulars
that I was looking for: a studio apartment, in Manhattan, rent one
thousand dollars monthly, with kitchen, four-burner stovetop and
oven, refrigerator, washer and dryer, bathroom and shower. This
was one of three options on the first site that popped up. It is a
first-floor studio apartment for rent by the owner. I liked that there
was no realtor on this one. On the low, I had spoken to a realtor
from a prestigious realty company, when I first considered moving
out of the Immanuel Estate. Even though I got plenty paper, when
she laid out the step-by-step process to buying a house, owning or
leasing a condo, or renting in an upscale area that meets my high
criteria, I realized that making my move out on my own would take

a time-consuming, careful, and expensive process, even involving background checks, committees of residents interviewing me and voting and deciding whether or not they want me in the building! I didn't and I don't like that shit. If I can buy my way into any building, there should be no further discussion. I hand you or wire you the money, you hand me the keys, fobs, cards, or whatever.

"How did you hear about this apartment?" the owner asked me as she opened the heavy locked buzzer-entry door. She is wearing a dollar store dress with teapots stamped all over it. On top of that bad decision, she strapped on a dollar store apron with four huge pockets in which she stuffed folded papers and what looked like a large round keyring with several sets of metal keys. Her eyeballs, abnormally large, both bulging, looked like they were trying to escape their sockets. It was as if she was frightened. Yet, she had a welcoming smile on her face.

"I saw it online," I replied.

"You know that the rent is twelve hundred per month," she said, and of course I caught that she added on a two-hundred-dollar nigga tax. A lot of businesses do that. They want the Blacks and Latinos of any shade to pay them extra just for being willing to do business with us. I'm not fazed by her or her two hundred dollars above the advertised fee. "There is a two and a half months' advanced rent and security deposit. Small pets are allowed, fish, turtles, and petite puppies, you know the kind that you can fit in your purse like Paris Hilton. And, of course we allow cats, primarily because they keep the rats away or eat them all when they show up. It's Hell's Kitchen, no need for me to lie about the vermin." The older white woman's hair was white and wild. The blue veins in her hands seemed swollen. But her hands were steady, not shaking. Her body was solid and her way of walking on her thick calves was smooth, as though she had been climbing stairs for her entire life. "Other than that if I must say so myself, my building is very clean and secure," she added.

"What do you think of this place?" I asked Dutchess, after taking the one-stop tour.

"It's probably too small for you," she said calmly. "Otherwise it's cool. I didn't see no roach or mice poop. When I turned on the faucet the water wasn't brown. I didn't see no streaks, cracks, or water leaks in the ceiling. The refrigerator gets cold, and the toilet flushes," she reported after searching around while me and the owner landlord had been speaking. What I liked the most was how Dutchess had observed and checked without me having to ask her to do it.

"So what's the process?" I asked the owner.

"Credit check, proof of employment, a strong reference, a signed lease, and I already informed you about the costs. Oh, and you pay your own utilities," she added.

"I work for the Network Entertainment Company," I began saying. She immediately got excited. "Oh my gosh I knew it. I can just tell. *You are a lovely girl.* So pretty the rich would easily pay you for your looks. Must be an actress or a singer. This building has a lot of people in the entertainment industry. Not huge-huge movie stars . . . but you know, Broadway singers and dancers, as well as jazz artists, musicians, and all of that. Oh how I love a great Broadway show!" she said and a speck of debris flew out of her mouth.

"I don't have pay stubs but I have a copy of my first check for starring in my new television show. I have not built up my own line of credit as of yet, but that's why I will pay for the whole year up front." Her huge eyes widened. "You look like a reasonable woman who appreciates being certain that she will receive her money." I smiled. "That's fourteen thousand four hundred a year," I calculated. Then I pulled out the envelope, which contained the copy of the first portion of my season 1 payout, which was wired directly into my account, a quarter of a million dollars. Her eyes did a blinking frenzy as she counted up those zeros and verified the embossed letterhead of the Network Entertainment Company. She looked at me like she couldn't believe it. So I went into my denim mailbag and picked up fifteen grand. I raised up the one-inch stack of new clean bills that fit between two of my fingers and manicured nails. All doubt left her eyes. She reached for the cash, I guess for a count. I pulled the stack back.

"Let's see the lease first," I asked. She pulled an envelope out of her apron pocket swiftly. "The apartment will be in my girl's name. She's the renter."

"Oh, yes, your girl. We welcome that. A lot of my tenants are two men living together or two women. Whatever, we *never* judge," she said, and of course I caught that she thought Dutchess and I are lovers. I didn't deny it. Saw that in this woman's mind, it works in my favor.

"Meet Dutchess Mitchell. She works for me. Today is her first day. She doesn't have credit or pay stubs." She suddenly flashed a second doubtful expression.

"What about the security payment?"

"What for? What's more secure than twelve months advanced payment on a one-year lease?" She looked at my hand holding my stack. I placed it in her hand and knew the lady was enticed. She counted. I poured on more honey, thinking how Santiaga said, "You get more bees with honey." "Dutchess is a good girl. You mentioned that she needs a strong recommendation." I placed my hands on my hips gently and said, "That's me."

"I'm too sleepy to eat," I told Dutchess. "I was out clubbing all night. I'll come through tomorrow and we'll talk about the job offer and whether or not you're interested. Besides that, we need to catch up on the ten months since we last saw one another."

She laughed. "You funny," she said.

"I'm serious," I replied lightly. "Take these 2Gs. Buy a couch and some shit. Pack up your refrigerator with whatever food you want."

"No I can't. You've spent more than enough," she said, dangling her new keys and waving her iPhone back and forth.

I didn't reply, just gave her a certain look, then began walking off, leaving the two grand in her hand.

"Don't you want my new number?" she called out after me.

"Tomorrow" was all I said. I didn't need to explain that my father had taken my phone that contained every important thing and did not return it yet. I bounced.

I know I dazzled Dutchess. Only I know why. She's worth it. She has the mind, the guts, the fearlessness, plus the communication and the people skills, and a real nice voice. I'm certain she will run my business team and company the way I tell her to run it. She had the look of amazement on her face when I first turned and walked away. Probably couldn't even believe all she had gained in two hours' time. And, I also am 100 percent sure, I had given her more than any nigga she ever loved, or only fucked, ever gave her. In fact, I had given her more than I ever have spent on anyone else. That was my secret guarantee that she would show up, stay, work hard, and stick to me like glue.

10
THE SHOEMAKER

I didn't go to sleep like I told her I would. Stood on the corner for five minutes and flagged a yellow cab across and down to the East Village. My mind was racing in both directions. I am thinking about the place I'm on my way to and reviewing how I first met the shoemaker.

Doing business brings the person doing business, that's me, face to face with people they never would have crossed paths with. Business pushes aside the personal opinions, prejudices, and the politics, plus other shit that keeps millions of people hostile, hating, and separate. A sharp businessperson, that's me, prioritizes and asks herself only, *Who is the best person for the job who can give me the top level results that I'm looking and paying for?* And fuck everything else.

The day I am reminiscing about (a word I learned in my teens from a hip-hop track by CL Smooth), I was wearing red-bottom Louboutin heels. Also, a black pleated miniskirt that showcased my incredible thighs, a black satin Victoria's Secret strapless bra that could be seen through my blackish translucent sleeveless blouse that rode my titties and accentuated my figure. When I told my driver, "Pull over, I need to check something out," I instructed my body-guard to chill in the whip. He hated that. I didn't care. I opened the back door of the powder-blue Range I was roving in, and stepped out, walking directly into "The Foot God." I was attracted by his location, as well as the play on words, "The Foot God," even though I'm sure that there is only one real GOD. His shoemaker shop was on the ground level. When I pulled the shop door open, some bells jingled and then a recording of some drumbeat on a loop played. I was like, *what the fuck?* As I stepped in I didn't see a store atten-dant but saw four colorful walls, each with a product related to feet. Such as costume jewelry: toe rings made of an assortment of things, including metal, brass, copper, beads, string, wire, lanyard, you name it he had it hanging there for sale. I didn't look down on it. I knew there's a market for costume jewelry. That's fine for everybody else. However, if I decide to rock a dope-ass toe ring, it's gonna sparkle with genuine clear diamonds. If I ever rock an ankle bracelet, it will be a diamond charm bracelet made for the ankle featuring every-thing precious, of course diamonds, gold, onyx, topaz, sapphire, rubies, emeralds, and the works. Or maybe only diamonds but clear ones, yellow ones, blue ones, and in any color certified authentic genuine diamonds can be copped in. I pulled out my small drawing pad that fits in the palm of my hand to quick sketch the design ideas that began swirling in my head for feet jewels.

The back wall featured organic nail polishes in every color. I liked that. I didn't necessarily trust that all the ingredients were healthy and pure, but I liked that someone had the business idea to create organic nail polish and market and position it in such a way that customers believe it's nothing but nature. Other than that, there were temporary tattoos for the feet, ankles, and calves. The packaging claimed that the ingredients were made from fruits and vegetables. Definitely not toxic and would last on the skin for only a week unless you intentionally wash it away sooner than that. It was all cool to me but I was searching for the shoemaker. I walked down the stairs that were off to my far left. The wall leading down was lined with shoes in slots. I wondered if people had not picked up their shoes after the owner repaired them? If they had abandoned them, what does that say about the shoemaker? Am I in the right place? I had an idea when I was locked that I would design and make my own line of shoes. When I researched shoe and other fashion designs and so on, I discovered that getting into the top fashion houses as a designer was next to impossible. It was and is a closed society. You had to know somebody who knew somebody, or worse you had to suck and fuck your way into some low-level intern-type position and forfeit your time, body, and finance since you were giving those houses all of your time and creativity and not getting a paid position until they had sucked all of the designs out of your head and blood out of your body. Since I knew I was starting late in the fashion industry and had already blew fifteen years of my life, I had to come up with an idea to enter and burst into the top tier. To not ask any of the fashion houses for a break or an internship or a job, but to feature designs so dope that I reverse the process, resulting in the fashion houses chasing me. Niggas have always known that all designs originate in the hood. We the hood dwellers are the most live, most creative, make the most out of the least, and release new styles and designs *daily*. Since we are not in the fashion market, and not in the money game, we see ourselves and our styles on the Paris runways as supermodels don what we invented, or turned up in the hood. They get the billions. Trademark our styles and creations. We keep nothing but the look. I'm not mad. Instead I'm on my money move.

"Those shoes don't need fixing." I heard the baritone voice before I could see him. "Unless you have some other shoes in your bag that I can't see," he said as I walked down further so he could see me and I could see him as well. His workshop was dark except for the lighted area where he had tools randomly scattered on the table. He was standing, a tall man bout six-foot-five. He must've been so black that I couldn't separate him from the darkness. But I could tell he had stood up from his lighted workspace to greet me.

"Achol Turyagumanawe," he said in a heavy accent. I'm like, *I guess that's his name.*

"Achol," I repeated because fuck me tryna say his last name. "I never heard that name before," I said to him.

"Achol, means in my language, 'the black.'" I liked his voice. Sounded like a freaking tuba. "What brings you into my shop?" he asked me.

"I'm a shoe designer. I want to make my own shoes," I said eagerly.

"Not with those hands," he said strangely. I didn't say nothing back. Then he said, "Come." Somehow, I was turned on by his command. I took two steps forward. He held out his huge hands with his palms open. "Put your hands here," he commanded. I did. Now my hands are over his hands, my palms facing his palms. He stared. Then he used his hands to turn my hands back over. He looked and then let them go. He walked to his workspace and sat down in the light.

"Come," he said to me. So I stepped closer to the lighted area. "These are the hands of a shoemaker." He placed his hands in the light faced down and then flipped them around palms up. He didn't need to say anything else on that point. I saw that his huge hands had been impacted and worn. But, I liked his hands.

"You have the hands of a young bride who has not yet prepared even one pot of cassava, beef stew, or even boiled any rice or potato or yam," he said, smiling with a mouth full of white teeth, one of them framed in gold. I liked what he was saying not because of the compliment or the meaning, but because it was completely unexpected. I like men who say and do things I welcome, but do not expect. Things that are not hateful or harmful to me, but are completely surprising. He grabbed one of his tools and said, "This is a shank. It's one of ten tools that you will always need to handle as a shoemaker. Your hands and the shank don't belong together," he said and I smiled brightly thinking he has no idea how many shanks I've held. I liked that he did not know, and couldn't tell. "How much did you pay for your shoes?" he asked, then picked up a flashlight, switched it on, and spotlighted my Louboutins.

"Three thousand, five hundred," I said.

"I already knew. Just wanted to see if you would be honest or if you would be embarrassed."

"Embarrassed," I said swiftly.

"Yes embarrassed at paying more than thirty-eight dollars, which is all it cost for a skilled workman like myself to make a pair same as those."

"Thirty-eight dollars," I blurted out. "C'mon," I said. "You should be honest!"

"Give me your shoes if you want to learn," he said. I hesitated, then I handed them over.

"Your feet are same as your hands," he said, spotlighting my toes. Then he pulled up a little seat and placed it beside him behind his worktable.

"Sit," he commanded. I sat.

"Did you pay 3,462 more than they were worth because the bottoms are red?" He laughed. "Is red your favorite color? What if I make a pair of these and the bottoms are green? Would you pay me 3,462 dollars for them?" he asked as he began using his various tools to take apart the Loubutins slowly and carefully.

"No I wouldn't," I said. "If you make a pair they would be knock-offs not originals and no matter how good you made the lookalikes everybody would know they're bootleg because the bottom is the wrong color. My father told me since day one, no bootleg knockoffs should or would ever touch my body," I said proudly.

He laughed a hearty laughter. I didn't know if that was a diss or not. "So you are paying for the name, not the shoe?" he asked, not looking up at me and still working his tools. "That means you are wasting your time to design or make your own shoes. Who will pay you thousands of American dollars for your name?" he asked.

I could tell he was one guy who wasn't playing dumb. Didn't really know who I am. I liked that he didn't know. I stood up and stepped forward. "My name is high value, even though you don't know it. If I design and learn how to make my own shoes, when I wear them first and everyone sees me wearing them, I can sell them for ten thousand dollars a pair!" I declared straight-faced. He dropped his tool purposely. He pointed his adjustable light towards my face. It was so bright it made my eyes close.

"Yours is the face of an unmarried beauty. Never suckled a new-born, or walked around the village in your bare feet, and never even met a real man," he said and it was as if he had hit me with his hammer.

"My father is a real man," I said.

"You can never ever marry your father," he quick replied.

"I . . . ," I began explaining. He cut me off.

"Any real man who is not your father would automatically marry you," he said. My cold heart melted. "And I see that you agree." He smiled and pointed his light at my titties, where my nipples were raised up beneath the black satin bra and thin silk see-through blouse.

"You are older than my father," I said, placing my hands on my hips.

"I am," he said. "But I am the father of the seven sons who I raised. All *real men* and I will marry you to my youngest." He said it like it was definite. I couldn't front, if his youngest adult son has a sexy voice like his father and pretty white teeth like his father, and huge hands that mean he's all good below the belt, if he's deep black, which is the complexion I favor, no, the complexion I deep lust . . . and a real man . . . ooh.

A bell jingled. The drumbeat played. "I have another customer." The big man stood back up. Instead of a customer, my bodyguard came stepping down. His presence swept away the heat I was feeling. I was pissed that he didn't follow my order to remain outside in the car.

"You good?" he asked me. "You were in here for a long time. Just checking," he said.

"You can take her. She will come back on her own next time," the big old beautiful black man named Achol said. And, he was right.

That's how we met. After threatening my bodyguard, or should I say enticing him with a pay tip, to remain outside no matter how long I was inside his shop, I came back as often as I could, and whenever I was out on the streets of New York examining and checking out styles and lack of style. I'd stop by and have unexpected, unplanned deep conversations with him, as well as creative back-and-forths about my shoe designs that I felt confident to show him. After we were in a creative rhythm I struck a deal with him. I will design the shoes. He will make the shoes. He will only make one pair of each of my designs in only my size. I will wear them and sell each single pair. The cut is sixty-forty in my favor. I will trust him not to steal my designs, not to display the shoes he makes for me anywhere in his shop or in any markets or stores or even online stores or anywhere on the internet. "They are for my eyes and feet only." He will trust me to get him his cut and to be transparent in the accounting, and if I license the designs to any conglomerate, he gets 10 percent of the licensing price on my big deal. It was a clean agreement we wrote down on a sheet of paper. He said he didn't need a copy because I would become his daughter in which case he knows I would never rob my father. I was like whatever. I still had not seen even one of his seven sons, and I was convinced that he had a crush on me himself.

I paid and tipped the taxi driver a hundred just cause he had the good sense to shut the fuck up through the whole ride, without me having to ask him. He gave off that excited feeling people give off when receiving unearned cash. This is New York. People give off that feeling but hide the smile and the gratefulness. It's replaced with New York cool.

It's Saturday early evening. As I eased down the shoemaker's stairs, Achol just looked at me and then pulled back his black curtain. He nodded his head towards his cot. I laid right down and he closed the curtain. "Please wake me up in ninety minutes cause at eight p.m. I have a date," I said.

"Oh ho! You think you've finally met a real man?" he asked doubtfully.

"No, with a pretty bitch who I like." Then I dozed off.

11
THE DATE

I left my Gucci hat at Achol's. I freed my hair from the plain ponytail. Walking in the dusk while the summer sun and moon are in
a rigorous tussle, it's nighttime and I feel more free. I'm still in the
Village, which is lower Manhattan, the arts and creative and dramatic crowd, Americans and every other nationality in the world.
No sunglasses shading my eyes cause I'm with the nighttime crowd,
which plays life more cool and people are more laid back. On a Saturday night they have already had a few drinks, popped a few pills,
or busted enough nuts not to give a fuck about celebrity sightings.

   I got my hair bumped and caught a vintage Jean Paul Gaultier
hand-crocheted black minidress from a well-known vintage clothing shop on 8th. I don't usually do vintage. In fact I never did before.
However, this dress was so mean on me in particular, I had to drop
3K on it. "It holds high resale value forever. In fact if you want to sell
it back to us after you've worn it, for a little bit less . . . ," the salesgirl
said, holding up her two fingers to signify a little less, ". . . we're open
to it, as long as it is not damaged in any way."

   "I'll keep this on and wear it out instead of bagging it," I told her as I dipped in the cheap denim mailbag to pay up. "Can I please take a photo of you wearing it?" she asked me, crossing her fingers like as in *pretty please.*

"Hmm that means if I resell it to you for a little less, you will use my photo to sell it to the next customer for a lot more!" We both laughed. I wasn't joking though. "How bout this, if you find me a handbag that goes with this dress exactly, and run down the street and buy me some black high-quality genuine leather freaking undeniably fashionable sandals to wear it with, I'll do the photo when you get back."

"Oh we have a fabby collection of handbags," she said. Then I pulled out my hourglass and flipped it. "I got a date in thirty minutes, go!"

I walked out feeling perfectly pretty. My dress-down Guess denim overalls, denim mailbag, and BX wear is now folded into an embroidered shopping bag. I intend to leave it in the pretty bitch's Mini Cooper trunk. That is if that little roller skate vehicle even has a trunk. I look more than good even though I feel naked without my jewels and cell phone. Of course I know that I could've just bought myself a new phone, but fuck that. I rarely think that I can teach my father a lesson. Tonight I will. I can't call anybody without my phone. *However*, nobody can call me either. Poppa will care much more that he can't find me after seizing my "tracking device" than I will care about being without my phone. That's facts. Not only him, but Porsche will *go crazy* and whoever else who will be wondering why I am not picking up, returning calls, posting or texting back.

Skeptical, I'm hoping she shows up. I already considered that she may have hit my cell to reschedule or confirm or anything, and not made the trip down here because of course, I couldn't hit her back. It's all a test, I'm thinking. Let's see what the pretty bitch do. Soon as that thought occurred to me, a vehicle moving on the other side of the street in the opposite direction of where I am standing, headlights lit up the interior of a doped-off pale pink Panamera Porsche. Those headlights exposed her parked there, sitting behind the driver's wheel, not looking in my direction. She's already parked. She had to have seen me waiting here for the past ten minutes, I thought to myself. I crossed to walk towards her. As I reached the car, I could hear a male voice speaking but only she was inside. I tapped the front passenger window. She turned and smiled at me. I heard her automatic locks click open. "Get in." I opened the door and placed my shopping bag on her backseat. Then I got in. The bright white soft leather interior was immaculate with maroon piping. I thought to myself, *That's more like it!*

"Okay, babe, we can talk about it some other time. Don't be mad." She pressed a button on her steering wheel and his voice disappeared.

"This beats the Mini Cooper," I remarked.

"Well hi bitch how was your day!" she said laughing. Then I broke out in a laugh thinking how I guess I am a bit rude.

"The Mini Cooper is Bijoux's. This is one of mine," she said. I was thinking *yeah that was the girl's name driving the bumper car.* Then I reminded myself that I don't know Pretty's name. I felt like a fool asking at the same time. I did anyway. "I didn't catch your name," I said.

She looked at me, smiled, and said my words from last night back to me. "Bitch, you know who I am." Then we both laughed and that relaxed me. But she still didn't say her name and I refuse to ask twice. Since I do know and I do watch what's going on around me, even though evidently Poppa doesn't think so, I would discover her name naturally before this night ends.

I also wanted to ask about these dudes who she said me and her partied with last night. Not only do I not know their names, I have no recall on their faces whatsoever. I figured if I was with a nigga I can't remember, he must be very forgettable. Once I see him tonight, I will know if I partied with him cause I know my taste. Besides I was concerned about what exactly we did with them? I hope I didn't get fucked for the first time in more than fifteen years and forgot because I was drunk and popped a pill and slept through it. I promised myself certain things that are a direct result of my death experience. I don't want no nigga to get me pregnant if he's not a man who I know and I love and wouldn't mind to marry. I won't ever again abort any life that takes root in my womb, period.

"How hungry are you?" she asked. "They'll pay for dinner. What kind of food you like? Italian, Chinese, Jamaican, Brazilian, French, American, Greek, Middle Eastern, Indian, or what? Tonight is your pick. Once you decide, I'll text them where to meet us."

"Fuck the food. Let's go to the casino."

"Casino! Atlantic City or Vegas?" she asked excited. Her eyes lit up like it's all an option.

I never been to neither. I'm trying to not get mad at the shit real niggas have enjoyed at age eighteen years young when I was locked, that I missed out on. But I've seen flicks of various casinos in Atlantic City and Vegas. I enjoyed critiquing the interior design, but more than that I like a casino floor jammed with men who put drinks on the table, smoke in the air, and have money to blow. Additionally, I had decided that I needed to meet these dudes Pretty had obviously linked us up with, in public, or in a packed place just in case they're fucking crazy. They'll be multiple exits, several ways for me to ditch em, and hundreds of eyes on us. Although the feeling of a powerful orgasm makes a bitch do spontaneous things, a speeding bullet to the head will make any bitch more cautious than she ever was before.

"You got a driver's license or passport?" she asked me, speaking rapidly and quickly looking up from her rapid finger-texting.

"Of course" was all I answered back. She kept texting, tapping, and swiping. I'm thinking how I do have a legitimate state ID which can be used wherever I go in New York State, most importantly at my bank. In two weeks I'll have the driver's license as well. In one month or less, my passport will arrive. I don't need to tell her all that.

"Okay here's the deal," she said, excited as she pulled out. "We will catch the nine-fifteen p.m. flight to Vegas. We'll go fifty-fifty on the flights and hotel suite. We take the red-eye back home Sunday night at eleven p.m. That puts our heels on the ground at seven a.m. Monday morning, in time for the opening of business. Cool?" she asked me, speaking calm but swift.

"Cool," I confirmed.

"Call Bijoux," she said strangely. But then Bijoux's voice filled the car.

"I'm listening," Bijoux said.

The pretty bitch told her, "It's a go. Book it." Then I heard the call click off, looked, and seen that her cell phone was mounted on the console that looked like the digital schematic for a spaceship heading to Jupiter. I laughed to myself.

"What? Let me in on your jokes," she said. I didn't say nothing. She began explaining. "While I'm driving the car I can't text. So I used the car system. I'm controlling it from my steering wheel." I didn't reply. I don't want anyone assuming that because I was locked up so long, I'm unaware or surprised by the technology. Although sometimes, I actually am. I'm in the car with her, but now mostly in my own head. I might as well live it the fuck up before Santiaga delivers on his new rules and restrictions, new bodyguards and a new driver. I exhaled. Then Dutchess flashed through my mind. But, I swiftly reminded myself that I had given her everything that she needs. Besides, oh yeah, I gotta packed Monday schedule beginning with some charity coordinator. Then, I reminded myself, *Feel good bitch. Feel good bitch.* I am calming myself, saying, *So what I beat Dulce's ass at my father's apartment. Santiaga should've never taken me there especially if he knew she has a key to show up anytime.* Next I'm praising myself. *You the only one in the world who ever got scolded by her father on the same day she made a million unplanned, unexpected perfectly legal dollars.* I laughed.

"C'mon, *what's so funny?*" she asked again.

"I need . . . the weed," I said talking like a funny fiend.

"No worries. Wherever I go I got da plug," she promised. That's all she needed to say.

Inside of the airport our first-class overnight tickets advanced us to the front of the bag check line. We sat our handbags in the gray tray so they could be scanned. The Pretty bitch's green eyes spotted a pack of Magnums in my handbag. "That's wishful thinking," she said smiling. We laughed. "And I got my Backwoods for—" I said.

She interrupted with a "Shhh, don't worry, I got you."

We hit some of the airport shops to buy what we needed, including a roll-on bag we could both use for our quick trip. Since she booked first-class tickets, which made me like her more, we bypassed going to the gate where all of the passengers on the packed flight would be seated close like sardines and waiting until after the first-class passengers were on board before they could move one muscle or one foot forward. The Northwest Airlines business and first-class lounge was plush, offering complimentary everything, bottled water in glass bottles, fruits and finger foods, as well as liquors, a meal, and desserts.

"I'm gonna grab a water. Want one?" she asked me.

"Nah." I waved it off.

"We skipped dinner. You better grab something," she said delightfully. But my eyes were on the flat screens mounted up high for all to see. I had already gotten flagged by TSA when processing through airport security.

"Miss Winter Santiaga, welcome. It seems a lot of people are worried and looking for you. That's none of our business as long as you are safe."

"Looking for me?" I had replied.

"Check your phone. You're trending." She held up one finger and said, "You're number one."

"I will," I said and walked through the weird machine that X-rays your body in public. I felt all eyes on me. Whatever. But now in the lounge with other first-class passengers, I'm seeing myself on the flat screens.

"Does life imitate art? Or does art imitate life?" the *Eyewitness News* anchor asked with a backdrop of some video some fool shot of me in front of the Network building being carried away by the rude and reckless but handsome dred-driver this afternoon, while the crowd of fans watched and both cheered and jeered and commented.

"This afternoon in Midtown Manhattan, reality television star Winter Santiaga was involved in what some fans reported as a kidnapping. Other fans thought it was just all part of a show, as the highly anticipated and wildly popular season 2 of *Bow Down Starring Winter Santiaga* debuts after this Labor Day. Our reporter is on the scene at the 17th precinct in midtown. Bob . . ."

Then the scene switched to the police precinct. A police captain was interviewed by Bob, the reporter on the scene, but he was not one of the cops that pulled us over. Of course I remember their faces vividly.

"Sir, it was not a kidnapping. It was a show. Our officers were on the scene outside of the Network building and everything was checked out thoroughly," the police captain said. Then the screen switched to a photo of me standing in my fire-engine-red Dior dress with the chief of police.

I felt like dying right there in the airport lounge. What the fuck? The location changed and the chief of police came on and thanked the citizens of New York for uploading and reporting in all of the Winter Santiaga sightings and post-incident videos and photos to social media that brought calm to the city. "Miss Winter Santiaga was and is safe and free." Then B-roll ran, a collage of photos of me in my morning Dolce & Gabbana, including wearing my Amore sunglasses. Also, photos with the other two police officers at the Irish Pub, and in the Gucci hat and Guess denim standing outside of the T-mobile as I waited on Dutchess. Even the dress I have on now, the Jean Paul Gaultier, showed up on the screen as I had arrived at the airport, damn!

"Winter's style is dizzying! Four or more terrific outfits in less than twelve hours!" a lady reporter exclaimed. Then she said, "Back to the chief of police."

The chief of police says, "I'm her fan. She is a strong young lady who embodies the spirit and fight of the best of New York. She came back from the dead and she looks absolutely great! I haven't seen such an amazing comeback since Gloria Estefan blew up Madison Square Garden dancing and singing as though she was not just paralyzed and at the brink of death from a horrific car accident."

That triggered a few suits to approach me, asking for photos and autographs, even though they were supposed to be part of the cool first-class clientele. I scribbled my signature maybe six times and stood side by side for their selfies. When I finished I looked back and Pretty was standing at the back wall smiling. I liked that she didn't have that jealous glare in her eyes that I used to like to see painted on the faces of bitches who I wanted to bow down to me. I love that she didn't ask me for flicks of me and her or try to jump into the photos with me and my fans. Now I'm just glad that there is somebody who could be and might become my friend, who has her own shit, her own money, her own beauty, her own credit cards, and her own elite whip.

"Yeah I'm sorry bout all dat," I said to her.

She laughed and said, "Bitch, I know who you are!"

"Yeah but where these niggas at?" I asked her. "Don't tell me we riding first class and them niggas is in coach!" I bumped her.

She pulled her phone out her purse and said, "They said they on their way half hour ago."

"Whatever," I said. "Bitches over niggas," I repeated her line. "And come to think of it, why bring dick to a dick extravaganza?" We both laughed.

Seated comfortably in the wide chairs in the air-conditioned cabin bout to take off, the plane captain's voice came on and the flight attendants demonstrated what to do to survive turbulence or a crash. But for me there was no volume. I can see their movements like in a silent film. But, I am in my head. A memory flashed through my mind. Me, sitting in the middle of two federal agents handcuffed and ankle cuffed, being transported to my mother's funeral several years ago.

The flight took off. I feel the gravity. Pretty is already knocked out. Guess she really did have a packed schedule and a wild day same as me. As soon as it leveled off, I special ordered two dirty martinis and threw em back. That deaded the dreaded images in my mind, and put me right to sleep.

I woke up to a darkened cabin. Hold up, there is a blanket over my face. I don't know why. I didn't cover myself. I pulled it down, unlocked my seat belt.

"Excuse me," the flight attendant whispered. "I hope you don't mind. I covered you with the blanket because a few of the passengers were standing by your seat watching you and a couple of them took photos. I didn't think you would like that. It's not a first-class experience," she said and handed me a business card. "If you ever need any special services . . . this is my contact info."

I recognize her as a young stunner on the come up. I might have had her same feeling right after my father got knocked and I desperately needed to make a connection with anybody who already had clout and was doing it. Back when I needed to flip my little itty bitty paper into some real cash to secure and protect my status. I understand her. I dropped her card into my handbag.

"Good looking out, thank you," I told her. As soon as she walked by, I stood up to walk the slim aisle to the first-class bathroom to pee. I'm glad it's dark. I'm sick of the attention.

Vacant. I pushed the tiny door in and stepped inside. Somebody stepped in right behind me and closed the door and clicked the lock. Two people can't fit in that small space. But now my ass is smashed against this person and I am so fucking vexed at fucking fans taking this shit way too far. I want to turn around and fucking scream to the top of my lungs and spit on whoever it is, but quickly a voice in my head said, *probably this lunatic has a cell phone camera up ready to capture my reaction in the fucking toilet room.* I neutralized my facial reactions. Then I turned, only my neck and head, and see it is a man, I get furious. I forced my body to face him. Now my breasts are pressed against his chest. We are so closed in that we are basically nose to nose.

"Back the fuck up. Unlock the door," I said, through gritted teeth. "Or I'll—" He covered my mouth with his hand. I grabbed his wrist but could not unlock his grip.

"Don't scream. It's me," he said and eased his face back from mine. It was motherfucking Bullet.

"I just wanted to talk to you one time," he said and dropped his hand from my mouth.

"We ain't got shit to talk about," I said.

"Then don't talk. Just listen. Hear me out."

"Hear you out in the toilet?" I said.

"There was no other way," he said solemnly.

"You damn right. *Fifteen years and now you wanna say something. Come on, nigga.*"

Someone knocked at the door. "Miss Santiaga, are you good in there?" the flight attendant's voice asked me. Bullet was staring into my eyes. I was staring back at him with nothing but heat and hate.

"Yeah I'm good. I'll be right out," I said calmly.

"Okay, just checking," she replied.

"That's why I fucking love you," Bullet said. "And I don't give a fuck who don't believe me. You the realest, most loyal, the baddest, and the best, and most beautiful bitch on the planet, word to mother." Then he smiled. "I don't care about no other bitch except you." Then his face turned serious. "I never did. That's facts. Anything I got, and I mean anything, *you can get it.*"

"Time's up," I told him. "I was locked up so long. I don't let no nigga or no bitch waste my time no more," I said. "Unlock the door," I demanded. He put his hand behind his back and I heard the lock click.

"I won't let no other nigga have you. I put that on my life," he warned. There was another knock at the door and then a push. I put my hands on his waist without saying let's switch places. He caught on, always was swift. We exchanged places and both turned to face the door. I unlocked the door and pulled it, but it couldn't open all the way with him standing pressed behind me and Pretty standing right there at the door. I know she saw him. She didn't say nothing, just looked into my eyes and stepped back. I stepped out in the small space she left open. She led. We walked back to our seats and sat.

"You always got some nigga following you," she said, like it was a real problem.

"I know. I can't even pee in peace." She laughed. I didn't. Bullet came out and "acted natural" as he used to say when he was dodging the feds and handing off packages of that white stuff and moving guns. He was in the first-class section, in the last seat by the curtain that divided the haves from the have-nots. I figured the chick seated next to him was with him. I couldn't really look her over because of the angling and in the dark. However, I'm glad he got someone to pay attention to, to keep his hands and his eyes off of me.

Of course I know the deal with him. On lockup I heard all the stories of him harassing and hounding and extorting major artists out of their paper, their music rights and masters and publishing and jewels, and even bigger shit like their land and their houses. I'm sure he swiped and used and then even discarded some of their bitches in the process. I planned my revenge on him with that in mind. Figured he needs to feel the same shit happening to him, blindsiding him and making him shake with fear, and shrinking his bank account, and humiliating his ass, and then tipping off the media so the whole world will be able to watch his downfall. Soon as I complete setting up my team, he's number one on my payback hit list.

Holding in my pee while seated and buckled, I'm thinking. Maybe Santiaga was right. I'm on the same flight with Bullet. Opposite aisle in the same cabin. I didn't even see him come in. It's a five-hour flight. I was deep asleep in the same room with my enemy. Not until he pulled up on me in the bathroom of all places, and locked the door, did I become aware of his presence. *Poppa is right,* I concluded. I might need to be driven everywhere that I want or need to go, accompanied by two big bodyguards toting four nines. What a fucking life.

12
THE BELLAGIO

We checked into the beautiful Bellagio at 11:30 p.m., Vegas time. They're three hours behind New York. After collecting two keys to our one one-night-only suite, we gave our roll-on bag to the bell-man. Then we dashed to the gift and designer shops, which were all open for late night business and located in the hotel and on the hotel property.

"You shower first," she said soon as we rushed through the door of our suite carrying designer shopping bags stuffed with our picks and pieces and of course more than we could wear in one late night early morning. I was already stripping on the way into the bath-room. I needed the weight of the warm downpour to wash off the invisible sludge that gets in the skin pores of all New Yorkers and big city urban dwellers who ride the buses, trains, or even walk our streets. Not to mention the germs that intermingle in the stagnant air on a packed flight. Once the warm shower cleansed and soothed me, I shocked myself with the cold downpour that wakes and alerts and alarms me, so I can fully enjoy the adventure of the night.

We hit the casino floor by 1:15 a.m., right when shit is bubbling.

"Ah it's gon be lit!" She was excited. "What about that weed . . . ?" I said in my make-believe fiend voice.

"It's already set. Took care of it while you were showering."

"That's what I'm talking about."

Hundreds of hands holding cards and drinks and placing bets. Before we arrived, all eyes were on the dealers, the chips, the spreads, and how much was being spent, lost, or won. But the blast of aroma that arrived when we arrived, and moved with us when we moved, caused a dramatic effect.

She is Fendi, all heat. I am Giambattista Valli, all fire. Our titties jiggling and bouncing, and our thighs shining, all eyes are on us. A split second was all that was needed to register a huge reaction. Drinks and bottles are being ordered and carried on silver trays and are headed in our direction. We ignore the Dom Pérignon and reject the Cristal on purpose. Each sway of our hips upping the ante. "Let's case it out," I said. "Then I'll decide which game I wanna play."

"Not in the Bellagio," she said, breaking a li'l bit of her calmcool. "You're going to lose all your money including these outfits we charged to the room," she warned me. "We will be walking back to our suite butt naked." I just stopped, turned, and looked at her and then we busted out laughing.

"Then why did you choose this place?" I asked her.

"Cause women like us gotta be in a setting where the dudes are all at least as competent as we are. Business is about getting the right connections and building relationships. Any man seated at any one of these high roller tables," she pointed with her eyes, "is a six- or seven-figga nigga dropping twenty to one hundred K in minutes. That's perfect potential clientele." She looked at me like, *Bitch, do you get it?* "We don't need to spend a dime. See right there? They're looking more than interested."

"Those two suited white dudes?" I said after I saw them staring.

"No, the two black dudes. But I don't discriminate. Anybody's money and status, as long as it's verifiable, is good with me. We just go stand by the money and when they smell our scent, and check out our look, it's game over," she said.

"You talk a lot of shit," I said playfully but now really I meant it. "What happened to the two dudes you said we partied with Friday night?"

"You happened to them," she said swiftly.

"What do you mean?" I asked, one hand clutching my handbag and the other riding my waist.

"Check this out," she said pulling up her cell phone, swiping, and then pushing it close to my face while she held on to it instead of letting go. I'm not mad. I get it. *People's phones are personal.* I looked at her bright screen. It was a text. "Tell your friend, she's gorgeous but she got too much heat. We don't mind spending, but we ain't ready to kill or ready to die for her."

"Something must've happened. Maybe one of them people following you threatened them," she said as she pulled back her phone and dropped it back into her handbag.

"Maybe they just some pussy-ass niggas who bout to be replaced," I said. Then a waitress walked up and announced, "The gentlemen at the ten-thousand-dollar-minimum blackjack table sent you a gold bottle of Ace." The waitress had a look in her eyes like, *What are you stupid? Jump on it.*

"See," Pretty said, elbow-bumping me.

"Is this a business trip for you?" I asked her.

"Every trip and every day is business for me. Even if I am really out to have fun, at least twenty-five percent out of one hundred percent of every fun day *has to be business.* Either an investment opportunity I discover, or I'm making money, deals, or earning free points and perks I'm getting for just being me," she said lightly and playful, but I knew she meant it. In fact, she sounded like me. I like her way of thinking. But still . . .

"We can buy our own bottles," I told the waitress with attitude after I saw her tapping her foot like she was rushing us.

"We'll take it," Green Eyes overrode my talk. As we walked over towards "the gentlemen," at her lead, she turned and told me, "There's a way to do Vegas instead of letting Vegas do you. First, you check into the five-star hotel, like we did. Mingle with the big money. Score some connects. Take everything of value that comes your way, like we about to do. Then, if you insist on playing the slots, we go off the strip to the Horseshoe or the Golden Nugget or some other cheap casino hotel. Right before dawn, you hit the slot machines. Suckers been playing and losing their wealth on em all night long. Round five a.m., before the machines reset, it's ching-ching. We hit and win all the money the losers who couldn't figure it out lost on those same machines all day and most of the night." She laughed, just as we arrived to the two men who sent the bottle. She was right. Their mood was lifted instantly with one breeze of our aroma. I think her smile melted their hearts. She thanked them with her eyes and body gestures before using her lips. The waitress popped the bottle and the Ace was flowing. Green Eyes eased into a seat right next to one of them. And, I bet she was more surprised than both of them, when I began walking right past their table. I'm really back in my head. *Have it your way Winter*, I told myself. *Don't let no one manipulate or monopolize your time anymore, even if they are acquaintances, friends, or family. I told Pretty I didn't come to watch. I came to play.*

Ever since I was seven years young, me and my girls (the same bitches who recently betrayed me), all of us who grew up together in the same Brooklyn projects, learned and played every card game in existence. From the easiest games like old maid, finding matching pairs, also a card game called war, and another named pitty-pat, all the way up to the most difficult like solitaire. By twelve years young, we would have all-girl spades cut parties, do dominoes and dice all the way up to strip poker with young dudes, who no matter how young they were, were still older than us. We'd throw a few dollars on a bet or a dare, or a wish. Whoever banked up would re-up for the weed and snacks. The memory brought Santiaga back to mind. Of course I did all of those things out of his eyesight, at whoever's house had working and away, or cracked out and roaming mothers with no fathers at all to stand watch. Still, Santiaga would come crashing my party, at least the ones that were in our same hood. So we found uptown niggas and partied at their projects instead. Maybe that's why right now I am walking past the blackjack tables and headed to the roulette instead. It was the only game we never played. Matter of fact the closest to it was spin the motherfucking bottle!

I glanced around and chose a dealer based on nothing but a feeling. Found one, whose eyes locked into mine during my search. The roulette table looked different than I had imagined it. I was thinking more like the spinning wheel on the old game show *Wheel of Fortune*. Then I reminded myself that this is my first time at a casino, my first time completely on my own, out of state, outside of the Immanuel mansion, no sister or father, stylist, public relations rep, no bodyguard or driver, no freaking cell phones or cameras aimed at specifically me. *Feel good feel good feel good bitch*, I recited in my own mind.

The table had numbers zero through thirty-six. I wondered why that particular number, thirty-six? And the colors to bet on were red and black. My eyes slowly moved over the chips. I wondered how much each chip was worth. It took me a minute of observing the play to figure out that the chips were not necessarily based only on monetary value. At the roulette table the chips are about colors, as I saw each active player has a different color or uniquely patterned stack of chips. With a blasé "money ain't a thing" attitude, I pushed my pretty fingers into my clutch and pulled out a stack that should impress the pros at the table. Or at least make them view me as an equal. I pushed it forward excited to see how many chips it would buy me. The dealer pushed me back a short stack, very short compared to what the other players had. Still, I smiled. At least he had given me all pink chips which matched my fine fabric . . . silk georgette micro-mini translucent pink dress. Without hesitation I picked a color on the board, of course it was black. Then I thought up a number, fifteen because that's how many mandatory years I spent locked up. Swiftly I placed my pink chip stack on 15 black. I don't want anyone to see me thinking and hesitating, then realize I have no idea how to play this game. The little ball went skipping and spinning and landed on the 15 black. Shocked, I lost my cool and raised both my hands to cover my mouth and jumped up once, landing on my hot-to-death heels. I couldn't believe that me, "the roulette virgin," won on my first pop. No one at the table could believe it either. They had all seen me just walk up and squeeze myself into their game.

"Place your bets," the dealer announced. I was like, *wait a minute!* The other players placed their bets like they were unfazed gambling experts. A uniformed man pulled up beside me. "We welcome you to continue your play. We set a tab for you against your win. If not, I will escort you to the cage."

"Cage," I semi-shouted. I do not want to go to a cage or a cell or a pod or any form of confinement.

"Step over here." He waved me over two steps. "You have won two hundred and forty-five thousand dollars. You placed seven thousand dollars on fifteen black and the payout is thirty-five to one. At the cash cage we will give you your total winning and offer to escort you back to your suite, or vehicle, or simply place the amount on your tab and keep it in play."

"Let's go to the cage!" I said, excited at this new shit. I'm going crazy that I won while also thinking how life is a little fucked up. When I was teen young and needed the money the most, like seriously-seriously, I couldn't get it, or I couldn't get enough of it, or I couldn't keep what I did get in my hands. Now that I have more than one million in my bank account, plus assets, I hit the number on my first play, like one, two, three in less than fifteen seconds I earned more paper than the twenty-eight thousand dollars I had spent on Dutchess yesterday, more than the haute couture fashion money that I spent in the designer shops at the hotel, and more than I spent on my half of this Bellagio hotel bill and the first-class round-trip flight to get here. All less than twenty-four hours after the extraordinary one-million-dollar bag from Kuntz that I negotiated and earned on my own. All of this is happening on the same weekend and it ain't even over yet.

"What made you quit roulette after your first win?" Pretty asked me, as we drained the last of the complimentary Champagne bottle we popped to celebrate my win. We are both up at the suite sitting in the middle of the huge king-sized bed with the crisp money stacks right beside me. I leaped up and stood on the side of the bed as she tossed me each stack playfully. I didn't drop one. Instead, once I had them all in my embrace, I walked over, opened the hotel safe, and pushed the two hundred and forty-five thousand inside. As I arranged the stacks, I answered her question.

"When security showed up at the roulette table and offered me to place a second bet and try my luck again, to me he looked like one of the salespeople working on commission in the department store, who tells you you look great even though you look fucked up in something that only looks good on the hanger or on their man- nequin." Then I made a face. Pretty laughed and so did I. We are both buzzed so it don't matter if I make sense.

"Every girl been in that shopping situation for sure," she added. "Besides you did the smart thing. Your winning could have been *only beginner's luck* and after that you could've lost everything you won and all the cash already in your handbag," she said. I didn't care what she was saying right now. I don't care about the reason I won, or the reason I walked away after only one play, one win. Just the fact that I won is good enough.

"It's almost 2 a.m., you want to just stay here in the room?" she asked like I was some old tired chick.

"Hell no!" I said as I took the fifteen thousand that I had left over from the fifty grand I had dropped into my bag early yester- day morning, right before the Kuntz meetup, out and added to the winnings into the suite safe. Two hundred sixty-thousand dollars, *nice*, I thought to myself. But if I had forty more stacks making it three hundred thousand total, that would've been even nicer. Either way, more than a quarter of a million in less than sixty seconds, awesome. Now I have purposely left only two grand in cash in my handbag for the quarter slots. That's eight thousand quarters! Do the slot machines still cost a quarter like they did when I used to see

a busload of Brooklyn grandmas getting in the bus to Atlantic City
with bags of quarters in their hands or handbags or fanny packs? I
bursted out laughing.

"You keep a lot of shit to yourself," Green Eyes said. "If it's only
a joke, you should share it so I can crack up, too," she requested. I
turned and looked at her. She was naked and easing into her RPRS
Jeans that we purchased earlier on.

"Bitch, you should put on some panties before that blue denim
dye rubs off and gets all in your pussy!" I snapped back. That was it.
We were both cracking up. She collapsed on the bed with the jeans
riding only her calves. I walked away from the safe and pulled a pair
of satin panties out of my Victoria's Secret shopping bag. I tossed
them to her. "I didn't use to wear panties ever," I confessed. "Then
once my pussy hairs got stuck in my zipper. That shit hurt. Now I
wear panties sometimes when the fashion situation calls for it."

"Your pussy not waxed?" she asked like she was shocked at my
little painful hairy story.

"Evidently it wasn't waxed at the time that that happened,"
I swift replied.

"I keep mine waxed and glossy," she said smiling.

"Well that's one of the facts you should keep to yo'self. Between
you and your nigga," I told her as she eased out of the jeans and slid
into the panties and eased back into her jeans again.

My attention switched to the four numbers I needed to select
to lock the safe. I put in fifteen-fifteen, figured that was easy enough
for a bitch who did fifteen, and bet and won on fifteen, to remember
no matter how much liquor she threw back or weed she smoked.
"I'mma change into my jeans also. Then we head to the other side
of town. I want to hit the slots and get all the money the suckers left
behind," I said all confident and cheerful. She was fully in her jeans

now but topless, her 32 Cs almost as nice as my 32 Ds. She agreed but had a trace of a sour look.

"Don't worry. I know we said fifty-fifty on this trip. But Vegas was my idea and I got you. I'll pay the whole bill, one hundred percent, *with my beginner's luck.*" She overlooked the jab and got excited all over again. I don't know why. She seemed like a rich enough bitch. But then again Lana Santiaga would say, "There's no such thing as enough or too much." And when Poppa would say less is more, Lana, in her sexy playful way, would say, "No, more is more!"

In the Bellagio courtesy limo, which actually is a mean-ass Volvo, me and Pretty are dressed down and chilling in our jeans, with sexy strapless haute couture bras made of ribbons; one long ribbon dangling right over our bare navels, bellies, and lower backs. Our feet are in comfy Air Maxes since we are headed to the *we might have to run* side of town. When we first walked by the valet stand to exit the main door and hail a cab, a young twenty-something-year-old white guy stepped up wearing a basic black suit, white dress shirt, slim black tie, and hard black cheap shoes. For some reason he removed his black captain hat and held it over his chest like he was doing some type of salute. He introduced himself as Jeff, and had declared himself as our Bellagio complimentary designated driver.

"Where exactly are you ladies headed?" he asked. His blue eyes beamed on us through his rearview mirror. "I know the whole town. No need for navigation," he boasted.

"The Horseshoe Casino," Pretty replied.

"The Horseshoe," he repeated. "If that's what you want . . . ," he said as though he felt sorry for us, "I'll drive you girls there, although we don't recommend *that area* of town for our five-star VIP Bellagio customers. Of course it's just fine for everybody else."

"Just pull up to the Horseshoe Casino entrance and we will take it from there," I said calmly.

"Sure," he said and pulled out, while still watching us through his rearview mirror. He said hesitantly, "I figured beautiful five-star young ladies would be headed to the M Hotel. Tonight they had 50 Cent, Eminem, and it's rumored that there's also a special guest appearance."

Me and Pretty just looked at each other. She checked her rolly. "It's probably over now," she said.

Then the white boy said, "After the show it's the after party. After the party it's the hotel lobby . . . ," singing R. Kelly's joint. Then threw in a head wiggle to let us know he had his dance moves. We laughed.

"Well take us to the after party spot," I said without hesitation.

Pretty leaned into my ear and whispered, "Good choice. That's where the real money is moving. It may not be instant like the slots, but get the right hookup, a chick could be set up for life."

"How you know 50 and G-Unit gon be at the after party?" I asked her softly.

"We bout to find out," she whispered back girly-giggly.

"Wish I could come with you. The cost of the show tickets, man, my whole paycheck. I didn't care though. I'da paid whatever. Just couldn't get any of the other drivers to shift shifts with me. Almost lost my job over it. I'm a huge 50 fan. And, what if the secret special guest is Dr. Dre!!! He ain't been doing no shows lately. I'll kill myself if he showed up and performed tonight and I missed it."

"You seem like a cool dude. Don't ever kill yourself for any reason. Suicide is for suckers," I said, surprising myself. I am definitely not the type to hand out advice to anyone. However after my death experience . . . there's just certain things I know for sure.

"Look at that crowd," he said and tried to find a place to pull over.

"We can just hop out," she told him, "and mingle." We both went for our door handles at the same time, but they were both locked.

"No, I want to make sure you ladies are secure," he said strangely.

"We're secure, just unlock our doors," I said. Now I am having flashbacks from the fake kidnapping just yesterday and thinking, *Not this bullshit again. I should have just went straight to playing the slot machines.* He parked. Our locks popped. He beat both of us out of the car and went to his trunk as we eased out. "Your're going to need a ride back," he said as he swiftly peeled off his suit jacket, loosened and removed his tie, unbuttoned his shirt like he was old school Superman in the phone booth. "I might as well stay. The traffic is only gonna get crazier," he said and by now I peep that he's trying to use us as his reason to attend the after party while he is still considered on the clock at his job. Pretty slick, I thought to myself. I ain't mad at him. Besides he has some nice abs beneath that cheap suit, which made him nicer to look at. Still . . . I said . . . "Thanks for the ride," then walked over and handed him a hundred-dollar bill. "We will make our way back safely," I assured him. Pretty and me speed walked off towards the crazy crowd in front of the club.

"They should've had the after party at a bigger club. They knew Vegas would show up," one of the chicks in front of us, who had her hair done up like a rooster for some crazy reason, said.

"True but it's all these freaking foreigners fucking everything up. I bet they didn't even go to the show. That's how they got to the after party spot before us," another obviously local girl complained. They turned, and looked at me and Pretty standing close behind them. I gave them a look like, *What! We ALL in the back of a crowd of hundreds of people!* They didn't say nothing when they looked, but their unspoken conversation was written on their foreheads.

"We ain't no freaking foreigners, we're Americans," I said aloud.

"We talking bout anybody who ain't from here, Vegas!" she replied, and threw her hand on her hip. Her fluorescent green five-inch fingernails looked like weapons to me. I thought we gon have to beat these bitches with our designer handbags or with one of our kicks.

"Oh! I love you!" her friend blurted out. Her eyes locked in on me. "I know who you are! What are you doing back here with us! You should have gone straight to the VIP!" she shouted way louder than necessary. I am standing right here in her face.

"You remember her!" she said to her pissy girlfriend. She threw her green claws up over her mouth. Her hate melted. "Oh, sorry. You that bitch who got shot dead and woke back the fuck up. Oh my God, I respect that. Let me give you some dap." Her loud voice was growing louder. "Yup most niggas just stay dead," a new face and a new voice chimed in. "Vegas! Listen up! Winter Santiaga is in the house. Bitch so live, she playing the back with us Vegas locals when she could be inside with the motherfucking celebrities who locked all of us out," she yelled.

Some of them laughed. Some pointed. Some gasped. Some stared. I noticed one-by-one people turning around. Now they are no longer facing the club. They are facing me. A gang of cell phones went up. Pretty pulled me. I like that she knows that I don't like what's going on, without me having to complain, scream, show, or tell her. I don't know where she's headed. I figured neither does she. Long as I get away and out of the spotlight and about a hundred cell phone cameras filming me from every angle. Suddenly she curved to the left away from the crowd scene and down a block closed off by those orange-and-white "do not enter" cones. And all of the parking meters had been bagged and stickered with "no parking" signs. Now there's way more space, no street lamps, and no party crowd. However, once I looked back, I realized that we really didn't shake em. About sixty females were closing in behind us. Pretty sparked an L, hit it, and passed it to me. When the crowd of girls reached, I stopped smoking and handed it over to the first chick standing in front of me, the girl with the claws who caused this whole commotion. Passing her the weed influenced her. She took a pull and passed it to her friend. Now other chicks in the crowd, instead of stomping and stampeding, started stopping and pulling out their weed and lighting up, making our own party.

"Sign my shirt."

"Sign my jeans."

"Autograph my shoe." One of them threw her leg up and had the bottom of her heel facing me. *Everything in life is fashion,* I thought to myself and caught an amazing business idea.

"I don't know about y'all Vegas chicks. But I am a Brooklyn bitch and I came to party. I don't got no Sharpie or pens or papers. I got my MAC lipstick, my weed, and my condoms." I held them up and all them bitches started laughing and then going through their cheap handbags and holding up their condoms and lipsticks. I'm thinking to myself, *What a crazy fucking night. What a crazy crowd. How did I turn out to be the show after the show?* Then I remembered. *Nobody is paying me for this performance.* That shifted my mood.

Whoop! Whoop! The sound of the police siren straightened all of our backs. I took a final pull of my weed that had just came back to me. I dropped the bud and smashed it with my sneaker. Immediately after I moved my foot, someone bent over and picked up my leftover bud. The cops were down the block behind their cones.

Gave all us girls the seconds we needed to disperse. As I looked to my left, Pretty wasn't there. I looked around. I don't see her. The cop car was just parked, the lights spinning. Guess they just wanted to scare us, break up the crowd. Or maybe they were just waiting for backup and would storm us all and throw us in the paddy wagon.

I'm a loyal bitch so I'm looking for Pretty. I'm weaving in between the outside party crowd that was still standing around doing everything even though it had been long enough and made clear enough that they were not getting into this club tonight. As I'm searching for her, I feel a mounting crowd of girls just following me for no damn reason. I don't turn back on purpose. But I can feel and hear them all.

"Got you." A guy grabbed me. I turned towards him. He was black-hoodied up. String pulled so tight he was nothing but a pair of eyes, like a spook in a cartoon or a murderer in a horror flick.

"Let her go." A guy snatched me back like I am a rubber band. I turned my face away from the hooded one and saw a next nigga who was clutching my wrist. Before, I was surrounded by a gang of girls. Now I am surrounded by dudes. Both of the ones holding me dropped hands. Gunshots!!! Everyone starts running, some stumbling, some getting crushed and walked on and over. Everyone's moving, except me. I am froze outside of the club trembling. My hands shaking as I touched all over my whole body starting with my scalp, checking for blood or bullet holes. I'm hoping that I am not broken and bleeding and dead. Knowing for certain that I was already given a MERCY, and that I would not receive another free pass from death.

"Are you her guardian?" I overheard.

"No, but you can put my name down though. Jeff Tucker, a

driver who drove her to an event. There was a stampede. She suddenly fainted," I heard him say.

"Who will be responsible for registering her and payment?"

"She's a VIP customer from the Bellagio. She can pay for herself if you would just help her and make sure she's okay." I am being wheeled on the gurney. *Oh no, a hospital,* I thought to myself. I'm a hundred percent sure based on the hospital smell. A curtain closed. Seconds later the curtain opened. They lifted my eyelids, beamed them with a pin light. Something was wrapped tightly around my arm.

"Low blood pressure. Bring the saline drip." A clip was placed onto one of my fingers. Something was inserted into my nostrils and the inside of my right arm, then squeezed.

My eyes opened. "Do you know your name?" I was asked.

"Of course, bitch," I said instinctively then realized I shouldn't have.

"Excuse me?" she asked.

"What happened to me?" I asked.

"I'm asking the questions," she said. I knew it was a doctor. They get easily insulted if you don't bow down and kiss their ass. I felt around for my handbag. My body jerked once my fingers couldn't find it. Plus I hurt myself reaching too far based on the way they had the needle and tubes connected to me. I sat up. Then I saw my handbag on the table next to me.

"Please lay down. I will adjust your bed setting now," a nurse said. She raised the top half of the bed so that I am in the sitting position after she said lay down! "The police want to ask you a few questions." My eyes widened. The hospital room door opened. The doctor and nurse exited together. A deteck walked in. "Miss Santiaga, before your flight back to New York we have to ask you a few questions." Hmm he already knows my name and where I'm from. I already knew I wouldn't tell them nothing. I temporarily convinced myself, *I don't know anything anyway.*

"Why are you in the hospital?"

"I fainted they said. Low blood pressure," I added.

"Do you recall what happened before you fainted?"

"Yes, I was standing outside of a club trying to get into a party but the crowd was too big," I answered.

"And then what happened?"

"I heard gunshots."

"Did you have any weapons on you?"

"No. I'm not from here. I don't own or carry any guns anyway. Besides, a person can't fly from New York with any weapons can they?" I asked even-toned and blank-faced.

"Did you see anyone carrying or discharging a gun?"

"No."

"Why did you run?" he asked me with an accusation in his expression. I said swiftly, catching the word tricks the cops play all of the time, "I did not run."

"Why didn't you run?"

"Because I was an innocent victim of a horrible shooting earlier this year, outdoors and I was hit by a random bullet. Tonight when I heard shots being fired, my legs locked. I couldn't move. I fainted."

"Thank you for your statement and cooperation, Ms. Santiaga."

They left without me saying what I saw. I exhaled. The door opened again. *What now?*

13

THE MULTIMILLIONAIRES

"Good morning, Ms. Santiaga," a tired-looking woman with bags piled up beneath each eye said. She rushed in like she had gotten dressed in a hurry. "I'm Mary Scudder from the mayor's office."

"What mayor?"

"We were contacted by Mr. Elisha Immanuel," she said. Now she had my complete attention. "He landed here in the state of Nevada. It's my duty to have you discharged and escorted to him directly," she said, and her manner was like she was a servant and I am the VIP. Still . . . I gave her a look like I don't trust her. She doesn't know that that's my standard expression to any stranger who I am not making money with. She pulled up her cell phone, swiped then tapped her screen a few times, and pushed it forward to my face. On the screen is Elisha. "Winter, I sent a car and a driver for you. Ms. Scudder from the mayor's office will escort you directly to me."

Now I accept her. Love the way Elisha keeps it brief and gives orders without them sounding like orders. If a person wanted to disobey him, he leaves room for you to do that. However, because he is who he is, nobody would dare. I also love that he knew that I would not go anywhere with this lady unless I spoke to him or my father, or saw him, like I just did in the video.

I don't mind riding in the rear of a mean-ass black Maybach. I love the way even if it's an emergency or an incident, Elisha moves me around in the style I require. It's not a car. It's more like a cloud, the ride is so smooth, quiet, and comfy. As the majestic whip moved through the early morning darkness, it reached an airport. Not the same one I arrived at for sure. I'm thinking hold up, I'm not flying out without my things from the Bellagio. I have two hundred sixty thousand stacked in the locked safe in my suite. Also my overnight fashions, my stilettos, and the Pretty Bitch's things are there, too. Matter of fact what happened to her? Maybe she's at the hotel right now. Even if she is, she doesn't have the combination. But, she made the booking for the suite. So I'm sure she can work it out. What if she does work it out and robs me? I imagined. Nah she's a cool bitch. She got her own stacks and business. She won't rob me. But fuck, I don't know shit about her, couldn't track her down even if she did.

"Turn back," I spoke up to the driver. "I need to be driven to the Bellagio so I can collect my belongings before flying out." He did not reply. Neither did the woman from the mayor's office. *Fuck it*, I thought. I'll just tell Elisha. This driver works for him. He's probably not authorized to do anything different than what Elisha ordered. Elisha doesn't know about my cash in the hotel safe. If I had my cell phone I could just call the hotel, Fuck! *My phone*, I thought to myself. By now Poppa must seriously regret ever taking it from me. Bet he won't ever do that shit again.

The Bach pulled up three feet away from a black jet. It was not a 747, like the one I flew in on. And I feel like I'm already on the runway. But there is no lineup and no passengers from what I could see. Wait a minute. The jet is black and orange. The Immanuel Group logo is an enlarged black letter I shaped like a carrot and a lowercase g. Yes, the orange I see is a huge carrot. The air flew out of my mouth, the opposite of a gasp. This nigga owns a private jet! I'm so freaking amazed. The driver stopped the Bach, jumped out, and opened the rear door for me, like I'm a boss. I only felt a brief blast of the hot Nevada summer wind. Went from air-conditioned Maybach, to thirty seconds of desert wind, to climbing the stairs of a parked menacing metal beautiful black bird. I could feel my heart pounding.

A flight attendant greeted me. I guess that's who she is. I can't imagine Porsche allowing some badass chick to fly around in the sky with her precious husband. She helped me inside and directed me to one of the eight royal seats, with her silver-gray bomb-ass eyes. "Would you like some water, or orange, carrot, cucumber, or beet juice?" she asked. I just started cracking up out of nowhere. A sexy, curvaceous jet with a carrot on it, and a long, thick-haired, single-braided, silver-gray-eyed flight attendant offering me a vegetable juice instead of a Bloody Mary or a beer and an aspirin . . . anything that takes the edge off of one crazy night. She walked away unfazed and returned with a glass bottle of Voss Still water and a glass. She sat the glass on the table, twisted the bottle top, and poured the water.

"I recommend, we start with water."

"Are you a doctor?" I asked a li'l sarcastically.

"Yes," she replied, "I am." I was blown away.

"When Elisha shared that you were in the hospital, I changed my hat, so to speak," she said oddly. I like her. She has a good feeling to her and a stellar look. I don't like how she says Elisha's name though. Felt like with some affection in it. Now I know top niggas got bitches everywhere. Especially when they fly out of state and out of country on these so-called business trips. But Lana would say, there can only be one queen. Top niggas knew if they had extra bitches on the side, they better hide them on an island, send them to a faraway state or country. If the queen gets a call, or a glimpse, or a note, or a beep or now a text, or an email, that's a failure that could cause the fall of her king, and the crash of his empire. To me that meant, if there are some random bitches that Elisha smashes around the country or the world even, they could not receive his heart, his loyalty, his paper, or even his time, in more than extremely tiny amounts. More importantly, they had better not be top-tier women. They should *never be* the same caliber of woman who could evenly replace the queen, or worse, outdo his queen.

"Elisha forwarded to my phone your discharge record from your brief stay in the hospital today. I'm concerned about your diet, your hydration, and your sleeping patterns. With your permission I can assist you with that, just based on our relationship," she said softly, no bitch or slick mixed in it.

Still, I said, "Relationship!"

"Yes the Immanuel family and my family are very close friends. We love Porsche, and I am just meeting you, her lovely sister. Please drink," she asked holding up the glass of water.

As I accepted the glass from her hand and I raised the glass to my lips, I saw, through the window across from me, Elisha exiting from a black Suburban. He is wearing saddle-leather Ralph Lauren boots, that Brooklyn calls just "Lo boots with the buckle," dark green cargo pants, and a man-tailored shirt made from the same fabric as the pants. Looked rough and rich and cool to me. Definitely different than his business suits and golf wear. He is being followed by a handsome, younger cat, light-skinned, ice grill, pretty silky hair in a Caesar cut, carrying a green duffel bag. When they entered the jet, I could now see that the younger one's eyes sparkled like alternating light and dark brown, same as Porsche's, like a kaleidoscope. He lets off a very masculine feeling. He's wearing a Ralph Lauren thick denim nicely tailored shirt, and jeans, with Beef and Broccoli Tims on his feet. Yup, a next New York nigga, I thought to myself. Fashion wise, West Coast and Midwest and desert niggas will break down and wear sandals in the heat. However, New York, all five boroughs, stay in fashion no matter the weather, no man sandals, or mandals as some call em, when they cracking jokes on the non–New York wears. He brushed past me without his eyes moving even slightly in my direction, without saying one word, and sat in the back seat casually like he's used to walking into a room with a multimillionaire, boarding a multimillion-dollar private jet, and used to seeing top-tier women, like the doctor with the silver-gray eyes and, of course, like me. I didn't turn around to watch him. My eyes are now towards Elisha. I'm asking myself *what's next?* I'm bracing myself for it.

"Wheels up in thirty minutes," the doctor said. *Wheels up, is that the same as takeoff?* I wondered. I also noticed she now has on a green bucket Gucci hat and, beneath it, a Hermès pleated scarf, which she definitely was not wearing when I arrived.

"Where are the other three in your crew?" Elisha asked her. She pointed her head upwards and highlighted that they were walking right outside of the jet bout to climb the steps. Elisha, her, and me are now glancing through the jet window. Word to mother it looks like we are about to do a *Vogue* shoot. It's not every day that so many uniquely beautiful people are all in one space. Yet I see three more stunners coming, two maybe eighteen-years-young, exotically attractive females and one incredibly carved, deep black, serious-faced, young twenties man, who could make a bitch like me say, *I'll do whatever you want.* Instantly I became conscious of my own appearance, whereas I was all chilled out in my late night dressed-down jeans and ribbon bra and somehow Jeff the Bellagio chauffeur had delivered me to the hospital in his black suit jacket which I still have.

"Elisha! I need a change of clothes," I blurted out. He smiled and pointed. "Porsche packed your garment bag. It's hanging in the washroom." I jumped up and speed walked to the rear, pushed in and the varnished black bathroom door opened. I rushed in. Hmm . . . polished black wood and silver fixtures and three times the size of the tiny toilet space even in first class on the commercial airlines.

Porsche packed me a perfect pick of items for what she knows is my constantly caught-on-camera unpredictable predicament. The dress is Pucci. When I first heard of the Pucci clothing line, I thought it was a bullshit company try'na bootleg Gucci. I laughed to myself. A little research and I found that Emilio Pucci was the actual name of the designer who originated the brand. Since it was his real name, he jumped out of the bootleg bin in my head, and back into an old and classic quality Italian designer who either makes or recruits authentic colorful creations. At the bottom of the garment bag was a pouch with washcloths, all the soaps, pastes, creams, and butters, brushes, and combs I am accustomed to, that only she would know. I appreciate her for that. Then I felt temporarily tight at the thought that she was in my apartment, picking through my things while I was out. I wondered if she only went for packing me a garment bag or if she climbed the short stack of stairs to my loft space where I have my design table, tech and art supplies for the fashion company I'm about to launch. I don't want anybody seeing any of my original works (many of which I drew up in prison) until

I am set up and ready to reveal them. That is, unless they are professionally necessary and involved in the process, like my shoemaker. Speaking of shoes, I peeped that she only sent me my Hermès slides cause she knew that would make me have to come back home to choose the shoes that I really need for all-day wear. Oh, it's Sunday, so yeah . . . she would try to get me, at minimal, seated at their family Sunday brunch-dinner. While washing my face and shoulders, arms and hands, I'm calculating the five-hour flight and the arrival time. It works out that we should land around 3 p.m. in New York. While washing my pussy, switching cloths, and then washing my ass, then gliding down my hips, thighs, and my calves with my raw soapy fingers, I'm thinking of Dutchess and the rest of my new team and all of the work I have to introduce and assign based on my bitches' strong points, talents, and know-how.

I emerged after folding last night's wears and leaving them in the garment bag and of course tidying up because a bitch needs to be tidy about certain things even if she got servants. I feel more like myself and on the right level to be comfortable around these handsome niggas and, more importantly, exotic bitches that Porsche allowed her husband to fly around the sky with. The sky, a place where there would be no proof of human foul play unless you were there, or unless you were me, Winter Santiaga, being blindsided, stalked, and filmed by people who had zero permission to follow or film me, all day every day. The black-skinned dark dude isn't in here no more. Neither is the silver-eyed doc. Now taking up the seat in the rear is only the light-skinned ice-grill nigga. The two exotic young chicks are seated in front of him and Elisha is seated way up front, first chair.

"Seat belt please," a young lady who had been seated in a tiny flipdown chair said as I returned to my seat where Elisha is now seated opposite of me. She remained standing. Oh, so she must be the flight attendant, I thought to myself. I looked around. She's an employee obviously. As she began the standard safety routine, I zoned out from her lovely face and huge alluring eyes. Even my wondering about if her French bun was her real hair or not . . . faded.

"Elisha! I forgot to say that I left my clothes and things at the Bellagio and I need to get them before anyone else does."

"And you forgot to say good morning to me, or to introduce yourself to everyone here," he said calmly without it sounding like a scold, but it is. I know I'm a rude bitch. Besides, they all should have introduced themselves to me. They know who I am. But instead of my true thoughts, I just skipped over the criticism and said, "Good morning, Elisha," then smiled slightly. I looked at his reaction and read it as my simple greeting worked. He pulled out his cell phone and focused on his screen, a few swipes and taps and he's on the line . . . "Please connect me with hotel security . . . ," he said then waited. "I am Elisha Immanuel. One of my top artists stayed at your hotel last night, in suite . . ." He looked at me.

"2606," I whispered. I don't know what the fuck I was whispering for.

"2606," he said to whomever was on the line.

When his call was completed, he looked up at me. "Did you tell them your name was Bijoux Yorke?" he asked me. I started to answer back no. But then my thought raced and switched. "Yes," I lied to him. I don't know why I lied. While we were traveling, I had heard someone at the airport refer to Pretty as Ms. Yorke. I thought I had finally found out at least her last name. Now it turns out that she is *not* Ms. Yorke, who is actually Bijoux, her handmaiden. How come Pretty Bitch didn't use her real name?

"Well, if you gave me the correct suite number . . . ," he said with doubt.

"I did. I'm sure of it."

"The head of hotel security said that suite 2606 checked out at 6 a.m., which was an hour ago, and front desk management confirmed that the bill was satisfied in cash. We both know that couldn't have been you. You were here at 6 a.m. and before that you were in the hospital." He just looked at me without judgment but like he was waiting for my explanation.

"Well maybe if they could take a look if any of my belongings were left behind . . . ," I said. "And to check the safe . . . ," I added softly, from feeling like a fool for fainting and leaving the loot in any hands or bags besides mine.

"Security already offered and said he would check the suite and text me if they found anything and if so will forward your belongings to any address I give him."

"Cool, thank you so much, Elisha," I said and put on a polite smile that was not genuine. I was still thinking about my two hundred sixty thousand dollars. Would the security text Elisha back and say the safe is still locked? Would he surrender my cash, designer wear, and everything that was inside? Would he skim or outright steal my cash and things and simply lie and say they weren't in the safe or the room? Did the Pretty bitch get her hands on it?

"Winter, are you happy?" Elisha asked, snatching me back from my worries.

"Happy . . . ," I repeated as the jet began moving down the runway.

"Okay . . . ," he said in a cool way. "Let me rephrase that. Winter, how are you feeling in this moment and how are you feeling in general about your life?"

"I . . . ," I began answering.

"Don't say anything too swiftly," he said. "It's a five-hour flight, a little less because this jet is the fastest one out here. Take your time and give me your honesty," he said and my empty stomach churned. The flight pulled up. Each notch up I could feel. And because of the way Elisha spoke and positioned his words, my cold heart melted some. Still . . . despite taking five whole minutes of silence, other than the sound of the overhead air blowing in and the purr of the Rolls-Royce engines, all I answered was "I'm okay, Elisha." He leaned as forward as one can lean while seat-belted.

"Is there something that you want that you don't have?" he asked me and his eyes somehow appeared as though he genuinely wanted to know. Also, as if he believes that I *already have everything.* "If there is anything . . . tell it to me now," he added as though he is a genie from a magic lamp. Or as if his arms embraced the world and he could fulfill any request or command, or longing that someone beneath his umbrella, could ever desire. Since I know that Elisha is definitely "that nigga," but also from my death experience I know for sure that only ONE GOD is ALL POWERFUL over every person, living thing, and circumstance, I replied him something that I do want, that I also know that *he* could definitely never give me. Maybe I did that because I can feel that he wants to please me and keep me calm and cooperative because of his tremendous love of my sister Porsche and not for any other reason. I'm not mad at that. However, I want the nigga I choose, who I hunt, and who hunts and chooses me, to feel that way about me. The way Elisha feels about his wife Porsche. I don't want somebody else's nigga taking too good care of me, and giving me and guiding me in a way only my man should give and guide. So of course I'mma ask for something I know he can't give me.

"Well Elisha, I want three of me," I said. "That would make me feel more satisfied and comfortable. I want one Winter Santiaga to exist outside of the world of fame. She would be me, my original self." I placed my fingertips against the top of my breast to show that the fashionable, cool, and popular hood chick Winter, minus fame, is the real me. "I want a second Winter to build and run my fashion empire, that badass billionaire business bitch who'll design, style, dress, accessorize, and shake up the whole world." I smiled at the thought of it. "The third me, ummm, would be that celebrity bitch, who makes money rain from the sky, so I can scoop it up and hand it off to the other two mes," I said, then gave him an eyeball-to-eyeball serious expression that was also a challenge that I knew he couldn't reach or satisfy.

He didn't answer right away. He leaned back and released his seat belt. The jet had leveled off and I guess it was all good.

"I can present you with two Winter Santiagas who look exactly like you," he said, shocking me really. I laughed and released my seat belt. "Impossible," I told him quite confidently.

"No one would be able to tell that they are not you. Only you and I would know, and my suppliers. The only differences would be internal. For example, that they would not, and could never, have your same soul. They each would not have your same mind, feelings, or intentions. However, once we employ them . . . ," he chuckled, "they will follow all of your directions and complete the tasks that you find to be too much for one person to complete," he added, and I knew he was not bullshitting, although I still do not believe he could pull it off.

"My same look! Yeah right." I laughed then leaned back.

"You don't believe me." He laughed a man laugh, his white teeth, perfect, and his one embedded tooth diamond sparkling even in a dimmed cabin. I love that he only has one diamond in his mouth. It's more than a fashion statement to me. Everybody knows he's richer than mostly all the niggas whose mouths are diamond-flooded. His one diamond is a symbol of how discreet and smoothed out he is . . . and a subtle message that the one diamond is not an invitation. He's married.

"Hollywood can do almost anything that can humanly be done. Have you ever heard of a doppelganger or how about a body double? This is a huge world. There are at least two and up to ten people who have your same exact look," he said like it was a promise. There was a pause, then he asked me, "Do you think you are the only talented artist who feels overwhelmed by their own fame? Schedule? Expectations?" He leaned back. "Nah . . . it happens," he said, asking and then answering his own question. "This fame is a high-priced monster. I won't let it get the best of you." His promise of protection warmed me. I don't want to be warmed by my sister's husband.

"I'm curious," he said. "Which of the three Winters who you described would be the one who remembers her sister's birthday?"

Felt like he smashed a cream pie in my face without warning. I'm scrambling to remember today's date before I can even begin to remember the date of my sister's birth. I guess he's referring to Porsche's birth date. *I don't have my phone, my calendar, so I can't just glance down and spit back an easy reply. All right, so my last official workday was Friday . . . the 24th of July. I signed the new one-million-dollar deal on Saturday, the 25th of July. Today is Sunday, the 26th of July. That's it!* "July 26 is Porsche Luxurious Santiaga's birth date," I said aloud after an obviously too long pause.

"Which Winter is speaking?" he asked me too calmly.

"The original one" was all I said, swiftly.

"Cool, so when I bring the other two Winters to you, the original one will remember her sister's birthday weeks ahead of time. She'll either make or purchase her sister a thoughtful gift. Not because there is any one thing that her sister does not already have, but because she knows that if she disappears on her sister's birthday weekend, and her sister believes she is in some trouble, her sister Porsche . . . will cry. And even though her husband knows that his wife would be crying *anyway* on her birthday every year since her momma died . . . on July 26, on her birth date . . ." Bombed. I felt bombed while way up in the sky, riding on his jet.

"I had a private surprise party planned for Porsche for today at 3 p.m.," he said oddly. I'm thinking *Who parties on Sunday in the middle of the afternoon when everyone else is trying to get over their hangovers?*

"I know it sounds unique. My wife is unique. I designed the party based strictly on what my wife loves. A home-cooked Sunday brunch, but this time prepared by all of the people she loves and who love her back. I planned to ask you to prepare a special dish on Saturday night. Whatever you could handle," he said calmly.

"You never mentioned . . . ," I said softly, still feeling bombed, scattered, embarrassed, and cornered. Also feeling him saying "Whatever you can handle" meant he believes I am not even capable of cooking a side dish. Also, that comment means he thinks he knows for sure that his wife is better than me, more capable.

"You never returned after the Kuntz meeting," he said. "I thought it would turn out better if I allowed you to focus on and complete the meet and greet, and then I would've told you the Sunday birthday party setup. I kept it last minute on purpose because like I said it was supposed to be a surprise. I set up a spa day for you and Porsche at the Ritz. When my driver brought you ladies home, everybody else would be gathered and everything laid out and set up. My entire family, your father and family, even your brother young Ricky, who Porsche desperately wants you to meet face to face." He just looked at me. So I switched my gaze out of the window at the clouds. "For Porsche, you and young Ricky getting together for the first time would've been the gift she wanted the most."

"Okay Elisha, I'm a selfish bitch who fucked up. Is that what you want me to admit?" I asked, turning it around on him, which I know is deceptive and wrong but I'm still doing it. "Besides, I didn't know about the party and of course I know my sister's birth date. We grew up together. I used to be forced to babysit her and change her stinking diapers back when I was too young to babysit or change diapers!" I said in a way that I am making it clear that I need him to change the subject.

"What else do you need to happen to have a piece of your original self available to your sister and family?" he asked, as though my first wish of three selves is easy, doable, definite, and done. Now I am only thinking harder about the next true things that I want that he could never give me. The flight attendant arrived with a tiny trolly of glass-bottled drinks, condiments, fruits, and appetizers. I'm thinking I should challenge Elisha, and tell him to *turn back the hands of time*, but I am certain he couldn't ever. *Give me back the fifteen years that I lost in the pen. Raise Momma from the dead. Kill that bitch Dulce, who somehow snagged my father and gave birth to his bastard sidepiece son.*

"Seems like you want to fight. But you're too beautiful to be a fighter. And your bread and butter is in the beauty industry," Elisha said as he pushed a small plate of fruit forward, silently encouraging me to eat. "Even if you've fought before, you now have a more fragile constitution." He leaned forward. "Any sudden impactful wrong move or any blunt object upside your pretty head, it's lights out," he said gently, but it felt like he hit me with a brick and said, *Wake up, bitch.*

"Is that why you flew in with a doctor for me?" I asked. "You thought I was 'lights out,' in Vegas? Did all of the businesspeople think it was time to cash in all of those insurance policies you guys took out on me?" I said as get-back on feeling exposed and agitated.

"No," he said calmly. "That doctor is the pilot who is flying this aircraft right now. She's a licensed pilot who happens to also be a doctor. She's also Midnight's wife." BOOM.

"Her son, who was seated in the rear, is also a pilot. He's in the cockpit right now as copilot. The two young ladies, one seated behind you and the one who served you a fruit plate, are the pilot's daughters. They came for Porsche's party and to begin as freshmen this year at NYU and Columbia University. All of these people changed their schedule for you." He gestered with one hand and his pointing finger. "Oh, and seated in the last seat with his headphones on is your brother, who goes by the name Yung Santiago, aka YSL."

14
MY WORTH

I am monster. I wasn't before. I am now. Alone in my room wearing only my black panties, I'm seated on my stool at my designer table up high in my loft area. Hennessy XO in my glass, a spliff in between my lips, I'm trying to calm down after the craziest day of my life. Nothing floating in my head but numbers. The reason being, it was the first day that Elisha treated me as a liability, when he had previously *only* treated me as an incredibly valuable asset. But after the long meeting in the sky in the jet that he says cost ten thousand dollars an hour when in flight, I realized my Vegas trip had cost him one hundred thousand dollars. Even though at the time that he said it, I shrugged my shoulders a little and told him, "I purchased, with my own money, a round-trip Vegas ticket on a commercial airline. I didn't ask you to come out here and get me. In fact, it was *your wife* who costed you a hundred thousand dollars cause I believe you flew out here at her request, right or wrong?"

"Wrong," he had replied. "I flew out here after meeting with your manager and hearing that you were wandering around without your bodyguard or driver after going missing Friday night and showing up right before our golf tournament, in one of his vehicles, with a bullet hole in it and a replacement wheel." He was looking me dead in my eyes to measure my reaction. I was tight that Santiaga had told this information to Elisha. He's supposed to be my father and my manager. He had said he would take care of everything. Why was he diming me out and making me look bad, when he is the king of *less is more?*

Reading my mind, it seems, Elisha had said, "Your father didn't mention any of this until Saturday night when you popped up on *Eyewitness News* and pics were posted of you at the airport. Santiaga said he believed you were being targeted by someone while also traveling alone in a messed up state of mind and it worried him. He told me he had already sent your brother to Vegas to locate you and do shadow security."

"So if Santiaga said he was taking care of it, why did you set off on a ten-hour, ten-thousand-dollar-per-hour round trip, Elisha?" I asked him, to say and show how ridiculous all of this is and how it is personal not business. "It's personal that I decided to spend my weekend alone." I told him furthermore, "I am not interested in discussing my personal life and my personal choices. Let's talk numbers and business same as we have in the past." Elisha pulled up his calculator app and laid his iPhone on the small table.

"No, that's not why I set out on the one-hundred-thousand-dollar round trip to Vegas." He typed 100,000 into the calculator. "On Saturday night, I also received from CEO Kuntz a pdf which contained a fifty-page contract that you signed authorizing him to do a seven-day summer shoot before the debut of *Bow Down Starring Winter Santiaga* in September." BOOM.

"I signed a whiteboard with one paragraph handwritten on it," I told Elisha.

"I know. He sent the photo of you and him, the deal memo on his whiteboard, your signature and his bloodied fingerprint. That was the short form. The fifty pages is the long form. The fifty pages is my top television star, that's you, making a business deal without a heads-up or consultation with me, who has a sixty-five-million-dollar deal with the Network, with you as the cornerstone."

"So why is that a problem?"

He smiled. "Because you cut me out of the deal on a show that I created, produced, and directed, and made the number-one-rated show in America and in several global markets. You put me in an expensive awkward position with the Network, because I could easily place a cease and desist on this deal you signed, but then it would destroy the relationship I built with Kuntz, and business is all about relationships. My reputation in the world of entertainment, businesswise, is priceless. If I fight this show you signed up for, and trigger a number of lawsuits, rightfully so . . . not only Kuntz, but the television industry players will see me in a hostile light moving forward. Not only that, *you will be bitter* that I canceled out your seven-hundred-thousand-dollar bag."

"One million dollars!" I corrected Elisha.

"The million-dollar bag you negotiated, according to the contract, was really a seven-hundred-thousand-dollar bag. Kuntz got you to agree that the extra three hundred thousand covers three promotional events at his discretion." He paused. "Do you know what that means?" he asked.

"Of course it means by his choice," I said swiftly cause it sounded like he thinks I'm dumb.

"No," he answered back. "I am not asking you if you know what the word 'discretion' means. I am asking you, can you convert that three-hundred-thousand-dollar so-called bonus agreement into its actual value?" he asked, and I hate that I'm blank faced right now. "You know the Network has a film division, a music division, a theater division? Say one of their top million-dollar stars hits a slump. Their work is not selling or not selling as rigorously as projected. Now, since you are the hot article of the moment, Kuntz can require you, based on your agreement to three promotional appearances, to stand beside or show up with their star whose sales are low. He will use your 'heat' to reignite the declining career of their, say, top music artist. Now since the public loves you, Miss Winter Santiaga, and roots for you, Miss Winter Santiaga, by you appearing with, partying with, on camera with, that declining artist, he or she gets hot again, makes a song, sells a million copies, goes multi-platinum, gets ten million streams and likes and followers . . . PRICELESS," he said as he just placed his finger on the number 1 and then leaned on the number zero until the calculator lost track or could no longer hold the count.

"Not to mention all of the things you gave away that I didn't mention: Kuntz's ownership of the summer show footage, the shows that *he creates*, subscription services, streams, outtakes, bloopers, wave files, CDs, DVDs, merchandising . . . good God. You get a million dollars if you cooperate, but that's it . . . ," he said as though one million dollars was the same as ten dollars. "You get that one-time amount, no other streams of revenue, no back end participation, residuals, or royalties because it's reality television and more importantly it's what you negotiated because you don't know the game." BOOM.

I felt belittled but worse than that.

"After your prison release, the normal business route was for you to select an agency to represent you and make all your deals on your behalf. A big agency knows everything about this business, contracts, contacts, and can demand huge amounts that an independent artist can normally never negotiate. Furthermore, the agency only gets a small percentage for making you huge deals. You would be earning the lion's share of everything else with your name or participation on it and in it," he said.

Now I am beginning to boil, feeling like a fucking fool.

"But after our incident," he described my getting shot dead as "our incident," ". . . you didn't have the opportunity to interview agents and make a decision on which top agency you wanted to represent you for the next five years to a decade or in perpetuity. The Immanuel Group could not be your agent because it would be a conflict of interest as we are already in business with you in other areas." He looked directly at me. I know he knows he is talking circles around me and going levels above my head.

"So here's what we're going to do . . . ," Elisha said. And that was the first time Elisha looked like a fearless, ferocious, hungry tiger or a straight-up spilled-blood-detecting shark to me, not my sister's husband, but a dangerous creature from a foreign jungle or deep dark death waters. He wasn't asking about my thoughts or feelings like he usually would. Must be my fault, because I had asked him to drop the whole personal angle and deal with me as strictly business. Now I wanted a take-back, a do-over, a reset.

"I'll have my legal team vet and edit the fifty-page contract. I'll countersign the deal you made in the deal memo, which is the only way shooting the special can go forward. You in turn will do as I say on matters I have already discussed at length with Santiaga. First, you will accept and cooperate with the new security team Santiaga is currently negotiating with. They're a top global outfit, licensed and bonded to secure kings and queens, presidents and prime ministers, ambassadors and legislators, moguls, million- and billionaires and movie stars. The annual security price tag is heavy. It has to be paid in full before they arrive for duty. Your father has already told me he will finance it by forfeiting his percentage of your 2.1-million-dollar deal on *Bow Down* season 2 that he negotiated."

"Poppa said that . . . ?" I said quietly. I'm deflated.

"Next, you will need to see a therapist and cooperate with the treatment."

"I don't need no psychiatrist, Elisha," I spit back. "That's over the top. You guys are trying to punish me for a little Vegas trip on my own," I said.

"No, that's not it . . . It's a decision your father and I made after he told me how you jumped his youngest sister and left her bruised and beaten . . . for no reason at all," he said and waited for me to try and wiggle out or deny it. I couldn't. I had whopped that bitch's ass because I thought she was Dulce or some other bitch who was there stunting on my momma's dead body.

"Your silence is your guilt," Elisha said. "And, I came to Vegas to get you before you agreed or signed up to or for anything else without fully understanding who you are and what and who you are involved in and with. The therapy will help you to figure out why you are not happy when you have everything that you could ever want and are living the high life which is the opposite of being locked up."

"Security and therapy, that's it, right Elisha?" I said in a way that I know I am being blackmailed into it, in exchange for keeping the million-dollar bag I set up.

"No. There's two more items. We will build season 2 around your therapy and your search for true happiness. That will resonate with our audience. Seems millions of Americans, from the poorest to the richest, are battling depression and nursing suicidal thoughts.

Most people who can afford it are in therapy, fighting back from some trauma they experienced, of from some form of depression, or just fighting themselves for some unexplained reason," he said I guess to demonstrate that he thought I fall into that category.

"I create family-friendly content. That's not what Kuntz is going for, I'm sure," he said grinding his own finger on the small table that divided us. "Season 2 is sixteen shows. You give me the list of what kind of husband you are looking for. From a blue-collar guy who mops up the floors, to a king, or son of the king of any land, to a race car driver, or lion tamer, or doctor, scientist, or lawyer. I can line em up and film as you date, explore, and decide for yourself, what man matches, loves you, and brings you peace."

Sunday night while reflecting in the dark, I picked up my cell phone, which Elisha returned to me after my going through the motions of being a member of a tiring family. I still had not seen Santiaga. When I turned my phone back on, I had forty-eight missed calls. Then the screen lit up. *Incoming call from* PRETTY BITCH. Seeing the name I gave her brightened me up some.

"I got your money," she said, getting straight to the point.

"That's good. I was just about to ask, 'Bitch, where my money at!'" I laughed and she did, too.

"I know you was. That's why I started off with it," she said, showing how swift she is and how well she is getting to know me.

"Where did you go?" I asked her about the Vegas nightclub.

"I'm busy all week, all business. Let's link on the weekend. I'll show up with your paper ... unless you need it right now? I can get Bijoux to deliver it right now," she said.

"Nah I'm busy the whole week," I said. "And maybe even the weekend during the days. Let's hook up on Saturday night. Hold on to it and put it in my hand yourself."

"Let me leave you to your spliff," she said and it made me feel paranoid like she was there in the dark watching me. "I can tell by your breathing. Plus your voice sounds tired. Drink some water, bitch. Eat some food, bitch! Then go to sleep, bitch!" she said and laughed. "That's an order!" Then she hung up. I'm glad she called, not just about the money. I am glad that she's not connected to any other vein that's connected to me. With the exception of her, I'm tired of talking and tired of people talking to me. I'm exhausted of being a daughter, a sister, a sister-in-law, an artist, and I'm just getting started. That's why I'm about to turn this shit around, make every moment my moment. Yes, and every move I make will be solely in my favor from here on in.

Early Monday morning I'm soaking my body in the warm water of my wide bathtub when I see "Money Call" light up on my cell phone screen. Soon as I hear his voice, I can tell he's working out while doing his business. Sounds like he's running on a treadmill.

"Hey! Baby Girl! You're doing absolutely fantastic. The kind of publicity that you have been generating in general, but specifically over this weekend, AMAZING! Couldn't be better," CEO Kuntz said. He is calling me Baby Girl, a name only my father Santiaga nicknamed and calls me.

"Yeah, I was just living my life and it happened that way," I replied coolly.

"Even better. Even more brilliant, great!" he said with the energy and the confidence of a man who does not have one problem in this world. "And I love the fainting thing . . ." He laughed while breathing hard. "I wish more top talent and artists knew how to collapse *before a murder*. Now you're automatically above suspicion. You got to breeze through the investigation and skip the trial and the distractions."

"Murder? What murder?" I asked.

"That's it! What murder? That's perfect! Keep that line exactly like that," he said as though I was acting.

"Aight. You said anytime you call it's a money call. So what money you calling about?" I asked without the bitch and without the laughter mixed in it.

"Fabulous. Let's get right down to business. Our first show is tomorrow, Tuesday."

"Yeah I received the shooting schedule on my phone. What else?"

"There's a music artist named F-K-R. Mutha—"

"Named what?"

"F.K.R. Mutha," he repeated like that was some normal or fly shit for a nigga to name himself.

"There's an in-studio on-camera listening party for him tonight at ten p.m. I need you to show up there. You're his top pick. He's a fan. Thirty minutes, one hour maximum. I just sent the location. Check your phone."

"Got it. That's one. Two promos left" was all I said before we both cut the call.

Later, perfumed and perfectly pretty, I am in an all-white Hermès ensemble. The dress gives the illusion of being a blouse and skirt, but it's one piece, with pleats. I'm sporting the Hermès bag as well as the heels. Before exiting my villa, I looked over my collection of sunglasses and chose for today the Chanel chain-mail sunglasses. Sometimes I wear sunglasses so people won't automatically recognize me. Sometimes I choose sunglasses cause the sun is so bright. Sometimes I choose sunglasses to shield my eyes so I can be meaner and clearer than usual, which helps me to get my business done the way I want it done, without sympathy or empathy or feelings. I realize there is no place for feelings in big business.

"Expect me to ignore you," I said to Yung Santiago, the handsome one who I hate. He didn't say anything back. Its cool. He's comfortable being ignored *and* he's ignoring me. He opened the door to the Escalade. I got in. He closed it. His man was seated front passenger seat. I couldn't see nothing but his locks, and he didn't turn around to greet me. Santiago jumped into the driver's seat and pulled off. The final condition that Elisha demanded of me was that the guy who I did not know was my father's son would accompany me everywhere until the high-priced professional security team arrived.

"He's not a real bodyguard," I argued back to Elisha on the flight.

"It's not negotiable. You want my signature on the summer shoot contract, give in to me on my demands." So I gave in to Elisha's exact words. My father's son could follow me everywhere until the professional security team arrives. It's business not personal. Therefore I don't owe this guy anything as my father's son. I no longer will allow these personal entanglements to strangle me. I haven't seen my father since I got back from Vegas. To me, his son *is just a spy.*

15
EIGHT BITCHES

"Eight Bitches, that's the name of my new company," I said, placing a palm-sized hourglass on her desk and flipping it around to keep time. "Incorporate and trademark it for me starting right now," I ordered her.

My lawyer, Kai Stone, laughed. I didn't laugh. Her professional services cost one thousand dollars per hour. When I first met her, she offered me to either pay her per hour or she would earn 5 percent on every business deal she negotiated or handled on my behalf. "Take your pick," she had said dry and politely at the same time. Her firm is down on Wall Street. That's where we are both seated. It's Monday morning at 9 a.m. and I'm clear that time is money and money is time. Her back against the view of the World Trade Center, and the lower Manhattan cityscape, where the real gamblers, hustlers, and murderers earn, steal, and stash their cash, gives her confidence. Her firm's roster of powerful entertainers, athletes, politicians, and businessmen and women is the reason she does not tremble, back off, or bow down. I like that she doesn't bow. To me it means that when she's out there representing my interests, she's a shark not a guppy. Yeah, I am learning to talk like that.

"It's shocking," she said. "In fact everything about you, Miss Winter Santiaga, tends to be a bit shocking."

I smiled. "Life is a series of shocking events. That's what I believe. And, anyone's life that does not flow like dat, is one boring mother fucker," I added.

"I love it," she said. "What is the business of this new company that I will create for you?" she asked. "It sounds like the name of a rock band. Don't tell me you're venturing into music. Are you?"

"The company that you will incorporate for me, *and that I will own and create,*" I corrected her. She did not reply. Just waited for me to explain what I was asking her to set up.

"It's a fashion company where I will do all of my separate, non-television-reality-show business."

"Understood. So Lavender Sky is for your reality show and any other television or film or music production deals that may come your way in light of your escalating television popularity."

"Exactly," I confirmed.

"And 'Eight Bitches' is reserved for your fashion transactions and earnings and services related to the fashion industry. Let me ask what you had in mind specifically in your fashion business? Is it a design company, a manufacturer, a wholesaler, distribution company, or retail?" she asked, and my mind was speeding although my face was calm.

"It's all of that, a fashion empire that begins with *my look, my designs, my team* . . . ," I told her.

"You don't have to reinvent the wheel," she said strangely. "With your current clout, I could search out a licensing deal for you, wherein you simply license your name and your creative ideas for a filthy amount of money to an already well-established fashion house."

"How filthy?" I asked her, but I really am not interested in that route. I'm completely amped up on me and my new all-girl-convict team, starting with my first sketch, etched behind bars, and my first stitch, and then blowing up the fashion world. For me it ain't about following the icons. It's about becoming the icon that all the greats suddenly have to bow down to because *it's my time* in what was exclusively *their industry*. It's about twisting the trend, spinning the globe in the opposite direction than it is currently moving in. That's how I imagine it.

"Well then beat me to it," I challenged her.

"Meaning?" she asked.

"Present me your 'filthy fashion deal,' when you are specifically sure about it. Let it be so filthy that when you take your five percent cut, it's painless to me and the bitches I gotta feed."

"Love it. I'll get to work on it soon as you walk out of my office. But, not before you answer a few questions," she said. "Are the eight bitches you have to feed part owners of this company, full- or part-time employees, independent contractors, or consultants? What did you have in mind? And excuse my French, but are you one of the eight bitches?" she asked in her sharp, aggressive, but respectful, professional manner. I smiled, instead of answering her.

"That gorgeous smile of yours may make you rich, Miss Santiaga. However, if your business is not set up in an impeccable legal manner, the US government will disregard your beauty and celebrity and seize every penny you ever earned and grab all of your major material purchases, cars, properties, houses, jewels, and even your stunning shoe collection," she said, glancing down at my Hermès heels. "The IRS will investigate and humiliate you while the media will catch it all on camera while they are doing it. It will be *one shocking event* that you won't find exciting at all." Then she smiled at me, crossed her arms over her breasts, and waited for my reaction. I knew what she was warning was true facts. The US government had seized all of my father's belongings, using the excuse that it was purchased with drug money. Now that my family is legit, what this Wall Street lawyer is saying is that the US government has several different excuses to come and bag up the valuables of its citizens. Even small reasons like "the company was not set up exactly right."

"That won't happen to me. Not when I pay you a thousand dollars an hour or five percent per deal to guarantee that every single aspect of my life is set up legally. The owner of Eight Bitches is only me. The eight women I chose will be my full-time employees for as long as they do quality work. I have the W2 forms completed for my first and most important hire, and I will have the rest of the signed forms before the end of this week," I said.

"It's easy to hire. It's not as easy to fire. Did you happen to decide on which accounting firm will handle all of your business relating to your brand? I recommended Vernon of V. Brown & Company. He's excellent," she said. "I also gave you two alternative CPA firms, Koenigsberg and Padell. It would be easier if you remained within the professional network that our firm has established. An excellent, well-connected accountant will set you up with the best bank and banker, with the most favorable conditions. She or he will set you up so that your employees' paychecks are fully managed without you having to think about it at all. All of the proper taxes will be withdrawn in advance from their paychecks so that you never have to receive that ominous call from Uncle Sam. You will also need the proper insurance for every aspect of your business, including workmen's compensation. You're already an independently and properly insured artist via your reality show. Once you, however, create a new company and hire your employees, you become responsible for them, their health insurance, workmen's compensation, unemployment cost for those who you fire. Fashion is about all of the facets of beauty. But, say, one of your employees accidentally cuts off her finger while cutting fabric or sewing a dress you designed on company time? Or for instance, after you have hired her, one of your employees is diagnosed with an ongoing critical disease that requires unimaginable medical costs? I could list over a thousand what-ifs, but I won't because I can tell you don't have the attention span for these kinds of tedious thoughts." She gave me a tough stare. "Do you?" she then asked me, to take a little bit of the sting out of the slick shit she was saying in a way that I notice college bitches say things.

"I don't but you do," I said calmly. "So for the Eight Bitches brand, we will work on a five percent basis instead of your one-thousand-dollars-an-hour fee," I decided and said. She gave a tight half smile. I knew that's what she preferred anyway. "But at five percent of everything Eight Bitches, that means I have full access to your legal services on all fashion company matters. I don't care if you're home cooking bacon on a Saturday or in the middle of giving your husband a blowjob on a Sunday morning. When I call, you pick up. Deal?"

"Another shocking moment with my lovely client, Miss Winter Santiaga," she said politely. "And by the way, I stopped sucking my husband's dick years ago. You're not married. So, I know you would never understand the nuances of a married couple," she said as though she had somehow just put me in my place somewhere beneath her.

"No, I am not married yet. But I do understand that when a

woman stops sucking her husband's dick, his side bitch keeps sucking it, and his new bitch sucks it double-time."

"And his wife doesn't care who sucks it as long as it's not her,"
she laughed and leaned forward like, *duh*. "Young dumb single ladies
don't know nothing. And yes, I know this is incorrect English I'm
speaking. And I know that I have digressed after being lured by you,
Miss Santiaga. But since 'I'm on your side,' and I am a decade or less
older than you, and because I represent you, and furthermore since
you brought it up. Marriage is serious business. The wife wins it all.
The 'side pieces' don't get anything from his life insurance policy, don't
end up owning any or all of his properties, do not get their hands on
any of his inheritance. And even if the side bitch sucked my husband's
dick in his Mercedes-Benz, I will be the one who gets the Benz and
all of his cars in the end. She doesn't even get a chance to show up
and shed obvious tears while seated in the front row of my husband's
funeral. Side pieces are not wives or family to the deceased. A side
piece or a mistress, or whatever you would like to call her, is the same
as an undocumented immigrant, aka an illegal alien, a loser," she said
then cleared her throat. "Lastly, five percent of zero is zero. That's our
starting point, Miss Santiaga. And, even though my firm and myself
have no idea if your fashion venture will be lucrative, we still have to
begin working on its legal foundation and framing without any compensation. So keep that in mind when we are chatting."

Chatting, I thought to myself. Is that what we are doing? But
then I decided to stop going back and forth on her. She's right. She's
on my side. And, if she ends up owning 5 percent of my company's
gross earnings, she has a motive to do an excellent job. And if my
company does not earn massive profit, she would have lost all of her
time and professional services that she already put up.

"I have some other names and words that I want trademarked

as well," I said, ignoring a more direct reply and hinting at the fact that I do have a well-thought-out, tight plan. She should have confidence in me.

"Trademarking is tricky. There are a plethora of filing fees, which *you will have to pay* separate from the five percent I require. Those amounts go to the various trademarking agencies and courts. It's expensive and continuous and there are rules to be followed by any person or entity seeking to own a name, a word, a title, logo, or anything," she cautioned. But I was tired of her caution. I need her to *shut the fuck up and get it done.*

"McDonald's owns the name McDonald's. Burger King owns the name Burger King and Gucci owns the name Gucci," I said. "And no matter how much I like McDonald's, it's illegal for me to use the name McDonald's, which is already incorporated, trademarked, and owned by someone else. That's what I want for my brands, complete control over the names, logos, and items that I create," I said.

"Trademarking doesn't give you complete control over the names and titles that you trademark. Nor does it provide complete control or ownership of words exclusively. McDonald's is a food chain, a global franchise. It owns the name McDonald's in the hamburger restaurant business. If I wanted to open a law firm named McDonald's Legal Advisors, I could, because a law firm and a restaurant are two separate classes and types of businesses. Therefore you are trademarking the name, title, or logo specifically for the category of business that you are conducting. Someone else can trademark the same name to be used in a different kind of business in the marketplace. Do you understand?" she asked. I nodded.

"Look, you can buy a trademark for a specific category if it is not already taken, or not already in continuous use by another individual or corporation. However, you can lose the trademark if you are not actively using it for the category it was assigned. To get the trademark in the first place, you have to demonstrate that you or your company are already using it in the marketplace in the category that you are pursuing. For example, the musical artist known as Prince, all throughout the world, cannot stop a Prince clothing line from being trademarked by another person or entity if he does not have a clothing line using the same trademarked name. He cannot prevent an author from using the name Prince, as an author or as a book title, unless Prince the musical artist is trademarked as an author and or publisher who is in the marketplace selling books under the trademarked name Prince. Notorious B.I.G. only became Notorious B.I.G. because his previous name, 'Biggie Smalls,' was first trademarked by another music artist. It didn't matter that the other artist was a young unknown white rapper. The fact that he trademarked the name and used it in his little underground music marketplace was enough for him to keep B.I.G. from trademarking, using, or snatching the name Biggie Smalls from him."

The tiny hourglass I had flipped over the second after I had been seated and begun talking, at 9 a.m., was about to be emptied. I discreetly removed it and dropped it into my handbag. I pulled out my list, then stood up and placed it on her desk where she could read it. "I will also be using the following words, names, titles, and labels in my fashion business starting this month. So please start the process of trademarking them. I will supply samples of the merchandise that I will put into the marketplace immediately," I told her.

"And I will inform you, after our paralegals conduct an exhaustive search, of which of these words, names, and titles are even up for grabs."

"Thank you for your time," I said and stood up from where I was just seated.

She cleared her throat as if there was *still more* to discuss. "Have you considered an eponymous fashion company name? That would be easiest to own, incorporate, and have approved for trademarking," she asked, also standing up. Now I know this bitch knows I don't know what the fuck *eponymous* means. So I didn't reply. All in my eyes are the words *explain, bitch!*

"When you first became a client, I looked at your documentation of course and completed your passport application as well as many other matters. I noticed that your full name is Winter Victorious Santiaga. That sounds perfect to me, a real moneymaking name." She stared into my eyes. I relaxed into my game face; I was about to pretend that I had thought of that myself, when the truth is I never used my middle name before. Most Americans don't. It's just a name given at birth and not used in real life. But she's right, the middle name is hot to death. If I made a clothing line named Victorious, I could capitalize on an already established brand name, Victoria's Secret. Simply sounding the same would make my line familiar in millions of homes and minds. I'm remembering how my third grade teacher, when she saw my registration form, said, "Victorious is not a name, it's an adjective." Even back then I was like, "Bitch, shut the fuck up." Besides, I am middle-named Victorious. Porsche is middle-named Luxurious. Mercedes is middle-named Elegant, and Lexus is middle-named Elite. They are all adjectives and are all our government names printed on our birth certificates.

"Miss Santiaga . . . are you listening?" my attorney followed up. "In fact Victorious sounds more commercial and universal than 'Eight Bitches,'" she added.

"I planned to use Victorious on my clothing line. However, my company is Eight Bitches. No one else will have that name, I'm sure." I played down her incredible suggestion. Now that I am learning the game, I realize that top bosses pretend they thought of everything themselves, and that they are doing more for a talented artist than they are actually doing. Then they snatch the lion's share of all earnings. I can do that, too. I will.

As I began my walk out of her office, "Do you mind if I ask what is that scent you are wearing?" she said in a much softer tone than she had said everything else during our meeting.

"It's a scent for only single bitches like me, who are plotting out becoming married women, so that we don't have to be living the same as illegal immigrants."

"So swift with your words. You probably would have made an excellent lawyer if you had put your time, your mind, your studies and energy into it," she said sharply. I stopped walking and let her words just hit me the same as if she had thrown rocks at my back. "And remember, Miss Santiaga, being a successful artist is a rainfall of earnings, residual earnings, royalties, licensing fees, buyouts, etc. Becoming an employer, a CEO, a CFO, the chief, the boss, *the responsible party*, is a 180-degree difference. It's when you become the spender, the risk taker, the signatory. For some artists, who suddenly dip their feet into business, they regret not having left that business to the professionals whose singular training, education, and focus *is business*. Your choice as of today, by not simply remaining in the entertainer's receiving position, with the rainfall of revenue," she raised her thin arms up high and wiggled her fingers like raindrops falling, "is a whole new beast." She escorted me out to the firm's reception area. I saw her eyes lock in on my fake bodyguard. I didn't introduce him and she didn't ask. Even though she's an older bitch, I saw her look and her lust as her eyes lingered on him. Old bitches crave young dick.

16
THE SETUP

"I'm not going to ask where you been. I already know," Dutchess said. She's holding her cell phone up.

"Don't pay attention to all that noise and bullshit," I told her about the general and the social media.

"It's my job to pay attention to you, Winter. I already did a search and watched and read all of your online stuff."

"Oh! So you already saying yes to working for me. I didn't even tell you the job description or the pay."

"Whatever it is, anything except murder or anything that will get me back on lock, I'll do it." She drew her line. I like that she made herself clear up front.

"Anything except murder, huh," I replied jokingly. "You already did a bid for murder. That's not my line of work," I reminded her.

"Okay then we have an understanding. But I heard there was a murder out in Vegas. You told me you were too sleepy on Saturday afternoon. Then you hopped on a flight across the country? Girl, that's gangster." She laughed.

"A bitch needed a break," I said.

"Yeah, there's pics online of you sleeping on the flight."

"Whatever," I replied. "Of course I give a fuck but I realize if it ain't about getting more money, I shouldn't give a fuck. So I don't."

"Woah" was all she said.

"It's gonna be a whole lot of work. I planned to pay you a hundred thousand a year. Since you already agreed to do the job though, I should drop it down to fifty thousand. In this business I'm in and you are just entering, you will have to tighten up your negotiation skills and don't be so quick to show your hand and agree to anything or lowball our company or products."

"Got you," she said. "You'll see though, I would only do it that way for you. If you pay me one hundred thousand dollars a year, that's more money than my moms ever made in her lifetime. If you pay me fifty thousand dollars a year, that's thirty-five thousand dollars per year more than a minimum-wage bitch like me would ever be paid. That's facts," she said. "Now what's the work?" she asked.

"Executive assistant," I said. She smiled.

"Fancy," she replied.

"You will be in charge of doing, or causing, everything that I say needs to be done, exactly how I want it, for my new company. You'll be team leader, in charge of every other employee on my team. You answer to me. Day-to-day they answer to you." I gave a brief description which I knew did not give her a glimpse of how much work it will involve.

"First task is for you to go door-to-door and get the rest of the team recruited. I wanted to do it myself like I did with you. It's eight females, all convicts, who did time during the years we did time. So, I don't have phone numbers on any of them, just the addresses they gave me on the inside." I handed her my list. "I already recruited three including you. You gotta get the next four, get their W2 forms filled out and send them to the accounting firm. I'll give you all of my business contacts. They're confidential. Don't give out any information unless you check with me first. Once you got em, and if they agree—"

"You mean *when they agree,*" she laughed.

"Set a meeting for all of us. I'll email you my schedule."

"Got it," she said. "We meeting here?" she asked, holding up her right hand to show me how in two and a half days she had already painted and decorated her new place.

"This is *your* spot. I don't like nobody up in my spot. So I'll set up a separate meeting spot."

"No," she said. "I'll set up a separate meeting spot. Just give me the budget and tell me the type of setting you prefer." She smiled.

"Ah bitch, I love it. You're right! That's your job not mine," I said, and she looked down to read the list I handed to her.

"Yeah I seen you online getting Boobytrap from the strip club. I was like yeah, Winter always likes pretty bitches in her clique."

"Yeah Yeah, Booby will be the real estate coordinator for our company. She did her time for all of her illegal real estate hustles. We gon flip her legit. I plan on buying a store, maybe a whole building. I'll also own a NYC or downtown Brooklyn parking lot, as well as send her out to all of the hood bodegas so I can monopolize all of the unused, up for grabs billboard space in all five boroughs," I said, to let Dutchess know, I'm not paying no bitches just based on them looking pretty. You gotta bring money in based on the work that I assign and you carrying it out.

"What you recruiting that bitch Upside Down for? Her shit changes minute by minute. One bad second or mood, she could bring down your whole company," Dutchess warned me.

"Upside Down with a good paying job and a solid crew can exhibit some self-control," I assured her.

"Arson and murder and she had no reason for why she did any of it," Dutchess warned me.

"She had to have a reason. She just kept it to herself. I understand that."

"Okay, it's my job to warn you. Also, I'm not supposed to be around any other convicted murderers. But, I'll do it for you. That bitch better act right." She gave me a serious look, then said, "All good, I'll take care of it. What's your timeline?" she asked.

"Wednesday afternoon. That gives you two days to visit four spots." I handed her one stack. "Give each of them two hundred dollars to cover round-trip expenses. Even if they decide to catch a cab or Uber over to our meeting, that will more than cover the costs. You don't need to tell them nothing specific. Once you say my name, it's the same as money. I had told each of them on lock that I'd come for them after my release, same as I told you. Once we meet up, I'll hand out the job titles and any setup money needed." I handed her another stack. "That's your transportation and lunch and chump change to carry out your duties. Keep receipts for everything you spend or pay out. From here on in, for any amount I advance you, you have to hand back an expense sheet, dated, with all receipts attached. That's not me being a cheap bitch. That's me following the government rules. We legit now, a hundred percent and that's how it works."

"Chump change," Dutchess repeated counting up the cash. She slid it in her pocket and ran and put on her kicks. I reminded myself that I will have to spend, to dress and make over my whole team. Since they represent me in a fashion company, they should be fashionable. "We can head out the door together. I better get started right now," Dutchess said as we left.

I can tell murder weighs heavy on Dutchess's shoulders and on her mind. I could tell also that she felt, feels, and knows that the murder she committed was justifiable homicide. Therefore she holds herself higher than the common killers. At thirteen years young she gave birth to her only child, a son. By the time she turned fifteen, he was dead. She was holding his hand walking in baby steps down the street when he was hit by what the cops called a "random bullet." But Dutchess, the storyteller, said when you live on the block ain't shit "random." Every youth knows who did it, who was the actual target, what the street war was about. On lock Dutchess told her true story. She didn't deny that she murdered the triggerman. The way she put it was beautiful to me. "My son died in shock. I had to make sure the shooter died in shock. At the trial I saw his mother praying that he'd beat the case. I had to make sure that she would be as shocked as I was when my son got shocked and shot down, when I shock and shoot her son down. I wanted to make sure she grieved, like I grieved. Cause nobody who never had their son or daughter murdered in cold blood could ever know the feeling of the mothers who birthed them. I had to be sure she felt that feeling I was feeling every day, endlessly." It's the code of the streets, like that old Gang Star joint.

Dutchess's voice is her best thing. I realized that on lock, as she used to read aloud from her street literature collection to all of the lazy prisoners who did not want to read for themselves, or who just didn't know how. Dutchess would switch up her voice for different characters in the story. She could even make her voice sound like a man, woman, or child. In a complicated dialogue where her voice had to switch in seconds then switch back, she was amazing and we could even tell the age of the characters by the way she altered her tone and flow while reading. The listeners were also participants.

They'd get so excited and start calling out their thoughts to the rest of us. "Oh hell no that nigga gon get her set up!" Or "Yup that's the same shit that happened to me." Or "That's the exact bitch she shouldn't trust." After Dutchess's readings aloud, us prisoners would still be debating back and forth, asking each other crazy questions that only a gang of criminals would ask one another. "If you could only snatch one thing and get away with it, which would you snatch? The money bag, the guns, or the jewels?" Then they'd argue, how much money, what kind of jewels, what grade of diamonds, how many guns?

One night Dutchess had cramps and canceled the reading until the next night. So another bitch volunteered to continue reading where Dutchess last left off. The whole tier was like, "nah nah nah," in a passionate chorus. Dutchess, after being known as "the reader," and "the voice," also began helping other women in prison to locate and fight for their children, who were most of the time lost in the system. She was swift in the library. When we got the first computer access, she was the one who either learned or already knew how to fully utilize it. She was smart, organized, thorough, unselfish, and on a humble. That seemed to be the reason every one on lock loved her and the reason she made good time and shaved years off her sentence. Got released at age twenty-five.

"Who's he?" Dutchess asked as we exited her apartment. "I saw him standing out here while you were inside." She remarked about Ice Grill.

"He's nobody," I replied. He walked and opened the back door to the Escalade for me.

"Whatever you say. He looks like somebody to me. Nice lips and his smile is all diamonds. Handsome as a fuck," Dutchess uttered discreetly, positioning her face and lowering her voice and exhibiting no facial expression, reaction, or excitement.

As I got into the Escalade, Dutchess stayed back on the curb. She didn't ask for a ride or nothing. She knows how to play her position. She did ask me though, "Why me? Why did you choose me to run your business?"

"Cause you just a live bitch. At first, just for a few seconds when I heard about you coming upstate from juvy, I was tight that you got nine to twelve years on a murder, and I got fifteen mandatory on nothing at all. I like your style. Ever since I met you, I always did."

I just said it like that. I didn't want to put it into my truer words, which would've been *I love a bitch who's fearless. A bitch who has heart. A bitch who takes action, ain't nobody's victim. Who is not fucking just playing out here, and if you hurt her, she hurts you back.*

17
MUSIC

The studio was dark at 10 p.m. In my mind I'm like, *Where the party at?* I never been to an artist's listening party before and I never been in a music recording studio either. Just getting tight that I might have wasted my time coming through, escorted by two Network reps who I intended to ditch soon as I got inside where the other VIPs were supposed to be lounging and listening. "We'll be right back," Network rep one said and both of them left. I was more suspicious that they left my shopping bag with my gifts on the floor right beside me, like they were not really coming back at all. I had selected these gifts while in the Gucci showroom preparing a few picks for myself to rock on my million-dollar-bag summer shoot.

"Miss Winter Santiaga," a male voice came through on some kind of a PA system. I looked around but I did not answer.

"I'm F.K.R. Mutha, your fan. Thanks for showing up."

"Thank you for not showing up. Where the fuck are you nigga?" I asked. He laughed a little.

"I'm here. You just can't see me. Let's play a game," he said in a calm, playful voice. I felt a strong urge to bounce. My right foot was on pivot when I decided not to leave, reminding myself that *this is work*, a one-hundred-thousand-dollar encounter and the first promo I'm doing to fulfill my contract with Kuntz for the bonus three hundred thousand dollars. So I took a deep breath.

"I even like the way you breathe," his voice said calmly. "The mic is hot," he added.

Seize the moment, I thought to myself. *Make every moment your moment, Winter, especially when someone thinks they are using you. Turn it around and use them instead.*

"I don't trust women," he said suddenly. "But *I like you*. Girls can say anything about a dude. Make anything up about what a dude did when she was alone with him, especially when she know that dude is a platinum artist with a platinum bank account. So I'm checking you out first, before I step into the same room with you," he said cautiously.

Instead of responding, I dipped into my handbag and pulled out my hourglass.

"You got thirty minutes. You already used three" was all I said to let him know this is strictly business and I'm just tolerating him.

"Introduce yourself," he said.

"Nigga you know who I am . . ." I dragged each word out.

"Introduce yourself in rhyme. That's my challenge. If a girl is too tight to flow, I already know she's no fun, too old, or not nuthin nice. I like to have a good time. Show you something you never seen before. Get you doing something you never done before." I took another deep breath. I was mad and excited. I definitely had to clap back to him saying if I didn't accept his challenge, it means I'm too old! No fun! Nothing nice! *And, I'm on camera*, I reminded myself. I closed my eyes, pushed my lips up to the mic, and said my first original rhyme ever. Never written down on paper. I have no idea what I'm about say. But this nigga wants me to introduce myself. Here it go:

"Until you warm me up
I'm basically cold.
But if you that nigga,
My pussy is gold . . ."

"Ooooh . . . ," I heard him say, and I could hear *him* breathing now through the speakers.

"If you not Dat Nigga you can't have it.
Can't buy it either cause I'm well established."

"Oh shit you not looking to jack me . . . ," he said. I like that.

"If you want me nigga you gotta snatch my heart.
Make me feel some'm that sets you apart."

After I rhymed that, I felt good and my flow picked up more energy.

"From the average bitch nigga, cockroach, or maggot.
Forget me nigga if you undercover faggot!"

"Oh! Oh! Oh shit . . . ," he said, and I licked my lips realizing I was warming myself up, getting myself into it. Not really even talking to him. I'm talking to any nigga who wants to *capture me.*

**"Dat Nigga for me can't be nuthin sweet,
I like him strong and black a li'l rough in them sheets."**

The way he was reacting with just oohs and ahhs and breathing, I imagine he was jerking off to the sound of my voice or the flow of my freestyle. I didn't care. He ain't squirting on me.

**"I don't give a fuck if you went to college.
It's how you handle *this life*,
Sexy street knowledge.
Got stacks piled up cause you ain't no bum.
Use your head, look, and style to make me cum."**

Then I heard a sound that definitely sounded like him shooting his shot.

**"I'm true school nigga,
Still luv the dick-stick-shift
Feels more better than the lickety-split**

WORD . . ."

I stepped back from his mic. Felt like I made myself orgasm just getting certain feelings out of my mouth and off of my chest.

"Could you rhyme it one more time?" His voice reemerged.

"Nah, not even if I wanted to. I'm a rhyme virgin. That was me popping my rhyme cherry for you. You can only pop a cherry once. After the first time no one is a virgin anymore," I said, seducing the nation, cause I know I am on camera.

"I love you cause you can't repeat it," he said.

"You speeding nigga," I replied.

"Cause that means your flow came from your heart and soul. Now I feel like I know you."

"Believe me you don't."

"Can I take you out on a date?" he asked.

"No, cause your punk ass tried to set me up on a first date tonight by acting like it was a studio party. A nigga I like speaks with his own mouth to me directly. He don't have his handlers arrange some sneaky shit. And, if he gets me to show up *somehow*, he wouldn't hide," I said and pulled out two boxes from my shopping bag and held them up.

"Here go your souvenirs. I know y'all call this drip, but I don't. That shit sounds like a fucking pussy or dick disease. This the gear I copped for you to celebrate your listening party tonight, just in case when I got here your gear wasn't right and your pants were too tight." I grabbed my hourglass and held it up. It was half-finished. "Time's up." I waved it in the air then bounced.

It is 11:10 p.m. when the Escalade pulled up onto the Immanuel property and parked right by my villa. My father's son popped the trunk and him and his man both got out. They both carried the thirteen shopping bags I had from today's purchases. A few of the bags were filled with fabrics I selected and bought in bulk from the fabric district in Manhattan. One bag was filled with plain white T-shirts of various cuts, wifebeaters and short sleeves or long sleeves, or tapered T-halters. I plan to freak all of the materials I gathered with my own designs and styles. One bag was so precious to me, two pairs of shoes that I designed and my shoemaker made. I picked them up while in the Village, which is where I also buy old back catalog fashion magazines like *Vogue, Elle, Women's Wear Daily*, and even *Sports Illustrated* and *Cosmopolitan*, for my ongoing fashion library. One bag was all designer hats from various shops I visited today, and the remaining bags were designer tees which I designed, and designer picks I planned to wear on camera for the Kuntz seven-day shoot. I need everything regarding my look and appearances to be completed today. So I had exhausted the fake bodyguard and his man who took over the driving when my father's son had to accompany me inside or remain posted immediately outside of a location I was at. In one day, I did my accountant in downtown Brooklyn, my lawyer on Wall Street, my shoemaker in the Village, fabrics in Midtown, designer flagship stores on the East Side, Dutchess on the West Side. After all of that, I hit up a major pet shop to check out their puppies. My idea is to have eight female puppies as my logo. I'd get Dutchess to coordinate a photo shoot at the pet shop I selected that has eight purebred beautiful bitches. While at the pet shop, I stumbled upon a birthday gift perfect for Porsche. So perfect she would forgive and forget that I am twenty-four hours late in giving it, and that yesterday I ruined her surprise party.

"Good night," Ice Grill said to me. I didn't say nothing back. He didn't react to my silence.

His man said, "Your sister's mad rude." They both got back in the Escalade and off they went.

I looked up at Porsche's window. The light was still on. I took out my cell and gave her a call.

"I can't believe it," she said. "You're calling me first."

"Come out. Come solo. Right in front of my place," I told her, knowing she would come running even if she had a baby on her hip and was wearing her pajamas.

"What's all this?" she asked when she saw how many shopping bags were outside.

"I went shopping today," I said blandly.

"Oh."

"I'm glad you're still awake. I got something I need to give you before I can sleep peacefully."

"LOL, you think I need some designer bag in an emergency? Couldn't wait until the morning. You know I will stop by before you leave out like usual," Porsche said.

"Not tomorrow, I'm sleeping in late and going to the spa at one in the afternoon. Gotta get my look right before the shoot tomorrow night."

"You asking me to come with you, right?" She smiled and posed some cute look.

"Go over there." I pointed. She walked over slowly like she thought this was some kind of a trick. "Now lift the sheet," I told her. She lifted the sheet and gasped. She jumped up and down and bent forward to see more carefully into the cage. I was waiting for that damned bird to sing happy birthday like he did in the pet shop. The fucking thing didn't sing, just cooed.

"Oh my God it's a macaw, a blue-and-gold macaw." She lifted the cage door and placed her finger like it was a branch. The bird didn't go to her. I got mad and walked over and kicked the cage. I didn't like that the bird did all type of tricks 'n shit in the pet store, but in front of Porsche it was a wasted investment, a bust.

"Oh, Winter, don't kick it. It's a new environment. He's probably just a little scared." Then, the damned bird walked over and leaped onto Porsche's finger and sang out, "Your sister is mad rude. Your sister is mad rude. Your sister is mad rude."

18
THE BLUE HEART

By noon, as I was pulling myself together, I could hear the sound of some type of drill, a saw, and some hammering. I peeked from behind my curtain over towards the garden where the sound was coming from. It was Elisha and two workmen out there, a pile of wood, and a fountain that wasn't spouting water or even connected to the ground. It must be new, I thought. As soon as I let go of the curtain, I heard my doorbell. It's always only Porsche, but she doesn't normally ring my bell, just comes walking in if I've left the door unlocked, or uses her key. I opened the door.

"I'm going with you. The spa is no fun all alone," Porsche said. She looked beautiful, a braid down the center of her scalp and her eyes and skin glistening. She is wearing an off-white all-in-one satin short set, very stylish, and her hips and thighs are shining and in top shape. Even while pregnant she is still picture perfect.

"It's not supposed to be fun. It's supposed to be relaxing," I said, releasing the door so she could just walk on in.

"Well then I'm going to relax, too," she insisted.

"I'm surprised you are going to leave the house. What about the children?" I asked, trying to remind her who she is.

"Elisha the Second is at school and the other two are staying with Momma Elon for the afternoon. So I'm free." She opened her arms and held them out like to say, hands free.

"And the new diamond necklace?" I said. "Elisha gave it for your birthday?" I asked. I saw it sparkling on the satin. In fact it was the *first thing* I saw once I opened the door and the rock and the sunlight from the garden connected.

"No," she replied coyly.

"Then what?" I asked, knowing it could only be from Elisha.

"I got it from Poppa," she said, "Sunday, on my birthday."

I paused but not on purpose. The necklace was pure and perfect, the grade of diamonds that only Poppa would deal in. I should have thought of him first. And the diamond heart dangling was like oooh, wee, and bam. It couldn't be fucked with. I remembered Poppa had a gift box last Saturday in that little fucked up car. First I thought it was for me. Then I thought it was for dead Momma but ruled that out because Poppa would never leave a gift other than the bouquet of flowers at a grave site. Then when he didn't take it out of the car, I thought the gift was for some other bitch. In his penthouse, I had imagined the box was for Dulce. So the gift was in my mind while I was beating that bitch's ass. But she turned out to be the wrong one. All the while, it was a gift for Porsche, *which never even crossed my mind*. She removed her short-heeled satin ballerina shoes with the ribbons, same color as the shorts, crisscrossing up her pretty calves. She sat on the edge of my bed.

"You know we could have brought the masseuse here. I have a

spa room inside of my dance studio, set up for spa days," she said. "You would know that if you didn't reject my offer to personally escort you throughout the entire property," she reminded me.

"See, I know you don't really ever want to leave the property. *I like a change of scenery.* So I'm going to the Mandarin in Midtown," I declared.

"Yes, *we* are going," she said softly and certain.

"What's all the commotion outside?" I asked her, still tight about the diamond rock dangling from her diamond chain.

"Elisha's building me a birdhouse for Lovey."

"Lovey?"

"Yes, I named him Lovey, because I love him. Because I love you and I love that you know what I like and bought him just for me. I was gonna name him Love, but Lovey is prettier don't you think?" Porsche was smiling like the bird is the best gift she ever received. But in my mind, nothing can compare to that diamond heart. I loved that it is not flat and the edges are not a perfect heart shape. Instead it is jagged and imperfectly shaped. Still any and all could tell it's a heart. That feels like real life to me, a very precious and very personal gift for any girl to receive. But 99.9 percent of the females in the world from the youngest to the oldest will never receive anything similar or remotely like it. It's that rare.

"You're still staring at my necklace. Should I give it to you? I will if you want it. I was just happy that I finally got to spend a day with Poppa. It was my first birthday with him since I was six years young. He drove me in his really nice Rolls-Royce from his car company. We went to Long Island for an open house on a property," she said, and I purposely had my back to her. My face is in my shoe closet.

"And I ended up buying the house for us," she announced.

"For us?"

"Yes, surprise! It's Momma's house! Where we all lived before everything turned the wrong way," she said.

"*I'm not going to live in that house,*" I said, sounding a li'l disgusted.

"I am not either," she said firmly.

"Then why did you buy it?" I asked like *c'mon.*

"I made a promise to myself to get back all of Momma's things. If you come next door and upstairs, I can show you. Remember I asked you if you wanted to see all of the family photos? You said you didn't. But I knew one day you would. I hope the collection makes you feel good like it makes me feel good."

"I'm ready . . . ," I told her with my heels in my hand. When I opened the door, the Escalade was parked right out front, shielding us from the construction of the birdhouse. My father's son was leaning on the vehicle. I exhaled. His man was in his usual position front passenger side. He opened the back door. I got in first, then Porsche. As soon as my father's son, aka Ice Grill, aka Yung Santiago, pulled off, he pulled back to make a three-point turn toward the exit. Elisha stepped in front of the Escalade blocking it. Then he walked straight to the driver's side window. "Yo! Santiago! You trying to run away with my wife?" he joked. "Nah nah . . . never," my father's son replied.

"I'm going to the spa with Winter," Porsche called out sweetly.

"And leaving me here building a birdhouse," Elisha said and cool laughed.

"Do you want me to stay?" she asked him all lovey-dovey. Meanwhile I'm so disgusted I can feel it in my throat. *I hope she stays.*

"Nah, you have a nice day with your sister. But you know, man," he leaned into the young bastard's face, "only *my driver* can drive *my wife.* So pull back and park." Elisha got on his cell. Seconds later his Suburban was idling. Without words and a simple nod of his head,

Porsche jumped out to walk over to Elisha's vehicle. Her husband watched intently with obvious affection. "Follow the Suburban," he directed Yung Santiago. With only his eyes, Elisha signaled me to get out of the Escalade and join his wife. So I did. Seconds later I received a text from Elisha.

> "My wife loves the pet. He shitted up her salon and even pooped on my youngest son. Now I'm stuck here supervising the building of a birdhouse and a playground for the thoughtful 'gift' you gave. I peep your revenge."

On the massage table in a eucalyptus-scented room with everything relaxing, even some music that made us feel like we were in a forest, Porsche layed beside me. She wanted us to like *really be together*. I didn't really want the closeness or any talking at all. I had a trillion things to think of which I planned to unpack one by one in my mind until my mind was empty enough to really relax. Porsche pierced my vibe and asked, "How come you don't say anything to young Ricky?"

"What's there to say?"

"You know he loves you," she said.

"He doesn't even know me."

"Everybody knows you, Winter, and young Ricky is really smart and warmhearted. He's a loyal member of our family and besides he knows everybody on Poppa's family side, who we never got to know."

"Why bother saying shit to him? That's fake. I hate his mother for what she did to Momma."

"He hates her, too. I beg him not to. How can anyone hate their own mother who birthed them? But he says his mother was disloyal and deceitful and that's the shit he don't like. She accepted Poppa's proposal for them to get married in prison. That's the only way they could have conjugal visits. Poppa was so popular in population that he got approval for several inmates to attend his wedding. Dulce caused Poppa to lose face. On the day of the wedding, she had a change of mind and ran away and married some other dude. Currently they live in another country. Momma would've never done that," Porsche explained, but I was still stuck on him trying to marry that bitch at all.

"She ran away with some nigga and left both Poppa and her own son?" I asked cause I knew that he was born bout two years before Poppa got locked. That was my first encounter with the bitch, with the baby in her lap.

"Her new man didn't want him. Guess he looked too much like Poppa. And we all know the only thing her new man could've had over Poppa is nothing, except that Poppa was doing life and he was free. So Dulce contacted Midnight, told him she was leaving and if he wanted to he could 'go and get your man's son.' That's how she said it."

"That's why I hate that bitch. She broke up a family, got a portion of Poppa's wealth. Used it to live, and probably started fucking the next man, moving him around on Poppa's dollars."

"The diamond district please. I need to pick up something," I said to Elisha's driver after our spa date ended. Both him and my father's son, who escorted us back into the Suburban, jumped right on their cell phones. I love having two spies reporting in that I'm going off schedule. I'm a grown woman, who people expect to stick exclusively to some itinerary, ridiculous.

"Ms. Immanuel, you'll have to remain in the car," Elisha's driver said once we were seated.

"I know, Elisha just texted me," she replied. Right then my phone buzzed. Elisha texted "Go in with Santiago."

There was plenty murmuring when we walked into the jeweler's showroom on 47th between Fifth and Sixth Avenue. I know the exact counter I'm heading over to, yet other jewelers try to catch my attention. Besides there's a gang of niggas gathered at separate counters, even the counter across from mine. It feels good to me, young niggas getting money, able to spend major paper on some sparklers without it bankrupting them. At first they was just customers all looking down at the diamond spread. When we breezed by, all of them looked up. Guess they got caught up in my scent. Yung Santiago is directly behind me, and I see now his man is posted by the main door.

"Miss Winter Santiaga," the excited jeweler said with a foreign accent. I prefer if he wouldn't call out my name, drawing attention on to me.

"That's me," I said. "You got it ready?" I asked.

"Of course," he said and went into a little drawer and pulled out a velvet pouch. He spilled the diamonds into the palm of his hand and laid it out on a velvet placemat.

"Let me check your loupe," I told him.

"Oh you are very doubtful . . . ," he said. "You had the diamonds certified just last week," he said.

"Yeah, at the appraiser down the block. How do I know he's not your cousin? He's wearing the same outfit," I joked. But really I am not joking. He handed me the loupe. I put it on my eye like an expert, the way Santiaga taught me to do when I was a young girl going with him to Jeweler Khan.

"Do you know what you are looking at?" the jeweler asked me.

"Just making sure they're clean and authentic and that none of your workmen deceived you and switched the rocks I had already selected," I said smiling as I removed the loupe and placed it in his palm.

"I love it! I love it. Now pay me!" He laughed but of course he was not joking either.

Right outside of the jeweler market, some niggas that left before we did were standing around. Yung Santiago stepped out first and kept me tightly behind him.

"Yo, Yo, let me holla at you a minute," one of them niggas said.

"Easy YSL got the blicky," his man warned him.

"We got our blickies, too," the first one said. Then my father's son's man stepped up behind me guarding. Now I'm sandwiched between them.

"By the time you get to your car to get em, it will be too late," Young Ricky threatened him. "Get in the car," he told us.

"Yo, Winter, you made a record with my man. That shit is fire!" one called out. Just as I stopped to say something, Young Ricky's man grabbed me by the waist and pushed me forward. I leaped up and got in the truck shielded by him. He slid right beside me in the back seat. He shut the door and pushed me down, I guess so that I could not be seen by them dudes. My father's son jumped in the driver's seat. I'm thinking how F.K.R. this rap nigga hustled me into a rhyme of self-introduction then flipped into a joint and played it for more niggas to listen to in twenty-four hours. I might have underestimated the young nigga.

Santiago pulled off with a force, as he said to me, "When I tell you to get in the car, don't hesitate. Get in the car." I didn't say nuthin back.

"You made a record?" his man asked me.

"Yeah I did a collab with F.K.R. Mutha . . . ," I said and I was cracking up inside of myself. I knew nobody never heard of this dude.

"That nigga's nice. Crazy flow, plenty paper. He's independent. Blew up on YouTube."

While I was lying low in the backseat, I googled F.K.R. Mutha for the first time. I had purposely avoided doing so before and after his so called listening party. I prefer the face-to-face newness and friction. I even had Ola, one of the Network's many stylists, research his sizes so that the gifts I selected and purchased for him would be a perfect fit. When I mentioned F.K.R. to her in the first place, she got instantly excited about him. I was surprised that she even ever heard of him. When I had not.

I sat up and googled "F.K.R. Mutha, Image." Caramel brown complexioned, carved and cut, lean and mean, solid male body beautiful without a face. The flick was from the neck down. Maybe it's the cover art for his music? I hope that's his body not filtered or photoshopped, cause ooh. Seared on his chest in rough and bold black letters are the words, SON OF A BITCH.

19
THE REUNION, SHOW #1

They set it up like an apartment in the projects although it was only a television and film studio.

"Isn't set design simply amazing," a Network rep said to me. I didn't say nothing back. What the fuck these Network people know about the projects besides nothing. Of course one of my used to be girls had to have put em up on the look. The chairs were cheap. The tables were wobbly. The kitchen was fucked up, down to props placing the dirty dishes they had in the staged sink. I guess my bitches think this is cute. I don't. Santiaga's project apartment, where I grew up for sixteen years, was laced. Every year it was upgraded in one way or another. If anyone was inside of our project apartment, they would automatically forget that they were in the projects. But of course, over time, no one could get to the inside of our place. Each year, fam and friends had less and less access. That's how it is when your pops is top hustler.

"So Winter, on today's shoot, it really is like a sort of reunion," a lady who introduced herself as Tally, our assistant producer, said.

"And to start off and break the ice, since you girls really haven't interacted since your release . . ." I cut my eyes at her like, *Bitch, how would you know?* She seemed to sense the tension and went about rephrasing her words more carefully. "Um, it really should be a fun-fun day! There's a deck of cards on the table and you girls are gonna play a game that will help the audience to get to know you all as the longtime friends that you are."

"Are we going live?" I asked her.

"Yes, the show will be streamed so anyone in the world can watch it live. The rest of the subscribers can catch it on the Network platform anytime after that. There is so much anticipation," she cheered and overemphasized. I thought of Elisha's words about "streams of revenue" that Kuntz would profit from. I'm not mad though, long as I get my million. I understand that a million dollars is like one hundred thousand dollars to Elisha. But, clearly it's a million dollars to me. It's his chump change. It's my setup money for Eight Bitches and the streams of revenue that we will create to show motherfuckers how the bottom becomes the top.

After the director called action, I had to use the knocker and wait for someone to open up the staged project door. I knocked. Asia opened it and threw herself onto me like a creature with eight arms. The rest of my girls were seated around in various positions. All eyes are on me. They're cheering really, like this Manhattan studio is actually Brooklyn and they were finally welcoming me back home. I'm thinking, *Look at these bitches gone Hollywood on this fake project set*, even though it looked precise. Simone sparked an L. I'm thinking, *Can we really do anything on stage even if it ain't presently legal in the real world?* Then I answered my own thought. *Bitch, someone shot you on location on camera. So what the fuck? Pull up and hit it.* So I did. Asia opened her handbag and pulled out a mayonnaise jar filled with the rum punch she used to make when we was teenaged young. I'm for keeping it real, but I really was cracking up at the idea of her bringing the Hellmann's jar on the global stage. Reese pulled out the red plastic cups, same like we used to use. So it's on. We smoking and drinking.

"We pose to play a card game," Zakia said.

"We posed to?" Reese cut Zakia a *shut the fuck up bitch* look. Guess they were supposed to make the card game that Tally the assistant producer had just told me about look natural. *Too late . . . ha ha*, I thought to myself.

"Look at these cards." Simone lifted the whole deck off the table. On the backside of each card is a *Bow Down* logo. It looks dope. Then I thought to myself, merchandising, Elisha had mentioned another stream of Kuntz's revenue, merchandising.

"Shuffle the deck now that you got your big hands all on it," Natalie said. Simone shot her a look and shuffled.

"Cut the deck since you all worried about it," Simone said to Natalie. Natalie cut the deck.

"Put it in the middle. We spose to pick a card and do whatever it says," Zakia said. Guess she didn't give a fuck that she had already blown up the spot and exposed to whomever was watching that this card game is a part of the show.

Simone plucked a card. "Share a funny memory about anyone in the game," she read her task aloud.

All my girls were scanning each other's face at the table, when Zakia pointed out to Simone, "You shuffled the cards. You weren't suppose to go first."

"I am first," Simone spit back. "Yo! Remember when Natalie's mom . . . ," Simone started saying with a wide smile on her face.

"Let's leave mothers out of the game," I said. "Cause if somebody

say anything about my moms, we gon throw hands," I said. Everybody except Simone and me laughed.

"You wanna make new rules? The game already started. Or do
we all have to change the rules, cause you the star of the show?"
Simone asked me, but really she was showing off to the girls and
more importantly to the global audience.

After a stupid staring contest between me and her, I said, "Go
'head. Play it however you wanna play it. Let's see what happens,"
with a threat tucked in it. I'm in my thought now, wondering if
the producer had done what Kuntz had agreed on, told my girls
that there was a budget cut and only one of them could stay on the
show?

"I remember when Natalie's mom got beat the fuck up by one
of her mens . . ." Simone chuckled. "Natalie jumped in to help her
moms out. When Natalie knifed the nigga in the ass, her moms
punched *her in the face*! Nat showed up at my house with not one,
but two black eyes. She was so pissed at her moms, she slept on
my couch for a whole week without saying how her face got broke
up like dat. I found out the story after her swelling went down
and there was no more blood in her eyes." Simone leaned back and
pushed the deck to Reese to pluck a card.

Reese said to Simone, "How the fuck was that a funny story?
You're supposed to play by the rules and answer the actual question
on the card or do whatever the card says to do. That wasn't funny.
You should get a penalty."

"You should get a penalty," Simone mimicked Reese and said,
"Y'all all prissy now that we on television. I'm da realest." Simone
posed up.

Reese plucked her card and read aloud, "Name something that
you would never do." She looked around, for about two nervous

seconds. "I would, uh, I would never let a nigga fuck me in the ass," Reese blurted out.

"Bitch, you lying," Natalie blurted out.

"That's facts and I never did," Reese defended.

"Oh please . . ." Natalie puffed out a weed stream.

"You just think I am lying cause you a nasty bitch who will do any goddamn thing," Reese said.

"This is a getting-to-know-you game we playing. Why y'all saying only fucked up things?" Asia asked.

"Every bitch at this table is nasty," Natalie spit back, then shot a look my way, her eyes landing on my bright white wifebeater tee that rode nicely over my bare pretty titties and featured the word UNIQUE in bold gold letters. She must still be mad that me and her ain't the same. She can't reach my level and everybody knows it.

"But you the nastiest!" Reese said. "That's the difference. There's some things some of us would never do. But *you do anything*. And I wouldn't've said shit about your nasty little ass if you didn't comment on *my turn* when I was only talking about *myself*."

"What about you, Winter?" Simone asked me.

"That wasn't my card," I said straight-faced.

"And don't ask Winter nothing about fucking . . ." Asia jumped in. "She was locked up for fifteen years. She gets a do-over. She's the same as a virgin!" Asia claimed.

"A virgin!" Natalie screamed back and busted out laughing.

"Yeah I heard if a bitch don't fuck for ten or more years the skin grows back. She gets a do-over cherry," Asia said, then we all cracked up. Asia broke up the tension in the too cold studio, lessened the freeze by a few notches.

"We ain't seen Winter since her release day," Zakia said. "So really we don't know if she has a man or if she's intimate or not."

"You think somebody snuck into the hospital and fucked her?" Toshi asked everyone.

"Y'all all stupid. She was in a coma. Who gon fuck a girl who can't feel nothing, who won't throw her hips back and hump nothing, can't suck or lick nothing, and can't even moan when her G-spot get tugged?" Asia asked.

"As you can see she woke up! Once she's awake anything could've happened," Natalie said.

"Okay, okay, back on the topic," Reese said and pushed the deck to Zakia.

Zakia plucked a card and read aloud. "Tell one secret about yourself that you think no one else knows." She looked around the table. After a long pause, Zakia said, "That no one else knows ... Y'all know mostly everything about me. I'm pretty obvious," she added.

"Answer the question!" Natalie barked on her hard.

"Um, okay, okay ... I ah ... think about killing myself every day, so I'm on meds. The meds make me feel worser. I'm glad our clique stayed together through thick and thin. Being with y'all, and even on this reality show, is the only thing that makes my daughter look up to me. So I push through." The room went silent.

Simone broke the silence by clapping. "That was good. You tryna win the game *and* one of those weird dickless Oscar statues. I respect that," Simone said. Now each of us is looking at Simone like, *shut the fuck up.* "Whatever, man. I think people who want to kill themselves, kill themselves. People who talk about killing themselves are looking for some type of sympathy or reward. We Brooklyn chicks. We don't do suicide. We taking it from whoever's making it. We merck whoever gets in the way of the money flow," Simone said with full confidence.

"We what ...?" Toshi asked Simone. "Cause I ain't no murderer.

If a bitch is from Brooklyn, that doesn't mean she's the type of chick that could kill someone."

"Are you that type?" Zakia asked Simone. Simone gave her an *open your mouth again and I'll kill you for you* look.

Zakia said, "One of the things that makes me wanna leave this world is having to live side by side with a bunch of overdoers. I think Brooklyn is more about being cool than killing somebody. And I think a lot of problems could be solved if the overdoers didn't outnumber us regular people who only want peace."

"You never answered Zakia's question," Toshi said to Simone. "Are you the type of bitch who would murder a person?" Toshi gave her a look that if the camera caught it close up, we are moving closer to the secret of who murdered me. The fact is I did flat-line and was declared dead before being revived and falling into a coma. That means that I was dead even if it was for seconds or for minutes.

"Like Winter said a few minutes ago, that wasn't my card. You don't get to ask me any questions that's not on my card. That's the game," Simone explained to Toshi.

"Yeah but we are allowed to discuss each card between ourselves, remember that?" Reese said.

Zakia pushed the deck to Toshi. Toshi was still deadpan staring at Simone. She plucked her card and read it aloud. "Name something that you would like to do but never did." Toshi's anger broke and she smiled, thinking. "I wish I could be Winter for a year. No, that's too long, for a few months. No, that's too long, too. I'd be happy if I could live her lifestyle for one week," Toshi said then added, "That's facts."

"Which thing?" I asked Toshi swiftly. "What part of my life would you like to have lived? The fifteen years, cause I did more time than everyone at this table. Or would you like to live in the part where my father, my favorite person in the world, got locked up and served seventeen years? Seventeen years I never saw him except at my mother's funeral," I said and the room went back to freeze.

I'm not emotional. I'm strategic. I didn't like the global audience getting the idea that I'm some pampered princess. I was at one point, but I took my knocks like a real street bitch should.

"There she go showing off because she has a father," Simone said then smirked. I purposely igged her. She gon end up catching herself in my trap.

"True dat," Toshi said. "I always wanted to be you back when your father would throw you those big birthday parties at fly hotels and ballrooms and even the big-ass block party on the block. So that's my answer. I'd like to be you for one week, from way back when your father made everybody bow down to you as princess of the hood."

Reese and Zakia and even Natalie and Asia started clapping like they vibe with what Toshi put out. Toshi pushed the deck of cards to Natalie and she read aloud.

"Tell one secret about someone else that you think only you and that person know." Natalie pushed the cards back. "Who wrote these fucking questions?" she asked.

"It doesn't matter who wrote them. The cards were shuffled and you cut them right in front of our eyes," Asia said. "Now answer the question, Nat," Asia ordered.

Natalie looked around the table with gloating eyes and a gloating smile. I know Natalie thinks she knows every little thing about every person in the world. But the part of the question she plucked, that said for her to tell something that *only she and that person know*, was the problem here. Natalie runs her mouth so much and tells everybody's business to whoever will listen because that's how she builds her clout. "Okay, well the time that Simone talked about where my moms was a victim of domestic violence and I ended up getting two black eyes . . . the part that Simone left out . . . ," Natalie said, staring at Simone. Simone covered her eyes with her left hand. That was unusual. Simone doesn't get embarrassed or shy. She embarrasses everyone else. Natalie then blurted out, "Simone tried to fuck me on my last night sleeping on her couch. She came out with a strap-on with a big long rubber dick, like *she the man!*" Natalie accused.

Reese fell out her chair. Toshi helped her up. Everybody else cracked up except for Simone, who was now covering her face with both her hands. "So I might be the nastiest bitch at the table . . ." Natalie stood up posing. "But there *are* a few things I won't do." Everybody laughed.

"You should've let me fuck you with my rubber dick. Then you wouldn't of had to have sixteen abortions!" Simone stood up and spoke through a threatening grimace. Natalie jumped across the table and bitch slapped Simone. Me, Toshi, Reese, Zakia, and Asia all jumped back, the cheap legs of the wooden chairs scraping the floor and making scrape sounds. The cards fell onto the floor. Simone punched Natalie in her stomach. "My bad, Nat, you right . . . it was eighteen abortions not sixteen." Them two fought brutally, but Natalie is short and Simone isn't. Simone's hands are heavy and Natalie's aren't. I know. Simone has longer reach and harder impact. She's a fighting beast. Tally, the assistant producer, never showed up to stop the swinging. Neither did production security. No one else did either. Simone's face was scratched and bleeding. Natalie coughed and a li'l blood came up which she spit onto the studio floor. That's when me and Reese stepped in to separate and hold back both of them and break up the battle. Then Toshi and Asia helped also. Reese was holding back Simone, who actually couldn't be held back unless she wanted the fight to stop herself. "Natalie, watch your back," Simone said stupidly for the whole world to overhear.

"Shut the fuck up," Natalie spit back.

"I didn't get my turn," Asia called out delightfully as if the rumble never occurred.

"But the cards ain't right no more," Zakia said, picking the deck up from the floor.

"Just shuffle and cut em. Winter didn't pluck a card yet. Let's hear what she has to say since she ain't really been saying shit," Simone said with her hair all tossed to one side, looking like a pirate after a gang war.

"It's my turn anyway," Asia said, then plucked a card while saying, "I hope I get a happy card." Then she read aloud. "If you could have sex with one celebrity from anywhere in the whole wide world, who would it be?" Asia was wiggling in her chair and super-excited. She always been the most boy crazy one in our crew. When we was young she was the only fat girl we let roll with us. We protected her. She loved it. At thirteen, bam! Fat gone, tiny waist, crazy curves, thick thighs, and her real pretty face that had been buried got revealed.

"Elisha Immanuel!" she screamed like she couldn't help herself, then turned and looked at me like *Sorry, Winter!* Everyone laughed, even Simone. I just smiled a little. I know she's never ever gonna get it. Asia pushed the deck to me. I plucked a card.

"Cut," the director called out.

"Oh that's bullshit," Simone said. "We all answered these ridiculous questions and now y'all say cut right before Winter's turn? It's rigged," she added. I was thinking Simone must really not care if she gets picked to be the one friend of mine to remain on the show. Either she had no idea that that's the setup, or she was incapable of restraining herself and strategizing so that she could keep earning more paper than she was gonna get from anywhere else without wearing her ski mask, toting her 22, and risking her freedom or her life.

"Gather up, girls," Tally said as she approached us. We were already gathered. "Simone, I am sorry if you think today's show was rigged. The truth is, if you and Natalie had not fought each other, Winter would have gotten her turn to answer her question. This is a business. We are on the clock and only allotted a very specific amount of minutes. The good news is, tomorrow, you all will answer the questions from the audience that will stream in live," she explained. Simone and Natalie were both still salty but not running their mouths.

"And while we are all here in the same room, I'd like to explain that due to Network budget constraints, only one of you girls will be cast as a full-time member of *Bow Down*. That doesn't include Winter, of course, since the show is built around her."

Now all of my girls are staring at me like I am the villain. I guess I am. Meanwhile I'm tight because the Network was supposed to inform them of this from the jump, back when I first came up with this idea in Kuntz's office. That was the only way they wouldn't suspect me of getting rid of them. So I put on my acting skills, even though I'm not no actress.

"How come the Network did not tell us about this decision before our first show?" I spoke up to the producer, pretending that this was my first time hearing it.

"Great question, Winter!" the producer said.

"Great question, Winter!" Simone mimicked her.

"We really designed this first show to be very organic. We had no way of knowing who would work best on camera beside Winter because in season 1 of *Bow Down*, Winter was in a coma, and then in recovery until the grand finale. As a consequence, we were uncertain as to what is the status of each of your individual relationships with Winter. Thus the *getting to know you, walk down memory lane* card game. And, sorry, time's up. This set will be broken down now and another show will be utilizing this studio space."

As I exited the studio with my father's son, I could hear my ex-bitches talking. They wanted me to hear. "It's a ass-kissing contest. I know all of y'all gon do it, too," Simone said.

"If you weren't stupid you would kiss Winter's ass, too," Asia said.

"I don't think it's about ass kissing," Reese said. "Its just a job and our job is to make Winter look good," Reese further explained.

"Same thing," Toshi stated.

"I don't know what you all could be thinking about, but we all got new apartments from season 1. It's been hard enough maintaining through the summer until season 2 starts in September. How we gon pay our rent if only one of us gets to stay on? I already know they're not picking me," Zakia said.

"Do you think that self-pity works?" Simone asked her. "How the fuck do you know that they're not gonna pick you?" Simone challenged Zakia.

"Cause I just know it," Zakia said.

20
THE FRIENDLY COMPETITION, SHOW #2

The look in their eyes was different when I took my chair on set for show number 2. It was like each of them was less furious, less bold, and less comfortable. I'm thinking, *That's right, yesterday was nothing. I'm waiting for each of you to betray one another the way all of y'all betrayed me.* The location and the set for this shoot was also different. Gone were the projects; the ugly chairs and broke-down kitchen and the deck of cards. Now it's high-tech and fancy seating. We can see the screen where the viewer comments are posted, as well as their questions.

"Is there anything else we should know before we get started today?" Simone asked Tally.

"Well on our *Bow Down* page, fans of the show are voting on who their favorite girl is on the show, as well as who *they choose* as Winter's best friend. It is possible that the two don't go together."

"*Who they choose* as her best friend!!" Natalie said.

"Is that it?" Simone asked.

"Yes, aside from the fact that each of you has a bottle and a glass on your high table. Feel free to pour yourself a drink."

"Rémy Martin Louis XIII!" Simone said, as she walked over and hailed up the bottle. "I thought y'all had budget constraints? You could of got one bottle of Paul Masson Brandy for way less than twenty dollars. You could've spent less than a hundred dollars for Paul Masson and used the twenty-four thousand dollars you spent for six bottles of Rémy Louis to pay for two cast members to stay on instead of one," Simone criticized in her most possibly polite voice and tone. She's correct about the numbers. She's a career thief and she knows how much she could get for the six bottles of Rémy even on the black market.

"The bottles were donated and we are featuring them on today's show. You are under no obligation to drink," Tally said. Now I'm thinking, *yeah, there goes one of those endorsements or product placement deals that Elisha mentioned.* The producer was saying donated, because she probably knows we don't know the business. But, now I do know.

"Cast, take your marks," the director called out. Somebody from props appeared and took the bottle from Simone and placed it back on the table she took it from. We all went and sat on our seats, which had our names on the stool top. "Quiet on the set. Action!" the director called out, and the girls instantly all faced the cameras and flashed forced smiles.

Most of the initial comments were fans who adored me and wanted to know about and compliment either my "amazing recovery," my hair, my look, even my legs and thighs. I realized they could see each of us full body today, as we each had our shoes positioned on the lower level of our bar stools. I laughed because if you were watching, you could see the status difference between each of us by simply looking at what shoes we are wearing. Today my feet are laying in Jimmy Choos.

The first real question was crazy. "Winter, how did it feel to get shot?"

"Shocking, cause I could hear the gunshots. Suddenly, I realized that it was me who took the hit. Honestly, I didn't feel any pain at all. I just knew that I was dead," I said and the amount of comments and questions after that tripled and sped up onto the screen. Also the silence in the studio was very loud and unusual.

"Probably it was more painful for us, her friends. We were all there. It hurted a lot," Simone said. And I was like . . . *if I had a hammer . . . I'd bang that bitch in her head.*

"But there was a snowstorm that day. So we didn't really get a chance to see it, even though we were there," Reese said.

The next question on our screen was, "Winter, now that you are in the celebrity world, is there any celebrity you're currently dating or looking to date?"

"Not exactly, but I hear there's a lineup of celebrity dudes and athletes who want to date me," I said then giggled. Then I placed one pretty finger on today's tight tee that read STRICTLY DICKLY.

"Winter, what do you want in a man?" was the next question.

"The man she wants doesn't exist," Toshi blurted out.

"He exist! She just couldn't pull him," Natalie said, her words dropping out of her mouth without even thinking about the stakes, it seemed. But she knew and knows how crazy I was and am over Midnight, and somehow it was as if the fact that I couldn't pull him made her feel better about herself.

"None of us could pull him," Asia jumped in and said.

"Maybe he was undercover," Simone poked.

"Like you!" Natalie blurted out. The director, off-screen, pointed at me that I should answer the question since it was directed at me.

"The man I will have in my future should be unpredictable,

unforgettable, adventurous, and unregrettable" was the true description of what I am craving.

"See I told y'all! Y'all know a man like that don't exist," Toshi
said.

"Yeah, cause he could be unpredictable because you couldn't
predict that he was gonna steal your rent money or rape your daughter," Zakia said, moving the energy in the room to a darker place.
"That also would make him unforgettable, because you couldn't get
the shit he did off of your mind for even one second and then you
have to take meds to try and forget and that medicine would make
you feel even worser," Zakia added.

"And he could be regettable because he's the adventurous type
in the way that he's fucking you and three other chicks on the same
block or in the same building or on the same floor and you really
liked him," Natalie said.

"Yeah and ask any girl if she regrets any of her exes. She'll be
like yeah, 'all of them,'" Reese added her opinion.

"So what y'all saying?" I said seated upright and gesturing with
my hands. "You girls got no more love for men? Winter Santiaga is
strictly dickly," I announced as I leaned back and crossed my legs. "I
can please a man and he can please me, too. When I find that right
one, he'll put a rock on my finger and his heart . . . in my hands," I
said, cupping my hands together, really so the audience could throw
some respect on my dope-ass manicure. I'm strategic.

"Winter don't know. She was locked up for too long. It's war out
here between niggas and bitches," Reese said.

"That's because the new niggas are bitches, and the new bitches
are the niggas. Shit switched up on us when we were on lock," Natalie announced dramatically.

"So don't get your hopes up too high," Zakia said. "That's really when you fall hard," she added.

"Winter, do you feel afraid because the person who shot you never got caught?" I looked on the screen. The person who was asking this question was the same name who asked me how does it feel to get shot.

"Bitch, would you be afraid if someone aimed a 357 at your head and pulled the trigger?" Natalie asked staring straight in the camera grimacing at whoever sent in the question, as though she was protecting me.

"Was it a 357?" Reese asked Natalie.

Then Simone cut her eyes at Reese.

"I think a bitch should be fearless even if she been through some shit. That's how we grew up in the hood. Even though people got beat down or shot up, we still had to walk on our streets, sit out on our benches, and live our lives in the same spot where the chalk outlines where the body dropped," I said.

"Oh she's going deep," Zakia said, and then the comments and questions tripled to the third power.

"True dat," Natalie jumped in and said, "A bitch should be fear-less but everybody out there should know not to come at Winter Santiaga cause she do got bodyguards and tight security." Natalie said it like she was on my side, but I know she's really trying to blow me up like I'm a fake lying-coward bitch who can't go anywhere without guards.

"Winter always had security. Her father ran the whole hood and she had the most family in the hood," Toshi said.

"Winter, who and what's on your playlist?" was the next ques-tion. I felt stuck. Truthfully I only listen to the top performers in hip-hop from *my era* at sixteen years young. But, I couldn't say that. It would make me seem old. So I said, "F.K.R. Mutha . . ." without thinking. I hope they do not ask me what song. I never listened to even one of his tracks. I just found out he is a current multi-platinum underground artist. My girls were looking all blank-faced like, *Who? Who? Who?* On the screen the topic flipped to F.K.R. Mutha, and the next question was, "Which track?"

"The track I did with him just the other night at his studio. Wait to y'all hear it!" I said gleefully.

"Don't tell me you into the music business now? What's next?" Toshi asked.

The next on-screen question was "Winter, why do you think God brought you back from the dead?" Zakia, who was the first one to pop her bottle, stood up and walked over and poured me a drink. I needed one. The question shook my soul. I don't want to talk about God or religion in public. When I first got home from the hospital, I would say a prayer each morning and each night. That lasted about two weeks. Once I got in the work rhythm and the schedule began stacking up, I had forgot all about it. But somehow, I felt within myself at that moment, if I didn't say what I know for sure, which I learned from my death experience, *which was real*, I'd go outside of this place and something horrible would happen to me, like a fatal car accident, a random shooting, a freak accident, like a scaffold collapsing right over my head, something horribly bad.

"I believe in one God," I answered. And held up one pretty finger. "I didn't always believe. When I got shot and flatlined, I had the awareness of God placed in me. It was more like the fear of God, put inside of a fearless bitch like me. Maybe the ONE brought me back from the dead just so I could announce and *admit that* to the whole world."

"Woah, she all brand-new," Simone said. "Y'all heard that!"

"Word!" Natalie said.

"Seems real though," Zakia said. "I can feel it," she added.

"Yesterday I said Winter is a do-over virgin. Today, Winter says she's born again!" Asia said clapping her hands together joyfully.

"No, *you* said that," I corrected Asia. I didn't like her trying to make me seem like I'm some holy rolling religious freak. Between the virginity and the born again comment, I'm thinking she's moving me further away from my fan base.

"Don't get me wrong, Winter, I'm all for it, your virginity, your new religion. You deserve it," Asia replied.

"See that's that ass kissing . . . ," Simone said under her breath while mic'd up.

"Do you think your friends know who shot you, since they were there?" We all had our eyeballs glued to the next question on the screen. I took some seconds to think and said, "Well, I don't know. But, if one of my friends knew who shot me and did not tell me who shot me, well then they would not really be friends would they? They would be fakes, just clout chasing and pretending," I said with a burning honesty.

They each reacted to my words without words but with awkward body language and avoiding eye contact with me at that point.

"If one of them knew and decided to tell me, *even now*, then she would definitely be my best friend, no matter what anybody else says." I threw all of them a "get out of jail free" bone. "Winter Santiaga, I'm that no-snitch bitch, so it's not even a police matter to me. *Still I want to know*," I said calmly and pleased with how my strategy was evolving.

"We all got investigated. So no, we don't know who shot Winter, and yes, if we knew we would tell her," Reese lied and said.

"And it was a snowstorm day, we already said that, and that's what we told the police. We were having a snowball fight when she got shot. We were freezing cold that day and a li'l bored because it was our first day on set and there was a lot of waiting and waiting . . . ," Toshi added.

"Maybe the snowman you made shot her," Simone said laughing.

"That's not funny," Asia scolded her then flipped back into happy mode. "We wouldn't've been bored if we could tell who was who. You know like celebrity sightings and shit. But e-v-e-r-b-o-d-y was all North Face, Moncler, Jansport, Columbia up. I mean like hats and gloves, ski masks and scarves, and snowsuits and boots and shit," she laughed. "There was no way for none of us to tell who was regular invited guests like us, or who was in the VIP crowd or the camera crew or whatever."

"And some of us had our children up there even though we weren't supposed to bring them. Why would one of us shoot Winter while our kids were there?" Natalie asked, sticking her cheap shoe and her whole foot in her mouth.

"No one said one of you shot me," I swiftly said to Natalie, leaning forward.

"Well that's what it feels like," Reese said, trying to cover for Nat. "People are insinuating that it was one of us and that we are not your true friends even though every bitch in here grew up together with you and we even served some time together," Reese added.

"All I know is, I didn't shoot her. I would never shoot anybody. If you don't believe me, give me a lie detector test," Zakia said. The director yelled "CUT."

"Wow this was a great show. Very intense and super sensitive," Tally said. But none of us replied. We were all paused looking at each other even though we weren't on camera anymore. I'm sure they are now all mad at each other. Each one of them gave away something even if it was a tiny piece of guilt. My father's son, who was stage right the entire time, walked on set, not speaking to anyone else. "Let's go." He linked arms with me. I didn't resist.

"She messing with young niggas now," Natalie observed.

"Young fine niggas," Asia said.

"My nigga is young, too. It's trending!" Toshi said.

"Yeah your nigga is young, but he's not fine and his teeth not diamond flooded," Reese pointed out.

"Ain't that the truth cause he's living offa you! It's more like you his mommy," Zakia said.

"You got so much to say, Zakia. You should just shut the fuck up and play the side like you used to always do," Reese barked on her.

"The competition got Zakia fighting *us* now. She tryna win," Simone said, and then I couldn't hear no more of their desperate off-camera comments.

"So it was your friends who set you up," Young Ricky said as he peered at me for a reaction, through his rearview mirror in the Escalade.

"Santiaga bought you this car?" I asked changing the subject purposely.

"No I bought it," he said in an even tone.

"You hustle?" I asked him.

"Nah. I'm a young businessman. Got my own company."

"Doing what?"

"Hood loans. Debt retrieval," he said.

"A loan shark." I made it plain. "Why dem niggas at the diamond district called you YSL? That's your top designer?" I asked him.

"Nah, just a street name aka Yung Santiago."

"And the L?" I asked, hating his half-ass brief replies.

"Loyal. That's my government middle name, so I threw it in there."

"Hmmm . . ." was the sound I made.

"I branched out. Most of my paper is in video games."

"Video games?" I repeated like is he fucking kidding me?

"A billion-dollar industry. Tournaments, and I do developing and coding. I can create and finance one for you. Your story's dynamic. You're the villain, the victim, and the hero. That's worldwide paper," he said in a serious tone.

I smirked. He didn't.

"The young generation figured out what y'all couldn't figga," he said like it was some riddle. "How to get rich before we turn eighteen. How to stay rich after we turn eighteen, and how to keep the fuck out of prison."

The same night, I am seated in silence bare butt on my stool scrolling on my phone. I get a call from "unknown caller." Most of my calls are labeled the exact same way, "unknown caller" or "scam likely." Normally I don't pick up, but . . .

"Oh, you picked up. You must have felt me," F.K.R. Mutha said.

"Don't exaggerate nigga," I said in my flirtacious voice. "How'd you get my math?" I asked him.

"Shit it was hard work," he said, laughing like a man. "Everybody I asked quoted me a price."

"A price, to get my number. That's crazy."

"Yeah like cash or favors or tickets or whatever."

"How much did you pay for me?" I asked him.

"I'm tight with my cash. I gave somebody one hour of my time for a meeting they been trying to have with me that I never had time for."

"A bitch like me knows that time is more valuable than cash. Maybe you would have been better off to slide her some paper."

"Who said it was a her?" he asked me.

"Oh it was a man who sold my number . . . Must've been a business man. That is possible. I'll probably be wracking my brain all night trying to figure out who is out here selling my digits." We both laughed.

"So what you calling for?" I asked him.

"First cause you wanted me to call you. You probably was staring at your phone waiting on me. That's why you picked up my call ain't that right?"

"I'll play along with your fantasy," I told him and laughed a little.

"I like that. A woman capable of cooperating."

"What's the other reason for your call?"

"Can we link this weekend? I hope so, before you blow up so large that you won't even speak to a nigga unless he's Leonardo DiCaprio."

"Leonardo DiCaprio! He's cool but not my style at all. Let's talk about *you nigga*. First of all, I'm working through the whole week and even the weekend, except for maybe Sunday." I'm making him taking me out easy on him. The bold black brand on his chest in the one image I saw doesn't seem like a tattoo or a photoshopped image, filter or artwork. It appears like the black letters were embossed into his skin by an extremely hot metal, like how a once wild beast, after a battle then capture, might be branded with intense high heat by its owner. SON OF A BITCH. I like that. Makes me want to pull up close on him, touch it and be sure that it's real.

"Aight, text me where to pick you up from on Sunday at eleven a.m."

"That early?"

"Yeah like eleven to eleven."

"Cool."

Soon as I hung up, I started picturing me and F.K.R. and my father's son or the new security team if they arrive by then, all going on a date. What a bunch of bullshit. I'll have to make my plan to shake security, him or them. I will.

21
BILLBOARD

By 6 a.m. I received a text about a schedule shift. Instead of heading to the studio, I am to go down to a brownstone in the Village for a photo shoot regarding my billboard appearance. Oddly the text is from Elisha'a office, not from the Network. So I phoned Elisha.

"Yes it's a go. Kuntz and I are on the same page on this one," Elisha said as soon as he picked up my call.

"What about show number three? I . . . ," I began saying and Elisha cut me off.

"It won't affect your contracted payment, counts as your third episode. Everything you need is there including hair and makeup, clothes, and accessories. This particular photographer is favored by Kuntz. He's only in New York for today. Tonight he flies out to Sweden. Do a great job. Times Square, this is the big one. My driver and my security will drive you down and remain parked outside since my wife will accompany you," he said and it sounded like an order.

*   *   *

"Your face is lovely, but we don't need it," Ulrik Olsson said to me. He is a tall, bright-blond-haired man with a solid fat-free carved physique, a too-tight T-shirt, white karate pants that only reach his ankles, and no socks, no shoes. He speaks with a strong I guess Swedish accent. I had to listen carefully or face the wrath of asking him to repeat himself. I am the star but he acts like he is the universe. "Send the hair and makeup girls away. We don't need it. All I need is you, no distractions." He ordered them out. Meanwhile, I'm thinking *he needs me without my face?* Porsche escorted the hair and makeup team out while speaking some overly polite words. But, of course, she remained. Ulrik looked at her and said, "Gorgeous, why are you still here? This is not your day."

"You're right. This is not my day but this is my sister who came out our same mother's womb," Porsche said and he laughed.

"Okay, gorgeous sister, say no more. Stay out of my way as though you are invisible." Then he swung his arms open like a magician who was actually about to make her disappear into thin air. Next he brought both of his palms together, then pushed them out forward. "You must not absorb any of the energy in the room or even a speck of the light." Porsche walked into the corner and sat comfortably on the floor of this all-white, extremely high-ceilinged room with nothing but a block of white marble in the center of the floor, a screen and the lights and umbrellas and Ulrik's cameras, and computer laptop.

"Undress," Ulrik said to me.

"What?" I said even though I heard him. His masculine, powerful voice was impossible to ignore. The look in his translucent blue eyes was not sexual. It was like his whole face was saying, *I am a professional! Are you a professional! If you are not, don't waste my time!* He pointed towards the bathroom. "Go in, undress completely, and shower. Do not towel yourself dry. Come out with the water jewels still sparkling on your skin," he said, and I had only ever heard Porsche describe water on skin that way. I looked at her. She smiled.

In the immaculate bathroom, I removed my clothes slowly. I was looking at myself in the mirror. My mind is flooded with thoughts. Why am I listening to this photographer? Is it because he speaks only in commands and leaves no space for options or thoughts? He wants me naked. Is he trying to do some porn move on me? How do I feel about being photographed naked? Naked without a face? Where the fuck is he going with this? Did Poppa and Elisha already know that *this* is the direction he would give? Of course they don't. Elisha had said hair, makeup, and wardrobe would be here for me. How come neither of them showed up for such a big shoot that the Network dropped such a big bag on, to feature me? Then I tried to erase all of my thoughts. I got in the shower, first a warm downpour and then shifted to cold. Now I'm standing in the bathroom in a light puddle. *Fuck it*, I told myself. Maybe if I do a naked billboard, it's better than doing a billboard wearing the top designers, who didn't give me a penny or a dime to advertise their brand. *Yeah, fuck it.* Maybe a fashion brand placement fee was paid out to Kuntz instead of to me. Maybe if I do it naked, and it blows up, I can get all the designers in a bidding war to dress me. I laughed a little. I could hear the echo of my voice. I opened the door trembling from the cold water and the air-conditioning and big, wide open space, my nipples are raised up from the freeze. I walked out facing forward. Purposely avoiding eye contact with Porsche. "Stand on the marble platform," Ulrik said to me, like my nakedness was nothing. "Turn your back to me," he ordered. I gladly did that. "Now squat," he commanded while he had a huge camera pressed against his face, and the camera clicking away, only photos of my backside.

"Sit on your knees," he ordered me. I sat. "Perfect. Imagine you are a statue in that position. You have a magnificent back!" He's clicking away. "You! Gorgeous sister. Pick up the spray bottle and come," he instructed Porsche. She brought it over without any back talk. "Spray her. Refresh the moisture. She should glisten like a newborn. I saw this in my dream," he said oddly. Porsche began spraying me from my neck down, until he yelled, "Enough!" After he said that, she took off her big diamond rugged heart, hanging on her 54-inch sparkling thin diamond chain, and placed it not on my front, but on the bare skin of my back, the heart-shaped blue diamond dangling right over the split in my ass. "Orgasmic!" he exhaled. "She is like a newborn baby but better."

"She's a rich newborn baby," Porsche said. "Born royal," she added.

Ulrik's camera began clicking like crazy. So fast I lost count of the number of photos he was shooting.

I was in my head. "The shoes," I said suddenly to Porsche.

"Even rich babies are not born wearing shoes," the photographer paused and scolded me. "You are both *interfering* with my vision." Porsche arrived with my shoes, the ones I designed and my shoemaker made. She slipped them on my feet while my feet were behind me. It was a bit awkward but it worked. I positioned myself nicely. "The shoes . . . ," Ulrik said. "Not red bottoms, Louis Vuittons or Louboutins. Not Chanel or Fendi or Choos. Stillettos with your autograph on the bottom, perfect. Now you have owned this session. You made it all yours!"

"Don't mention about the shoot to anybody. Can you do that for me, Porsche?" I asked her.

"The only person I would mention it to is Elisha and he usually already knows everything."

"Well if he doesn't ask, or even if he does, don't tell."

"Everybody's gonna see it anyway, Winter. It's your art. Your skin is a beautiful canvas. That's how I look at it."

In the Suburban, I removed the diamond necklace that no one who had ever seen it could ever forget. I placed it back in Porsche's palm. Then, she handed it back to me. "You can keep it. The whole world will see it as yours because you looked so dope wearing it on the sexy curve of your beautiful back."

On the inside I felt like my organs were boiling. Like how milk and lemon or oil and water don't really mix. But people throw them together anyway and wonder why their stomach is about to explode. It isn't just that I'm a little hungry and refused to eat anything before the photo shoot. It's the way Porsche's presence affects me. It's like my head knows to love and appreciate her. My heart rejects because somehow, her love is different even though we full blood related. She could give away her six-figure jewels like it was nothing. She pushed away all her fame like it is nothing. She gives all of her beauty to only one guy, like she couldn't care less how many hundreds of thousands of niggas sweat her and envy Elisha. It's almost like she somehow knows that everything she already has means that she had already won every competition, defeated every competitor, trumped all of her admirers and detractors and conquered the whole world. That irks me *the most*.

"I'ma hop out here. I have a meeting to attend before heading home," I told Porsche, then removed her necklace from my body and handed it back to her. She looked sad. "Who's going with you?" she said with a worry that irritates me.

"Your father's son. He's right behind us, look," I said to assure her.

*   *   *

"Take me to McDonald's, the one at Washington Square Park," I told Yung Santiago.

"That's where you want to eat?" he asked me.

"No, I got a business meeting in there with some females," I said in a serious tone. He laughed a little and pulled off. I know why he thinks it's funny. When Dutchess recommended that we meet at Micky Dee's I laughed, too. But she was like, "Winter all this money you earned is *your money*. You can't let the girls start off too high. Then they will think your money is their money. Let's feed em in small doses, make them prove themselves to you and the goals you have moving forward." I had liked the way she put it. So I flowed with the location. "I'm leaving my bags in here and going in," I told him and his man.

"We'll be right here. I'll give you fifteen before I come in and sit in the corner just in case," he said. I was glad he was being cool about it. I want to arrive alone.

Upside Down is pacing and smoking outside of the meeting spot. She looks the same as I remember her but everybody looks better outside of Department of Corrections rags. Her hair is half-blond, half-black. Her jewelry is braided strings and her accessory is three red bandanas. She's five-six, thin but sturdy, and her clothes are basically Walmart.

"Bitch! You know I can't sit still. What's this about a meeting? The other chicks are inside. I figured I'd get the jump on them since I know, ya know, you tagged me to do the dirty-dirty." She hugged me but her hug turned into a body search.

"Bitch, stop. I'm not holding, or bladed. I'm on some new shit. Some get-legit-money shit. You don't have to get dirty for me. Just shadow my movements. I get real bored without a certifiably crazy bitch around me." We both laughed.

"Yeah you saying that and okay I up for dat. But what about your friends? You gon need some work put in on them tramps. Most of dem should get dumped right in the dumpster."

"What you heard?" I asked her.

"What I heard? All seven of us watched your show today on Dutchess's phone. Them bitches was wilding out about the lie detector tests. The ones who took the test was all lying, I don't need no machine to figure that out." Then she made a face like she was asking and checking to see if I had seen the show and if I am stupid enough to have missed the fact that my ex-friends was guilty.

"Oh really," I said flatly . . . on purpose. "I didn't catch the show. I was working in another session," I said.

She leaned into my face and said in a passionate killer's whisper, "They obviously set your ass up on your release day. *That shit is fucked up*. We need to clean up and wipe them out," she said releasing a stream of Newport smoke.

"We got better shit to do with better benefits." I threw my arm around her and walked inside to my new crew of bitches.

22
DIVIDE TO CONQUER

"Use the key," Santiaga said as soon as I picked up the call. There was a pause. I'm thinking *what key?* But don't want to say that and sound stupid. So I'm thinking further.

"You left with it. Come back with it." He helped me out. He's talking about the key to the penthouse elevator. Yeah ... that's right, of course I have it.

"When?" I asked.

"ASAP, there's a lot of new business on the table. I could make all these decisions, but I think you should be aware before I confirm new contracts."

"Oh you want to hear my opinions," I asked a little joyfully.

"Of course, you're the artist. You are the face. None of the contracts will matter if you don't show up," he said seriously.

"You're right. That means I have final say. Does that include about my security?" I asked.

"No," he said solidly.

"Poppa, I ... ," I began saying.

"Face to face, less is more. Don't worry about nothing," he said and cut the call.

My show schedule update came in. The next day of shooting is in a studio at the Network building tomorrow at 10 a.m. I texted the info to Dutchess and Upside Down. Both of them will be on point. We will walk in together. Upside Down, who Dutchess required that she use her birth name for all business, will be introduced as Rosibel Guardado, some fucked up name she had from her home country, which she said is "El Salvador, the land of volcanoes." Dutchess told her being known as Upside Down worked in prison, but on the outside in legitimate business transactions, that name would work against our goals. "Everybody will see you coming and distrust you automatically."

I don't give a fuck what we call her. I know when she shows her face side by side with mine, along with bombshell Dutchess, my Brooklyn bitches *will know* I'm not fucking playing around. Upside Down is smart. Of course I wouldn't say I tapped her to do my dirty work. I know that her reputation, rap sheet, and insanity is written on her face, a caution and a warning to all bitches who know. I also know, when I feed a bitch good, she will in turn feed her own crew, and that's even plenty more niggas riding for me.

We walked into the green room, the waiting location before the shoot. Natalie and Asia were getting made up. Reese, Toshi, Zakia, and Simone were seated around. Zakia was nervously tapping her foot. Simone was staring and sizing up Dutchess. I could see the irises in her eyes go into rapid recall and recognition. When she looked at Upside Down she didn't need any time to recall. I could see the instant impact.

"Whassup?" I said breaking the silence. No one said nothing back.

"You don't usually come in our green room," Reese said.

"There's only one green room booked for all of us today," I responded.

"I wonder why," Reese said.

"They probably filming us right now," Zakia said.

Then Upside Down burst out laughing. "Oh you the crazy one that didn't take the lie detector test on the show yesterday."

"Who you calling crazy?" Toshi defended Zakia, but she don't know Upside Down.

"That crazy bitch right there. Yesterday on the show, she got in the room to take the lie detector test and bugged out talking bout she has claustrophobia and she was shaking and shit. I thought it was funny. I was like this bitch faking a breakdown!" Upside Down continued. Meanwhile Simone is eyeballing me. Natalie is watching me through the reflection in the mirror where she was seated having her makeup finished.

"I would take up for you, Zakia," Reese said. "But like I told you yesterday, if you wouldn't have suggested that *you* would take a lie detector test, *none* of us would have had to take it. You brought it up first. Like for no good reason!" Reese screamed and shamed Zakia.

"Yeah and then we all took the test but she didn't," Natalie said, piling more pressure on Zakia.

"I didn't. But, I also *didn't* shoot Winter!" Zakia pushed back.

"Oh so you saying they agreed to the test cause one of them shot Winter? But you didn't take the test because you didn't shoot Winter," Upside Down said throwing a curveball in the mix.

"No! That's not what I'm saying," Zakia raised her voice.

"Okay maybe you didn't shoot her . . . ," Upside Down said. "But you obviously *know who shot her*. Aha . . . that's why you refused to take the test. You're loyal to the shooter. But you not loyal to Winter." Upside Down grilled her.

"Are y'all coming on the show?" Natalie asked Dutchess and Upside Down, slickly and softly changing the subject.

"No, the Network ain't got the budget for no new cast members."

Simone finally spoke. "Isn't that right Winter?" she asked without looking at me.

"That's what they said," I answered.

"We have other business with Winter. We're not part of your thing." Dutchess said her first words in their presence.

"I *am* loyal to Winter," Zakia blurted out.

"Why not shut the fuck up, Zakia?" Reese checked her.

"Can a bitch who shot a bitch in her head on the day she got released from the joint, before she even got to have a private bath, a great meal, and a strong drink, call herself loyal?" Upside Down asked. "Even on death row, they give a prisoner a final meal of whatever he chooses before frying his ass in the chair till he shits it out," Upside Down narrated. "So do what your girl said and shut the fuck up!" Upside Down barked.

Tally opened the door. "Five minutes to time, girls!"

"Tally, you two-faced," Natalie said, her cosmetics all finished and she looked like a clown to me.

"Pardon me?" Tally said.

"Pardon me," Simone mimicked her.

"You got us all gassed yesterday talking about we were doing a photo shoot for a well-known fashion magazine. You sized us up and let us choose from the fashions *y'all never offered us before.* Then when we were all ready, you whipped out those papers for us to sign for the lie detector test that we didn't know nothing about."

"I have a job to do. And you guys did do the photo shoot. It was great."

"Yeah but you said if we didn't sign and take the test, we wouldn't be eligible for the fashion magazine shoot." Natalie went in on her.

"Well I gave all of you a choice. Since yesterday's show was about the lie detector test, if you refused to take it, I did say that you would lose your appearance fee for the day. After all, if you refuse to appear on the show, how can we still pay you?" Tally said and finger combed her hair nervously and bunched it all up in her fist. "Okay, that's it, two minutes on your mark, girls," she said and turned and rushed out.

"Fucking sneaky bitch," Natalie said after Tally was already gone.

"You shouldn't call Tally a bitch cause they probably filming us in this green room. Member they filmed us in the elevator and we didn't know it?" Zakia added. "They used it in commercials for this summer special," she said, and it was clear to me that she is watching everything and this gig is very urgent for her.

"All the more reason for everybody to shut the fuck up and watch what you say." Reese glared at Zakia. "Have a great show," Upside Down said as all of my used-to-be Brooklyn girls filed out of the green room to hit their marks.

The studio is freezing, way colder than the cold it was before. The set design is an outdoor snow scene. My girls are all shivering in their short sets and summer dresses. I'm rocking jeans, Air Force 1s, and a tight tee that I designed that has only one word on it, "GOLD," in gold metallic curvy capital lettering. Today my natural fingernails are French manicure with gold instead of white. My hair is two side buns, one on the left, one on the right, because today I am featuring my face, and a light trace of lip gloss with gold sparkling specks. I feel confident. There's only one piece of jewelry on me today. It's my short diamond chain with the platinum-and-diamond hourglass filled with the gold sand. I'm on my mark, which is off camera behind a door that leads to the stage. I have no idea what's about to happen next. I hear Tally's voice say, "Attorney Monica Brown is your point person today. Please follow her instructions and lead."

"Action!" the director called out.

"Welcome, ladies. Today we are going to do a reenactment to assist in our search for the truth. On the table to your right are hats and gloves, scarves and coats. Select the items that match the most what you were wearing on the day of the incident," I heard her say. I wish I could see the faces of my ex-friends. I can't. And there is nothing but silence and dead space for seconds, which I know is not good for television. Then I could hear feet moving.

"No, I had the red gloves," Zakia said.

"There's more than one pair of red gloves on the table," Toshi said.

"We spose to pick the pair that matches what we wore that day," Zakia reminded them. "Me and my daughter were the only ones of us who was wearing red gloves that day."

"Okay now which one of you can place the snowman in the exact position he was in on the day of the incident?" the lawyer lady asked.

"Me!" I heard Asia's voice answer. "Cause I did the most work on making the snowman. Me and my daughter," she bragged.

"Okay so the door to your left is the prison release door. Place the snowman in the position it was in, in relation to the prison release door," the lawyer instructed.

"My snowman was better than this one. This one is fake," Asia said as I could hear her lifting it.

"Was the snowman Asia and her friends made wearing a hat or gloves or scarf or anything?" the lawyer asked.

"Not really cause it was too cold for any of us to start undressing ourselves and giving our gloves and things to a snowman," Reese said.

"Yeah but I put my supersize fries container from McDonald's on the snowman's head as a hat. Y'all remember that!" Natalie said and laughed. But the other girls didn't laugh.

"And I drew on eyes and a mouth with the ketchup packets," Asia said.

"And I pushed a boiled egg in for a nose," Toshi said, then added, "And y'all got all tight talking bout we could've ate that egg on the way back cause its a long-ass drive back to Brooklyn. Then Asia pulled it out and said, 'Why fight about it? Somebody can still eat it.'"

"Okay, ladies, put on your thinking caps and walk over and place yourselves in the exact position that you were in when the shooting happened," the lawyer instructed.

"No that's not where you were. That's where I was," Zakia blurted out.

"Bitch, you on meds. You can't remember where you was at!" Natalie said and the girls starting laughing.

"I can remember more than you think I can," Zakia said and that shut everybody up for some seconds.

"Zakia is right. That is her spot. And Natalie, you was over here by me," Reese said.

"Okay the white plastic balls that you see scattered there in our studio are snow, use them to simulate how you made your snow-balls and who and where you threw them," the lawyer insisted and there was that quiet again before I could hear anything else.

"How can we remember all that?" I heard Natalie ask.

"I remember Natalie you threw a snowball at me and it almost hit my daughter. So I threw one right back at you," Zakia said.

"Well damn, Zakia, you act like your daughter is some li'l baby. Her grown ass was sixteen during the fight and she was making snowballs and throwing them, too."

"Oh see you remember!" Zakia caught Natalie. "So let's just get started so we can get this over with," Zakia said. I could hear the tussle and laughter and balls flying about in the studio. I received my signal and walked out through the door. As soon as I did, shots rang out, that were obviously M-80 firecrackers. But the sudden loud continuous boom of the fireworks shocked all of us.

"Freeze!" the lawyer called out. Zakia and Asia were both ducked down on the ground with their hands over their heads. Toshi and Reese were both still standing but turned away from the prison release door.

"Asia, what are you doing on the ground?" the lawyer asked. "Zakia, what are you doing on the ground? Reese and Toshi, where are you headed right now? Natalie, you are facing the prison door. Did you drop the gun or push it into your pocket?" the lawyer shockingly asked Natalie. "Simone, you are still standing facing the prison door. Did you see what Natalie did with the gun?"

"I didn't have no fucking gun," Natalie said.

"I was on the ground guarding my daughter," Zakia said.

"And *my daughter*, who is only eleven, was beneath me. I was protecting her," Asia said.

"We was running back in the direction of where our rental car was parked," Reese said, pointing out that it was her and Toshi.

"Natalie, did you see Simone with the gun?" the lawyer suddenly asked, but somehow it did not sound like a question.

"She didn't see me with no gun," Simone fired back before Natalie could answer anything.

"Who saw the red blood on the white snow? Who rushed over

to help Winter?" The lawyer was firing out questions before she even received replies.

"I saw it," Asia said. "But I didn't want my daughter to see it. So I covered up her eyes."

"Winter had plenty of help because the workers all ran forward and the ambulance was already parked up there on the set before she even stepped out of the prison door," Reese said. "We just wanted to get out of there," she explained.

"And we all made it back to the van but the wheels were stuck in the snow," Asia explained. "I was the one who was driving so I turned on the ignition and turned up the heat and told them to get out and dig out the wheels," she said, making sure everybody would know she was the hero of the scene.

"Did they help?" the lawyer asked Asia.

"All the adults dug out the wheels except for Simone cause she lost one of her gloves and said her fingers was too freezing. But I was like even though the rest of us still got our gloves, our fingers is freezing, too."

"Simone, where did you drop your glove?" the lawyer asked.

"I didn't really drop it," Simone said. "I was in the front passenger seat and I stuffed it beneath the seat and said I dropped it cause I just wanted to stay in the car by the heater," Simone said and all of the rest of them looked shocked. I guess it was new information.

"Simone, come close to me and show me the gloves that you selected off the table today which match the gloves that you were wearing on the day of the incident," the lawyer said authoritatively. Simone walked over like a young dude with swag.

"Which one did you stuff under the seat, your right-hand glove or your left-hand glove?" the lawyer asked her.

"What difference does it make?" Simone said.

"Answer the question," the lawyer persisted.

"The left-hand glove," Simone said confidently.

"Asia, when you returned the car to the rental agency, did you clean up and make sure there were no personal items left inside of the vehicle?"

"There wasn't. I cleaned it myself cause they was all going back to get ready for the party," she said and looked like she didn't mean to say that.

"What party?" the lawyer asked. Asia did not respond. "Were you ladies throwing a party after your good friend Miss Winter Santiaga was shot presumably dead?" the lawyer asked and she was dramatic about it. She had a disgusted look on her face. I was thinking damn they must have gave her a fat appearance fee because she's getting into it like she is my lawyer or friend and heartbroken for me. And all of my girls' reactions were written on their faces.

"Asia is the one who gave the party. I thought we should have canceled it. I said that. Y'all remember?" Zakia asked them.

"Ah bitch shut up. You was right at the party with the rest of us," Natalie said. I'm thinking she's so stupid. She just confirmed that they was all there celebrating on the night of the morning I got shot.

"So ladies we can conclude that Miss Winter Santiaga doesn't have one true friend among you? Is that right?" the lawyer asked all of them. I could see the camera panning the girls' faces.

"That's not how the hood works, lawyer lady," Asia said. "Winter is the one who paid for the party. She put me in charge. Even before we drove up to watch her prison release, the party was all set up. Winter bought the liquor and the food and even got me a new couch. I wouldn't have done all that work if I wasn't a true friend." Asia campaigned for herself.

"Asia is right. Niggas get shot in the hood every day. So we pour out a li'l liquor for our friends who get gunned down. It wasn't like a joyful celebration," Reese said.

"Yeah it's *our* way of mourning." Toshi added. The girls' faces shifted. It was as though they felt relieved showing the global viewing audience that the lawyer is not hood, and that is the problem here, *not them.*

"The police, from the upstate prison location . . . ," the lawyer began saying. When she said, "the police," everybody's eyes widened and sparked up. "The upstate police were kind enough to overnight us the box containing the items found at the scene of the crime as well as some key photos of a few of the items they could not release." The lawyer bombed them. "Let's take a look." The lawyer walked over to the table and opened a sealed brown box. The camera followed her. The first thing she pulled out was a red glove. Simone started laughing. "Look at that, Zakia, you said you and your daughter were the only ones wearing red gloves. And the police got the red gloves right there in that box."

Simone laughed and then added some more gas onto the fire. "You never said that you didn't get back in the van with *your* red gloves on, or maybe your daughter didn't get back in the van with *her* red gloves on."

"Simone, do you know that Zakia is the shooter? Did you witness her pulling the trigger?" the lawyer asked swiftly and passionately and Simone's laughter dried up.

"No. I'm just saying you pulled out a red glove. That eliminates all of the rest of us from suspicion because Zakia already admitted that she and her daughter were the only ones wearing the red gloves," Simone defended.

"That could be anybody's glove, like from the camera crew or

caterers or any of the workers," Zakia said, then pointed at each of
my Brooklyn chicks. "I said me and my daughter were the only ones
wearing red gloves between us, *Winter's VIP guests at the shoot*," she
clarified. "And leave my daughter out of it. Keep her name out of
your mouth! That's the limit for me," Zakia threatened, trembling.

"Let's remain calm. There are some other items in the box," the
lawyer said delightedly and pulled out one black glove.

"Look at that!" Zakia jumped up and shouted.

"Simone, let's compare the glove that you selected as a match for
the gloves you wore that day of the shooting incident and this black
glove in my hand." The lawyer held the gloves up side by side. The
glove from the police was in a plastic ziplock.

"They're similar. Would you ladies agree that these two gloves
are similar?" The lawyer held them up for the girls to see but really
for the close-up shot for the cameras. Nobody spoke or nodded.

"That could be anybody's glove," Simone said, hopping on
Zakia's previous defense and smiling like she's a nice person.

"Fortunately, we can run both of these gloves back through
forensics and do what obviously was not done at the scene of the
crime or during the investigation of this case since you ladies were
not considered persons of interest or suspects. If Zakia's or Simone's or any of you ladies' fingerprints match what is on either of
these gloves, and if there are any traces of gunpowder or blood . . ."
All the girls looked terrified. "I hope all of you understand that
this is not only about who pulled the trigger. It's about how many
of you may have conspired with the triggerman, so to speak, in a
conspiracy to commit murder. Conspiracy to do any crime is an
extreme criminal offense with dire consequences, should there be
a conviction," the lawyer said then raised up the black glove for all
to see the shredded hole in the fabric of one of the fingers. She

held her right hand up to show that the glove was a right-hand glove.

"Cut," the director of the show called out. However, the lawyer did not comply.

"We can take fingerprints right here today," the lawyer said to Tally and to the director. "Since all of you ladies have volunteered to be a part of this process . . . ," she continued.

"No, this is bullshit," Natalie said. "I'm not about to be finger-printed on a reality television show. We supposed to be having fun and y'all got us cooped up in this cold-ass studio like we guilty of something."

The lawyer turned and said to Tally, "All of these ladies are convicted felons so the police have their fingerprints on file."

"Winter is a convicted felon, too," Simone shouted.

"True, but she obviously did not shoot herself. Her victimization is recorded on camera. Her friends' actions are not on camera," the lawyer spit back furiously.

"Okay let's wrap it up. The director already called cut. See all you for the fifth show tomorrow. Keep checking your schedule for updates."

We ended up all waiting at the elevators. When the going down light switched on and the doors drew open, everybody was looking around like, who's getting in and who's not? So I stepped in. Dutchess, Upside Down, and Yung Santiago stepped in right behind me. Then, my ex-friends and cast members all pushed in on some *we ain't scared of shit*, Brooklyn-type energy. At first there was silence. Then Simone said, "I guess you ain't never coming back to the Brooklyn block. It's all fake studio projects and fake studio snowstorms, and fake studio investigations. *They must be paying you a whole lot of paper.* Now you scared of the real world *and* you scared of the hood."

"You left out fake friends." Upside Down was the only one from our crew who replied.

"Yeah you right. Once *any* friend is on the payroll, it's the same as being fake friends," Simone said, calling out Upside Down. Upside shifted and looked Simone dead in her eyes and said:

"You know what's not fake? How the Colombians machete a bitch's mouth out and leave her tongue dangling. But the M-13's are not so creative. They just chop a bitch's body into thirteen not so pretty pieces and feed it to the mutts."

23
THE FANS

It's a mob scene outside of the front door of the Network building. None of us knew why. All of us stopped walking right before funneling through the revolving doors. "Must be some type of a show," Natalie speculated.

"Those men with their backs to us are police officers," Zakia warned.

"Yeah but the boom mic, light umbrellas, and cameras are set up out there," Asia pointed out.

"It's definitely a show," Simone said.

The Network ground-floor reception area security arrived. "Good afternoon, Ms. Santiaga. It's your choice. The crowd is waiting for you. We can reroute you if you would prefer to avoid them," he offered. But Simone had just said in the elevator that I'm afraid of my friends and my hood. If I don't roll through even to face and greet my fans, her accusations of cowardice would be confirmed in front of my new crew and my ex-crew. Besides I'm not afraid of my escalating fame. It's exhausting, but it's what will make me a double-digit millionaire rich bitch.

"The Escalade is a straight shot," Yung Santiago assured me. "Open up the straight door," he told the reception security man. "We will cut down the middle. Follow me," he said as he grabbed my hand and held it. Dutchess walked close behind me and Upside Down behind her. My ex-girls just tagged onto the back. Security opened the straight door so we could file out without jamming in the revolver. The crowd began cheering. I waved with my free hand continuously like bitches in beauty pageants and princesses in parades do, and kept walking forward. I heard a commotion behind us. I looked back. Dutchess looked back. Upside looked back and we all saw the crowd swallow up my ex-girls and begin pushing them around with the weight of their numbers. "You fucking bitches! You tried to murder her! Lock them up! Lock them up! Lock them up!" the crowd chanted. Yung Santiago yanked me forward. Dutchess pressed her hand against my back pushing me forward and UD kept pace. Now we're in the Escalade. I wanted to watch, but YSL's man pulled off. Upside Down turned and sat on her seat on her knees cracking up at the last images of the police and Network security attempting crowd control. All I know is those Network cameras set up out there and random cell phones are still rolling.

"Where we headed?" Yung Santiago asked me.

"I hope today we get some grub," his man said.

"I'm down for that," Dutchess added.

"We gotta get to B&H. I'm gonna buy a camera for our new company. I'm tired of people filming me without paying me. I'ma make my own movie with footage of my lifestyle that no one else has, and sell it," I said.

"You could just use your cell phone," Santiago said. He held up his iPhone and said, "This little device does everything."

"So why they don't film the reality show with cell phones?" I asked. "I want a camera with the quality of the cameras the Network aims at me."

"They actually could film the show with cell phone cameras," he said. "But the old heads be stuck in their ways. Besides, when you got people making money one way, if you change the arrangement, and if it affects their profits and payday, then it's war," he said, sounding like my father.

"All of your business could be handled with higher quality short cuts. The shoes you designed could have been made with a 3D printer. Cut out the back and forth between you and the shoemaker."

"We still heading to B&H?" his man asked. It was the first time I saw Yung Santiago let him drive his whip. My cell phone rang. "MONEY CALL" stretched across my screen. I picked it up.

"Baby Girl," Dick Kuntz, Network CEO, said to me. "What's your location?" he asked.

"Why?"

"I need you to head over to New York Presbyterian Hospital on York Avenue."

"Hospital for what?" I asked. He laughed.

"I love the way you never know what's going on," he said. I didn't like the comment so I didn't say shit back. "There was a full-blown riot outside of the Network Complex. Your cast member Simone punched a fan in her face and really messed up her eye. She got arrested," he said.

"Arrested!" I reacted.

"Yes, her and your other cast member Reese stomped a couple of girls pretty bad. All three victims are in the hospital. I sent a camera team over there. Now I need you to show up to distinguish yourself from the violence. And one more thing, a big number of your fans were arrested, the ones who were not attacked by your cast."

"For what?"

"Disorderly conduct. Unlawful assembly, simple assault, disobeying police orders."

"This is number two then, of your special requests," I said coldly cause I'm cold.

"I don't think so," he said. "Since we will capture your hospital visit on camera, and you will be met by reporters and we will capture that as well. I think we will use our footage as show number five and air it tomorrow as the Saturday live show."

"Will that be enough content for an hour-long show?" I asked him.

"My super producers will do a super edit and the bomb is when you meet with Zakia after the hospital and reporters."

"Meet with her for what?"

"Your plan worked. She wants to make a deal. Tally told her she couldn't have a private meeting with you about the show. This is reality television and if you meet with our star . . ." He chuckled. "That's you. It has to be on film," he gloated.

"So if I agree to all of this, my Saturday shoot is canceled?" I asked, trying to conceal my excitement.

"You get a day off. Plus five of your cast members are locked up. Two are very serious charges. The other three got swept up in the melee. So, it works out perfectly."

"Okay so Monday Tuesday is show six and seven then it's a wrap. On Wednesday my numbers will show up," I said as a roundabout way of reminding him he's contracted to pay me my million at the conclusion of show 7.

"You got it, baby," he said and cut the call.

YSL's man was staring at me through the rearview, and six eyeballs were burning the sides of my face.

"Pull over. Dutchess, make sure Upside Down gets hooked up with everything she needs to be in business with us," I said as the driver was pulling over.

"I'll take it from here," YSL told his man and hopped out.

Dutchess and Upside Down jumped off as well. "Let me know if you need to use me for my offer," Upside Down said, reminding me that violence is the best response. "Clean house, all trash in the dumpster . . ." She laughed and they left.

"As quick as you can, head over to New York Presbyterian Hospital on York Avenue, east side," I told my father's son. I liked that he switched seats with his man, is now driving, didn't ask me no questions, just drove me there.

At the hospital the cameras greeted me at the emergency room entrance and followed me in. "Here she is, ladies," Tally said to the nurses who were all staring at me like I'm a goddess, instead of tending to their patients. There were even doctors passing through and stealing glimpses. I am smiling politely, and lying, "Nice to meet you. Nice to meet you." I'm touching hands, and "Thank you for your hard work," which is the sincere part.

"Miss Santiaga, we will escort you to your injured fans," one nurse said and led the way. One camera is in front of me and one is behind. As we make our way through the doors and down the corridor I noticed the number of people tagging along is steadily increasing. When the nurse stopped in the curtained off area where the fans must be, I turned to the entire group, but mostly the cameras, and said, "Let's respect the patient's privacy." Everyone except the camera crew fell back. I pulled the curtain. There was a teenaged girl in the first bed holding her ribs. At my arrival she had a painful look on and then she switched her facial expression to hide her hurt. "Oh my God, you came. I can't believe you came," she said and covered her eyes and began to sob. I wasn't sure if she was performing. *Is this real?* I asked myself. She lifted her shirt revealing black-and-blue smudges all around the left side of her rib cage. I gasped for dramatic effect. But I'm like, *Damn, Reese stomped her like that?* I'm thinking this girl must've called Reese a string of bitches or motherfuckers or spit in her face or something foul. But I swerved around those thoughts and asked, "Can I touch it?" She nodded yes and I extended my hand and felt it lightly with my fingers. "Will it heal?" I turned and asked the nurses. They all nodded yes. The teenager said, "It's no big deal compared to what they did to you." The girl drew the attention back to herself. "I'm going to heal and survive the way you did," she said and the nurses began clapping. "Cool. When you heal and survive call me. I'll get you tickets to *Bow Down* season 2, we can go back-to-school shopping together, and I'll treat you to lunch!" I offered. She screamed, "I feel better already! I can't believe you showed up. You're the realest! Winter, please dump those girls. They don't deserve you!" she said with an enthusiasm mixed with love and hate and hate.

Each of the three victims were over-the-top excited. The one who Simone punched couldn't express it the same way. She was in with the doctors. Her eye was fucked up. Simone is heavy-handed, I know. When she's mad, she's vicious.

"I don't forgive her. I won't forgive her. I will sue her and I hope you drop her ass from the show," she said as she held her head steady for the doctors to examine the severity of the damage and whether or not surgery was necessary.

"If someone from my show did this to you, I take full responsibility." I turned to the doctors and said, "Please give her the best care available, on me."

Tally appeared. "Winter, it's time to go."

"I won't forget you. Tally, please give all three girls my number," I said my exit line.

"Major decision here," the Network public relations manager said, when I arrived for the meeting with reporters, that I had agreed to with Kuntz. "We have the *New York Times* reporter promising to lead with your story in the Sunday *Times*, that's huge! Like global! Then I have *Eyewitness* local news offering to air live with you at 6 p.m. today, that's television so super-effective!" She's speaking like she's completely turned on by this shit.

"So what's the decision?" I asked her.

"Well the *Times* wants an exclusive and they have basically one hour before it's too late for them to get it into the Sunday paper . . . but they want us to waive the *Eyewitness News* interview for obvious reasons."

"Obvious reasons?" I repeated.

"Sure, yeah well, it's because they want to break the story and one-up the television stations."

"But if there was a riot at the Network and people got hurt, everybody already knows. So what sense does it make for them to request an exclusive? By Sunday it will all be old news." I said my true thoughts.

"The incident will definitely be televised on today's afternoon and evening news. However the exclusive and the thing that makes it all a super big deal is the *New York Times* gets an exclusive interview with you and television does not."

"Okay, if NYT is global, let's go global."

24
THE WITNESS

"Zakia, we could dead the cameras and just talk one-on-one," I said on camera. "We have known each other long enough to have a private conversation." I looked directly into her eyes.

"That's what I wanted at first. Just me and you, a private conversation. I didn't want to be known for what I'm about to say . . . ," she said sadly.

"Turn the cameras off," I said to the two cameramen.

"No don't. I need the appearance fee," she said. The cameras remained on. I was thinking fast about whether or not I should offer to pay her the appearance fee from my personal funds and have them shut the cameras off. But, I didn't want to be too eager, or seem even slightly like I'm overdoing and faking it.

"Is anyone forcing you? If so let me know. I'll fix the problem right away."

"No no no it's nothing like that," she said and I felt like now I had said and done enough not to look bad to my local or global viewing audience.

"I'm going to turn myself in," she said. I stepped back. I was

271

shocked by her words. What does she mean? *She's not the shooter.* Is she planning to take the fall for me getting shot?

"I already taped my confession at the Network. There's no turning back from it now. So I'm not here to get your permission or anything like that," Zakia said.

"Confession of what? Don't try and tell me . . ."

"No I would never aim a gun at anyone's head. Truth be told, I'm not the type to pull any trigger," she said. "I couldn't even do that to myself even though *I wanted to die so many times*," she added.

"Stop saying that, Zakia. Suicide is for suckers. I promise you. If you kill yourself, it's not a peaceful ending to a painful life. The pain will continue after death. I'm one hundred about that. Facts." I told her sincerely and passionately what I had learned from my own death experience that I don't discuss with any human being, but that I am completely sure of.

"So what's the confession about and why bother confessing to me?" I asked softly.

"I'm guilty because I know who shot you. I saw it with my own two eyes. I'm guilty because I went to the party even after we all thought you were dead. I didn't want to go, but I went. I'm guilty for holding it in for all of these months, and for playing dumb in the first investigation that the police did right after it happened. I'm guilty because I was more concerned about the money I could earn for being part of the show than anything else." She is crying silent tears now.

"I'm telling you and on camera because I want my daughter to know that I have not been an angel in this life, but I never murdered a person or even attacked a person. When I did crime it was just taking what other people earned and using credit cards that didn't belong to me. I went to prison for that. I paid for that. But I don't want to be known for being a part of a conspiracy to murder a girl who I look up to, who I think is so fly and so fortunate and so cool. And I don't think it's right the way the authorities group a whole gang of people together to be punished for a crime that only one person committed."

I stood up and hugged Zakia. In my ear she said, "I beg you to give my daughter a job in your new business. She young and pretty and good-hearted. If you give her a good job and a great experience, I promise I won't kill myself."

I whispered back in her ear while still embracing her, "That's blackmail, bitch!" then I pushed her away and we both laughed.

"I'll do that," I gave her my word.

It's late Friday night and I'm not at the club. I mean lounge. Like I was last Friday after an exhausting day. I can't really believe how much shit happened in just one week. That's why I'm in my lavish bathroom in my private villa, with the bathroom door locked just in case Porsche suddenly appears. I'm bout to pee on my early pregnancy test stick. I bought ten tests. Since I never know how many people, staff, security will follow me into the pharmacy when I make my personal purchases. This way, I always have a test on hand and it's only my business. I'm not expecting to be pregnant of course. That would be foul play. After the pink pill blacked me out, I'm not sure if some nigga fucked me or not. I am sure though that I damn sure don't want to be pregnant by some nigga I don't even know, whose face I couldn't even recognize. I am sure that if for some fucked up reason I am pregnant, I'm not going to abort the anonymous baby. So please, please, please . . . let it say negative. Otherwise I played myself and would be embarrassed in front of anyone and everyone, especially the child for who I would have no explanation whatsoever, and no father to raise and love her, the way I was raised by my father, thee Ricky Santiaga. I waited.

It's negative! Alhumdulillah . . . oh I haven't said that word in weeks. In fact I only said it once since I woke up from the coma I was in after my death experience, which led to my full recovery.

Now, I can feel relaxed as what Asia called the "born again virgin." Then a text came in under the name "My Sister's Man."

"Winter, here is the name of the doctor. Your appointment is on Sunday morning at eleven a.m. I already checked your schedule and you're open at that time. Afterwards let me know if you're comfortable with her or not."

I read his text twice. It fucked up my mellow mood. I don't want to see a psychiatrist because I already know there's nothing wrong with me. And why does this family continue to think that if there's nothing on my work schedule, it means I'm free. I'm not free on Sunday. I got a date with F.K.R. Mutha from 11 a.m. until 11 p.m. So, I turned on the shower. The sound of the water soothed me. Eventually I undressed and got beneath the downpour. I suds up my fingers and massaged my shoulders. I slid my fingers in the hidden spaces like beneath my 36D's. Soaping and sliding, sliding and rinsing, and soaping and sliding again. I remained wet for forty-five minutes while calmly concocting a plan.

Once I was beneath my cold sheets, loving the way they make my naked body feel, "PRETTY BITCH" called.

"Just checking, we still on for tomorrow night and where should we meet up?" she asked me.

"Yeah unless you are available tomorrow morning? I suddenly got a day off," I said.

"Morning, what do you have in mind?"

"Dress casual, wear kicks," I told her.

"Oh no. Are there gonna be some dudes chasing you and I'ma have to run, too? Hopefully no riots or shootouts or kidnappings!" She laughed like for a long time.

"What, you scared of me now?" I asked her.

"Bitch I'm not scared of you. It's the cartel or the Mafia or the Bloods or the Crips or the zombies or your ex-niggas hunting you down that's a little unsettling." She laughed again.

"Dress casual, pack a change of casual clothes and a few bottles of water in your car," I bossed.

"Yeah okay on one condition," she said. "You're going to have to eat some food. I'll pack a picnic basket," she added.

"A picnic basket! Just don't pack too much. We ain't a couple of fat bitches. And, when it's hot we don't need heavy salty foods to slow us down," I said.

"What about the money then?" she asked. Should I just stuff it in the picnic basket beneath the food?"

"Oh yeah I forgot about that."

"Wish I could forget about more than a quarter of a million dollars." She laughed.

"Leave it in a safe place, like wherever you had it locked all week. I'll get if from you tomorrow night once we about to part ways."

"Okay cool. Where we meeting up?"

"I'll text it to you."

"Copy dat," she said.

I hit up Dutchess to give her the business rundown. Also, to hear her business updates.

"McDonald's is interested in recruiting you for a nationwide TV commercial campaign," she said, and I can feel that she feels good about it. "I spoke to the rep. He saw the pics I posted of you in McDonald's and hit me up. I forwarded his information to Manager Santiaga."

"You posted the pics?"

"Yeah, after you told me to cop that movie camera, I thought about how smart you are. Since everybody is making money off of your image and actions, your team should be banking the most. You know McDonald's and Burger King be battling, burger wars . . ." she laughed. "McDonald's trying to snatch you up first."

Afterwards I texted my father's son to let him know what time to come for me early morning, to drive me to meet up with Pretty.

25
THRILL ME

Hot out and I love it. The sun is blazing. No pregnant clouds or signs of rainfall, perfect. I'm in an all white tennis shirt and white tennis skirt and no racket and no balls! Ha ha, I don't play tennis but I'll sport any badass outfit. On my pretty feet are red low-tops, Air Force 1s, a Nike–Louis Vuitton kick collaboration, fire! No jewels today on purpose and two ponytails, just because it's been a minute since I had em. Plus it keeps my hair out of my face. I got a bright white Fendi canvas bag riding on my backside with not much in it. Not carrying my usual ten-inch pile of paper. Just enough to do whatever I want to do today, a clean white facecloth, my sunglasses in the case, cell phone, wallet, and two blow pops just for fun. Yung Santiago picked up my emergency change-of-clothes shopping bag (cause you always gotta be ready for anything when you top bitch), and loaded it into the Escalade. His man was asleep in the shotgun position.

"Holland Tunnel," I told him.

"Got it."

*   *   *

"I'll get out right here," I said when we arrived. Pretty was leaning on a BMW SUV. "There go my ride." I jumped out real quick with everything in my hand and ran across the lane where his car could not maneuver. I did not look back. He knows it's my day off. I'm glad he didn't say nothing. That's what I need, a cool security who knows a bitch gotta breathe at some point.

She's dressed in a white linen Safari jacket-shirt and white linen shorts with camouflage Nikes. The arms of her sunglasses slid outside of her pocket.

"Good morning, bitch!" she said to me joyfully. "Get in!" she said as she got in. I walked around and dropped my change of clothes in her back seat.

"You really packed a picnic basket! Baseball bats and balls!" I said.

"I only need the bats to swing on whoever's chasing you today!" She laughed as she pulled off through the tunnel.

"Where are we going?" she asked.

"Weren't you supposed to ask me that before you got us stuck in a tunnel?"

"Why would you ask to meet at the Holland Tunnel if we weren't riding through it?" she said, making too much sense.

"Six Flags Great Adventure," I cheered. "New Jersey Turnpike to exit 7!"

"You really are a teenager!" she said.

"Better than being two old bitches," I said.

"We are both too young to be anybody's old bitches," she said with a seriousness.

"Play some music!" I demanded. She did. "What the fuck is this? I asked her.

"You don't know it. It's Maroon 5, come on!" she said and began nodding her head to the rhythm while driving. Maroon 5 flowed into a next thing I never heard.

"What is this?" I asked.

"It's Nirvana!" she screamed.

"What about hip-hop?" I asked trying to talk over the music. "You were all amped to go to the 50 Cent after party," I reminded her. She lowered the high volume of her music some.

"Yeah we got duped that night. That wasn't even the official after party. I wouldn't have made any strong business connects in there."

"Well then we weren't the only ones who got duped. The crowd was massive," I said not liking the idea of being part of any group anywhere who is getting played.

"Well there actually was a show inside. It was DMX and the Lox so that's still gonna draw a huge crowd. I think it was a shady promoter who threw confusion in the game to double up his money. Like he put out the rumor that 50 and them would show up there."

"So *you do like hip-hop?*" I asked, confirming that I don't have her all wrong.

"It depends on my mood." She dragged her words out in a funny expressive way which made me laugh. Then eased the volume back up while saying, "This is playing from my iPod. I programmed it for certain songs. All my playlists are based on my moods. Relax and listen. You'll start to love it. I promise you," she said. "Do you like to listen to the lyrics more or the beats and music more?" she asked talking over some next crazy song.

"Both! They go hand in hand," I told her. "What sense would it make to listen to the powerful beats and samples on 'Who Shot Ya,' without listening to Notorious B.I.G. rhyming, 'I can hear sweat trickling down your cheek. Your heartbeat sounds like Sasquatch feet.'" I rhymed it over her music.

"Okay, okay, okay," she laughed. "I'll switch my mood for you somewhere in the middle."

"Somewhere in the middle?" I repeated and she switched to R. Kelly singing "Fiesta" with Jay-Z rhyming. Immediately the music matched my mood and I was good with her new playlist for the ninety-minute drive down.

"I hope you ain't scared of the big rides," I asked and teased her.

"I ain't scared of shit," she said and that made me love her more.

When we saw the face-painting table near the entrance of the park Pretty Bitch said, "You should get that. People already pointing you out. I know you heard them, talking bout you on the ticket line?"

"I heard em but so what."

"Oh, you scared not to be the prettiest, most noticeable, causing the most chaotic reaction famous bitch all the time huh?" She poked at me then smiled.

"Since you said I'm the prettiest," I gushed. "I'll do it," I said and headed straight to the face painting fool.

"Make her go Goth," she told the face painter. I didn't know what that meant. But, based on her challenge, and really not wanting to be fucked with while I'm having maximum fun, I let the guy start drawing on me after confirming that the paint wasn't poison and having him show me how to get it off soon as I want it off.

"Don't look in the mirror!" she insisted.

"Make her face match her camouflage kicks," I told the painter and pointed down to her feet.

"I didn't say I was getting it, too. I don't need a disguise! I'm not famous!" she complained.

"Yeah but you *almost* the prettiest bitch in the park so get it," I demanded. We laughed and she got it. She looked like she was on a secret military mission trying to blend in with bushes in the forest.

It really worked. We went from ride to ride and no one recognized me or sweated me or asked for autographs. Even the dudes in the park didn't pay the two of us no mind. I love it. I'm here to have fun and to forget.

"I'm not getting back on this crazy shit!" Pretty complained. "That would be our fourth time. We not kids. My organs are switching position. My brains fell in my mouth and my ovaries fell down to my ankles," she said and we cracked up.

"Okay we'll do something mild. Let's get on the flume." I pulled her towards it.

"It's still a roller coaster," she called out.

"It's a water coaster, damn near a baby ride," I challenged her. We got on.

"It's cool and relaxing. Less drama, finally," she said smiling. Then the log pulled up a steep incline, the camera clicked and flashed, and we dropped down and into a pool of water. All wet, we walked out laughing and ringing out our clothing while we still had it on. We were drenched. I purchased the photo of us two at the height of the ride at the drop. When I opened the white cardboard photo frame and saw myself I was like, "You bitch! You got me looking fucking nuts out here," I screamed at Pretty.

She laughed and lied and said, "You didn't look like that before the water ride. The splash fucked up your look!"

"Yeah right! Let me find out what 'make her go Goth' meant cause that's what *you said*."

"Let's go to the washroom and take this off. I have cosmetics. We can repaint each other," she suggested. So we did.

In the dim-lit bathroom we used a whole roll of toilet tissue to get the face paint completely off. One whole sink was piled up high with colored tissue because of us. The trash cans were already full. Pretty Bitch lined up her cosmetics on the next sink and was like, "Okay no revenge. Let's discuss what we are going to make each other look like."

"Oh now you want to discuss it," I called out her slick ass. As we laughed, two teenaged girls entered the restroom. One went in a stall. The other one waited. I watched her watching me through the mirror. Then a mother with two little kids entered. When the first teenager came out of the stall, the girl who was watching me whispered to her. Then it was on. Pretty packed up her cosmetics and said, "Let's be out!" But the two teenaged girls followed right behind us without either of them washing their hands. A small group of teenagers were outside of the restroom I guess waiting for them. They signaled them and one shouted, "It's Winter Santiaga!" and that set off a chase. Pretty Bitch dashed like she was Flo Jo. I mean she was gone. I was surrounded once again.

"We watch your show," the young white girl said. "Your friends are pretty lousy," the other one said. "How come you let them hang out with you?" the next one asked. "We would make better friends than them. For sure, right?" one of them asked as she was filming me with her cell phone. "Let's get a selfie!" one said and they charged, hugging me, and my wet tennis outfit, while clicking pics with their phones.

"Okay, girls. Thanks for watching my show. But I lost my friend who I came to the park with and I have to go and find her."

"Aren't you going to offer us tickets to your show?"

"I don't have any with me today and the season begins in September. You all will be back to school," I said and they groaned.

"Give us your email address. Do you want us to help you find her?" they offered.

"You don't know what she looks like," I told them.

"She's almost as beautiful as you and she has green eyes," the one who was staring at us through the mirror said.

"Green eyes! Let's help look for her," and they scattered. One remained behind. She said, "I asked for the email address because I still want tickets even though we will be back to school. My best friend said don't ask for tickets cause Winter's show friends will beat us down."

I laughed even though I knew it was inappropriate to laugh. I put my finger over my lips to quiet her and said, "Come September, *they won't even be there*. Don't tell anybody. It will be you and my secret."

"Great! Your email address?" She was relentless. So I gave it to her.

"There she is . . ." Pretty Bitch pointed at me as I approached her standing there kicking it, with Yung Santiago and his man. I slowed down my pace as I tried to figure some things out swiftly. What are they doing here? Did they follow me? Apparently they did. How else would they know where I went? Why is she talking to them? Do they know her? Did they just meet her? Did they ask her if she seen me or knows me? What the fuck is going on now?

"She is my friend who I was looking for," Pretty said as I approached. Meanwhile I'm searching eyes and body language.

"There they are!" Eight or nine white girls came charging. "You found her before we did!" They were huffing and puffing. In my head, I'm like, let me find another face painting stand.

"Nice to meet you," YSL's man said to me. I took that as a signal that him and my father's son were playing dumb about knowing me, and probably they just saw the pretty bitch roaming and tried to push up on her.

"Which one is your boyfriend?" one of the young girls asked me.

"The most handsome one," one of the kids said, and they all pointed. Funny thing was some were pointing at my father's son and others at his man. "Hey what are your names?" one of the girls asked the fellas.

"I'm Benito," YSL's man said. I didn't even know his name.

"You didn't tell us your name? And your teeth are like sparkling. Like BLING!" one of the young teenagers said, staring into my father's son's light brown eyes like she was mesmerized. All the young girls giggled and swooned.

"Hey isn't there a counselor or group leader or camp director looking for you young ladies?" Pretty Bitch asked the girls.

"Oh my God." One of them looked at her watch. "It's five p.m. We're supposed to meet at the fountain." Then they all dashed except for the one who I gave my email address. She stayed back like me and her are friends. "Okay, Miss Winter, I'll email you," she said and then ran to catch up.

"What time are you and your friend leaving the park?" Yung Santiago asked Pretty.

"Depends, this girl wants to get on every freaking dangerous ride," Pretty said.

"Let me get your number," YSL asked her after pulling up his phone. The sun was sparkling on his diamond grill.

"No!" I blurted out before I could stop myself. "She's married," I said. I grabbed Pretty's hand and said, "Let's bounce." I started running and damn near dragging her along.

26
HER

I made sure we were back in her BMW at 7 p.m. "I'm sorry we couldn't stay to see the fireworks," I told her. "I have a date tomorrow, actually in the morning at eleven a.m."

"Oh you have a date? Yet you were cockblocking and telling the one I was talking to that I'm married," she complained without playfulness or a trace of laughter.

"It was just a feeling," I said. "He seemed like he was too young."

"As long as we are all adults, no one is too young," she said.

"I guess so," I replied. She started her car and pushed some buttons on her dash. When I heard the song, I thought it was a money call so I started opening and searching through my bag for my cellular. It wasn't ringing though. It was off. I kept it off all day and underneath the passenger seat. "What's this song?" I asked her.

"It's old. 'Stairway to Heaven' it's called," she said, then pressed another button that triggered a digital display that identified the song title and artist. "And don't complain about my music on the way back. After just riding with you *three times* on a machine that is 242 feet tall, swings us in a 98-foot circle at 43 miles per hour, I earned the right to be the DJ," she said and I didn't argue back.

Instead I just said, "It sounds like drug music."

"Drug music!" she exclaimed.

"Yeah like not weed music, but like some hard drug like heroin," I explained.

"The artist was probably doing heroin. Fame is a hard life. So famous people use hard drugs." She said it like she knows it for sure. I tried listening to her song, which is the same as CEO Kuntz's ring tone choice. But the music gave off a druggish feeling and the lyrics were not relatable to me. I thought about what she said, "Fame is a hard life." But soon I was thinking, *Fuck that, being rich and famous is exhausting,* but it's not the definition of a *hard life.* I know some broke, broken-down, poor, brutalized niggas and bitches who are *really* living or had already lived *a real hard life.* That's something different. That's facts. Besides, I had already decided that I need my weed, but real drugs, addiction, and the way it makes a person react, act, look, and spiral down, the way it wipes out a memory . . . that shit is not sexy or cool. If my life gets more challenging than it already is, I have to find other ways to get real thrills. Maybe I'll have to buy a house down by Great Adventure. Wake up and race right over when I'm feeling down. Get lifted 242 feet in the air, then swung in a 98-foot circle at 43 miles per hour ten times! Or maybe that thrill will come with a real love, a real heart, a real dick, a real good fuck, a real feeling, a real man.

"Oh, don't forget my money," I said.

"Only you could do that," she replied. We are driving north and had arrived just about at the beginning of the New Jersey Turnpike.

She switched over from the high-speed lane to the slow lane and exited. The sign said "Leonia."

"Where you headed?" I asked her.

"To the place where I stashed your cash," she said. She was driving uphill in a tree-lined area. Beautiful trees of multicolor leaves, orange, white, pink, but mostly several shades of green. The leaves were lit up by the lampposts that lined up the entire route.

"I was right," she said suddenly, lowering the music a little lower than it already was.

"About what?" I asked.

"The usual. Somebody is following us. I thought so when we were on the turnpike. But, with so many speeding cars, I couldn't be sure. That's why I exited where I exited," she said placing her right hand on her rearview and adjusting it. "It's a black Escalade," she said and I exhaled.

"Damn. Just ignore them," I said matter-of-factly.

"Normally I do. But your money is at one of my places. I don't want your random stalkers knowing any of my addresses." She said it like there was a reason she needed to be mysterious.

"Okay forget it. I'll get it from you tomorrow," I said, not because I'm careless with my paper. I don't want her to meet up with my father's son. I want to keep her as a true friend, a separate reality, no links to my work or family. Only belonging to me. Even as I am thinking it, I know it sounds weird. However, since this fame shit, I feel like everybody thinks I belong to them and that my life is a shared space. *It's not.* Some things got to be *only for me.* I don't want to experience Pretty's reaction to Ricky or Elisha or Porsche or my father, or my producers, or anybody else who seems like a permanent part of my family or business life.

She made a sharp left turn and sped down a dark suburban

block with trees everywhere. She made another sharp left turn and stopped behind a huddle of trees and bushes. Immediately she switched off the engine and deaded her headlights. Now she's cracking up. "I knew I could shake em. This is an alcove and a dead end," she declared triumphantly.

"Why speed down a dead end? That means if they pull up, there's no exit for you either," I said. "We'll be trapped."

"This my territory not theirs. I know all of the nooks and hideouts."

"You sound like you love this," I said.

"Hell yeah cause why should I let them fuck up my schedule," she said smiling just as some bright-ass headlights began to shine through the trees and bushes. "Shhh," she said to me, but I wasn't talking. The headlights became brighter and brighter and seemingly got closer and closer. I like the idea that she was running from the same nigga she wanted to hook up with, Yung Santiago. If she knew, she would have pulled over and linked. Then all of a sudden the headlights began to withdraw.

"Haha, they're reversing. They couldn't see us. That's right motherfuckers. I'm *the best* at playing hide-and-seek," she said excited. Just as she pushed a button to turn on her ignition her car phone rang.

"Where are you?" the male voice said, filling up the atmosphere in the car. She reached and opened a compartment. "Out living my life," she said into the air of a call on her car speakerphone.

"Our son . . . ," the male voice said. She swiftly pushed a button and then another and put an earpiece in. *Too late,* I thought to myself. Now I know the bitch has a son. Like Porsche, her body doesn't give away the fact that she had pushed out one or more babies. She looks young, single, and fit, and more beautiful than most bitches, except me. I laughed to myself. She didn't react to my laughter. She was just calmly listening, then, feeding the voice on the other end, blah-ze, one-word or one-sentence responses. "Whatever. Yeah. I know. I knew. No. Nope. Nah. That's what you think. I decide. Watch me." She cut the call, pushed another button, and the digital display read "Nirvana, 'Smells Like Teen Spirit.'" The guitar led into a drum-heavy track. The music seemed to get her amped up. She pulled out and down the darkened block and made a left uphill on the lighted road, passed a sign that read "You Are Now Entering Ft. Lee, New Jersey." I'm listening to the lyrics of this song that I had never heard before. I have no choice. Her sound system is so mean, I felt like I had orchestra tickets and was seated at a live concert. She's only facing forward, no talk only music. Her digital song list displayed a new cut. It is Pink Floyd, "Comfortably Numb." We are driving up a winding road that reached a peak and then wound downward past a sign, which read "You Are Entering Edgewater, New Jersey." Smoothly she drove down another dark road then parked her car up against some wall of huge rocks. All I can see in front of me is darkness. There was one lamppost way down the road, but because of the huge distance, it was of no effect. She opened her door and said, "I'll be right back with your cash." But, I didn't like being left sitting in the darkness in a completely unfamiliar location alone. I had done more than enough of that during my death experience. The thought of being back in that position gave me the chills.

"I have to pee!" I shouted out of my window and opened my door, which was parked so closely to the wall of rocks that I had to wiggle and squeeze and jump out.

"Hold it in," she said coldly. "I'll be back before you know it."

"I can't. I'm coming with you," I said and began walking behind her. She stopped.

"No you're not!" she screamed. I was like *what the fuck.*

"You want me to pee on myself?" I asked her. She kept walking and igging me.

"Is this your man's address?" I asked her. "I won't get in your business. I don't need to meet him or nothing. Just show me to the bathroom. I'm in and out," I said.

"Get back in the car!" she yelled in a way like she doesn't even know me. Like we didn't just have the funnest, wildest best day together that two bitches could have.

"Bitch, I'm wearing a white skirt. The interior of your car is white leather. You want me to fuck up my wears and your whip? Or, are you saying for me to squat and piss in the dirt like a fucking dog!" I asked her. She bursted out laughing. Went from furious to lighthearted. It was strange to me. But I flowed with it and followed her down the dark street to a single house that looked like it was newly built. It was doped-off so crazy. The front is made mostly of glass. It is embedded into more huge rocks and boulders and there were three stacks above the ground level. Or I should say, a total of four floors.

"I know you don't have to pee, bitch," she said. "You walking like you carefree. You just want to check out my spot."

"You want to come in the bathroom with me? Listen to it trickle? How the fuck you know what's going on in between my legs," I said calm and bold. She cracked up, then reached into her purse and her garage door opened. Her Porsche parked inside. I followed her into the garage. We walked past her whip and she covered a keypad with her left hand and punched in a code with her right. The door clicked unlocked. We entered.

"Run straight ahead. Don't look left or right. The guest bathroom is right there. When you're finished, stay in the bathroom with the door closed until I knock," she said all serious faced. I laughed so hard, a little pee pushed out. So I focused and ran straight and didn't look left or right and pushed into the bathroom. Her toilet is ceramic and cold. My bare ass is shivering. I'm sitting here peeing as I look around the guest bathroom that is so clean and brand-new that it looks as though it has never been used. Next to the toilet I'm on is another toilet. Like two people would ever sit side by side and have a nice convo while pooping, no divider, no doors. There is no window in here and only a ceramic basin with faux gold fixtures, and a tight *you better be slim* stand-up glass shower stall. One bath towel, one hand towel, both embossed with the name Searle, both unused and a stack of brilliant white facecloths on a rack. It's like the message in here is "Don't stay too long. Don't get too comfortable." I'm thinking everything luxurious is on the top three levels. The toilet paper is thick and soft and has a nice light scent. On the sink is a small basket of miniature multicolored perfumed soaps. I turned on the water and leaned on the sink as I tend to do, sudsing up my fingers, cleaning beneath my nails and enjoying the warm water even after my hands are thoroughly cleaned. I hear a noise, a door slamming open or slamming closed. I turned off the water so I could listen better.

"Jinzi, come down here," I heard a male voice call out. I'm thinking finally I know her real name, Jinzi. Of course it's unique and exotic, same as her. A name I never heard of before.

"No, you come up," I heard her scream back.

"You said the second floor of the house *I bought you* is off limits. So bring yourself down while I am trying to be nice."

"I'm not scared of you!" she screamed out.

"Well I'm scared of you. I'm standing right in front of the door.

Just come down. It will take three minutes or less. We have something to discuss."

"Aubrey come upstairs," she screamed out her command.

"Aubrey stand right here," I heard the guy say. "He's leaving with
me," the male continued.

"No he's not!" She screamed her words even more frantically
and I heard feet running down the stairs.

"This is my weekend," he said.

"Then why did you come back here. That's dumb," she said.

"First of all when I got here to pick him up this morning you
weren't here."

"So what!"

"Look at how you talk. I told you not to leave our son with any
of your friends. I pick him up from you. I hand him back to you.
That's the agreement."

"Bijoux is not a friend. She's my employee!"

"That witch is whatever and whoever you tell her to be. *I don't
like her.* You know that. You disregard my words, undercut my
authority, and try to drive a wedge between me and my son, when
you don't even want him."

"Aubrey go upstairs!" she yelled. Now I can tell that they are all
standing together at the same door that I came through.

"Aubrey stand right here next to me," the guy said. "Why did
you take his baseball equipment? You knew we had a game scheduled for today," he asked her. She didn't answer. "Why did you take
him to another audition? I told you no show business for my son,"
he complained passionately.

"Show business is lucrative. It only makes sense. Ask anybody!
Ask him. Everybody says he's the best-looking kid they ever laid
eyes on," she spit back confidently.

"So what. I don't care *what everybody else says*. Aubrey is my son. No auditions, no show biz, no tap shoes, no piano lessons, no cutting or curling his hair. I take him to the barber or I cut it myself or leave it alone. It's my decision as his father."

"Says who?" she said sarcastically. "You get two weekends a month to be king. That's it! That's what the court said. Every day of the week and for the other two weekends a month, I make all of the decisions. I take him wherever I want to. I send him to whoever I want to. I get his hair cut if I want to," she said, and I imagined she was all up in his face.

"Aubrey go sit in my car!" I heard him say.

"Don't move!" I heard her say. Then a door opened and then a door shut. I guess the kid listened to his father.

"See he knows what kind of a bitch you are. He listens to me," he said, changing his tone more meaner now that their son was out of the picture

"He's four! He'll listen to anybody who buys him a slice a pizza and a toy truck!"

"I taught him better than that," the guy said. "He respects me. I came to tell you face to face. He told me he wants to live with me, not you."

"Who cares what he wants!" she spit back.

"He's getting older. Next week he turns five. He's not as gullible as when you used to give him anesthesia and leave him knocked out on the bed while you went out to play around," he accused.

"Shut the fuck up!" Pretty demanded.

"You don't like hearing about yourself. Then you shouldn't do the shit you do. It's evil. Our son caught on. He doesn't even want to come back here to this empty loveless house," he said.

"Get the fuck out. Bring my son back Sunday by six or you will be sitting right in front of the judge, trying to explain yourself when you already know the court will take my side every freaking time," she said and sounded like she was 100 percent confident and sure.

"That's because they don't know you. Nobody knows you. Nobody can live with you. Yeah you're well educated. Yeah you're an unlicensed doctor. Yeah you look good but you're a conniving, heartless, greedy, reckless, scheming, evil bitch." Sounded like he was spitting out each insult.

"And you're nothing but a glorified drug dealer. So what now!" she yelled. Boom the door slammed open and slammed closed. There was a pause. Then the sound of her feet moving. Then, knock-knock-knock on the bathroom door. "Here," she said removing the strap of the Birkin bag from her shoulder and pushing it forward to me. I took it, opened and checked. It's my cash stack. I lifted the stack out and flicked it like a deck of cards. After measuring it with my eyes, I don't need to do a count.

"What's all this?" I asked her after peeping a pill pack beneath where my money was at, along with a small zip lock of pink powder. Looked like pink cocaine.

It's my gift to you. Each one will make you feel like you're riding one of those crazy-ass rides you had us on today."

"I don't need em," I told her.

"It's rude to return a gift. Besides, I thought you're a get-money chick, same as me?" She challenged me with her eyes and her stance.

"I prefer powerful, potent weed."

"If you gifted the same thing to me, and I didn't prefer to use it, I'd still thank you for the gift and seize the opportunity to sell it. That's what real business women do," she said, widening her pretty green eyes for emphasis and with an air of superiority that she never had with me before.

"Well thank you bitch," I replied mostly to shut her up. Didn't like her posing to be smarter and better than me.

"Come out. I need you to do me a favor," she said but not looking into my eyes anymore. She turned and walked away like she's sure I'd follow. She's wearing a tight half tee over only her bare titties. Her beautiful back and belly exposed, and only a teeny-tiny pair of pink panties that couldn't cover or contain the jiggle and wiggle of her ass. She's barefoot. I followed her. My thoughts racing. The fact that she returned my money made me respect her even more. No bullshit excuses or slick game. She led me into a very wide living space. Through the ceiling-to-floor thick glass window wall, the trees across the street cast shadows into her space. She pushed up a dimmer and very little light came on. BAM! The walls were stripes. I never seen anybody's house, not even in the interior decorating magazines I've studied, and read over and over again, have three wide tall walls with stripes; a thick pink stripe, then a white stripe, then a red stripe then a maroon stripe, then a purple stripe, then another white stripe. While those stripes ran diagonally, the next wall had horizontal stripes; a thick black stripe then a thick gray stripe, then a silver stripe, another thick black stripe, then a red streak of a stripe, and on and on and on, bizarre. The third wall had stripes like waves. Similar to um . . . the Oodles of Noodles shapes. They were all thin and of each and every color, more varied and captivating than salt water taffy, ribbon candy, or a real rainbow in the real sky. And of course in a huge striped room that must have been painted by a mad but imaginative, precise painter, the entire ceiling was all colored polka dots of varying sizes, all surrounding seven or so pink halogen lightbulbs. What the fuck? Each wall was lined with backless, armless low-riding couches of varying colors. The rest of the area was wide open like it was meant to be a dance floor that could fit more than fifty people easily. The whole place opened up into to an open kitchen where she is now standing. The design makes me feel dizzy and my mind flashed a déjà vu, as though I had been in this space before. Yet I'm telling myself if I had been here before, I definitely would remember because, Hell, this place is *unforgettable*. When I stopped looking up at the dizzying design on the ceiling, she was standing there with a pound of bagged weed. She tossed it to me. I like that it only took her three seconds to provide the gift that I actually preferred. In her other hand is a tube sock with something in it. She handed it to me.

"Hit me," she said.

"Hit you?" I replied.

"Hit me!" she yelled.

"Nah, I'll pass on that," I said calmly.

"No you won't. Either you hit me or I'll make you hit me," she said oddly. I laughed.

"It's okay. You had a fight with your ex. Everybody fights, no big deal," I told her. "Bitches over niggas," I reminded her so that she could shake out of this dark mood and know for sure that *I'm on her side*.

"I ordered an Uber to take you back to lower Manhattan from here. You got three minutes to do me *the only favor* I ever asked you to do," she said and her green eyes were widened. "Hit me."

"Bitch, hit yourself." I tossed her back the tube sock. She caught it and whacked me across my back. I rushed her, slapped the shit out of her. She smiled. "No not like that." She said it as if my full power slap meant nothing. "Punch me with a closed fist like a man." She smiled at me. "Or just use this." She handed me back the tube sock she had just slammed me with.

"In your face? This shit is hard as hell. What's in here?" I asked her.

"An apple," she said casually like this was some normal scenario. "Right here." She pointed to her eye with one pretty finger.

"That'll fuck up your face."

"Bitch, stop talking and start swinging." She goaded me. I cracked her right in the eye with the apple in the tube sock. Seemed like she was challenging me, wouldn't respect me if I didn't hurt her.

"Ow . . . ," she screamed. "That was perfect," she cried. "Now pinch the back of my thighs," she asked me. But I was tired of this psycho shit. I dropped the tube sock to the floor on purpose.

"Crazy bitch, I'm leaving . . . ," I told her and turned to bounce, my head spinning. No wait, the room is spinning. No wait, the lights are spinning. No wait, the red and white spinning lights beaming through her glass window wall are spinning and are completely familiar.

"*I called the police*," she said and that stopped me in my tracks. "I didn't call the Uber. I called the police," she repeated. My thoughts were rapid-fire. Here I am with a pound of weed, a bag of pills, pink coke, two hundred sixty thousand dollars cash in a Birkin bag with no receipts. She didn't even give me back the tax form I had in the safe, along with this cash back in Vegas. My fingerprints are definitely on the side of her face cause I power slapped her. And, definitely on the apple sock cause I hurled it at her. And her eye is fucked up from the impact. I turned and looked at her. Couldn't believe I'm getting fucked over and didn't see or sense it coming. I dashed out of the designer space with the panic of the fifteen years I never wanted to revisit. I'll toilet dump and flush the drugs. I won't dump my cash though.

"Not on you, on him," she said, speed walking behind me. "So hurry up and pinch me. I need more bruises to be more convincing."

*   *   *

"Ma'am, did you witness Marlon assaulting Jinzi?" the policeman asked me. She glared at me to go along.

"No I didn't witness the assault. I was in the bathroom but I heard them arguing."

"How many voices did you hear?"

"Two" was all I answered back.

"What was the argument about?" he asked me.

"I don't know exactly because the bathroom door was closed."

"When you heard the argument, why didn't you come out of the bathroom?" he continued.

"I was nervous because I heard the screaming, and I have been a victim of violence before. So I hid," I told him. The police officer got right on his walkie-talkie and told whoever was on the other end to issue a warrant for the arrest of Mr. Marlon Monterossa for theft and domestic violence and he gave all the details that she had provided including that he had stolen a registered gun from her, along with her cell phone. She had also given the cops the make and model and license plate number of his 600 series Mercedes-Benz. The cop reported that the pretty bitch's man was armed and dangerous.

*   *   *

"Don't say nothing, bitch," she said to me. We are back in her BMW heading to lower Manhattan. I had already texted Yung Santiago to meet me at the shoemaker and drive me home from there to Brooklyn. Like her, I don't want her all up in my private life, all inside of the Immanuel Estate, or even dropping me off outside the gate. She's fucking crazy and gorgeous and mean. Bold, I would never ask someone to fuck up my eyes or my look or to leave a trail of bruises on my thighs like she has right now. Or the bruise that I am sure I have on my back right now. For the short while I've gotten to know her, I can feel that she cares about me. She packed me a picnic lunch and even insisted that we take a break to sit still and eat. In Vegas she could have stolen all of my paper very easily. In fact, when I asked her how she even got it out from the hotel safe, she answered, "It's obvious you're obsessed with the number fifteen so I played with that number until the safe clicked open." I just looked at her. When I thanked her for holding the money for me, she said, "No need to thank me. I added forty thousand to it and flipped it into a bond that earned me a nice portion of it to keep for myself." I stared at her, amazed really. "If you'd like, I'll show you how to do it, even though you already rich," she said. "Matter of fact, if you want, you can buy your way into my all chick consortium."

She's useful. I'll keep her as my private adventure friend. She needs to remain anonymous to everyone else I know. Touched in a gentle way, or handled incorrectly *she's lethal*. We still in her whip. She is holding her cell phone she had just reported had got stolen. I don't know if she also has her registered gun, or even if she ever really had a gun, or simply made that shit up. I know she never mentioned no gun when they were arguing. Neither did he. The dirty slick-tricky way she had set up the father of her son confirmed some facts in my mind. *She'll set a nigga up.* A nigga who she had a baby for; a nigga who been all up in her, who she must have loved at one point or another. And she *fucks* with the police. She seduced them. Pretended she was so hurt that she had forgotten that she was standing in front of them in only her thin pink panties and tee over her bare breast. She seduced them with her tears as she told her made-up story. She sent them after him with hard dicks and an aggression even though her five-year-old son is riding with him. We from the streets know that when you sic the cops on anyone, everything could easily go south. They could pop a bullet in the young boy's back and get away with it. They could lie and say that her ex pointed the weapon at them, even if there is actually no weapon in his car.

When they were arguing, she called him a glorified hustler. What the fuck does that even mean?

Of course I knew from the first time I laid eyes on her, and that watch she wore that cost triple the price of a common person's little house, that either she hustles or her man hustles. But *an unlicensed doctor*, all of the details that spilled in that argument painted a complicated story in my mind. I now know one thing for sure. She's a college bitch.

"Now we're even," she said all out of the blue.

"How are we even when you had me talking to the fucking police?" I shared my real aggravation.

"So what! In Vegas, you had *me talking to the fucking police*. I had to make a statement to the police," she said and I didn't know that that ever happened to her.

"Bitch, I'm on your side. I never told them that the dead nigga outside of the fake after party, who was sprawled out on the ground next to the same spot where *you fainted*, was the *same nigga* who was squashed up with you in the first-class cabin bathroom of the airplane we took to get there."

She turned on some song. The digital display on her dash gave the song title: "It's My Life," by some guy named Bon Jovi.

27
THE DATE

"Your lips are beautiful," he said, which of course caused them to open and spread into a natural smile. He smiled at my smile. I didn't tell him, but his lips are nice and thick and look warm and comfortable. When he smiled, his teeth were white, like his bright white T-shirt, and his mouth seemed clean, which is the first thing I check out on any man.

"You just gon stare at me?" I asked him. I need to break the spell I obviously have on him. Plus I am covering up the fact that my eyes were also paused on him for some seconds, as I was checking him out thoroughly. His hair is wild and wooly, like black cashmere, but not locked like a dred. His edges are cleaned up nice which works for me cause messy gives off that homeless image which I hate. I laugh a little.

"Nah close up, you're even prettier. Like damn," he said coolly. "The details *matter a lot*," he added, looking me over like a painter and sounding like a real artist to me. His complexion is the same as MAC Lipstick, the bronze. His facial bones are pronounced and rugged, like an unfinished carving. Then I remind myself that yeah, he is carrying a shopping bag which is always good. But he's not wearing any jewels, not in his teeth or on his neck or on his wrist even. He's either shook of getting robbed or ridiculously humble or broke as a motherfucking joke, I warn myself.

"Well nigga, you get a close up because this time you showed up," I teased and laughed a little about how he hid during our first meeting at his so-called studio listening party.

"C'mon." He held out his hand to me. I stood up from beneath the umbrella at a sidewalk cafe where I had been seated as discreetly as a celebrity bitch can be. My hair tucked beneath a bad ass reversible blue-black Burberry bucket hat. My eyes shaded by Chanel. I call these sunglasses my 10,000's, cause that's how much I had to lay out to cop em. From shoulder to ankle, I'm in a 100 percent linen, sleeveless black jumpsuit, with deep pockets and a gathered waistline. On my feet are high top Prada classic kicks, cause that's what goes with this specific outfit that I'm showcasing today.

"No handbag. We traveling light," he had said. Since he said it, and for other good reasons as well, I left my cell phone at home and switched off. I ignored my unrivaled, superstar handbag collection and my stacks. Instead, I had folded twenty, 100 dollar bills, grabbed my credit card and ID, and slid it down in the corner of my jumper pocket. His ideas for our day seemed to match my plan, which was to ditch the psychiatrist, Yung Santiago, my guilt and all restraints that could possibly ruin my day, and my first real man-woman date since being released from prison and under hospital care.

We are walking on a tree-lined block in Inwood, a few blocks over from where Yung Santiago had dropped me off to see the psyche. I entered the building as he watched. I turned from his line of vision, waited till he pulled off, and then walked straight out of the rear of the same building to the cafe where F.K.R. and I had agreed to meet.

Purposely, I am a few steps behind F.K.R., checking out his walk in his deep blue five pocket True Religion denim. Those high-priced jeans are currently dominating, but I plan to replace their line with my own line of jeans that no other designer ever imagined or put into existence. I feel excited just knowing the impact my denim wear is gonna have on America, in Europe, and the entire world that follows.

I wonder where he's leading me. Guess we about to get in his whip wherever he may have parked it. Or, since he was on some "no cosmetics, dress casual" type vibe, maybe we gon hop on a train to wherever he planned for us to go. I like not knowing. I like no cameras and feeling free.

Suddenly he stopped walking, waited for me to catch up, then stepped off the curb to a BMW R1250 spaceship-motorcycle. The sexy black machine has an alluring physique. "Do you mind if I ride you?" he asked me. Got my blood rushing a bit. I didn't answer. I was feeling the tingling sensation. He pulled one of the two helmets from the BMW, a sexy red one. "Let's trade," he offered me, extending his hand.

His eyes asked me to remove my hat and my shades. So, I did. I watched his eyes dance as my hair, which I had specially for him, crinkle-curled, bounced out and dangled over my shoulders. He seemed amazed and was staring into my now unshaded eyes. He pulled up his cell from his back pocket and tapped the voice record function. He spoke into his phone. "Winter Santiaga, would you like me to give you a ride?" He pushed his cell over to me playfully.

"Yes," I spoke into it.

"Yes what?" he asked.

"Yes, F.K.R. You can ride me," I said and smiled a little. He placed the helmet on my head gently and moved my hair back with his fingers. He strapped it below my dimpled chin. From his shopping bag, he pulled up a red leather, waist-length tapered, designer jacket. Looked pretty and ultra feminine. I checked the label. Ethan Bauer is the designer. I'm not familiar with him, which made me mad at myself. I work hard to know and examine all top designers and their design style.

"Put it on," he said, as he put my hat and shades into the shopping bag and dropped them into his black leather saddle bag attached to his bike. He pulled out a blue leather. Looked like the masculine version, by the same designer.

"Put it on if you want to," he adjusted his words. As he put his on, I put on the red leather cause it's bad ass and don't clash with my black linen.

Still, the whole time I'm thinking, *it's Sunday August 2nd and it's surely summer hot!* "Get on," he said, as he revved it up to a hum. I lifted my leg up, mounted, and slid behind him. With the engine on, it feels like his seat is massaging my pussy. I'm fascinated. Never rode on a real motorcycle before. "Lean in," he said, and I pressed my breast onto his back.

"Hold on," he warned. As he thrusted forward through the light traffic, I pushed my hands beneath his jacket and finger locked them over his abs. Immediately, I love the feeling of looking at the people through the face shield instead of the people staring at me. I love feeling anonymous for a moment. I love the excitement of riding without the protection from the outside world like how we are protected inside of a car or SUV or even an airplane. On a motorcycle if I hold my hands out, I don't feel a door or a door handle. I only feel the force of the wind. If I fall, all of my bones will break and that's it. I don't want to fall. I am not a suicidal bitch but I love the thrill and the challenge. I love riding with my legs opened. Maybe I also love doing something so risky with a stranger. I don't really know F.K.R. Yet, I'm pretty sure that since he is also somewhat famous, he will not turn out to be a rapist or serial killer. I love the look of Riverside Drive and then the incline onto the Henry Hudson Parkway for seconds, which lead to the George Washington Bridge. I love the feeling of instability, while feeling tremors of a huge bridge hanging over the Hudson River, a long drop down. Where is he taking me?

"You good?" he turned his head slightly and asked me in a raised voice. I answered by tightening my fingers.

"Don't let go," he said. It felt like it meant more than don't release your grip.

A swift right exit onto Jones Road and it was as though we were riding through a garden. Trees everywhere, so big that the leaves of the trees on the right side of the road interlocked with the leaves of the trees on the left side of the road. Beds of multicolored flowers and manicured lawns and I'm feeling like he's taking me to his house and *he lives in a rich neighborhood.* We rode through the trail a bit before he crossed over a main road and began weaving in a suburban area of mansions galore. He's showing off, I thought to myself. Letting me know that he's rich enough to live in an area reserved for only the filthy rich. Looked like a family could live in any of these houses and not even see or speak to each other for a whole year. I laughed.

"What's funny?" he called back to me.

"Nothing." I played it off and began thinking how this area trumps the Elisha Immanuel Estate, Park Slope, Brooklyn neighborhood. That made my cold heart swell. I love the idea of bagging a nigga who is in the league of my brother-in-law and other brothers-in-law to be.

He slowed down but we still riding. He stopped at the only tiny house, on a sharp triangular corner. I bursted out laughing. Just when I thought I hit the jackpot, this nigga stopped at what had to be the servants' quarters. But really it was too tiny for even a handful of maids or butlers. It simply did not belong in the area. Everything was low. The gate was tiny and the doors and windows were small. I kept laughing. I was like, *what the fuck!*

He took off his helmet. "I'm glad you having fun," he said smiling. I took off my helmet.

"What's up with your house?" I'm still laughing. "You're like six feet tall, and the doors here are like maybe four feet low. We gotta duck just to get in there. And how come only this house is tiny and every other house is massive?"

"Maybe this is all I could afford. But, I got big dreams. If I surround myself with the rich and famous, it will force me to work harder to get what they got!" he said lightheartedly.

"Yeah but . . . ," I said.

"Yeah but what?"

"It's a li'l embarrassing."

"Embarrassing. My neighbors treat me good! Sometimes when I get home, there's care packages left on my front door with some real good stuff in it like caviar! And the clothes they gave away only been worn one time. I rock what matches my style and sell the rest. It's a come up," he said. Now I'm really cracking up. Maybe I'm not laughing at him. I am laughing at myself. What are the fucking chances!

"I'ma cook lunch for you," he said smoothly.

"No that's okay," I said. "I don't wanna bump my head on your ceiling."

"Oh you looking down on me now," he asked.

"You're whole hood looking down on you. You in the center of huge houses sitting on hills. They can't see you unless they *look down*. Or maybe if they got binoculars!"

"So what? I pay high property taxes just to live in this spot. I earned my position!" he bragged?! Just then the tiny front door opened. Out stepped a tiny man. Um . . . like a small man . . . um like a midget, or whatever we spose to call them. I tried not to laugh.

"Show some respect for my father!" F.K.R. said, suddenly angry.

"Get from in front of the house," the little man said pointing his little fat fingers. Sorry, dad! F.K.R. gunned his engine and pulled off. Slowly we are riding uphill with our helmets off. He pulls up to a mansion that took up half of the block. Super-wealthy, so much so it was completely guarded and surrounded by a cement wall. We could not see inside. The metal plate on the wall said, "BUBBLE HILL."

I'm delighted. This nigga is funny. He had this multimillion-dollar spread, and took me to the midget's house to see how I would react. I don't feel bad. Hell yeah I'ma react like that if a nigga got a tiny crib I couldn't even stand up straight in. And what would I look like moving out of Elisha's estate and in with him and his midget father. This place is more like it!

"It's me" was all he said as he pressed the button and showed his face on a security TV screen embedded in the wall. The gate slowly opened. He got back on and we rode inside. Now I'm doing the opposite of what I did at the tiny house. I'm quiet and acting like this is what I am accustomed to. Like I'm not super-impressed, even though I am.

"This my brother Monty." He introduced me. I just smiled and nodded my head, didn't really look at his brother on purpose.

"You ready for today?" Monty asked him.

"Bro, you know I stay ready."

"What you here for?" Monty asked him.

"Studio," F.K.R. said matter-of-factly. "Get Paul to set up some drinks. We'll be in there," he added and walked me through his incredible empire. *These young niggas getting it* was all I was thinking as I'm walking through multiple living rooms, actual movie theater rooms and even an indoor basketball court, indoor bowling alley, and an Olympic-sized pool. *His whole family must be rich* on top of what F.K.R. earned for himself in music. We went out a door and ended up in a garden. We walked the footpath and it led us to his studio. In the foyer of the studio were glass-framed photos of real superstars and athletes that everybody in the whole world knows, like Whitney Houston, Michael Jordan, Janet and Michael Jackson! Now I'm thinking . . .

"What you drinking, water, lemonade, ice tea, Kool-Aid, Coca-Cola, Pepsi, orange juice . . ."

"Okay, okay, I get it. Just water please. Where's the washroom?" I asked. He pointed. I went in. After peeing, washing my face and hands, I'm staring in the mirror. Not really looking at myself. Just feeling my feelings. I'm having a good time. He's funny and he makes me laugh, like shoulders shaking and shit like that. I don't feel as cold as usual. It's like I'm normally at zero degrees, and now I'm just approaching normal body temperature which is not normal for me. I do wonder why of all of the rooms and buildings on his estate, he has us in the studio? However, I guess rap niggas stay in the studio, to keep that money flow.

"Why I'm in here and you in there?" I asked him. He had me standing behind a mic like how I was when we first encountered one another. He was standing behind the glass where all of the digital boards were located. "This is how I want our relationship to go," he said and I could hear his voice in the booth I'm standing in.

"Our relationship?" I repeated.

"Yeah," he said. "How I look?" he asked me smoothly. I started smiling. "Oh shit, you think I'm ugly!" he said in an excited voice. I laughed.

"Okay you not feeling me," he said calmly. That was sexy to me. The way he was handling his doubt, or his rejection. "At least we can still work together. I want to produce you. I think you got it. You're already big. Add music to your accolades, man you'll be the highest high, queen of the . . . nah fuck it. You'll be king," he said.

"Show me some skin," I asked in a way that he could feel my feminine curiosity about him, the man. "You asked me if you're ugly. I got to see something to give you my reply," I said. He got a big smile on his face. He pulled off his T-shirt. "Turn up the lights," I bossed him.

"Hmm?" he said and the lights went bright on his side. "Now dead the lights in the booth where I am," I said. Now I am standing in the dark and he is standing in the light. I can see him clearly. My eyes are roaming around his caramel skin. His clavical is pronounced. *Maybe I'll start there*, I thought to myself. I'm imagining placing my lips on his collarbone. The branded black words SON OF A BITCH, somehow burnt into his skin, that's where I'll move my tongue into the grooves of the lettering. I exhaled. Felt suddenly super warm in the dark booth.

"Nice setup. I can tell that you didn't just start working out when you met me," I said. He replied with his breath, I could hear it in the booth, magnified. "That body was made by repetition," I complimented him. I have my hand on my front right shoulder, above my breast. Bare shoulders, arms, and back in my crushed black linen halter. He clicked a button or flipped a switch.

"Say, Born Again Virgin?" he asked me. Just as I was about to ask *why should I?* I decided to let him lead me. Men like that feeling. He had given me a good feeling so why not give him a good feeling, too.

"Born Again Virgin," I said. I saw his fingers moving. Then he played it back and I could hear my voice saying "Born Again Virgin," three times, like on a loop.

"You got a thing about virgins?" I asked him.

"I got a thing about you," he replied. "Now tell me about it?" he said.

"Tell you about what?" I asked.

"Tell me the story of a born again virgin."

"Hmmm . . . ," I said thinking.

"You're in love with the rhyme," I accused him. He didn't say nothing back, just watched me and waited for me to comply.

**"Born again virgin, but not the nervous type.
I ain't ascared of the dick and I know what I like."**

I rhymed out my thoughts. He turned off the bright lights on his side.

"I'm not down with Teddy don't turn off the lights," I added. He played it back.

**"Born Again Virgin, Born Again Virgin . . .
But not the nervous type.
I ain't ascared of the dick
And I know what I like . . . like . . . like."**

"That's fire," he said. "Tell me more," he said, but he was still in the dark.

> **"Keep the lights open**
> **You can see what I have,**
> **What to hug, what to rub**
> **What to snatch and grab"**

"Woah," he said egging me on and moving his hands and fingers over his digital board.

"Born Again Virgin, Born Again Virgin, Born Again Virgin." He played the hook and dropped in what I had just rhymed:

> **"Keep the lights open**
> **You can see what I have,**
> **What to hug, what to rub**
> **What to snatch and grab"**

Without him telling me I delivered the next lines:

> **"Believe it or not I want to look at you, too.**
> **How you stand, how you ride, how you**
> **do what you do. Born Again Virgin,**
> **Born Again Virgin, Born Again Virgin.**

> **"When you're inside of me**
> **Go on and close your eyes.**
> **Feel the universe between my thighs.**

**I'm the moon. You're the sun
Shoot them stars in my sky!
Born Again Virgin, Born Again Virgin**

**"I'm the Earth.
You're the Wind
Together we Fire.
I love the feeling
Of you taking me higher, higher, higher . . ."**

Then I started breathing seductively into my microphone.

I had heard one of them old bitches moaning on a hit record when she was young and sexy. Her song was worldwide at that time. Those were Lana's days and she was part of Lana's music collection and needless to say, *I am Lana's daughter.*

"Now show me your goods," he invited me to . . . strip?

"Nope," I said. "It was you who asked me if you're ugly. I didn't ask you to evaluate me."

"Perfect answer," he said. "If you would have started stripping in the booth, on our first date . . . at Eddie's house . . . I'd have to . . ."

"Eddie's house?" I repeated.

"Yeah, this is Eddie Murphy's house," he said. My jaw dropped. I busted out in laughter. I said, "Eddie Murphy's house! *Why are we in Eddie Murphy's house? Where is your house?*"

"I showed you my house and my father. You laughed at me. Eddie is my neighbor and my brother Monty is one of his house security guards," he explained. I just looked at him. I didn't know what to say or do. "After the hit we just laid down in Eddie's studio, we can buy a house in this neighborhood that's not as tiny as my father's but not as expensive as Eddie's!" he said straight-faced.

"You wanted unpredictable, unforgettable, and unregrettable, those were your words right?"

"Exactly," I said.

"That's me. So follow my lead. Let's see if you really mean what you say."

*   *   *

His motorcycle pulled up a ramp and onto a huge stage. It jerked stopped and spun out a little. Felt good. He pulled off his helmet and the roar that happened when his face was revealed was horrifying and sensational at the same time. He moved back and forth across the stage spitting some bars. I heard of having front row seats, but he parked me center stage. I couldn't do anything without being seen by a sea of thousands upon thousands of people. What the fuck! After he performed what I could tell is one of his hits, title "F.K.R. Mutha," the music changed and I then heard the boom of my own voice enter the arena.

"My pussy is gold
My pussy is gold
My pussy is gold."

"Bow down for Miss Winter Santiaga," F.K.R. Mutha said, and the crowd went wild. He raced over and grabbed off my helmet and lifted me off the back seat of his bike. Now I'm on my own feet standing and facing a bigger crowd than I ever faced.

"Give them you ma!" he said over the mic. I walked towards the front of the stage. I looked to the right and saw the image of myself on a gigantic digital Jumbotron screen. I looked to the left and I was on the gigantic digital Jumbotron screen on the left as well. Overhead was not my image, but the words to the song I had made up for him on the first day we met in the studio. He put the mic behind his back and said only to me, "Unpredictable, it's now or never." He handed me his mic. I grabbed it and held it like a hard dick. I did my feminine strut cause I'm a woman not no man.

"Until you warm me up
I'm basically cold.
But if you dat nigga,
My pussy is gold."

Then thirty thousand voices were spitting back at me, "My pussy is gold. My pussy is gold. My pussy is gold."

I felt a surge, a feeling stronger than the strong feeling I felt at Six Flags on their wildest ride. My heart is racing.

"If you want me nigga you gotta snatch out my heart.
Make me feel something nigga that sets you apart.
From the average bitch nigga, cockroach, or maggot.
And forget me nigga if you undercover faggot!"

Total eruption now, at least twenty-five thousand bitches of every race and nationality are pumping their fist, cell phone in the other hand, filming me. Facial expressions are like the ecstasy of sex and agony of struggle.

Then they chant what I realize now is the hook. "My pussy is gold. My pussy is gold. My pussy is gold." Their reciting gives me time to catch my breath and wipe my sweat cause I see my wet hair lying down soft and shiny on my face on the Jumbotron.

"Dat Nigga for me can't be nuthin sweet,
I like him strong and black a li'l rough in them sheets."

This time I used my hands to dramatize my words, especially, "a li'l rough in them sheets."

The roar and applause threatened to burst open my eardrums. Now they reciting "My pussy is gold. My pussy is gold. My pussy is gold."

I spit,

"Don't give a fuck if you went to college.
It's how you handle this life,
Sexy-street-knowledge.
Got stacks piled up cause you ain't no bum.
Use your head, look, and style to make me cum."

I saw girls rushing the stage. Security is pushing them back. Bitches piling up on each other's shoulders sitting three-bitch-high.

"My pussy is gold. My pussy is gold. My pussy is gold."

"I'm true school nigga,
Still luv the dick-stick-shift"

I placed the mic by my pussy like it was a dick and shifted it around like a stick shift.

"Feels more better than the lickety-split
WORD . . ."

And while most repeated the hook for the last time, "My pussy is gold. My pussy is gold. My pussy is gold," some bitches started arguing and then fighting each other.

F.K.R. flew out from side stage and whipped the crowd into a cheer of just rhythmically reciting my name, "*Winter Santiaga Winter Santiaga Winter Santiaga . . . BOW DOWN.*" As they chanted, he grabbed my hand and walked me back into the center absolute front of the stage. He pulled up a rock, turned his wrist back and forth so that the diamond displayed to the hundredth power on the huge screens. He then raised my hand and placed it on my finger. "Before you marry your FAME, marry me, Winter Santiaga."

Shocked, I looked out as thirty thousand people chanted, "Say yes! Say yes! Say yes!"

I had so much adrenaline racing around my body that I was dizzy. With the rock now on my finger, he handed me the mic. I held it, my diamond sparkling in my eyes and in the huge lights that hung overhead. I can't think. My heart is speeding, and even my toes are curled in my Prada kicks.

"You'll have to ask my father."

28
BENTLEY

I met him behind the metal barrel of his nine millimeter . . .
undoubtedly, a powerful weapon. He didn't need it though to convince me to step away from F.K.R., who was chopping it up with his
boys backstage while preparing to exit the stadium, where he had
hands-down destroyed and stole the sold-out, blow-out, ongoing,
noon-to-midnight summer concert event.

I knew the fact that I was quietly waiting for F.K.R., as his boys,
who each tried and mostly failed to keep their eyes off of me, was
bigging him up bigger than he already was in their minds. I like
that they respect him. I love that they admire me, felt a spark of
jealousy plus curiosity that he has me. They're wondering how he
pulled it off. Real niggas got bitches galore, but 95 percent of their
bitches be skins to hit and split, jump-offs, temporary hookups, or
online transactions, acquired with a li'l itty-bitty paper and zero
effort. Same as ordering a pizza to your crib. I, on the other hand,
have F.K.R.'s rock in my palm, and a receipt of his confession of love
out in the open air, on thousands of cell phones for any and all to
witness, replay and confirm and understand. *I am not a cheap bitch*

who any nigga can click or swipe for, or bang out and be gone, or pick up and drop, or throw away, unless I say so.

He entered quietly and remained silent. Obviously he talks with his body and his barrel, and his backup, as his armed man was both blocking and guarding the door. F.K.R. and his boys didn't say shit. Their eyes revealed that they know these armed men have the drop on them. His man in the back said one word, "Santiaga." The gunner with the wave of his weapon and the tilt of his head ordered me to leave with him. I'm not confused. This is the new security team my father hired. There was no smiling, laughter, courtesy, or requests. It was all serious and threatening. Yet, there was no hate or violence or recklessness that would happen if these was some niggas just about to run F.K.R.'s whole crew for their jewels and their pockets. These men are here for me. It had my heart back to speeding and thumping with excitement. Another shocking event in the life of me, Winter Santiaga.

Now I'm dolo in the backseat of a beautiful blacked out midnight-blue Mulsanne Bentley. I'm squeezing my thighs together. I'm having an intense orgasm. Just the profile of the smooth, silent, black-skinned, chiseled-face young gunner has me moist. The heat and energy that pours through his pores, and the bright light that beams through his eyes, even through his rearview, has me forgetting that I had just been proposed to in front of thirty thousand hip-hop fans, by a man who is *not* this armed driver, who my father already approves of enough to handpick him to snatch me away from all men and secure me.

Now I am turning my eyes from his shine, the same way a person turns away from the strength and power of the sun, although it's nighttime. The Bentley is being flanked, by two on the right, in the middle lane, and two at the rear; all four are black Lincoln Town Cars. No one is on our left cause my armed security guard/ driver is speeding in the third lane. Four police cars are also speed- ing but keeping pace, in the first lane, where cars are meant to drive with less speed and aggression. Guess that means they're escorting me back to my father. I exhale my frustration at the reality of this. I can't even count how many police I've been forced to be involved within the past two weeks.

Just as I felt aggravation creeping up in me, a motorcycle forced its way into the slim space that separated the Bentley from one of the Town Cars. I pressed my face up against the tinted win- dow and saw the helmeted driver gunning it, dangerously leaning left and then straightening. Then the Bentley and the Town Car tightened up the distance between them and I got scared that they would squeeze and crash F.K.R. to death.

"Don't," I blurted out instinctively to my dark driver. He didn't respond, just kept easing closer while the Town Car, which was obviously being driven by his man, did the same. F.K.R. popped a wheelie and pulled up and out of the tight space. The Bentley and the Lincoln sped up. Then F.K.R. reduced his speed and purposely fell behind. When I turned to watch him out of the rear window, I saw that it was not only F.K.R.. There were about sixty-seventy motorcycles trailing our motorcade. Must be F.K.R.'s followers or friends or fans or flunkies from the show. They advanced weaving in and out between the Town Cars and even the police cruisers. They weren't just driving. They were maneuvering their motorbikes masterfully. It was like a threatening performance. Like these young dudes were fearless but more than that. They're showing off. I'm captivated watching their show. I'm wondering why the police cars don't siren up like they normally do. Pull them all over. Lay them faced down on the pavement like they normally do. Pump a barrage of bullets into one or two of their bodies and think nothing of it, and serve no time for it, and get paid while they doing it and even if and when they're suspended pending a so-called internal investigation. Then, I swiftly reminded myself that in order to pull over the motorcycles, the cops would have to either detour from or completely abandon the celebrity escort detail, and not one of the policemen was willing to do that. When the police get the opportunity to interact with a major celebrity, who has maximum exposure, that's me, even the cops turn into clout-chasing groupies.

However when we reached the sign and the line that divided New Jersey and New York, the NYPD swooped in like eagles out of nowhere. They took over the tunnel, causing some of the motorcycles to skid, disperse, and even crash. I'm feeling fucked up now. Thinking, *Is he dead? Did he get away? Is he cuffed? Is he lying faced down on the pavement and under arrest? Is he the one who they pumped twelve bullets in his back?*

Attorney at war, cause that's how I think of her, Elon Immanuel is Elisha Immanuel's mother but most importantly is the chief financial officer of the Immanuel Group. Consequently, she is also Porsche's mother-in-law. Obviously she is not my mother-in-law. So, I wonder why after shouting to my driver, "Take me to my villa first," I am on her side of the property and being delivered directly to her.

"You must be deaf!" I complained without shouting but packing each of my words with passion and attitude even though most of me feels like surrendering to him. He drove through the gate, which opened immediately upon his arrival without any interruption or process. He stopped, placed the spaceship in park, and eased out and around to the back door where I was seated. Opening my door, he extended his hand to help me out. I'm looking at his powerful hand and thick long fingers. Really I'd like to grab it and pull it between my thighs and show his hand how to find, touch, and jiggle my clit. Instead I pushed past his hand and stood up using my own effort and energy and elegance.

Elon must have read the query and the anger in my expression. I'm all what the fuck and defiant and impatient and a little explosive.

"This is my car," she said softly, before even saying, *hi bitch*! "Fresh out of the showroom it's 695,000 U.S. dollars. With customizing and detailing and bulletproofing, it's worth two million," she added as she walked slowly around the car like a buyer in the showroom who was deciding whether or not to buy it, or to put the two mil towards purchasing a dope-ass house!

I'm thinking another old bitch flossing and flaunting and flexing and competing with me for no reason. I get it. I already know she's a rich bitch. I already know that she's the only one in the Immanuel family who pushes a Bentley, although I had never ever seen this two-million-dollar Bentley parked on the Immanuel property or in the Immanuel garage. She locked eyes with my armed security driver. He walked off heading to get back into the spaceship.

"How do you like your new bodyguard?" she asked but like it's a question she didn't even want or require to be answered. Meanwhile I am thinking, How can I have a bodyguard who without talking or touching me causes me spontaneous orgasms? How can any bitch remain steady or focused with this, I feel to say god, but instantly my mind canceled that cause I learned better not to ever call any man god, but damn. He's royal.

"Follow me," she said and turned to walk into her place without even looking back to see if I would actually follow her. We entered her mahogany-décor den. Yeah I said den. She's a ferocious lion or tiger or bear or beast. Either that or she's a she wolf, or worse, a hyena, or queen cobra.

"Sit." She said that one word. I didn't sit. It sounded like a command an owner or a trainer gives his dog. I'm standing up. My arms are folded across my titties and I purposely remained that way. I got my game face on now. Decided not to allow her to see my anger. I'm back to cool. Nah, I'm back to cold.

"How much do you think I paid for it?" she asked.

"Paid for what?" I responded, hoping she couldn't possibly still be talking about her car.

"Two million," I responded like it was the same as two dollars. She laughed. I'm feeling tight but not revealing it.

"Guess again?" she proposed.

"Two and a half million," I said dryly.

"Wrong," she replied, seemingly very pleased with herself. "It cost the Immanuel Group zero dollars and zero cents," she said proudly. I didn't say nothing back. "The owners of the Bentley Corporation gave it to Elisha for free," she said and seemed to want to study my face as her words sank in. "That's what an impeccable reputation as a global businessman, film director, executive producer, master of intellectual properties, real estate mogul, celebrated artist, and worldwide influencer can yield. Tangible gains, real power, and material respect."

"Thought it was your car. It's Elisha's," I said in a casual tone with a stab disguised as a laugh.

"In fact probably everything you say *you own* actually belongs to Elisha," I said, pushing the knife deeper into her side.

"You're right," she said suspiciously graciously. "You and I are similar in that regard," she added.

"Me and you similar?"

"Yes, like you said, everything I own *actually*," she emphasized the word "actually," "belongs to my son Elisha. The same way every opportunity handed to you, and everything you own, *actually* belongs to your sister Porsche. Let's face it. You would not be standing here in Park Slope and no one would have known or cared about you if not for your sister," she said accusingly. "In fact you may have even ended up at a halfway house or homeless shelter." It was like I got hit with a missile. My game face melted. Felt like I had no covering or mask, just burnt flesh.

"No, I earn my own paper, on my own show. I built my own reputation with my own actions, presence, and personality," I spit. She clapped her hands together, like sarcastically.

"Exactly, me too" was all she said to withdraw the *knife* I had thrown first, like it was a weak butter knife with no blade. I caught her meaning. However, it's not like I'm gonna apologize to her.

She lifted a short stack of newspapers off of her desk where she stood. She's walking them over to me. When we are eye to eye, she plopped the newspapers down to the low-rise wood-grain coffee table. "Have a seat." She rephrased herself from earlier. But, I am still tight. So, I am not going to sit. "Is it that you don't like to read or is it that you cannot read?" she asked, pretending that her words aren't a new round of insults and daggers.

"Old people read newspapers. I get the news on my cell phone," I jabbed back.

"Oh then can I assume that you have already read the articles in the *Wall Street Journal* and in the Sunday edition of *The New York Times* and even the front cover of the Sunday *New York Daily News* on your cell phone?"

"No, I left my cell phone home today. It's my day off," I said, letting her know I'm not fucking enslaved to this entertainment shit. Now we are both just staring at one another, without blinking.

"It is my car. Bentley gave it to Elisha. Elisha gave it to me. That makes it mine. I plan to use it to protect Elisha and all of his people and assets, as I see fit," she said. I know she is trying to reinforce in my mind an understanding of how much Elisha loves and regards and listens to her. I'm thinking but not saying the truth, which is that yeah Elisha loves her, but he loves my sister more. That's the unspoken reason that she can't throw me out even if she wants to. Obviously she doesn't know me. I'm actually only living on this property as a favor to Elisha, who begged me, so that he could please his wife with my presence.

Now she is back behind her desk. She placed her hands on top of it, her fingers spread out but pressed deeply into the desk surface. I notice that her chair behind her, which is made of taut, heavy leather, is stationary, without any wheels. It doesn't lean back or swivel to the left or to the right like most office chairs tend to do. It's stiff and stuck and straightforward just like her, *a one-position chick*, CFO.

"You're making a lot of money and a lot of trouble for the Immanuel Group," she said and finally sat.

"Which do you prefer?" I shot back swiftly.

"Hopefully, same as you, Miss Winter Santiaga. I prefer money over trouble." She said it like it was both a question and a statement. "In fact I have a clear, clean professional way to eliminate trouble from IG. I defer to the contracts that all artists and talent on the IG roster have signed and notarized eagerly. Your contract, same as theirs, contains a clause concerning *behavior*."

"Behavior," I repeated aloud. Does she think I'm a child, her child? Are all artists and talent supposed to be treated like children by our so-called sponsors and handlers?

"Yes, behavior unbecoming of signed talent. Behavior that damages reputation, image, marketing, sponsorship, or even likeability." She said it like she was reading me the rights same as when any of us is getting cuffed and hauled off to the police station. Then she opened a desk drawer and pulled out some money stacks. "This is the one hundred thousand dollars cash that you left for Elisha, as a payment for violating the agreement you made with him, to see the psychiatrist this morning." She stood up gathered the stacks and walked over and plopped them on the low table where I was still standing. "This isn't enough," she said, talking down to me.

"That is the one hundred thousand dollars to cover the expenses of Elisha flying his jet out to Vegas to get me, ten thousand dollars per hour, ten hours round-trip. I didn't ask him to do that. And, I thought about it, and decided to pay him back for doing something for me that I did not ask him to do. I'm also taking back the promise I made about the psychiatrist in exchange," I explained. My mind is racing. I'm feeling fucked up about how she flipped it on me and got me feeling guilty and explaining myself to her.

"It's not enough," she repeated herself. "According to our contract, the behavior clause, we can sue you for damages and recover the amounts that your behavior costs IG. We can even sue you to cover the legal fees it cost us to sue you. Imagine your life after arbitrators legally force you to give back the million you earned from season 1, and 2.1 million from season 2, and on top of that . . . ," she said, calmly calculating, her eyes like two drills pushing my eyes to the backside of my head.

"What behavior are you talking about!" I screamed, interrupting her. She smiled at me finally completely losing my cool. She backed out of my face and walked back towards her chair.

"Let's face it, Miss Winter Santiaga, our relationship is quite an anomaly," she said, and I know she knows I don't know what the fuck anomaly means. And, I am so sick and tired of all college bitches. "For example . . . ," she continued. She turned and is looking at me with a twisted smile. "You live on my property, gratis! That makes our relationship personal. You signed the contracts I authored for IG. That makes our relationship business. The fact that you live here, we live here together, de facto means that my son is responsible for you and your guests whom you bring onto his property. In the world of business, you are currently one of IG's most impactful image-makers. Every word out of your mouth, every choice you make, every action you take, impacts IG. Whatever wrong that you do, as the *small screen* star that you are, results in IG being culpable, guilty by association."

"Yeah well you already said that I am making a whole lot of money for IG. And yeah I am a small screen star. But cell phones and laptops are small screens. There are billions of small screens and way, way less movie screens and movie houses. What's your point? It's nearly midnight and I gotta go to work in the morning, *for IG*," I emphasized.

"F.K.R. Mutha . . . what is that?" She made an ugly ill face. "F.K.R. Mutha . . . Who is that? Marry who? Marry you! He wants to become a part of the Immanuel Group, family and team? Be welcomed onto the Immanuel Estate? Impact the Immanuel fortune, image, marketing, reputation? Miss Santiaga, do you have even half the sense that your younger sister has? Woman to woman, what makes a young lady carry on a relationship, much less a marriage, with a man who obviously named himself . . ." She screamed out only the word "*Motherfucker!*" and it was laughable to hear how she pronounced and pushed out the word. I smiled.

Mimicking her deceptive approach, I softly and calmly corrected and bombed her back.

"No, actually it's the other way around," I said. "His name is Fuck a mother!"

"You're alive . . . ," I said in my real sleepy but sexy voice.

He laughed just one beat. I hear his breath escape over the phone. "Makes me feel good. You're excited that I'm alive," he said. "I'm not an easy kill. I'm cautious."

"Cautious huh. You was pushing that bike like you was *ready to die*," I reminded him.

"Not yet. There are a few things I need to do and feel before I check out."

"Like what?"

"Guess?" He threw it back to me.

"Ah nigga I don't know," I said like I'm too lazy to think, cause right now I am.

"I'll let you speak on it first," he said. "There must be a few things you definitely want to do before your soul moves into an entirely different space?" I didn't say any answer to his question. It was too deep. Besides I had already had a death experience. I did die once in this lifetime. It's a fact, not a dream, or a nightmare, or even a coma. It was an actual death. I'm not telling no one about it. I already know it would cause them to think of me as completely crazy or too scary, or maybe even as bad luck.

Even though I went silent on him, instead of asking me why I stopped talking he waited, didn't say a word. Somehow, I liked that.

Had me catching feelings. "I'm going to build a fashion empire. I need time to do that. I already started, but for me to reach my billionaire status, it's gonna take at least a few years."

"Yeah I know you dead-ass," he said. "And I know if any female could do it, you could. I was waiting for you to stroke my ego and tell me you want to have my babies after accepting my marriage proposal. But I'ma switch gears. Tell me just how much you love designer drip and designing your own clothes, cause I noticed you always freak everything you wear with a uniqueness," he said. Then I heard a beep.

"Are you recording me?" I asked in a more alert tone.

"Anytime you hit my phone, it's set up to record. Your voice got me feeling like uuuh ummm." He made a word out of a humming sound that really did convey his feelings to me. "I don't wanna miss capturing it on the track." Oh I could tell he wants to play. So I played with him the way he likes it, in a rhyme.

"In my bed alone, (I exhaled my loneliness)
Like a princess in a castle.
Got guards securing me,
and my family is a hassle.
I wish a nigga would . . .
pull up and untrap me.
Pistol waving, guns blazing . . .
C'mon nigga. Kidnap me.
You say you want it, you want it . . .
and you know how to get it.

"It's your move, make that move
Forget. You'll regret it.

"Got niggas galore looking to bed me
Got F.K.R., attempting to wed me
I'm not for sale, But do you gotta house?
Money matters, respect, and clout
Buy me out, buy me out.

"Are you sure are you sure
that you love and adore me
strong back, strong stroke
and you'll never bore me.
I'm already on top
How high can you take me?
I be the realest bitch.
No nigga can fake me
Make me laugh, fuck me right
excite and amaze me."

"How's that?" I asked, a little out of breath. My sleepiness mingled with my off-the-top of my head, or tip-of-my-tongue romantic rhyme challenge to FKR. However, FKR wasn't saying nothing back. I mean he is dead silent on the call.

"You aight? Need anything? . . ." I broke the silence between us. Then there was even more silence.

"One thing," he suddenly said. "If you give it to me, then I'll know something. If you refuse to give it to me, I'll know something else," he said in riddle mode.

"Maybe . . . ," I said softly, not knowing what he is about to ask me for. "Some things can be given. Other things a nigga just gotta take," I teased without laughter.

"Believe me, I know what to give and what to take and how

to take it," he said in a confident, cool manner. I liked how he was arranging his words. Because of the way he said it, I said to him, "Tell me what you want." Then added, "And I'll give it to you."

"Text me your father's number," he said. Then he cut our call. I texted him Santiaga's number. Seemed like I should. Seemed like if I didn't, he would cut me off the way he cut the call. I'm saying, I don't know if I'll marry this young nigga. However, while I'm deciding, I don't want him to throw me away. The fact that Elon hates him entices me. She wants me to fear her and drop him. Based on that alone, I may marry him, move out, and drop her.

Right when I went to make a next call, a text came in from F.K.R. with no words, just a phone number. So I ignored the number and called him back directly. "Whose number?" was all I asked.

"What's that noise? I asked after hearing a loud beeping sound.

"It's a truck backing up," he said casually.

"You outside!?" I asked, surprised. Thought the nigga was laying in his bed like I am. Thought he was thinking bout a brilliant scheme to snatch me away from security, Santiaga, and the whole scene.

"Why you breathing like that?" I asked, feeling suspicious.

"I'm at FedEx. These boxes be heavy," he said, and I heard voices and sounds of other men moving around.

"FedEx." I bursted out laughing. "What the fuck?"

"I'm full-time. Night shift! I got health care and benefits," he said in a straight tone without laughter. "What?" he asked me as I continued to crack up.

"But you just performed in front of thirty thousand people. You must have gotten paid."

"I did. I gotta save that up to get my wife a house. It seemed like you didn't like the house I grew up in," he said and now I am speechless after laughing my empty stomach into pain. After a long pause, where he was just breathing and lifting boxes, I guess . . . I asked him, "Whose phone number did you text me? Was that a mistake? You meant to text it to some other bitch?"

"It's *my father's* number," he said. Now I'm just staring at my phone. Then I broke out in more laughter. I realize right then that making me feel light, happy, and filled with life and specks of joy is F.K.R.'s charm. He takes me away from my game face, the game, and the watching and scheming that, in my position, must be done. Like now, I'm imagining a conversation between Santiaga and F.K.R.'s father. I'm cracking up. What the fuck can I explain to my father when that midget, or no, dwarf, or no, little person-man comes out to face him and he's only as tall as Santiaga's knees? Would Santiaga be his normal cool self with a man who could not see eye to eye with him literally? "Good night nigga!" I said, and this time I cut the call.

Now I'm wondering if laughter is enough for him to win me over. *Why did I* answer his center-stage proposal with "You have to ask my father"? I'm actually questioning myself. Was I stalling? Was I worried that him and the concertgoers screaming "Say yes" would turn against me if I said, "Hell no!"? Or is the truth that I only like him a little? I don't even really know him like that. But I do know that doesn't really matter to me. A nigga could be totally anonymous to me, but the look, his energy, his stance, his complexion, and his action could overtake me and cause me to give myself to him, like the armed bodyguard, driver. Yes, I am a woman. We calculate. Beware fellas. You can give a girl a gigantic sparkling diamond, all the drinks on your tab. You can wine and fine dine her, take her shopping and the whole nine. You can propose to her in public or private. You can give her an only thirty-dollar cheap justice of the peace or court wedding. Or you could blow a million on the nuptials. You could fly her around in your jet or yacht her across the seas. But bitches like me be having men like Midnight deep-buried in our hearts. Even our ex-lover, who we loved so much we hate him just as hard, and hate and hide how we still love him despite the hate. You could be on a honeymoon with a bitch like me on an exotic island, but still . . . I could have one man in my heart, one man in my mind, one man in my pussy, and none of them is you! You could truly-oohly love a bitch, but you better find out who that bitch really loves.

"Baby Girl!" Dick, CEO, said, but his voice is an excited whisper. "I'm blushing," he said. "Is this a booty call?" he asked me. "It's uh, two eighteen in the morning," he said and chuckled.

"I'm going to the courthouse in the morning to bail out my fans that got arrested on Friday after our show," I told him.

"Super spontaneous, sexy spectacular idea," he said, his enthusiasm increasing by the second. "I'll hop on the horn and get the shooting location changed for show number six."

"Yes, let's meet outside of the courthouse in lower Manhattan instead. I'll be on my mark at 8:45 a.m," I stated and then cut the call.

"Yo Dutch!" I said, barely awake. "Meet me right outside of the Manhattan Courthouse tomorrow at 8:30 a.m. Have Upside on point with our new camera."

"Got it!"

29
JUDGMENT

It matters how you arrive and enter a scene both on camera and in real life. I know that. I have to arrive like an unexpected breeze on a hot, humid, breathless day. I have to look like light or better yet like lightning, causing all eyes to see *only me* at first, and wanting to linger on me, but unable to ever capture my light or look, that captured them.

Issey Miyake is the designer of the dress I'm showcasing today to achieve my goal. It's a gentle off-white. It's sleeveless, with the tiniest most delicate pleats that instead of fanning out, lay close outlining my body perfectly. It glides over my breasts like a suggestion but not full exposure. It hugs my waist but gives way for my hips and ass while concealing my thighs as though I am a modest girl on an official mission. But then, the tiny pleats ride tightly, hug, highlight, and invite the eyes to delight at the curve of my calves. Valentinos on my pretty pedi, while my right wrist is dangling an off-white Fendi with a mean-ass intricate floral embroidery, cause that's only right. The handbag is not too tiny like a clutch. It's not overwhelming like a saddle. It's sized and designed just enough to

tote my cash stacks for the court fees of my arrested fans, and any
major bailouts for the bitches who concealed the murder I experienced for a few horrifying moments. And, maybe even for the one
who actually murdered me. I'll see how it flows.

"How would you like me to address you?" a new bodyguard
asked me when I stepped outside of my door in the dawn of morning. My eyes, instead of landing on him directly, searched around,
over, under, and beside him looking for the black beauty who drove
me to orgasm in the Bentley last night.

"Where's . . . ," I began saying. Then I made a mental note and
pressed it firmly into my mind. *Bitch! From now on, find out the name
of any and every person who you allow to stand right beside or ahead
or behind you.*

"He's night shift. I'm workday." He cut right to it. His comment
brought my eyes back to him. I scanned. They really are like night
and day. This one is light-skinned and rugged with a pronounced
jawline and green eyes. I stared at them for some seconds. Is it okay
for a man to have green eyes? Does that make him bitch pretty, like
Pretty Bitch? After moving down his physique, and especially his
back, which is as built as his abs, shoulders, and arms . . . nice, I
decided he looked like he could secure me, if I decided to cooperate
with him.

"What do you and him call me when you are talking behind my
back?" I asked him.

"Him?" he repeated.

"Night Shift," I reminded him and emphasized.

"Do or Die," he answered straight-faced.

"Why that?" I asked. He half smiled.

"Born in Brooklyn, the section you already know you were born
into, and 'Do or Die' were your father's words to the men on our

security detail. Some took it like a death threat. That's the type of work this job is anyhow," he said with masculine nonchalance.

"And what should I call you?" I said, actually reminding myself to ask and get a definite response.

"You won't need to call me. I'll be up close to wherever you are," he said. *See, that's the type of answers I get and that's how I end up not knowing people's name who are standing right next to me,* I thought to myself.

"Name?" I asked again.

"Ameer," he announced, and when he did he must've have received a voice in his earpiece. He straightened even straighter than he already was and escorted me into a blacked-out pearl-white Ford Explorer parked parallel to my front door. I don't hate it or love it. It does match my attire, and I am wearing three of the crushed authentic pearl bangles with the pure gold bezel, of the set that Mercedes sent to me.

"You must be a cop," I said after he seated me and then seated himself front passenger side. He didn't answer back immediately, which to me meant a confirmation. "Whips can't be completely blacked-out anymore, in the state of New York, like this one is. But if you all are cops, then that would explain the windows and the weapons," I said softly, letting them know that I'm alert while also knowing it's a heavy accusation and/or reveal.

"*Mucho gusto, Mami.*" The driver turned to the backseat to introduce himself. Felt like it was an on-purpose change of subject. "*Me llamo Selva,*" he said. His name sounds like Silver to me. I don't speak Spanish, however fifteen years on lock, no matter who you are, you gon learn some Spanish from the Spanish-speaking bitches.

To my left, in the backseat beside me is another, I guess, body-guard. When I was entering the vehicle I took one look and recalled he was the one pushing the Lincoln Town Car that kept pace with Night Shift pushing the Bentley. I had faced him evenly after pressing my face against the thick glass of the back window of the bulletproof Bentley. "Name?" I asked him.

"Sir," he said. "Just call me Sir," he added and said nothing more.

"Think of us as *your* private police force. Much higher clearance than the NYPD. So nah, not cops," Ameer Daylight said with cool and impeccable confidence.

"We are here for the singular purpose of protecting *your* life and *your* business," Back Seat Sir added on.

"*Yo tambien.*" Selva confirmed that he's part of my security team. "*Music, Mami?*" he asked pointing to the radio. "Or *silencio*, or news?" he offered.

"Whatever," I replied. It doesn't matter to me. I'm in my head preparing myself mentally to go to court. Any courthouse anywhere is dreadful to me. After the graveyard, it's the next place I least want to ever be. The courthouse represents irreversible judgments against my life or any person's life. The courthouse is the place where our circumstances are being measured by people who never actually been in our circumstance. The judge in the courthouse is not GOD but somehow has the power to erase years of our lives, even decades, or decide for certain ones of us, death. *Be brave bitch, be brave* . . . I'm reciting to myself. Go get your fans who fought for you, out of the hellhole. Better yet do it on camera and make more fans and more ratings and more money! I smiled to myself.

"Former kingpin Ricky Santiaga spent Friday night in the 17th Police Precinct. No the ex-gangster was not under arrest and not in the holding cell. Instead he was serving a catered meal to the prisoners behind bars and to the police officers who arrested them," the 1010 WINS news reporter said over the radio. "Hear all of the news at the top of the hour."

The report snatched me out of my head. Poppa and the police . . . again? Feeding them and the locked? I turned on my cell phone and hit number one, which of course is Poppa . . . He doesn't pick up. That's weird. He always picks up my call. He *knows* anything could be going on if it's me. I try again, nothing. Third time I leave a voice mail.

"Poppa . . . I . . . ," I began saying. Then I remembered that I haven't seen Santiaga since I whopped his sister's ass in his penthouse. "Poppa I . . . ," I said again. Then I remembered that he had asked me to bring back his penthouse key to his elevator. "Poppa I . . . ," I said as I was about to apologize, but I couldn't. I know it is bullshit to leave an apology voice mail. That's not what a real bitch would do. Then I remembered that Poppa had told me that me and him need a face-to-face because of all of the recent business deals I've been offered. *Why didn't I follow up?* I asked myself. Then myself answered myself. *Because you feel guilty, bitch, and can't look your father in his eyes like you always used to do. Because you are angry at him about Dulce fifteen fucking years later, and you don't feel sorry for beating his sister's ass because you just needed to whoop any bitch's ass with the hate you held on to for Dulce.* I smiled, yes . . . that's me.

"Daylight," I spoke out to day shift bodyguard Ameer. "Please, I want to stop by my father's place. You know it?" I asked him.

"Mami, it's almost 8 a.m. 8:45 arrival at the court with traffic . . . ah *muy bueno. Quieres* stop . . . *no bueno,*" Selva said.

"No answer," Daylight said. "Your father is not picking up. Therefore, we will stay on schedule," he determined like he's the boss who I work for!

"Father, of reality television star Miss Winter Santiaga of *Bow Down* fame, will do anything for his superstar daughter. On Friday afternoon, fans rioted outside of the midtown Manhattan Network building, protesting and pelting Winter's co–cast members who they suspected as being the ones who conspired against Winter and fired the almost fatal shots that sent her into a long coma. Ex kingpin Ricky Santiaga showed up in solidarity and protection of his daughter's fans, and turned the 17th Precinct into a festival, for even those who were being held for various other crimes, who did not deserve to celebrate. The dubious dinner was also enjoyed by the NYPD, allegedly with the permission of the chief of police. Politics makes strange bedfellows and the streets are saying that Santiaga had always been known as The Charmer, a most well-mannered hustler who built a multimillion-dollar empire based on his ability to win over the minds and hearts of the men he moved around," the 1010 WINS reporter said.

"Baby Girl!" Kuntz answered my call that way. "We're all set up in front of the courthouse. We couldn't get a permit to film the proceedings but we don't need it. We'll capture you in the lens, coming to rescue your fans. The reporters have already been briefed that this was all your idea."

"So I'll go into the courthouse off camera," I said, but it wasn't really me asking him a question. More like stating it to myself.

"Yes and you'll come out victorious with your released fans at your side. My team will catch you going in and coming out. The whole world is going to Love You!" he said with high-volume excitement.

*   *   *

Business for the downtown Manhattan Courthouse is good, but bad for niggas. I see mostly men clutching their criminal court paperwork. Mothers are here with all of their earnings or savings or what they pawned or were gifted or stole. They're stress-strolling into the courthouse to snatch back their sons from the grip of the grippers who specialize in never letting go. I know. I also know that the key to this celebrity on-camera life is to pretend like I don't know . . . nothing at all.

SHOW 6

I spotted two cameramen from my show fully set up and already shooting as we drove into the crowd of walkers, the no-vehicles-allowed, high-security space. Back Seat Bodyguard leaped out. Now Daylight Bodyguard is opening my door and hand lifting me out into the center, where I presume my mark is located. Purposely, I am looking meek and demure and humble. Reporters suddenly swarm in like busy bees. Action! I call out in my head. I step back one step, as though I am startled.

"Winter over here!"

"Over here!"

"Over here!"

Each of several cameras wanted me to face them specifically. So I turn to the left, the camera from my show, first. Then, in tiny motions with half-second pauses, I eventually am facing the right, having allowed each camera to click their best shot of me, including the second camera filming me on my right side.

"Winter! You look amazing. Can I get a long shot?"

"Describe what you are wearing today?"

"I am wearing Issey." I placed both hands on my waist while the

Fendi rode on my hips. I stepped my foot forward and looked down
at my own Valentinos.

"Winter! Your scent is so tantalizing," a lady reporter said. "Can
you tell us the name of it?" she begged. I pulled my pretty fingers to
my lips signifying that my scent is a secret.

"A real lady has to keep some things to herself," I said sweetly.
"Don't we?" I asked, hoping to make the lady reporter feel included.

"Winter, what brings you to the courthouse today?"

"I'm here to bring my fans out of custody. They're innocent.
They are only guilty of loving me too much." I laughed lightly and
heard tens and tens of cameras clicking.

"Winter, have you seen this?" A male reporter pushed out the
cover of the *Sunday Daily News*. My eyes zoomed in on Poppa. He's
on the cover! Not like when he got arrested way back when I was a
teen. He's on the cover looking so handsome and so strong.

"What do you have to say about your father spending the weekend with your fans at the police precinct?"

"I'd say, Poppa is killing that Ferragamo suit!" The reporters
shared a group laugh.

A young black male reporter jumped into the opening. "Winter, I'm Kojo from the Hip Hop News Network. Do you have an
answer to F.K.R.'s marriage proposal?" he asked me. All the reporters' laughter turned into chatter. He had flipped the mainstream
news into the social media hood vibe. Even I was a li'l surprised
at the twist. However, I played it off, smiled politely, and said, "It
would not be fair to answer another man's proposal to any man
other than him."

"Ooh . . . ," the hip-hop head replied as the bodyguards took it
as their cue to whisk me away and walk me towards the building.
Without turning back I could still hear them asking one another,

"What's this about a marriage?" "Which concert?" "What happened?" "Who is F.K.R. Mutha!"

When I arrived at the entrance to the courthouse, I saw Dutchess waiting there on the right side, and Upside on the left filming with her cell phone instead of the movie camera. None of us greeted each other. We cool like that. So after my escort, Dutchess walked in behind Backseat Bodyguard, and Upside Down behind her, and I could hear the remaining Eight Bitches team-rushing up the rear. I feel good. I feel brave.

30
HERE

Exempt from the metal detectors and scanners at the entrance, my bodyguards breezed me straight through. That's what I'm talking about, genuine, actual clout. My girls went through the entire search process calm and cool and even their faces revealed no reaction to the obvious privilege my celebrity brings me. I waited for them.

You know who they are right? Upside Down asked me with her eyes. I looked towards the crew of niggas processing behind my crew who just finished. I really don't know them but I can feel their anger and heat and powerlessness all at once. My bodyguards separated and shielded me from everyone and walked me through the dreary corridor towards the even more miserable gray courtroom. I know. Meanwhile, my scent, my gait, my trot, my fine fabrics, my heels had everyone moving behind me in the same direction, even though there are several different courtrooms, and not all cases would be heard where I am heading. I had learned during my death experience that a bitch has to create her own atmosphere to rule the room or area she's in, and to distinguish herself. Moreover to compete with the rare exotic bitches who know how to do the same.

Seated in the front row, center position in direct eyeshot of the judge, who hadn't arrived yet, is where I am purposely. "All rise . . . ," the court officer called out and the judge strolled in sideways from his private chamber. *He has his own atmosphere*, I thought to myself. It's like he is surrounded by deep black smoke swirling around his black robe. "Order in the court . . ." and there is a long list of names recited. Out trails the first arrested person who, I know from having been there, came from a holding area where she was wrist and ankle cuffed and chained to the rest of the arrested. Standing before the court she is no longer cuffed. "Disorderly conduct, illegal assembly, trespassing . . ." Her charges were read off. "She's one of ours," Dutchess said softly, leaning forward towards me from the row behind.

"Do you understand the charges? Do you have an attorney? If not . . ." Then a well-suited young white man stood up.

"He's our lawyer . . . ," Dutchess said to me softly. I turned my eyes slightly in her direction. Without speaking, I'm asking her, *How do you know?*

ROR, released on your own recognizance, the judge decided. And one by one, each of our fans, whom Dutchess pointed out, and whose charges were the same, received the same treatment and were released. The illest thing was after they received their paperwork and the lawyer settled the court fees, they remained in the courtroom. Normally an arrested nigga, set free until his next court date, dashes right out the door as swiftly as possible. But these mostly young women, eighteen to twenty-three, I'd guess, all squeezed in the rows behind me as though they were waiting for all of the fans from the incident to get set free, same like I am.

"She's the last one," Dutchess leaned in saying to me. Then, there was a murmur. The quiet courtroom flipped to quiet whispers. The whispers grew to chatter. The chatter grew to excitement. The excitement grew to movement. The gavel slammed. "Order in the court. Settle down or you will be removed."

The random people who had been seated began rummaging, getting up, removing themselves, and exiting. "Don't move," Daylight Bodyguard ordered me. I didn't. Because I did not move, the whole eight-bitch crew remained seated, as well as the fans. Everyone else cleared out. Meanwhile someone charged with a DUI is standing before the judge. But that guy ain't with us so we don't give a fuck.

Out in the corridor now and it's jammed with all types of people. My crew, crowd, fans, and friends and family of fans are following me out in a huddle, separated only by my bodyguards leading the way. "Elisha Immanuel . . . Elisha Immanuel . . ." I keep hearing his name on the lips and out the mouths of the crowd moving in the opposite direction of where I am being moved. "Stay focused," Daylight Bodyguard orders me. Dutchess is moving our crew and crowd, and reinforcing the bodyguard's instructions and movements.

Outside of the courthouse building is a mob. A wall of police, a swarm of reporters, tens and tens of people who appear to be curious workers and passersby. Brooklyn dudes, Uptown dudes, and even professionally outfitted women, plus hood chicks from everywhere like they're waiting on a music performance. I'm like *What the fuck?* "Winter Santiaga! Bow Down!" one of my crew screamed out. Then all of my girls were like running in place shouting it out. The energy caught on. Now other crews are shouting, at the same time, "Winter Santiaga Bow Down!" At the thunder and echoing of my name, my heart began racing. I tried to catch my breath. The facial expression of the chanters, and the passionate and wild way they are pushing my name out into the air, got me lightheaded. Police whistles turned into police sirens. The scream of the sirens pushed against the chants of the people. I'm sandwiched between the bodyguards. The huge crowd is stirring. The megaphone goes up. "Clear the area."

"Winter, I asked you to eat the breakfast I made for you before you went out today. I wish you would have . . . ," Porsche said to me. I am in my villa on my king-sized bed, undressed beneath my sheets. "At least the wheat toast and butter, or just a boiled egg with salt would have kept you from fainting outside of the courthouse," she added softly, desperately, and with a trace of scolding. "You always need to have water as well . . ."

My eyes dashed to my digital clock as my fingers searched for my cell phone, only to discover I'm on the fucking IV drip again. "I know you hate it. I hate it, too," Porsche said. My memory began reminding me of today so that I can confirm that I am not dreaming like a dazed and confused bitch. I am alive, not in a coma and not dead. Oh yeah right, Porsche let herself in the villa this morning on one of her regular intrusions. She had a bird on her head and her youngest son on her hip. I threw her ass out cause of the bird. She left, put the bird in its own house outside by the garden, and barged right back in. While I was getting ready, she washed her hands then cooked up a quick breakfast for me, that I didn't want or ask for. She sang her son to sleep and then insisted on doing my hair. I remember clearly. I'm alive and all is well, I tell myself.

"But if you don't give your body the proper nutrients so that you can stay standing on your pretty feet, then you get the nutrition through this freaking *drip!*" Porsche said, still talking while I was checking myself instead of listening to her. She's right about one thing though. I definitely rather had ate something than to have embarrassed myself by collapsing on the ground in front of what seemed like half of the city.

Now I'm feeling angry, so much so that I don't want to ask my sister for the details of exactly what happened to me and everybody else. I know if I stay silent, she *will tell me everything*, even the shit I don't care to hear. I sat up, pulled out the IV, and pulled back the sheet and blanket and placed my feet on the floor. Porsche handed me my cell phone. "Please lay back down," she requested softly. I stood up, swiped my silk robe from my closet, and headed straight into my bathroom and shut and locked the door.

"I'll set your table. Since you're not doing the drip, you gotta eat something," Porsche said through the closed door.

"Yo Dutch!" I said when she picked up.

"Hey girl, you aight?" she asked. "You won everybody over," she added. "You look-did so pretty laying on the ground. It was like a real movie star moment even though it was real life. How you feel now?" she asked.

"Bitch I'm fine," I said.

She laughed. "You must be. You sound like your true self," she said.

"What about?" I began asking.

"I took care of *everything*. Your fans ain't about to sue you. They riding hard for you. And the whole New York all boroughs is like dead set against your cast members, so-called 'friends.' *Even the law is on your side*, picture that?" she added.

"Meaning?" I asked.

"Meaning, Elisha Immanuel came to the court personally to bail them bitches out. I don't know why he did that. He got Asia, Toshi, and Natalie out. Simone and Reese both still behind bars, bail denied. They got assault charges, plus . . . maybe they being held on them charges while the prosecutor piles up evidence about the shooter who fired on you on your prison release day. At least that's how I think they're moving," she speculated. Purposely, I didn't say nothing back on the matter. "You listening?" she asked me. "You aight?"

"I'm here. Thinking" is all I said.

"Don't think too much. Me and your father have everything all hemmed up."

"My father, you talked with him?"

"Definitely, he's your manager. I'm your executive assistant, it's our job to make everything perfect and easy for you," she said with a loyal sincerity that I can feel.

"He called you?" I asked her, still feeling some type of way about any woman talking to my father for whatever reason.

"You sent me all of your contacts. So, I called and introduced myself to him and told him my job description on Friday after we left the Network building. We organized the situation with the arrest of your fans. Your father said, 'We have to secure and feed the fans before anyone else feeds them. Whoever feeds them first and feeds them well will earn their allegiance. For the protection of Winter, we have to be first,'" she said, inserting the tone and seriousness of Poppa when he's speaking on how things should run, that he's running. I know for sure those were Poppa's words. Charming words, that choke a bitch up to tears. That's Poppa's way.

"Episode six was live and lit like a motherfucker," Dutchess continued. "Zakia's confession, footage from the riot outside the Network building. You visiting the hospital, checking on the ones who Simone and Reese beat down. Fans and your cast members getting cuffed, and pushed into the police wagon. Your father showing up at the 17th Precinct . . . Oh! And let me tell you!"

Dutchess is excited. I know by giving her the power and position in my company, I had pushed her life into a whole new universe that she would never have imagined while sitting up in her Bronx foggy project apartment that she comes from. "Your cast members had a brawl in the holding cell where they was locked. Those silly broads fought each other. Today Upside Down caught their faces on camera, black eyes, dried blood, and bruises. Word to mother, them bitches are dumb. *Everything* they got caught for, is them telling on themselves, making stupid mistakes while everybody watching."

"Dutch, I gotta go. I'll hit you back later." I cut the call. I turned on the shower, cleaned up, and was hoping when I unlock my bathroom door Porsche will be back in her house, not mine.

31
SANTIAGA

Illegally parked outside of Poppa's penthouse beneath the sign that says "NO PARKING NO STANDING ANYTIME," I'm in a blacked out Lincoln SUV, which I had never been driven in before. The summer moon is full, lighting up the dark sky. I'm ringing Poppa's cell phone for the third time, no answer. Black Beauty bodyguard aka Night Shift is behind the driver's wheel. He's silent. Seems like he doesn't like me or doesn't care. Won't even waste a word on me, not even greetings. His man, Backup Bodyguard, is riding shotgun.

I wanted to arrive alone to see Poppa. A private, unannounced face-to-face with the man whose face, and specifically eyes, I have been avoiding. However, the powerful black bodyguard was posted immediately outside of my front door, when I eased it open to creep beyond the Immanuel property and through the gate where my Uber would be waiting like I ordered. Exhausting process. Protection, that is pressure, possession, and prison. A love that is choking me to death. I don't want death. I hate death. I don't want prison. I hate prison, handcuffs and chains, co's and bosses. I hate slavery.

I hate following orders. I like myself. I want to use my own mind, face the risks alone. I want love that equals life and freedom. I love Poppa more than anyone. I'm asking myself if a woman loves a man, say her father, does that mean she has to obey him? What are the ingredients in love? What percentage of love is obeying the one who you love? I don't know. All I do know is I love Poppa and I want our legendary love to either remain as it always was or to deepen. More than my fame, money, friends, and even my fashion . . . I love my father.

"Santiaga is not picking up his calls," Backup Bodyguard said.

"I'm going in," I said, simultaneously reaching for the door handle to ease out. Night Shift's powerful hand adjusted his rear-view to watch me. Of course he knows that I am locked in and cannot step out without him pushing the power lock release. Backup Bodyguard jumped out swiftly and opened the back door for me, extending his hand. "Allow me . . . ," he offered. Bypassing his hand I stepped onto the curb. "I don't need you to escort me to my own father's apartment," I said without any emotion, like a boss. This new security had flipped the power dynamic as though they control me. I'm flipping it back. He followed me into the regal old building anyway. I breezed by the concierge and his sign-in book. *He knows who I am.*

"Excuse me sir. I need you to sign in and show some ID," he said to Backup Bodyguard. He stopped and pulled out his credentials. I kept walking. When I reached the elevator, I pushed the button and looked and saw the concierge's eyes widen as he read the credentials. He looked so impressed as though he had seen a badge issued by the FBI or CIA.

"What floor and the name of the resident you wish to visit this evening?" The concierge followed up with his routine questions expressed in exaggerated politeness and gestures of servitude. Voluntarily he was placing himself way beneath the level and status of the bodyguard. The elevator arrived. I stepped in, swiftly pressed door close, and inserted the key to go straight up where no one could enter without an elevator key.

There's a mirror on the ceiling of the elevator and on the back wall. I'm facing the wall, then looking up and slowly spinning checking myself out. Casual but camera ready, I'm wearing a Roberto Cavalli bomb-ass floral mini. Fabric so light my own breathing can raise it up, push it out, or open and give a peek or peep show if I want to. Bare thighs, and my feet are lifted by Miu Miu, a company by that famous designer bitch Miuccia Prada. If she saw me, she'd kick that supermodel Brazilian bitch Gisele to the curb and write me a blank check to replace her. I laugh. When I reached the top floor, right before the doors drew open I could hear loud music. Poppa is a real music lover. No surprise that he has his whole penthouse wired or Wi-Fi'd up, to pour out the sounds he loves the most, not through headphones or earbuds but into the atmosphere of every single room.

It can't be Poppa, I thought after the elevator doors drew open to a darkened living area where the music was too loud and too rough and too crazy, not smoothed out like my father or what my father would like. Santiaga's mellow mood music was more like "Moody's Mood for Love," the finale cut played every night on WBLS by Frankie Crocker, "The Chief Rocker."

Oh shit, I forgot to consider that the bitch, I mean my father's sister, whose ass I beat, might be here instead of Poppa. I looked down and laying to the side of the elevator are this season's pair of Christian Louboutin Sandale du Désert four-inch high heels. I pulled out my cell phone and switched on the flashlight feature. With the elevator doors now closed, I can't see. The light illuminated the blue, pink, lavender, and seawater-green design of the leather shoe that featured a wrap-around-the-ankle crepe satin Melancholia ribbon. Fucking gorgeous. I placed them standing up onto the floor, same way they would be standing and displayed if they were in the show-room. Even if I don't respect a bitch, I respect the heels and fash-ions. I dropped my cell phone back into my handbag and pulled out the can of Mace Porsche had left for me on my vanity table. If San-tiaga's sister is behind one of the closed bedroom doors, or maybe even hiding to get her revenge, I will spray the bitch to stop her, confuse her, and temporarily blind her enough for me to apologize without her getting any get back on me. Hell, I had already passed out earlier today. I can't let anyone poke or stab me in my vulner-ability. I stepped out of my own heels and put them to the side. In my bare feet with the dazzling rainbow French pedicure that no other bitch had or has, I walked towards the room where I had pre-viously found her suitcase and pushed open the door. I felt around for a light switch, felt a flat ceramic rise in the wall, and pressed. The lights are on now and no one is in there. I stepped inside. The music wracking my brain, I opened the dresser drawers, still empty. I opened the closet doors, still packed with haute couture fashions, but no suitcase, laptop, cell phone, and fuck it no perfume, creams or lotions, or flowers either. *Good*, I thought to myself. The bitch left. I exhaled. I'm walking around more freely after turning off the lights and shutting the bedroom door back to its closed position. The song changed, still loud but a different type of annoying. I'm in the kitchen. The table is set for two. Looks like Poppa, and whoever, got interrupted in the middle of their meal. One plate had a steak that a couple of slices had been cut from and probably eaten, but seven-eighths of the steak remained on the plate. The other steak had been half eaten. There's a mostly empty bottle of . . . Cabernet Sauvignon. I smelled it, a red wine from um . . . 1958, woah, more than fifty years back.

My mind switched, a romantic meal and a very expensive bottle. Had Poppa lied to me *and even to Elisha?* Did he say that the bitch whose ass I had beaten was his sister, just to cover up that she is his lover even though she is not Dulce from more than fifteen years ago? I remember how I had lied and told a fat bitch that I was her man's cousin, so that she wouldn't find out that I had been fucking him and even staying in his house for a couple of weeks even though I was not his girlfriend. I am not and was not his sister, cousin, or blood-related in any way.

So maybe the bitch is here. She's in the master bedroom, my father's room, cause of course if Poppa's fucking her, she would be in the master bedroom like she the Master's queen. I grabbed a butcher knife, same as she had the day we fought. But I'm not really the same as her. She was too late, couldn't get close enough to stab or jab me. I'm not late and the crazy bitch doesn't even know that I'm in here cause the music is too fucking loud. I rushed through the master bedroom door.

Topless with teeny-tiny panties the bitch was seated atop of Santiaga's king-sized bed with her badass beautiful toned thighs glistening and a perfect pedi. Her body remained calm in the yoga type position that her legs were positioned in while her hands held a few pages of papers. Her hair is long and beautiful but not as long as the bitch whose ass I beat. Her shoulders are exquisite and I imagine Santiaga was drawn into the contour of her clavicle even more than every other man would be drawn first into her green eyes. Yes, Pretty Bitch is perched on Santiaga's deep blue satin king-sized comforter, comfortably, like she belongs there. It isn't her first visit here for sure. She smiles that seven-figure bitch smile I had been drawn to. Her top-tier designer wears are flung about the floor like they are dollar store cheap.

"Say something, bitch!" she says to me . . . same as saying nothing is strange, wrong or out of place, especially *not her*.

"What are you doing here?" I asked her strongly through the bang of her rock music.

"What *are you doing here?*" she said at the same time as reaching for the remote and lowering the volume of *her mood* music. "I thought you were in the hospital after fainting on the court steps."

"Whatever, why are you in my father's apartment?" I asked again.

"Do you want details?" she asked smiling coyly. She placed her papers aside and touched her own titties, then held them lightly like they are precious, plump, succulent . . . weapons. "You and your father both needed help relaxing," she said and reached for her joint that was parked in a marble ashtray, bedside.

"Toke?" she offered me as she relit it with a lighter lying there on the end table. "I know you want some," she teased me. I do want some. Yet, I don't like her talking like she knows what I like, even though I know she knows. The whole setup is foul.

"Where's Santiaga?" I asked her. She laughed. "He's out taking care of your business. Both of you are *clearly obsessed* with one another." She diagnosed and I am remembering that her ex called her an unlicensed doctor. I am also feeling love and hate towards her at the same time. Feels like the hate is winning the love over. "Lay down the knife. We're friends aren't we?" she said with no visible fear of the blade. "Or is somebody chasing you as usual?" she added, laughing lightly and reinforcing the fact that she knows all about my life. I tossed the knife out the bedroom door behind me. I'm not gonna toss it to her for sure. Now I am thinking how I know *almost nothing* about her. When and how did she meet my father? Why is she in his penthouse alone? Does he trust her that much? Must've known her a long time. Even behind a weed cloud she's gorgeous. Yeah, but fuck that. That's not the point. The scent of the plant is enticing me. Her weed is more powerful than anything I copped. Doesn't she know Poppa can't have anything illegal in his crib? He's not a regular cat. He's a man sentenced to life in prison, pardoned, and any small illegal thing can cause him unthinkable consequences. I grabbed her foot and dragged, more like slid her off of the dark blue satin duvet. She laughed. "I hope we're not going to fight. I'd rather kiss you," she said pouting and puckering her lips. "Let's share a kiss before . . . ," she began saying playfully. I'm thinking how the bitch been fucking my father, tried to get fucked by my father's son. Now she's inviting me to a tongue-and-clit swap. We both heard the sound of the elevator doors drawing open.

"Come on out Baby Girl," Santiaga's voice said calmly. Pretty Bitch leaped up from the floor after pulling her lavender papier-mâché minidress towards herself. She swiftly tossed it over her head and gathered up what was left of her loose hair and held it in a limp fist.

"Say something, bitch," I repeated her line to her.

"He's calling for you not for me," she said, giving me a steely confident stare. I turned and walked out into the living area where Santiaga's voice was coming from. He locked eyes with me, commanding me to shut his bedroom door. So I closed it, leaving Pretty on the other side. Hmmm, now it's her turn to be locked out of the main convo, the same way she had ordered me to stay locked in her bathroom at her glass house imbedded in the mountain rocks. Me, I'm curious and furious, watching and waiting to see exactly how Poppa plans to handle this moment.

"First, how are you feeling? Did you eat something good before coming by?" he asked smoothly, like nothing unusual is happening here, or like he has no idea that Pretty is in his bed. I'm sure he knows. I know he even overheard me and her talking, when he arrived, and even now she has completely muted the music she had still had at lower volume while she and I were talking.

"I came to hand you back your key," I said like that was all there was to it, and letting him feel some of my coldness. "Here it is." I reached into my handbag and pulled it out. He opened his palm. I walked up closer to him and placed it there. "Poppa about . . . ," I began asking. Then I stopped my talk, recalling that I don't know her name. Then I remembered what her ex called her. "About Jinzi . . ." I pointed towards his master bedroom door.

"Jinzi?" he repeated like he never heard of her. Then he stooped down and lifted the blade I had tossed.

"The girl in your room," I clarified.

"Why would you concern yourself with a woman who's in my bed?" he asked me, allowing me to feel his coldness. Moreover reminding me that more than being my father, he is a man first.

"You're a woman who has more food on your table than you could ever eat. Tomorrow is a million-dollar day for you, isn't that right? Your shoot starts at six p.m., final episode of the show *you set up*, brilliantly." He complimented me. That caused me to loosen up some. He walked the knife back into his open kitchen and into the drawer. He leaned against the countertop, his pastel-blue leisure suit outlining his physique nicely. His deep blue leather Gucci driving shoe mean as a motherfucker.

He's right, tomorrow when the show wraps, one million dollars will be direct-deposited into my business bank account. "In the morning you have a medical exam because of what happened today. I'm concerned about you. Security will escort you there. Afterwards, you'll have more than three hours to hit up the salon and shop for your final appearance wardrobe. Or, you can take a look in the bedroom over there." He pointed. "I handpicked and purchased every single outfit hanging in the closet for you, including the hand-bags and heels. You won't be disappointed." He smiled. Now my guilt is bubbling up in my throat. Is that what happened? I beat his sister's ass because I thought she was Dulce and I believed that all of those designer clothes Poppa had purchased for Dulce, or for some other bitch . . . while acting all emotional at the grave site where dead Momma was buried. *I wasn't right. My bad. My mistake.* I thought to myself but didn't say it aloud to Poppa. "Poppa I . . ."

"Less is more," he said, turning and opening his refrigerator, and then pulling out a small glass bottle of Voss water. He reached into his cabinet and pulled down a glass. He opened the sealed water and poured some into the glass. Then he handed it to me while looking into my eyes. "Don't worry about anything. I got you," he said like he is king of the world.

"I'm sorry. I messed up. My bad, I didn't even know you had a sister. I'll apologize to her, to her face . . . if you want me to."

"Have some water." He urged me to drink. I sipped some because he said so.

"Although, if I was her . . . I wouldn't listen to my bullshit apol-ogy," I added, and laughed. "And, I wouldn't be satisfied until I beat and bite a bitch back," I said emphatically.

"Look at your fingers holding that glass," he said oddly. "I can't even imagine how you got all of those colors precisely painted on only the tips of your fingernails. And, the rest of the nails are white and glazed. Fingers like fine jewelry. Your pretty hands are not meant for violence." My heart melted. Poppa always loved the top bitch, who walks into any room or even down the street and causes all the men to pause and even cars to crash. That was of course Lana, the showstopper, the stunner, the cyclone, the baddest bitch *of her time*. Yes ... that's right. And *I got next*. That's me. Even Poppa has to acknowledge it. Matter of fact, he just did. I'm smiling. Swiftly I snatched my smile back, angry about Pretty Bitch in his bedroom. Doesn't that mean Poppa thinks she's top bitch, giving her his dick and Lana's crown?

"If you even think you have to fight anybody, it means I'm not doing my job right. If you actually had to lift these hands to fight, it's an insult to me. And, anything you don't know about me *is on me*. Any family I have that you never met *is on me*. There's only two types of men in the world, the responsible and the irresponsible. That's what my father taught me ... the hard way."

Poppa rode down in the elevator with me, carrying the outfit I chose from the room he filled with designer wears *just for me*. I feel good.

In the reception area beneath the chandelier stood Night Shift Bodyguard. His profile caused my pussy to stir. Once he and Poppa were facing one another, Poppa said, "Son, take good care of my daughter. She's more than your client. She's family." Then Poppa turned to me and said, "This man will become your brother-in-law. He's young, licensed, and lethal. I trust him. He sought out and earned my approval to marry your sister Mercedes."

32
BACK ON THE BLOCK

"Your father worked for my father and now you work for my father," I said to Black Beauty aka Night Shift, talking down to him purposely. He's seated beside me, radiating his man heat. We're back in the Lincoln SUV. Of course I'm hurt. Feel like I got dropped kicked and stepped on. I lusted him automatically, like from first sight. The feeling he gave me was above my control. And what!!! He's marrying my sister! He's another Son of Midnight!! Brother to the black-skinned Pilot Prince who pushes a jet through the skies! That means I got both of them by more than a few years. Everything about their presence is a crushing insult to my royalty.

"Drive me to Earline's," I told Backup Body Guard, who is now behind the wheel. I'm talking in a mean tone, but it is not meant for him.

"Earline's?" he repeated, questioning me. Just as I was about to bark on him for not using his phone to look it up, Night Shift spoke out loud the address to him.

"Oh, so you do have a voice. You can talk," I said sternly. He didn't reply.

Earline's was renovated. It's in the same location it was in before I got locked and of course still has the same name. I can see through the front window that there is an after-work crowd of ladies getting their hair done. The hood salon can be open and operating even up until midnight. Hair game is serious. I haven't been here in fifteen years. I could see that other businesses in the area had closed or been replaced by new businesses. Some were even torn down along with the stores to their left and right and replaced with one large market or supply shop. Earline's on the other hand was thriving and seemingly untouchable. I'd expected it to be here. Even upstate, we got the news about what is or was popping in our hood. Who's in, who's out.

"Don't tell me . . . ," Earline said as I pushed through the door leaving my bodyguards both posted on the other side. Her three much younger hair technicians looked up from their customers' scalps and reacted only with their faces. That's Brooklyn. Earline tapped the woman who was in her salon seat and began removing the cloth that shielded her clothes from getting messy from the cut. Instantly the lady's expression turned foul.

"I'm good," I told Earline and gestured for the lady to sit back down and for Earline to fasten the cloth and continue her cut. Earline laughed and said, "I must have took you for Lana." After she said that, and I didn't join her laughter, she deaded her laugh and her smile. "Your hair already looks perfect," she complimented me.

"Where's Judy?" I asked her about one of the hairdressers, aka Big Booty Judy, who used to be the youngest beautician back in the day. Earline always employed young workers to keep the hustlers financing and flowing through her salon.

"She opened a shop right across the street," she said and rolled her eyes and exhaled.

"Seen any of my peoples?" I asked, keeping it vague on purpose.

"Nope. They all moved to Atlanta. A lot of people from your time moved south."

"What happened to all the photos you had? Your whole shop was plastered with them, every wall, every window, and even the ceiling."

"Your sister bought them all."

"What?"

"Porsche came through rolling heavy. She the one paid for Lana's whole family to move south. She came by here and made me an offer I couldn't reject. She even bought up the photos in my overflow crates and shoe boxes, cause there was no open spaces for them," Earline said matter-of-factly.

"Matter of fact, the whole hood know y'all Santiagas is re-caked up. I'm surprised you came around here. Everybody you bump into need either a loan or a job or both." Earline laughed and so did her customers.

"You know that's right. I was just about to ask her," a customer said.

"Who needs a loan?" I said cheerfully to everyone. Their prideful stances melted away. I opened my bag, pulled out three racks and handed Earline the three thousand dollars then said, "All the hairdos is on me." Earline folded the bills and pushed em right into the crease of her big titties. I thought about how those big warm things used to press against my back or the side of my face every now and then when and while she was doing my hair.

"You heard that! And don't none of y'all try to upgrade from what you said you wanted. If it's a wash and set, it stays a wash and set. Either that, a perm, or braids BUT human hair, weaves, and lace fronts not included!" she said, now with hearty laughter, but every customer know she's for real. "I guess the next time we see you will be on TV." She said it like an announcement.

"We already know. Show bout to come on again right about now," one of the teen girls said.

Of course I saw the ones who were "secretly" filming me with their phones. I let it go. I want them to post it. Fuck Simone saying I was scared to ever return to the hood. It's nighttime *and I'm in my hood.* I'm taking photos with whoever asks, letting cell phones film me, and throwing around a little paper that means nothing to a bitch bout to see one million in less than twenty-four hours. I'ma hit up all my li'l spots I ever visited, played in, stayed in, and even fought at, when I was teen princess, first daughter of the king and queen. Why not? I'm with the young licensed and lethal bodyguards whose guns are as big as their dicks.

By the time we arrived to the Immanuel Estate, it was only me in the backseat and Mercedes's orgasmic husband-to-be driving the whip. He parked. I was surprised when he got out and instead of coming around back to open my door and help me out, he walked away from the car and towards Elisha's villa. I pushed the car door open and carried my clothes in myself.

"Yo Porsche, why you didn't tell me that one of the new body-guards is the man Mercedes will marry?"

"Winter, you called me first!" she said gleefully.

"Answer the question!" I demanded.

"I try not to tell you anything that will make you angry," Porsche said. "There's *so many things* I haven't said," she added softly.

"Why would you, telling me he's marrying Mercedes, make *me* angry?" I asked in a tone to let her know she's ridiculous, although I know she's not really ridiculous and I am definitely angry.

"Because he's so handsome, like his father who you always loved. And because, you didn't even answer Mercedes's wedding invitation from a month ago." She said that even softer, sucking the accusation and insinuations out of her words to soften the blow to my crown. "She asked you to be her maid of honor. That's really special," Porsche continued. I cut the call.

Late, late night in my villa in the dark . . . now the personal me, not the celebrity bitch or the fashion empire builder, is back to feeling blank. Blank soul, blank mind, vacant and empty and needing something to give me a jump start. I opened my refrigerator. All of the foods in there were prepared by Porsche. I slammed it shut. I opened the freezer and pushed my head inside and held it there for some minutes. I still can't feel my own pulse. I pulled it out and dashed over to the weed. *That's the answer.* Then I tossed the bag back down remembering that Pretty Bitch had given it to me along with a sack of her mysterious, multicolored pills and what looked like a quarter kilo of pink cocaine. Then I heard voices. No, I heard only one voice, the voice of Elon Immanuel saying to me, "Actually everything you have belongs to your sister. If not for Porsche, you would not even be standing here on our property. You'd be somewhere in a halfway house or homeless shelter even, and no one would even know or care who you are." BOOM.

I feel like screaming and breaking shit. Throwing all of the glasses and bottles against the wall and burning my own curtains and cutting up the shades and stabbing up my pillows and shaking out the goose feathers. But I don't do it. I'm reminding myself that

I always thought bitches who lose their mind and break up the shit they paid for and stab up material items that ain't got no feelings, or shred their own designer fashions, are fucking stupid idiots. And yeah I know I could pop one of those pills and forget it all, then reset in the morning. But fuck that. That's right, I ain't no druggy junkie bitch. That just ain't me.

"What!" I shouted. My cell phone had been vibrating all night.

"Uh-huh that's the real you," F.K.R.'s voice said. Swiftly I switched my mind.

"Have you been calling me all night?" I asked him sweetly.

"Why would I? We was together the whole day," he said strangely.

"Who was together?" I asked quickly. He laughed.

"What's so funny?" I asked him.

"Your father is a mastermind."

"You don't even know him," I replied rudely.

"Maybe *you* don't know him," he said calmly with a rude force in each of his words.

"Meaning what, nigga!" I asked him. He laughed again. I'm getting aggravated. I cut the call.

"Baby Girl, let me say first, this is *not* a booty call. I figured it was fine to hit you late cause you popped the booty call cherry!" Dick Kuntz laughed. "I'm learning how to be cool from your show," he said as he winded his laughter down.

"Is this a money call?" I reminded him.

"Definitely," he confirmed. "Accounting wise, I have 'two wishes' remaining with you, each worth one hundred thousand dollars, making up the three-hundred-thousand-dollar bonus, agreed?" he calculated.

"You already know it," I said in a tone like he better not be saying anything that amounts to me not getting my million dollars in less than twelve hours.

"About Elisha . . . I can't seem to beat him. I need your help."

"He's my brother-in-law," I reminded him in a tone like, *c'mon jerk what the fuck you talking about?*

"Another media group, in fact two other media groups, are trying to sign your cast members to do their own show."

"What? Why?"

"When you're a huge success like you are, anybody who's part of your team, hell even your crumbs are small nuggets of gold that a platform not as successful as the Network will eagerly pick up. I tried to shut it down to protect you because you and I have sworn allegiance to one another, business-wise," he said, exaggerating.

"And?" I urged him to spill out whatever . . .

"And it turned out that back at the creation of season 1 of *Bow Down*, Elisha Immanuel had gotten his lawyers to have the girls to sign contracts that give him exclusive control over anyone who appears on your show, for more than three episodes, which obviously is all of them. In which case Elisha ends up being the monster mogul who any other media group will have to please and pay to make any pilot, show, spin-off, involving those girls."

I thought about what he is saying, what I know about Elisha from interacting with him, and replied, "Well, Elisha created *Bow Down*. Nobody would have ever known those girls if not for Elisha (I really meant if not for me), so if they're going to blow up and get their own show, Elisha *should get the lion's share*. So, what business did you call me about?"

"I don't want to be slow to the draw ever again," he said strangely, like a cowboy from an old flick bout to do a gun duel. He lingered.

"I've been doing everything possible to sign F.K.R. as a Network music artist. No fuck it, to get him to sign up for our version of a 360 deal. We'd like to handle everything concerning his art. Now I hear that you, my good friend, are poised to marry F.K.R.!"

"Maybe, maybe not," I replied off the top. I don't feel comfortable discussing anything about my personal relationship with anyone except the man I might get with.

"But in between your maybe, maybe not, F.K.R.'s been meeting with Elisha and your father. I think the 'Genius Genie' Elisha Immanuel is planning a coup d'état?"

"A what?"

"A colossal takeover, a monopoly, an oligopoly even, the entire kit and caboodle!"

"And so . . ."

"I want to spend one of my wishes to get you to talk to F.K.R., butter him up, and get him to take a meeting with me, ready to say yes to the most enticing, exciting deal ever offered to an independent music artist by a powerhouse conglomerate."

"Hmmm, those are big words, a little tricky though. What if I convince him to take the meeting and he meets with you but rejects your offer?"

"Have you and F.K.R. already discussed me?" The volume of his voice amplified.

"Not at all," I said calmly, but in like a *don't be a paranoid freak* tone.

"So why use the word 'reject'?" he asked me. "He has already rejected my last two offers that concerned only his music career. Hey I introduced him to you, and I paid you to meet him in the first place," he said even louder. He's right, he paid me a hundred thousand dollars to attend what was supposed to be F.K.R.'s album

listening party. Swiftly my mind is mentioning to me that maybe
F.K.R. had demanded Kuntz to introduce him to me, in exchange
for a face-to-face between him and Kuntz. Then after he met me,
he still rejected Kuntz's offer. Then when he wanted my cell phone
number, maybe Kuntz is the one who sold it to him for a second
meetup. Still F.K.R. rejected him after he had my digits.

"And you got a husband from my kindness!" he pushed. I
laughed to break up the tension. "Seriously, help me out here. If you
marry him, it's the same as you getting half of my amazing offer in
your own treasure chest. That's what marriage means, half!" he said
convincingly. Of course I'm thinking about it. Of course I'm wondering how much exactly is Kuntz's enticing deal to F.K.R. worth?
However, I decided to play it down.

"I'm not his wife yet. I said maybe, maybe not."

"Because you haven't seen the footage of the cozy interview
Santiaga did with him. And the whole world knows if your father
says yes, it's the same as you saying yes." Dick Kuntz is right. I didn't
see the interview. What interview? I never knew that it was an idea
or that it already happened. Poppa didn't say a word earlier this
evening when we were face-to-face.

"I had to cut a deal with Elisha in order to film that interview
at the Network. Why? Because Santiaga is signed to the Immanuel
Group with a big film deal based on his life. Elisha would not agree
to allow me to use Santiaga on the summer special, without him
owning the content of the episode Santiaga appears in."

"So episode seven, that is supposed to air tomorrow, is now
owned by Elisha? But *you are still paying me my money* in full tomorrow," I stated. It is not a question.

"No . . ." He said that one word.

"NO." My volume went up ten notches.

"Tomorrow evening we will film episode seven of the summer shoot, which completes your contractual obligation. The footage of your father interviewing F.K.R. in front of a live audience will air before your final episode, which will air, starring you, immediately afterwards. And then Friday is the wrap party for the summer shoot and all of the front-of-camera, behind-camera, and A-list celebrities and media in attendance."

"So that's eight shows! You're filming the wrap party?"

"I won that in the deal I cut with Elisha," he said.

"Yeah but, *settle up with me*. You started off saying I owe you two wishes totaling two hundred thousand dollars. Okay, I'll ask F.K.R. to meet with you, but not like on some slick shit. I'll ask him straight out to hear you out and take you seriously. That's one of the two leftover 'wishes' I owe you. The wrap party is the third wish, since you are filming after my seven-show obligation is complete. And tomorrow is the due date for the million even though I'll agree to attend the wrap party on Friday. How's that sound?"

"You're getting good at this," Kuntz said solemnly. "Yes, full payment tomorrow for the summer shoot. I already triggered the payment. You can stop thinking about it. And, I have a condition to your 'how's that sound.' If I don't have F.K.R. sitting in my presence ready to negotiate and favorably poised to sign the biggest deal of his lifetime, by 3 p.m., that's two hours before his Network interview with Santiago airs globally, I'll assume that I've lost him to the Immanuel Group. *I am a sore loser.* I don't blame myself because I always put the maximum effort and maximum investment. If I don't win, eesh . . . I hate even the sound of those words . . . you Baby Girl will owe me for one additional big wish of *anything* I ask you for."

"Anything?" I repeated. "Anything concerning entertainment," I stated firmly.

"It's all entertainment, isn't it?" he said, and somehow it sent a chill through me, a cold bitch. "And?"

"Is there more?" I asked, growing tired of him late-night low-key pressuring me.

"Yeah, let me throw some hot sauce on our covenant."

"Covenant?" I repeated.

"Whether or not you marry him is your business. However, if you convince him to sign with the Network, I'll pay you a confidential signing bonus of one million dollars."

"In cash," I said without even thinking.

"You still with me?" That's what F.K.R.'s late, late night text said when it came in. I just stared at the phone screen, my finger hovering while my mind was debating whether or not to respond. Then, I reminded myself that I need to persuade him to meet with Kuntz ASAP. Then I put the phone down. Didn't want Kuntz to be the reason why I text or call him back. So I called him.

When he picked up my call, all I could hear was the sound of trucks, then the piercing bleep of what he said was the sound of the truck backing up. Bout eight seconds flew by and then his voice being pushed by his labored breathing.

"No breakup over the phone. Only face-to-face," he said. Then added, "That's one of my rules."

"Oh yeah well I don't break up with a nigga I don't even go with. That's one of my rules and that's not why I'm calling you. And, are you at FedEx?" I asked incredulously.

"You already know I'm on my night grind," he said as though there is nothing wrong with a successful hip-hop star, even if he's an underground artist, working at fucking FedEx.

"I wanna see you tomorrow," I said.

"Damn!" he said in a raised voice.

"You heated my heart. I dropped the box. Hold on . . . ," he said and I listened to the sound of his movements. "We was thinking on the same wavelength. Tomorrow is the day I'm gon kidnap you," he said calmly. "I even got one of my dudes to do my shift while I'm tying you up and writing my ransom note," he said, and because he was saying it in a serious and hushed tone, I'm not sure if I should believe him. I am excited though, and I pinched my bare shoulder to be sure I haven't fell asleep and entered a dream. *I'm awake. I'm alive, this is real!*

"I gotta be on set tomorrow at six p.m.," I told him as suddenly as my mind reminded me. There was a pause separating him from me, but the background noise on his side was still evident. Yet, he opted to rhyme. With the sound of men moving, heavy machinery and vehicles, high-pitch beeps, horns, and even the sound of waves for some reason, the feeling of his flow was all true school Public Enemy. *His talk* isn't about politics or government though, which I don't give a fuck about. It's about *him and me* and I like that *way better.*

"A man like me is all about fun.
A man like me gots tah be number one.
In your mind, with your time
In the bars that you rhyme.
In your lips, fingertips,
Your thighs and your hips.

"When I say I'm coming through
No room for debate.
Get it right, keep it tight

Be excited, and wait.
Not one word . . .
even if I'm late.
Sometimes a man
Can catch a case.

"I think it through, thought it through
Made me a master plan
Some men move bold
Without the chrome
In they hand.

"So follow me follow me
And do what I say.
When I say go, go!
Say no! Then you stay.
If you want and you love me
Trust and OBEY.

"I won't mislead you Winter Santiaga
Fight or fuck up your face.
I'm not a bully, a thug
or regrettable FAKE.
F.K.R. be dat guy no nigga
can replace.

"Follow me follow me
And do what I say."

He cut the call.

33
DRESS REHEARSAL

Soon as the SUV pulled through the Immanuel gates I heard the hum of a motorcycle following. I got excited. I didn't look back though. If it's him following, I don't want to blow up his spot.

Dr. Lesley Buff is located on 59th and Fifth Avenue in Manhattan. His nosebleed high-rent Central Park address matches his nosebleed elite private medical practice pricing. I have a top-notch entertainment health care package, so I don't think twice about it.

I'm naked beneath the ugly medical gown, seated on the leather-top examination table, with the thinnest tissue paper crunching and crackling beneath my ass. A neat nurse with an iPad, not a clipboard, is asking me way too many questions. "Have you eaten breakfast this morning? Please walk me through what you ate yesterday, beginning with your morning meal." I'm not answering. Bitch best be glad I already allowed her to draw my blood and urine sample. "Where's Dr. Lesley?" I asked her, in a tone like, *don't waste my time.* She caught it and exited. He rushed right in, then, calmed his stride immediately upon arrival. Extending his arm, his Rolexed hand, he handed me a hard caramel candy in a golden wrap. I pop it right in. "How's my number one patient, the lovely Miss Winter Santiaga?"

With the caramel moisturizing my mouth and melting on my tongue and spilling onto my taste buds, I feel sugar energetic. In a split second, I enjoyed a flashback of intimacy with Bullet, as he sucked a caramel candy out of my mouth and used the scent and the sweetness and moved it around to eat my pussy. Or was it butterscotch? I smiled. "You look great. Tell me how do you feel today?" he asked.

"I feel good. I didn't even want to come in and waste your time. I fainted yesterday but I'm fine really."

"I saw you on the cover of the *New York Daily News* first thing this morning when I was having my coffee. You were being carried by a strong handsome-looking man." He deepened his voice when he said "strong handsome-looking man," then gestured with his arms as though he was the strong man carrying me. Then he chuckled.

"Yeah, my bodyguard," I said matter-of-factly. Truth is, I didn't know I made the cover again. This morning I had purposely pushed earplugs in and laid my head against the backseat headrest in the SUV, to cancel out any noise that wasn't my own thoughts. Additionally, I remained in that pose to make it apparent to the driver and the two bodyguards not to say shit to me today. Just get me to my appointments and that's it. They would never know it, but I had fireworks going off in my soul. F.K.R. said he would kidnap me today for sure. His words made my pussy pound. It also fucked with my mind. How would he? How could he? My armed bodyguards *play me so close*. I don't want him to get himself clapped up coming for me. Yeah I know I said in my rhyme for him to do it. But it was just a rhyme expressing my true feelings but not expecting him to actually follow through! With my eyes closed, and no music playing into my ears, I felt guilty for asking him to arrive with his guns blazing. After all, these are Santiaga's men, licensed and bonded . . . to kill . . . and get away with it. For a split second, I had a second thought. I should text him and dead it. Tell him I was just playing and teasing. But I didn't. My heart was racing with expectations, and even my nipples were plump beneath my ink-black silk dress, which ties on my side for easy release . . . for my doctor's visit. Besides, when Porsche had barged in early this morning, her soft talk, and questioning and advices that I could tell she had pieced together along with her overbearing mother-in-law, "Momma Elon," got me determined to revolt.

"What did you eat yesterday for breakfast?" Dr. Lesley asked me.

"I had an important early morning appointment yesterday so I did not eat."

"Did you drink anything, water, orange juice, coffee?

"No."

"What did you do at your appointment? Did it involve any physical activity?" he asked me and I thought it was a crazy question. Is he asking me if I was out fucking?

"No, I went to court," I said dryly.

"Were you nervous?" He immediately followed up. "You didn't answer. I'll take that as a yes you were nervous," he said and rolled back to his desk on his wheeled chair that could swivel and swerve in any direction swiftly.

"Just a little bit," I replied. He typed in notes on his iPad.

"What activity were you doing right before you fainted yesterday?"

"I was standing still, in a crowd."

"What did you eat for lunch?"

"I didn't each lunch. I was asleep and woke up on the IV drip from the Immanuels' doctor."

"Dinner?" he asked.

"I had to skip it and run out to handle an important matter," I said recalling how I had raced over to Poppa's place.

"How important? More important than you?" he asked. I didn't say nothing back.

"Exactly. There's *nothing* more important than you," he said with affectionate sternness.

"How often do you drink water? Do you carry a bottle around as you do all of these important meetings and photo shoots and shows?"

"Somebody near to me will always have water available to me if I ask," I said. He took a pause.

"Close your eyes," he said out the blue.

"Why?" I said out of my natural resistance.

"Sometimes closing your eyes can assist you with clear recall. I'd like you to think back to the day before yesterday," he said. I closed my eyes. A smile spread across my face. That was the day I had the date with F.K.R. It was my first time on a real motorcycle. My first time on stage in front of thirty thousand people. First time performing. First time seeing myself magnified on a massive screen, and hearing my voice amplified on a microphone. First time hearing so many people screaming my name and cheering for me in a manner *I never ever felt*. First time any man, face-to-face, seriously asked to marry me, presented me with a rock in front of so many witnesses.

"Miss Santiaga, you should be recalling what you ate on Sunday. You seem to be recalling something else." I opened my eyes. He had his stethoscope over the gown and close to my heart.

"I drank some water on Sunday," I think I lied.

"Did you eat or drink anything the day before Sunday?"

"Yes!" I said, recalling that I had a few forced sandwich bites from Pretty Bitch's picnic basket. "A sandwich," I only half lied.

"A sandwich and water?" he suggested.

"Um maybe, yes."

"Miss Santiaga, have you been prescribed any medication from any other doctor besides me?"

"No."

"Have you taken any pills that you may have acquired on your own?"

"No," I lied, recalling the pill the Pretty Bitch gave me weeks ago, that caused me the memory blackout and a whole bunch of other shit.

"Do you drink alcohol?"

"Sometimes . . ."

"When is the last time you had alcohol?"

"Saturday night I had Hennessy X.O."

"Do you know that if you mix drugs and alcohol it can be fatal?" He looked into my eyes through his designer prescription eyeglasses.

"I never thought about it," I said honestly.

"Do you smoke marijuana? Or use any narcotic?" he asked, still straight-faced and pleasant. Now I'm just blank staring him.

"I'm your doctor. I'm here to heal you, not interrogate or arrest you. I took a professional oath to keep all of your private medical information confidential. I'm also a scientist. It's extremely important for your health and diagnosis that you answer each question honestly."

"Weed yes. I don't do dope, no narcotics, never," I replied passionately.

"Have you ever had your marijuana laced with any other substance?"

"No."

"Are you aware that sometimes it is laced and you could be oblivious to it? This is a warning. I see *a lot* of high-profile patients. The unimaginable does happen. Be careful who you allow to prepare your smoke, cook your food, serve you, or pour your drinks. If they drug you, they become your master. In the past few years, we have lost major talents and phenomenal human beings like yourself from voluntary and involuntary ingestion of fentanyl and opioids. You've already had an amazing recovery. Let's keep it going."

"Thanks for letting me know," I said sweetly. For the important people, Poppa says, "sometimes feed em honey."

"I'll be examining your blood count and your blood, sending out samples to the lab, requesting a quick turnaround. At first I thought you might be having a major crisis because of the tiny fragments of metal that we were not able to have surgically extracted from your brain. That would be disturbing and challenging to say the least. Fainting would be the easiest part of it. After hearing your responses, I am happy to say that I don't think this is a major problem, unless you don't follow my advice. Dehydration is a gateway to all kinds of health disturbances. Starvation affects your mood, your nutritional wherewithal, your immune system, and can even lead to mental illness. We can cure this, if you want to live. Miss Winter Santiaga, do you want to live?"

"I want to walk," I told Daylight Bodyguard.

"I like Central Park." He looks like he's against it. It doesn't matter. I'm walking regardless. He called the driver and told him to follow our path slowly, which I knew is next to impossible in New York City, where everything is aggression and congestion and traffic is in a constant state of jam. Backseat Bodyguard is already across the street from us following along as though he is not with us, but his eyes are on the crowd and passersby.

"Oh my God it's Winter! Can we get a pic? Do you do selfies? Oh look. It's her handsome bodyguard, awesome! Can you get in the photo?"

"No," he answered back without any emotion or concern or regret.

"Can you at least sign my *Daily News* then?" And those were the people who asked. Everyone else just did what they wanted. Taking video of me and stopping my path and clogging up the path of people who just wanted to get where they were going. Before I got locked, and back at age sixteen, I never imagined a world where every single person from kindergarteners to senior citizens, from the poorest to the richest, would have some brand and type of camera in hand all day and all night, every day by way of their cell phones and tablets. But this is the present tense and I have no choice but to accept it, I tell myself again.

"Next time we will take the car even if you're going a short distance," Daylight Bodyguard said. I had demanded that he sit at the table with me at a small café that I noticed as we walked. It was tucked below a Whitestone town house. He refused to sit at first. Then, he refused to order food. Now he's sitting and gulping his coffee. Guess he realized that standing guard over me, after being on the cover of the newspaper, attracts more attention than sitting down facing away from the constant crowd of eaters and onlookers. "We can't prevent people from snapping your photos and posting them," he said. "For security reasons, you should not post or allow others to post your location. If you want to post on your social media for publicity, always post from the past. Maybe three or so days back. That lures all of your potential attackers to the wrong location."

"Attackers," I repeated.

"There must be a reason your father hired us," he said with solid confidence. "What are you waiting for? Order some lunch for yourself," he commanded.

"I'm about to," I said and he flagged the waiter over. The same way a bitch has to create her own atmosphere, a celebrity bitch like me has to create her own appetite. Immediately after becoming famous, I observed that celebrity bitches, supermodels, actresses, and all rich chicks don't eat. I went to a business lunch with my lawyer Kai. That bitch ordered a tomato as her whole meal. The elite restaurant where we ate charged her forty-five dollars, for one red tomato, sliced up nice and fancy.

"I'll take chicken Caesar salad and an orange juice" I told the waiter. The answer to my doctor's question was "Yes, I want to live." Now I am following his advices while creating an appetite for myself. *I got no choice* now that Dr. Lesley has also referred me to, and had his nurse book my appointments with, a designated nutritionist, cardiologist, and a fucking psychiatrist. Instantly I decided, *Fuck that. I'll just focus and feed myself.* I know how to do that. I am uncomfortable with the "stupid crazy celebrity bitch personality" that celebrities put on, or actually have, where we gotta pay a bunch of professionals obscene amounts to babysit us and teach us how to do what every broke motherfucker in the hood already knows how to do and does herself for free, with no help at all, every second, minute, hour, and day in the hood.

"What time and where is your shoot tonight?" F.K.R.'s text came in. "Any schedule changes?" he also asked me in his text.

LOVE AFTER MIDNIGHT   385

"6pm at the Network," I reply texted.

"Where you at right now?"

"A Central Park cafe. Afterwards, headed to Bergdorf Goodman's to shop."

"Hit me if any of your plans change." I started looking around, imagining he was here watching me somehow, and just texting and checking to see if I would lie about my whereabouts.

"What's happening?" the observant bodyguard asked me.

"Nothing" was all I said.

Bergdorf's is a wealth and beauty battle. I saw celebrities shielded behind shades, as well as the children of celebrities, and the teen and grown-up children of wealth. Foreigners streamed up and down the store making it apparent that they had money to burn. Because of course, if any of us did not have money to burn, we wouldn't be in here where a pair of driving gloves could cost three to five thousand dollars, and a skirt six thousand dollars, and a mean-ass dress ten thousand dollars, and for the designer heels, well . . . just cut your whole foot off and leave it at the register *with* your black card. I laugh to myself, and as I am suddenly sucked in and staring at an Alexander McQueen–designed dress so feminine and colorful and revealing and badass that I have to have it. I got another text. Wait no, an email from my bank. One million dollars received by digital deposit into my business account for Lavender Sky. I'm so excited I keep staring and reading and rereading the brief bank confirmation. Daylight Bodyguard is watching me gloat but he doesn't know what the fuck is going on unless I tell him. I won't.

"Would you like to try it on?" a sales rep asked me, approaching discreetly. "Although you really don't have to. Your figure is exquisite. It's obvious that Alexander designed this specific one just for you," she said softly, and she is right.

"I'll try it on."

She gently took the dress from my hand and led me to the ladies' dressing room. "Although there is nothing similar to this one, shall I pull some other options that suit your figure?" she asked as she placed the hanger on the hook and held the curtain.

"I'll need the right six and a half heels for this one," I told her.

"Perfect! I'm on it!" She closed the curtain and disappeared. As I peeled off my wraparound dress, which I wore for a comfortable and immediate undressing at the doctor's office, the sales rep pulled open the curtain slightly and dashed in. Now I'm aggravated. I turn around, and a white girl, who is not the saleslady, plasters my mouth shut with black duct tape. *What the fuck!* I go to punch the bitch, but she presses a pistol into my ribs and whispers. "Stay still. This is for your benefit." A next bitch eases through the curtain. Now, we three bitches. My bodyguard is outside of this ladies' dressing area. Bet the nigga has no clue what's going down. The second bitch who entered removes her wig and shades. My eyes are widened with anger and terror and I can still feel the cold metal on my bare skin. I don't want to get shot again. She and her burner are so close on me, even if she's a horrible aim, and just held a gun in her hand for the first day, that bullet won't miss me. She doesn't look like a murderer. But she doesn't look like this is her first day holding the steel. The second bitch begins undressing. Her body is beautiful, but that's not the point. Her face . . . her face . . . looks . . . same as mine. "Drop your dress," the white girl orders me in a cold whisper in my ear. My dress was mostly off already. I'm thinking, *Is that what you want? This dress!*

"Don't try anything slick," the white girl threatened. I dropped the dangling dress off of me. The girl with my same face, now nude, swiped it from the floor and put it on. "Take the jewels," the white girl told my look-alike. The fight is in my eyes. The white girl raises the gun to my head. I'm trembling. "He told me not to hurt you. So don't worry," she said strangely while holding the weapon against my temple as the 'me bitch' began unfastening my diamond-flooded hourglass chain, then tugged my ear one time before unscrewing my ear shines. She squatted and swiped my handbag that has my stacks and my cell phone. She stood back up, snatched the Alexander McQueen dress, and dashed through the curtain as though she was never there in the first place. "Get dressed slowly," the white girl said. I'm thinking, *Slowly?* I don't move. The gun is still there on my head. Besides, I don't see how I'ma get dressed when the me-bitch took the clothes I was wearing and the dress I was buying.

"I mind my business, but sweetie I think there's something going on in there," I heard a scratchy older female's voice say. The white girl pressed the metal in and darted her eyes down to the floor of the dressing room where the Me-Bitch's clothes, bag, and wig were discarded.

"I'm Mandy from the shoe department. I have some great picks for you. May I enter? Or will you step out so I can have a look?" another voice said, and I could tell she was standing right up with her nose on the curtain. The white girl eased the gun down and pushed me back against the wall with the metal, opened the curtain slightly, and stuck her head out. "I didn't ask for those," she said. "Me and my girlfriend will be out in a moment. She's getting dressed." She was talking politely, her right hand extending, pointing the gun at me but no longer pressed against my temple. I could only see the back of her bobbed blunt cut. I know her face got some phony-happy expression. She shut the curtain. I hear the shoe bitch walking away. By the time the white girl is facing me, I have already removed the duct tape.

"What the fuck do you want?" I asked her.

"F.K.R. is waiting for you," she said.

"So why the fuck you holding me at gunpoint if he's the one who sent you?"

"He told me not to." She held up the gun. "He's naïve. Thinks you're a pretty pussycat. I know you're a beast. Get dressed," she ordered me.

"Shut up bitch," I told her. "You don't know me." I'm not trembling anymore. I'm back to bold. Now *I know* she won't squeeze the trigger.

"Everybody knows you," she said sharply. "And unlike everybody else that buys into your act, including F.K.R., I see the demon in your eyes."

I'm staring straight into her blue eyes. They give her an advantage. Her blond blunt cut is precise, frames her striking feminine face on a unique angle. I'm wondering what her relationship is with F.K.R. But I cancel that line of thinking. I'm tight at this nigga now. He better have my cell phone, handbag, jewelry, and my stacks. And I don't know how I'ma make him pay me back for making me put on some other bitch's clothes and a platinum wig. And my bodyguard . . . oh shit.

Her silver-steel CCX Koenigsegg whip caused me to forgive her. Car has supermodel curves and looks so mean, I feel good being driven in it. Maybe I'll cop it for myself. The deep black leather seats, each one the price of the everyday man's standard vehicle. I *never seen* one of these in Santiaga's collection. The silver-steel stick shift is shaped like a hard dick. She's clutching it and moving it around like a hand job. The whole scene had me quiet for a minute, just eyeing it all with my designer eyes. An exotic whip and a pistol which she dropped in her crocodile saddlebag that she didn't bother to tuck in the trunk. She simply threw it onto the backseat. A whip that can't do shit but attract nonstop attention, a famous bitch on shotgun, and a concealed weapon. Blues eyes, plus her skin complexion must give her the assurance and freedom, riding dirty, that no nigga would easily have.

"I hope you're worth it," she said to me without taking her eyes off of the road. "F.K.R. is a *really nice catch.* A lot of women are gonna be burning mad at you. Hope you can handle him."

"Are you one of the angry bitches?" I asked her.

"If I did dick, I would do him for sure. But we don't do dick," she said in a calm, smooth way.

"We?" I asked.

"Me and my partner. You'll meet her. We are moving in her direction now."

"Is that where he's at?" I asked her. "I definitely need to see him, not some other chick. I *do dick,*" I said forcefully.

"No. That's where you need to go to get ready for him," she said like he is doing me a favor by choosing me. Like he is better than me, too good even. Not a tone or words I'm accustomed to. Matter of fact, Porsche was saying the exact opposite. Early this morning when she barged in as usual, she asked me, "Who is this guy that asked you to marry him? Why would you?" she said like he was nothing.

"Why can't I?" I said back to Porsche in a sarcastic manner to let her know that I don't need her approval to marry any nigga I want to marry. Furthermore, does she think that she and Mercedes can have it all their way, *and I can't?*

"I didn't mean that you can't marry him, Winter," Porsche had said in a soft apologetic voice. "I meant that, I can't feel your feelings for that guy. I mean when a man and woman love one another, especially in the beginning, anyone with feelings can feel it. It oozes out of their eyes." She did a dance move. "It's all in their body. It's like feelings that can't possibly be hidden, even if the love is forbidden. I don't feel any love in you, Winter . . . for him." She placed her face in too close to mine, nose to nose.

I never replied to her hot comments. I don't like her whirling continuous storm of feelings to cause me to feel or react. Besides, I considered myself a little guilty. I couldn't say that I love him, but I like him a lot because of how much he likes me and the way he makes every moment different from the last, and incomparable to any other man, nigga, or dude I ever knew. And of course I have considered that if he does a deal with Kuntz, he could become *my Elisha*, a double-digit millionaire with several streams of revenue to keep a bitch like me satisfied. I don't want a nigga who's financially beneath me. A dude like that might actually hate me, be using me for my capital, then beating my ass out of anger cause he can't compete, earn, or even meet me at my level. Exactly, that's exactly it.

She pulled up to a marbled out mansion in Englewood Cliffs positioned on the curve of the alcove. "The House Of Doll" was inscribed beautifully on the awning. The expensive pink redwood double doors were embossed with a silver plaque that read, "FOR WOMEN ONLY."

"I'm Doll," another stunner said. "Welcome to my house." She walks like a belly dancer dances and uses her fingers, hands, and arms like some type of ballerina with fluid flexibility. She's inviting me to take in the luxury of it all. "Hmm I can see why F.K.R. loves you," she suddenly said. "You're very sexy. Your body exudes sexy." She was doing a 360 walk with me in the center.

"Don't fall into her trap," the blue-eyed girl said and folded her pretty arms across her breasts. Doll stepped close to her and kissed her on her lips.

"No jealousy allowed in the House of Doll. Here we only serve and *perfect* women." Then she touched and held my hand like we are two preschoolers on a school trip. Pulling me along gently, I'm cooperating, reminding myself that blue eyes has the burner and obviously she plays the masculine role in their partnership, even though she has an ultra-feminine beauty and look. She wouldn't shoot me over F.K.R., but she may easily blast me with the force of her jealousy over her flirtatious lover.

"Everyone with the marriage package starts here," Doll said, releasing my hand in front of a door.

"Where is he?" I asked, tensing back up about F.K.R. controlling things from a distance.

"When the package he prepaid for is completed, we will deliver you directly to him."

"What time is it?" I asked like a fucking fool who had been robbed of my cell and jewels and no longer could tell time. It's 1:15 p.m.

"I need to make a call." I said it like an order, not a request. She pulled up her cell phone that had been riding on her pelvis in her low-waist jeans. She drew in a password design. She pulled up the keyboard screen, then held it out to me. As I stared at it, I realized that I don't know F.K.R.'s math by heart. "Don't know his number?" She smiled. She is the one who exudes sexy. "Works out perfectly," she said in a whisper of a voice. "He asked us not to put any calls through to him until you're totally ready. But you can text him." She pulled up his contact and handed the phone for me to type my message.

"Nigga what!" I typed, then deleted it. "I gotta be on set at 6," I typed and texted. She pulled her phone back.

"I'll let you know if there's a reply," she said like she and I share a secret.

"Blood and urine sample?" I repeated. Behind the first door in the super-clean, well-designed, and perfectly lighted office with the powder-pink walls and luxurious furniture. "Are you even a doctor? What for?" I was getting irritable all over again. She pointed. Her medical degrees were mounted, Princeton University and Yeshiva Medical School.

"What for?" I repeated.

"You have the marriage package. We examine blood and urine to assure our client that his or her partner is healthy, not in a current state of disease or even pregnancy . . ."

Each room in their luxurious life-sized dollhouse was designed and furnished more elegantly than the previous. Their services included everything women. I even got my pussy waxed for the first time. Hey I got locked up so young. It was back when niggas loved the "nappy dugout." I smiled, remembering Ice Cube, a West Coast nigga, murdering every track on *Death Certificate*, to the point where all twelve and thirteen years young bitches had to listen, even though we was all-day-every-day-certified New York, East Coast loyal.

The last service was through double doors that led into a white marble showroom, where the most expensive designer wedding wear was displayed and available.

"Circulate," Doll, who reappeared, said to me. "Choose the dress that lures you to it. It will be a choice that you will cherish forever. And, over on the right side is the 'Jewelry Box,'" she said as she pointed out a side room with a golden door that displayed a sign that actually said "Jewelry Box." "Don't worry about costs of course. F.K.R. has covered all," she assured me as though she thought of him as a member of the millionaire's club, while I know he's still doing the night shift at fucking FedEx. Of course I hesitate. Why do I need to pick out a wedding gown right now? I can do it closer to the time that he inks a deal with CEO Kuntz. That way, when we get married. I mean . . . if I decide to marry him . . .

Fully adorned like a bride ready to walk down the aisle, I think of Poppa. "Can we take photos and perhaps a bit of video of you as you exit the showroom and through our front doors?" Doll asked even though her cameras were already poised to roll. When I paused to think about it, she threw the bait. "F.K.R. is waiting for you."

"He's here?" I say while spinning swiftly in the Vera Wang dress of perfection. Of course I see the video camera following me out. I don't care, I'm gonna see him about everything that happened today. I lifted and held up the dress gently so it would not drag and I would not trip. With Doll on my right and Blue Eyes on my left I opened the pink redwood doors and F.K.R. was right there leaning on a, on a . . . trailer! My fury and concern turned to laughter.

"Nigga what!" I shouted out. He smiled, stood up from his leaning, and said, "You asked me if I got a house. This . . . ," he pointed, "is our temporary house. I know you like privacy and don't want to live with my father."

"Nigga what!" I said again as my knees buckled and I squatted down to the ground in a twenty-thousand-dollar wedding dress. Doll and Blue are holding it up, even though their wide white stone walkway is totally clean. As I am still laughing and watching F.K.R.

walking towards me, I see that I am even on two more cameras that were on the left and the right of the trailer ahead of me. The two behind me are still there as well. I see a Ducati hoisted on the back rack of the trailer. So I know for sure *it's his*. Extending his hand, he helps me up. Then pulls me towards him and hugs me. His cologne smells nice. Not too heavy. Not too light, and a little arousing, I can even smell the scent of his haircut and could tell that he got it maybe ... moments ago. I touched the back of his shirt collar, lifted it, and saw the Giorgio Armani label. I pull back from his embrace and say, "Nigga what?" He grabs my hand and escorts me into his trailer.

"What is this?" I asked him when I got inside of the first trailer I've ever been in.

"This our kidnap wedding," he said still smiling.

"What in here? Right now? You want to get married in here?" I asked and I'm in a state of complete disbelief and laughter.

"No, next stop is my father's house. But after that, we'll have our honeymoon in here," he said with full confidence. I just laughed so hard tears came out of my eyes.

"What? You don't want to?" he asked and held his arms open like he was all swag. "I told you I'm saving up to get you a house that you'll love. Until then ..."

"Until then?! How long will that be?" I asked, laughing and screaming.

"By the time you have my daughter or son in you, I'll have the house ready, so you can have a peaceful say six months."

"Are you serious? No seriously. You have to stop playing and be serious for once."

"I am serious," he said without laughter. Then I heard the trailer door open and the engine start. "He's my driver. I don't want to wrinkle my suit. Let's stand facing each other," he suggested at the same time the trailer pulled off, causing me to sway to the left. He caught me and pulled me back and held me. He then pulled a certificate out of his interior pocket. "Check this out," he said to me. "This is ours." I took it and flipped it over and read it. The title says "MARRIAGE CERTIFICATE . . . UBALDO PINCHAS KUTZNEKOV and . . ."

"Wait a minute! Who is this person?" I asked him.

"What person?" he replied.

"Um . . . Ubaldo Pinchas Kutznekov?" I tried pronouncing.

"That's me!" he said and I dropped the certificate.

"That is not your name!" I shouted and started laughing all over again.

"It is," he said casually.

"Your Bald Though Pinch Ass Kutznekov . . . what the fuck!!! That's not your name. Stop playing. I told you to get serious," I said but even I am laughing.

"Did you think that F.K.R. is my real name?" he asked me.

"No!" I said, "but not this! It's impossible. How can I become Winter Kutznekov! My whole career would be over!" I exclaimed without any anger, but waiting for him to scream, "Psych!" it's a joke. Instead he lifted the certificate from the floor. And held it so that I could continue reading.

"This is the official joint. Check it out," he said. I read "Winter Victorious Santiaga" in the space for the bride's name.

"How did you know my middle name?" I asked after finally finished laughing.

"It was printed that way on your passport," he said.

"My passport," I repeated. *I didn't even get it yet. Should receive it any day now,* I thought to myself. Then I knew this is all a staged joke. Props at the Network could easily design a fake marriage certificate, same as they made those *Bow Down* playing cards and even the Brooklyn project set. So I decided to play along with him. Just as I was about to get started with my jokes, the trailer stopped moving. He opened the door and got out and held his hand out so I could step out also. I am glad to get out of here. Who ever heard of a honeymoon trailer!

When I jumped into his arms, over his shoulders, I saw . . . oh no. Not this . . . He's going too far. We are outside of the midget house with the tiny picket fence in the luxurious mansion area of Englewood Cliffs.

"Put me down," I told him. "Really, stop playing now."

"Pop! Pop! We're out front!" he hollered. Now on my own two feet, I see more cameras set up outside of this little house. This is definitely a Network trick. Midget Father hobbles out in the tini- est tux I ever seen. Behind him comes an even tinier lady with little fat broccoli stalk legs and a too tight dress that hugged her chubby hips. I tried to run back into the trailer, but it was hard to hurry and maneuver the wide skirt portion of the dress. He pulled me back by the waist and held me in place, kicking and screaming.

"Dad, Mom, this is my new wife. Winter Kutznekov. Say hello to my parents," he then said straight-faced. I'm trying to swallow my laughter and disgust at the same time.

"Mr. and Mrs. Kutznekov, nice to meet you," I lied. I don't want to have my real thoughts and my real attitude on film, and get attacked by all little people worldwide.

"She's so gorgeous," the tiny lady said. "Come here darling. Give your mom a hug." She opened her arms. They are as fat as her legs. Oh no! But F.K.R. and his parents were not laughing. So I bent over to give her a hug. She embraced my neck and wouldn't let go. I stood up and had a human hanging around my neck like a necklace! "Are those real diamonds!" she exclaimed, her weird face facing the diamond choker I have on, from the loaner jewelry, from the House of Doll Jewelry Box, her little elf shoes pressing against my pure white dress and my waist. F.K.R. lifted his mom off of the dress and placed her back down onto the ground.

"I'm proud to have you in our family," the little guy said. "I hope you and my son have a long marriage same as me and my wife. It's been twenty-nine years now."

Immediately my mind began calculating. If they have been married twenty-nine years, F.K.R. is probably twenty-eight.

"Will you come inside?" his mother asked me. But I had reached my limit. I won't be able to stop laughing. What if they have tiny beds and tiny toilets? I'd rather get back into the trailer. And . . . what time is it? My thoughts were racing trying to conjure up some excuses.

"We have work today at six p.m. But we will have dinner with you tomorrow. Okay Dad?" he said to his father.

"Work is work. We certainly understand," his father said.

"We are looking forward to sharing dinner and our lives with you," his mom said.

F.K.R. grabbed my hand and we walked back to the trailer and are both in the center of the camera lens.

"Okay what's the setup?" I asked him once we were inside.

"Setup?"

"Seriously, of course I saw all of those cameras. Did you happen to speak with CEO Kuntz?" I asked him, thinking *obviously they are working together.*

"Nah, not recently," he said like Kuntz is a non-factor-nobody.

"Oh, he wanted to speak to you urgently. I figured the two of you had spoken and that was the reason for the whole thing today, especially the cameras."

"No, this footage is for you and I to show our children one day. If they ask us any questions, I want to be able to show them visual proof," he said strangely.

"You are thinking way ahead," I told him.

"Got to. I plan to make a good marriage and a beautiful family," he said with a scary sincerity.

"Isn't that what a woman usually says?" I asked him.

"Depends on who the woman is and who the man is," he answered without laughter.

"Where is my cell phone? I need it now. And oh yeah, why did you tell them to take it? That and my jewelry and handbag? And I see you seem to know a lot of pretty bitches. Who was the girl who resembled me who dipped out with my shit?"

"She's my wife," he said. He lifted up the certificate. "She had your passport. Looked just like you. I thought she was you. I married her."

"What!"

"Monday morning when I met your father, *he was with her.*"

34
TWO MINUTES

"I gave you my father's number. Lend me your phone," I said feeling furious and anxious.

"What do you need your father for? You have a husband. There's been a transfer of power," F.K.R. said and now I'm just staring at him. True he's handsome enough. But he's not Poppa. And when anyone says anything about Poppa, or says Poppa said something or Poppa did something, I gotta check it with Poppa. Or, I don't believe it.

"So much doubt in your eyes," he said, dapper in his Armani suit and I love that he didn't opt to don a tux, isn't wearing a tie, and has his bright white tailored shirt buttoned only to his chest. His pearl cuff links lift him up higher in my fashion mind.

"I'll give you a chance. I'm F.K.R. Mutha, not a *motherfucker*. I would never trick or force a woman into marrying me," he said then paused . . . "your father did that though."

"If you wouldn't have told that other bitch to snatch my phone at gunpoint," I accused him and let my eyes linger on him so he could feel my seriousness.

"Your father has a tracking device in your phone. If I didn't tell her to swipe it from you, when I brought you over to me, your father would've known your every move and location." He had on his most serious face. "You didn't ask me to kidnap you, so that I could get tracked and merked by Santiaga? Did you? Either that, or end up serving a life sentence. Did you?" He let his eyes linger on me.

"Never that . . . ," I said swiftly. "I don't fuck around and set niggas up. That's not me. So I didn't, wouldn't, couldn't, and won't ever do that," I said urgently.

"I like the way you said that. That makes me feel good. It's five p.m. You have three minutes to make a choice." His eyes shot down to his Timex broke nigga watch, which doesn't match his rich appearance or pearl and platinum cuff links. "Either tell me right now, out from your pretty lips, that you want to remain my wife, in which case we show up hand in hand at the Network today at six p.m. *for your show*. Or tell me honestly, that you want to cancel our marriage, in which case we both will call our lawyers and mutually sign off on the marriage annulment. Then . . . you and I will be done with each other."

"Done," I repeated. "Why you speeding? What's the rush?" I asked automatically without filtering my questions through my normal sifter.

"I'm a man. I can't send my wife back into the arms of those men whose job it is to guard you, and lift you up from the ground and hold you in their arms," he said. Apparently he saw the *Daily News* cover shot with Daylight Bodyguard gripping me.

"Just say so. I'll drop you off on time and leave you with them. If I do, it's all finished for me." Then he looked at his watch again and looked up into my eyes. "Boyfriends are suckers. No props or dap or respect or relation. *Only your husband* has the authority to take

over, provide for and protect you once you leave the hands of your
father. You have . . . two minutes left starting now."

"I'm making a quick stop," he said as I could feel the trailer on an
incline. When it stopped and the ignition went off, he got out from
where he and I had been seated lap in lap. He lifted me off of the
trailer and carried me in his arms. He sat me on the hood of a black
"bow down" Bugatti. Once a bitch sees one of these in real life, all
she can do is bow down to the nigga who made moves to acquire it.
Santiaga ain't got one of these and neither do Elisha. I saw it featured
in *Vogue.* Hits more than two hundred miles per hour. The hood
of the whip is warmer than summer. My excitement, the heat, the
moment caused my entire body to tremble and tingle. If only . . . I
could have everyone but me and him to disappear, I desire to get
fucked on the hood of his missile. I exhale.

But Kuntz and the camera crew are waiting on me, and my million has already been deposited. "Don't give me that look," he said.
"Unless you want to miss your show." I could see the lust in his eyes,
and his hard stick shift. Still, he dashed away, and came right back
out with a huge very light-skinned older guy, who looked like he
couldn't fit inside of a Bugatti. He's so big in fact that he probably
always had to drive a Suburban, no . . . a tractor trailer. I laughed.
Two sets of eyes watched my smile.

"Chuck," the big man hollered. "Bring out the camera." A big
man, less big than the big guy, came running out with a Canon.

"Stand next to her," he told F.K.R. and F.K.R. did it. "Chuck
take the photo," he ordered the big, less big guy with the camera.
"Round here, we say 'money,' instead of cheese." The big man laughed.
I smiled and said, "Money!" The makeshift camera guy clicked away.

F.K.R. picked me up and held me. The camera clicked some more. I'm thinking all right, okay, enough with the personal favors for your neighbors. I could see Bubble Hill off in the diagonal distance. The light-skinned bear took two giant steps forward and gave me a bear hug. His hands stronger than bear claws. F.K.R. let it happen.

"Only my father is able to hug my wife. And only *my real wife* is allowed to meet my real father," F.K.R. announced and I was paused and shocked, all over again. His father released me, which was the only way I could get loose from his grip. He smiled wide and said, "Ricky's daughter. Beautiful! Tell your father I'd like to have him over to our house. It's been a long, long time."

"You know my father," I said, but it was not a question. He had just made it clear that he does. But who knows? Maybe he just watched the first season of *Bow Down*. When people see anyone in person, who they've seen on TV, they act real familiar like they grew up with you.

"Oh yeah," he answered my question in a deep affectionate roar. "Anybody who's somebody in this area of town knows *your father*. It's been years. He'll be surprised to see me. I'll be surprised to see him. Both survivors and thrivers and strivers," he laughed. "I'll throw him a big . . . well not too big, barbeque," he said, slowing his excitement down a notch for whatever reason. "Take the pickup truck. Your dudes hooked it up for you," his father directed him. "Let's show your father-in-law Santiaga how good you are treating his daughter."

I'm seated at the center of the back of a "Just Got Married" decorated black pickup truck, followed by about twenty-two motorcycles who all spilled down the driveway from the back side of my husband's mansion, where they apparently were parked and hidden just in case I had said no, and rejected F.K.R.'s offer.

I almost did. I knew that *none of this* fits my personality, or my way. None of these are the moves I would normally make or things or people I would normally gravitate towards. However, when F.K.R. said that me and him would be done if I did not accept the offer to honor the marriage on his certificate, it took the whole two remaining minutes that he gave me, for me to go deep enough and admit that I'm a top bitch, in a top-tier wedding dress, laughing and smiling. Me minus F.K.R. equals a heartbroken sad rich celebrity bitch, who feels betrayed by time, betrayed by my father, Pretty Bitch, my former friends, all at different levels of intensity of course. But still. F.K.R. is the *only one* who belongs to me, exclusively.

Besides, when I asked him if he would do a meeting with Dick Kuntz, who wants to offer him a double-digit millionaire deal, he said, "Nah, we don't need him. Watch how we gon do crazy numbers without him." I liked the feeling of a man who has the umph to walk on this Earth with no leash or chains or bosses over him. That got me excited in more ways than one. Then my mind switched into thinking about me and him having to hustle up and earn amounts that could be just *handed to him* if he signed on the dotted line. Even I will make an immediate cool million with the stroke of his pen on CEO Kuntz's contract, or thumbprint on his whiteboard, or initials from the digital pen pressed on an iPad. I calculated.

"But can you just call him and be like yeah you'll take the meeting?" I asked softly. He didn't answer. Just pulled up his cell phone and called him.

"What up Dickie?" he said as though he was making fun of Kuntz, or maybe just fun of his name. "My wife asked me to meet with you. I'm on my way. Set your cameras up outside. We're taking over the final episode. We have an announcement to make," he said, bossing the boss but joyful and gleaming, that he has me.

Maybe it was the word "takeover" that rang in CEO Kuntz's ear that caused him to set F.K.R. up? Maybe it was Poppa's version of protecting me that led to the demise of my husband. Maybe it was Daylight Bodyguard, who had to feel humiliated that F.K.R. pulled the slip on him and his partner, by snatching up VIP DO OR DIE from right under his eyes in Bergdorf. Maybe it was the black knight, Black Beauty aka Night Shift Bodyguard, son of Midnight living up to his young, legal, and lethal reputation. Maybe it was Natalie's mouth that killed him. Upside Down had said that the niggas processing through the courthouse security had been the boyfriends of my ex friends. They was all salty getting cut off from the summer special edition and even more vexed that all of their women, except one, were dropped from the cast of Bow Down season 2. Maybe it was one of Simone's family relations or friends, or Reese's? I know for sure it wasn't Zakia, her daughter, or Dutchess, or Upside, or Boobytrap, or any of my eight bitches. I had seen and counted each of them, mixed in the crowd so huge it shut down the block in front of the Network building in moneymaking Midtown.

Maybe it was the Me-Bitch, who looked just like me, who thought she was gonna become me and fuck my man and appear on my finale, wearing my Alexander McQueen and brandishing my sparkling jewels before her ass was deported back to Curaçao, wherever the fuck that is. No matter how far it is though, tabloid and bloggers, and podcasters, gossip girls, and fag hags and clout chasers all take her emails and calls and interviews she claims she's pregnant with F.K.R.'s baby. I know she ain't. When I asked him if he had fucked her, he smiled like he had. Then he said, "Nah I realized she wasn't you when I smelled her. Your scent alone makes a man want to pull up on you. After you left the studio when we first met, the booth smelled so good I just stayed in it whiffing instead of spitting." He laughed and had placed his nose in the nape of my neck and said, "Like dat right dere, gets me hard and high."

"You didn't fuck her?" I asked playfully like giving him the space to admit it.

"Technically I didn't."

"Technically?" I repeated.

"Once the smell was off, I knew she wasn't you. But she was standing right there looking like you . . ."

"So she gave you head," I concluded.

"Once she put her lips on it, I said might as well let her finish." He smiled. I laughed but hated it. "But nah, I couldn't fuck her. If she would've gotten pregnant, I'da been stuck with her. I never plan to walk away from a woman who got my baby on the way. I saved that privilege for you."

Maybe it was Elisha. Maybe it was Elisha. I had to think it and say it aloud two times, to even consider it. Elisha had said, "Be careful what you ask for especially if you ask me for it. You'll most likely get it." Then he reminded me that on his private jet, I had asked him to find two look-alike stand-ins to take the weight off of me having unreasonable demands and multiple simultaneous responsibilities, schedulings, and no time to be my real myself.

Maybe it was his mother, aka Momma Elon. She rivals me and wins, in her love of money. She thought me and F.K.R. were gonna crash her golden son, his reputation and empire. She wanted both of us far away from him and their property, finances, and fame. She wanted us unaffiliated, dead, trashed and forgotten.

Maybe it was Porsche, *no, not her*. One of the members of her "invisible all girl army," I laughed. Been a long time since I laughed. A laugh that only lasted a second or two.

Maybe it was some random hater of F.K.R. Although it seemed everybody who was aware of him loved him. Maybe the one or two who hated him just decided to pop him, to stop him. Just couldn't tolerate his shine or his rise. Maybe it was one of his ex-girlfriends, who I never heard of or cared, or knew anything about. One of the bitches who caused him to never trust women, and to order a blood and urine test and have me checked for AIDS, HIV, herpes, chlamydia, syphilis, and even a hidden pregnancy.

Maybe it was me. His father had said that the wrong woman can get a man killed for nothing. He's right. It was me. Has to be me. The blood is on my wedding dress, the one that crazy fans wanted to buy from my Victorious VIP elite shoppers site. Bids flew in like bullets. One VIP buyer offered a hundred thousand, five times the dress's value. I won't ever sell it though, not even for a million. *Maybe I did love him*, do love him. But surely, I didn't love him enough. I didn't know him enough to love him, or for him to lose his life for me.

I wish I could force time to rewind. I know from my death experience no human can do that. If I could just be granted one MERCY, it would be to have skipped the final episode filming, at the Network. I should've used my allure to lure him into his father's mansion, into one of the many, many bedrooms, and into me. Make love, and make life. Sometimes the best thing niggas and bitches can do is to stay the fuck still. Stay home and get into one another.

I never wanted to be like everybody else. A bitch has to either be born unique, or become unique. However, the fact that I love the man more in death than I ever did in life makes me the same as every everyday, ordinary, conniving, soul, and gold-digging bitch.

I pulled up my cell phone, bout to watch the footage of him again. I watch each day when I wake up and every night after my long workdays, before I finally sleep. I have to. I don't do dope. I don't crack, sniff, or pop no pills. It's just me and my millions, my weed, and strong drink occasionally. My memories and mostly this footage of him is my *only* narcotic.

35
LAST LOOK

There is a close-up of F.K.R.'s chest, with the words "SON OF A BITCH" branded into his skin. Then there is a voice-over saying, "This man wants to marry my daughter, Winter Santiaga." It's Poppa's voice. Then the camera pulls out and I can now see footage of F.K.R. on stage at a concert performing to a crowd so huge that the entire audience cannot be captured in the frame of the shot. He's young and perfectly nappy headed, shirtless, and perfectly fit. His expression and rhyme is passionate and wild, not calm and laughing how I experienced him. In fact, during this performance, it seems as though he is recalling some real-life incident as he makes whoever wasn't there when whatever happened to him happened feel like they was.

The lyrics to his rhyme are spelled out on the bottom of the screen as he rhymes it.

"I bite the fingers that feed me
I'd rather feed myself.
Stack my own chips.
Build my own wealth.

"No one can say shit
About what they gave me,
The sacrifices they made,
to keep and raise me.
Fuck you mother
U made me starve
Now I spit venom
All over these bars
To let the world know
What type of bitch you are."

The stadium exploded with young furious fans screaming the chorus, "Fuck you mother."

The shot switched. To my surprise F.K.R. is in the lens, nah he's in the Network studio live . . . seated across from Poppa, who is immaculate and superior.

SANTIAGA

"Son, I dig your opening line of your rhyme from your underground hit titled 'Formula Baby.' 'I bite the fingers that feed me. I'd rather feed myself.' I feel that," Santiaga said to him with a sincerity. "Probably every young man who's right about ready to stand on his own two feet, find his own way, make his own mark and impression on the world has reached this point and felt this feeling before."

F.K.R.

"Thank you sir. I respect you. I should say that first. I know who you are and what you've built," he added.

SANTIAGA

"But hold on," Poppa said in his smooth and calm manner. "I know as men, the action *we make* and the action we take in the streets earns us a name. How did you acquire the name F.K.R. Mutha?"

F.K.R.

"I know men are not supposed to say the truth about any woman. We are especially not supposed to say the truth about our own mothers, if that truth is not sweet. I push back on that. I don't accept that. A man should resist anyone who's trying to force him into a compromising, unacceptable position, or into a false reality."

SANTIAGA

"A false reality . . . break that down son."

F.K.R.

"Not all mothers are nice, friendly, dedicated, or good. Not all babies are breastfed. That's why I titled the song 'Formula Baby,' to let bitches know if from the beginning you are too stingy, selfish, or stupidly conceited to even offer your newborn your breast milk, and instead feed him some chemical powder, you on your way from the jump, to raise sons and daughters who can *easily hate you.*"

Then the camera switched back to FKR's concert footage.

"FUCK you Mutha.
You said my father was dead.

"Had random niggas and bitches fucking you in the bed.
Punched, kicked, and stomped me in my head.
Fuck you Mutha
You should've adored me.
Not the look of hate.
Every day you ignore me
Fuck you Mutha
And your fucked up condition.
I hate your eyes, your lies
And your nonstop addictions."

SANTIAGA

"You're a music artist. That means you must also study the music?"

F.K.R.

"I wouldn't say I study it. I'm a fan of great music so I play it and listen to the old joints all the way up to the new. There's some songs I listen to over and over again, cause either the instruments or the beats or the lyrics give me a feeling that *nothing else could give me*. That's an organic high."

SANTIAGA

"So you're familiar with the way the Intruders, the Temptations, the Ohio Players, the Isley Brothers, all the way up to Tupac Shakur, sang and rhymed songs about their mothers, as well as the ladies they loved, wanted to love, and even used to love? Does your music capture and convey the way you feel about women? Do you hate women, son?"

F.K.R.

"I hate the women who should be hated. And (pause) I love the women who should be loved." (thunderous applause)

SANTIAGA

"By the way, the Temptations sang that famous song,'My Girl.' It was a huge commercial hit. Big advertisers licensed it. Top movie houses paid to use it in film soundtracks from the twentieth century to the twenty-first century up to now. Music lovers love tributes to love, and to the women who they love."

F.K.R.

"But, the Temptations also made the song 'Papa Was a Rollin' Stone.' On the track they're singing and begging their mother to tell them the truth about their father. And that was way, way back then. So these bitches been lying, been stealing, and been hiding the babies *from their own fathers*, then lying about who the man they chose to fuck really was, what actually happened with him or to him or between them, or where he is or, better yet, who he is. That was then. Tupac wrote and performed 'Dear Mama,' made all the ladies love him. But, his mother was a lying bitch who lied to him about who his real father is. Musically speaking, he also wrote and performed 'Hit Em Up.' So he had to know that some bitches ought to be hated, and other girls who are loving, and who act and live right, deserved to be loved."

SANTIAGA

"That's heavy. Still I gotta ask if you ever heard some say, if you hate your own mother, hate is the most love you have to give to any woman? What do you think about that?"

F.K.R.

"Nah . . . When I was a little kid, every single day when I opened my eyes from sleeping, my mother would have this aggravated look on her face, like *oh it's you again*. Like she was pissed that I woke up. Pissed that I am still alive for one more day. That's different from a girl you like and the look she gives you. The smile she greets me with, the words she says to me, how she says them and the things her body gives away about how she feels for me. *I know the difference.* Why would I give hate to a girl who shows and gives me love?"

SANTIAGA

"Hate is a strong emotion and powerful word. Even if a mother is a little rough in the way she handled you, I mean you're a man after all is said and done. Shouldn't you just take it, and allow it to make you work even harder to become even stronger? Couldn't you work hard at improving yourself and changing the look on her face?"

F.K.R.

"In theory . . . ," he laughed. "But then if your moms is the type of bitch who treated you like an ashtray and put her cigarettes out on your bare skin when you were four years young, and beat you with an extension cord for opening a door without knocking, or knocks you over the head for drinking the last bit of Coca-Cola, whacks you ten times with the hose to the washing machine cause you didn't come running fast enough after she shouted *mother fucker get your black ass in here*. Or the type of psycho bitch who locked you in a room when her bum-ass boyfriend of the day or week came over . . . I mean, locks a li'l kid in, who didn't eat all day anyway, without food or water or even a jar of peanut butter, a radio or a TV to distract or entertain himself. Holding in your pee cause there ain't no bathroom where you locked up at. Too proud to pee on yourself or in the space where you're being confined. Looking at the plaster peeling off the walls. Wondering if it's worth the risk to jump out the window even though it's six flights down. Well then . . . you might become a 'rhyme animal', a young nigga named F.K.R. Mutha."

The in-studio audience clapped hard for him. The camera panned the faces of young females on their feet clapping, cheering, and co-signing on F.K.R.'s words.

SANTIAGA
"Doesn't sound like any woman or any mother or lady I've ever come across, or ever known."

F.K.R.
"Well sir, none of us can choose our mother. And no disrespect, you're Ricky Santiaga. I mean, I'm sure you had all the cream. I'm sure your moms is a gem and that you have known and had the best and most comforting, beautiful women worldwide."

Poppa blushed for a half of one second then snapped right back into his cool composure.

F.K.R.
"I love my father. My mother told me he was dead while he was alive and well. She wouldn't even tell me his name. She

said, 'He's dead. So, it doesn't matter what his name was.' When I asked her for a picture of him, she said she had long back burnt them all. I know how she liked to play with fire. Figured it was easy for her to burn paper photos since it wasn't nothing for her to burn a baby boy's flesh."

SANTIAGA
"You said he's alive and well. You must have found him?"

F.K.R.
"We been together since I turned twelve. Long story. Turned out he was searching for me the whole time as I was looking for him. I documented it on my YouTube channel same time as I released my first CD, titled *Son of a Bitch*. My current fan base of over three and a half million is made up of mostly youth who know for sure that some mothers are monsters."

The camera switched back to the chorus of "Fuck you mother, Fuck you mother."

F.K.R.
"After the DNA test confirmed us as father and son we been living life together in the little house we built. Pops is in construction, before that he was twenty-five years a longshoreman out on the piers of Newark, New Jersey, a real do-it-yourself dude with all types of stories of products from caviar to sugar to sushi, filet mignon, to furniture, exotic pets, cars, trains, planes, you name it being shipped out and received in and purchased throughout the world. I learned so much from him and admire him, more than

anyone else. How can a bitch attempt to keep a boy from becoming a real man because she's mad that his father looked at, or touched, or even had a baby with another woman? It's not right to threaten, hurt, and harm your children because of your petty jealousy. That's how I became F.K.R. Mutha. Someone had to tell these bitches that sons need their fathers, more than they need them. Fathers, if they get the chance to hold their sons, get to know them, grow to love their sons, teach them how to fight, build, earn, and survive."

The camera panned the audience faces, and the same females who were cheering before, now looked like they were all reflecting and thinking too deeply or feeling too insulted to react with applause.

F.K.R.
"I am here, to take your daughter off your hands and make her mine. Together we will make a real family," he said to my father Santiaga, as though it could possibly and easily be done.

SANTIAGA
"Do you think you're the only man who wants to marry my daughter?" Poppa asked him. The camera eased into a close up of Poppa's handsome face and serious expression, no blinking.

F.K.R.
"I may not be the only man. I'm definitely not a perfect man.

However, I am no doubt the best man for her."

SANTIAGA

"Lay it out son. Make it more . . . than talk. That way, the
men who want to challenge your offer will know what
they're up against."

F.K.R.

"I'm the man who causes your daughter to smile the bright-
est and laugh the hardest. I make her happy. That's priceless. I'm the man who caused your daughter to place her
feelings into rhyme and created and catapulted her into a
new top-selling musical career. I'm not about to offer you
any money for her hand. I know you're not auctioning her
off like that. That wouldn't be right, and I don't want to
get on your wrong side." F.K.R. laughed a stunted nervous
stutter laugh. "But I will turn over the money *she earned*
while performing with me in concert. I will turn over to
you the money she earned and stands to continue earning
from the sales and streams of our performance, and I will
produce the rest of her tracks that will solidify her position
at the top of all of the mainstream and underground music
charts, globally."

SANTIAGA

"Sounds like good business son. I respect a man who handles
his business. But there's one crucial thing you left out. You
didn't say that you love her. Isn't that the foundation? Can
you without even thinking deeply say right now on the spot
why you love her and why it has to be *my daughter for you?*"

F.K.R.

"Without thinking? That's a OG music lover's way of demanding me to freestyle?" he asked and laughed a cooled out laugh. He sat forward, then stood slowly. I see his eyes reacting to his mind pushing his freestyle together.

"Winter in America like Gil Scott said.
So fine fierce and fabulous bitches wanted her dead.
Hated her royalty and aimed at her head.
No bullet could rob her of her beauty or breath.
Grim Reaper turned Weeper
Jah gave her life after death.

"I love her more, than you'll ever know.
Like Donny loved music.
Like niggas love blow.

"She's my quiet fire.
She's so cold but so hot.
Not a bitch. Not a hoe
Not a slut or a thot.

"I'll put that crown on her head.
That rock in her hand.
Make her my wife.
To serve life is my plan."

F.K.R. looked at Poppa knowingly. Poppa was convicted and sentenced to serve life. Both him and F.K.R. look paused and serious. Then F.K.R. re-spit . . .

"C'mon Santiaga with all respect due.
You're her father and I know . . .
How much she loves you for true.
But I'll take her . . .
I took her.
What else would a young hustler do?"

F.K.R. posed.

"Still I step up
At the risk of losing my life.
I swiped her from you.
She's already my wife!"

Santiaga stood up and gave F.K.R. a handshake and pulled him
into a hug.

36
THE SESSION

"Miss Santiaga, are you going to only stare at your cell phone? These sessions are super expensive. Why come if you are only going to remain silent each time?" the psychiatrist bitch said.

Doesn't she know that these sessions are mandatory, same as the fifteen years I served were mandatory? To keep my millions flowing, and audiences growing, and customers spending and glowing, I have to come to the Network handpicked psychiatrist. They can force me to show up, but they can't force me to reveal the thoughts in my head, feelings in my heart, or my memories and secrets. All of the above are mine, exclusively. They are the only exclusive things I have.

I am back into my mind again. Back to my list of maybes and who done it, who did it, and why. However, my list is always thorough and always the same. I sat quietly some more. Thirty minutes passed and I asked myself the question, *Who did I leave out?* Whoever I did not consider or mention to myself, *that has to be the guilty one. Think, think, think . . .*, I'm telling myself.

"Okay this session is over," the psych said calmly. I'm still

421

scanning my list. My mind clicked. *Yung Santiago!* I thought. I had left him off of my list. Don't love him or miss him. Forgot to wonder where he even went after the new bodyguards rushed in. Didn't ask about him. I leaped up. *He's the one who gunned down Bullet in Vegas. I know* . . . A celebrity bitch has to act like she don't know nothing. Didn't see nothing . . . important. I'm good at that. I'm the gangster's daughter. I'm trained to be good at that.

"Miss Santiaga, your session is over," she repeated. "When do you think you will be willing to talk with me?" I didn't answer her back. She's a psychiatrist. I hate how everybody around me, and even not around me, does all types of crazy, scheming shit, then sends me to the psychiatrist and blames me for being the *realest bitch ever.*

Acknowledgments

I thank Allah first, foremost, and last, for allowing me to be a small mirror for us to look into and to decide if we like what we see . . . in and of ourselves. Alhamdulillah.

To contact Sister Souljah: souljahworkshard@gmail.com